Praise for *The*

Dr. Heiser answers questions that you didn't even know needed to be asked. *The Portent* will challenge you to come out of your slumber and be aware of the spiritual battle going on around you.

—Sharon B. Shipwash, Prayer Minister, Door to Destiny, LLC

There are plenty of ridiculous novels out there about Nephilim, Watchers, and aliens in today's world. *The Portent* (along with [Heiser's] first book, *The Façade)* is not one of them. Heiser brings his scholarly pedigree to the table of fictional novels like no one else can. This is a responsible, fascinating, and interesting novel series on the topic.

—Brian Godawa, Hollywood screenwriter and author of *Chronicles of the Nephilim*

A decade after he stunned readers with *The Façade*—with the fact that "they" are here and have been here for a really long time—Dr. Heiser again draws on his encyclopedic knowledge of Scripture and history, acute discernment of how biblical scholarship, science, technology and the paranormal intersect with societal and religious trends to ask: *What are they up to?* In *The Portent*, Dr. Heiser alerts us to ancient and modern cultural and spiritual trends, showing how the lines cross, converge, and perhaps reemerge with frightening clarity and vivid impact. In the end he shows us hope in the only place it can ever be found—the Spirit-filled human heart.

—Rev. Doug Vardell, ThM, Chaplain and Pastoral Care Coordinator

Fans of *The Façade* will not be disappointed. The Portent is another meticulously-researched thriller driven by biblical and theological insights that only Dr. Heiser would see. Picking up from *The Façade*'s cliff-hanger ending, readers finally learn the fates of Brian and Melissa and their new life off the grid. *The Portent* takes us into the mind of ancient evil (only Dr. Heiser could believably script a dinner conversation with a Watcher) to reveal a breathtaking global deception. If he's wrong, then this is at worst spell-binding fiction you won't put down. But if he's right . . . well, I just pray that he's wrong.

—Guy Malone, AlienStranger.com author of *Come Sail Away: UFO Phenomena & the Bible*, and founder of Roswell NM's Alien Resistance HQ

THE PORTENT

Volume Two of *The Façade* Saga

Michael S. Heiser

Defender
Crane, MO

The Portent
Volume Two of *The Façade Saga*

Defender Crane, MO 65633

This is a work of fiction. Characters, organizations, places, and events are either products of the author's imagination or, when factual, used in a fictitious manner. Any fictional character's resemblance to actual persons, living or dead—unless explicitly noted as such by the author—is purely coincidental.

Cover design: Patrick Fore
Typesetting: ProjectLuz.com

ISBN: 978-0-9991894-6-7

To my awesome kids, Amy, Molly, Calvin, and Simmi ("Summit").

You're all in here somewhere, named and unnamed.

Por · tent (pôr-tĕnt): An indication of something important or calamitous about to occur; an omen.

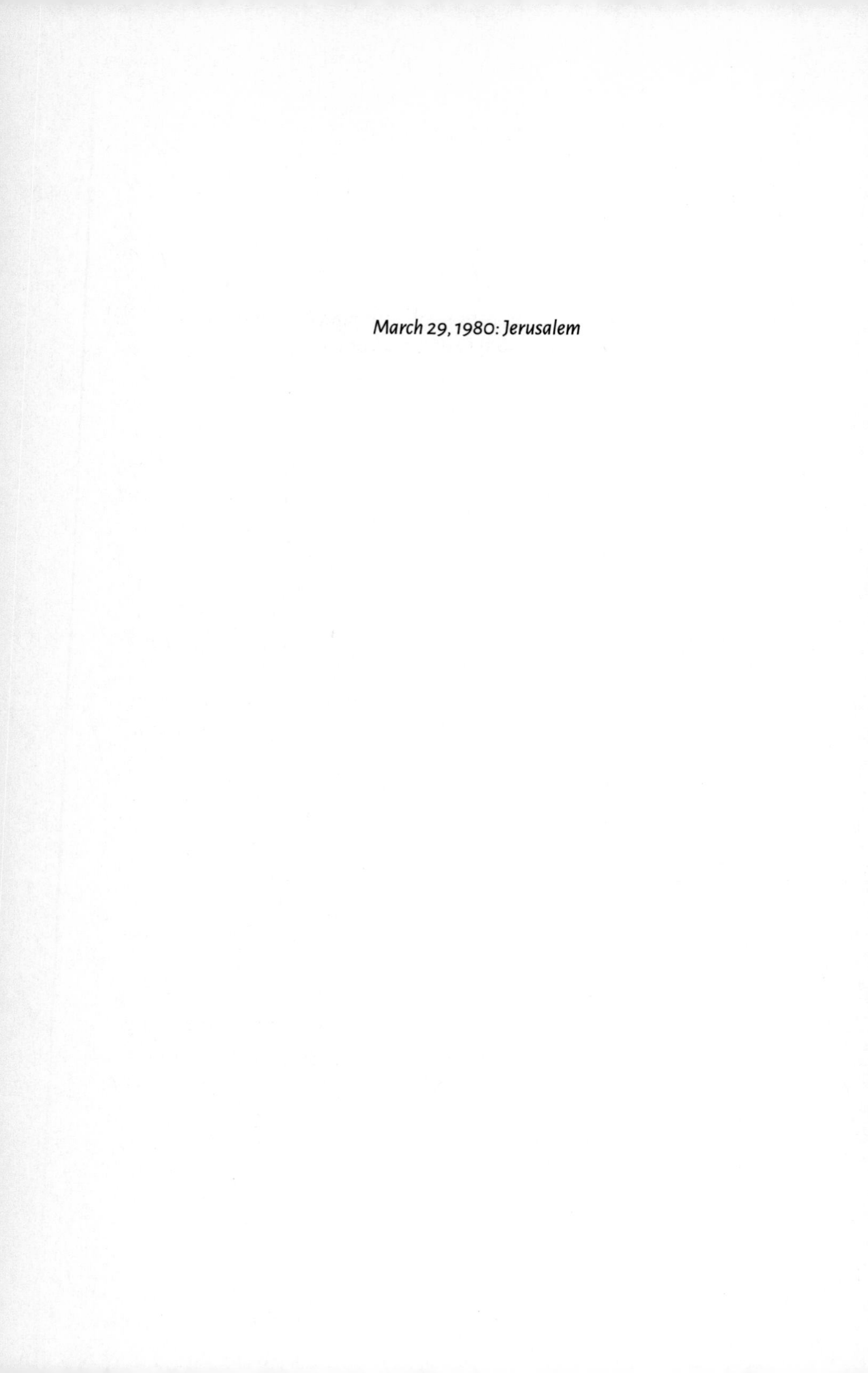

March 29, 1980: Jerusalem

1

In Jewish history, there are no coincidences.

—Elie Wiesel

"Don't just stand there, kick it to me!" the boy screamed impatiently. The target of his anger stood quietly, looking down at the round, awkwardly misshapen object that had come to rest at his feet, propelled there by an errant pass. He hesitated. It didn't seem right.

"Out of the way," an older boy in his early teens commanded, sprinting toward his tentative teammate. He was only a step ahead of the small pack in hot pursuit behind him. "I'll show you how to kick a ball."

"It's not a ball."

"It is today," he cracked, expertly timing his kick without breaking stride. The object fluttered through the air clumsily, hitting the ground with a thud about ten feet away. A cloud of dust rose up as more players scrambled for a shot, pushing and shoving for position.

"Stop that!" a woman's voiced suddenly broke through the ruckus. "Stop that *right now!*"

The boys wheeled around, startled, and saw an elderly woman, hair pulled back tightly under a stylish headscarf, rushing toward them with unexpected vigor. The woman paused for a moment, catching her breath as she glared at each one of the young male faces before her. "You should all be at home preparing for *Shabbat!*"

Her attention shifted to the ground. She gasped, her hand coming to her mouth unconsciously. She bent over and gingerly picked up a human skull, intact save for the jaw, which was missing. It was unmistakably old.

"Where did you find this?" she asked, her voice low and firm, barely concealing her contempt.

"Over there," one of the group pointed. "We'll show you. We didn't steal it—it was just there."

"I don't care if you didn't steal it!" she snapped. "We honor our dead. Do you hear me?"

The boy nodded, then looked at the ground, avoiding her gaze.

The woman followed several of the boys about fifty yards away to the location of their discovery. She saw the black hole in the ground, along with some boards and the tread marks of a heavy excavator. More bones were scattered about the surface near the opening. She peered down into the darkness and spotted a small, symmetrical breach cut into the rock below, about eighteen inches square. A demolition crew had apparently blown the top off a tomb. She'd heard the blasting two days before.

"Gather up all these bones," she ordered firmly. "I'll take them and call the authorities. This will have to wait until the end of *Shabbat*."

The boys complied and dispersed. The woman wrapped the remains in her scarf, tying the ends into a bundle. She shook her head as she embarked on the short trip to her home, fuming over the carelessness of the demolition crew. She was too preoccupied to notice one of boys lingering at the edge of the makeshift soccer field.

Once the woman was safely out of sight, the boy scurried to the location where he'd hidden souvenirs from his own excavation that day. Stuffing several handfuls of small bones into his pockets, he turned and ran home.

Two months before the end of The Façade

2

Coincidence is God's way of remaining anonymous.

—*Albert Einstein*

Neumayer Station III,
Queen Maud Land, Antarctica
70°40′S, 008°16′W

"Steady the other end when I pull in the rope," the bearded man directed, sniffing through the perspiration dripping from the end of his nose. The warmth of the lab compartments was always welcome, but it didn't take long for body heat, coveralls, a sweater, and a sub-zero parka to make a man sweat like he was in the tropics.

"Got it," the man at the other end of the slender, metallic drilling tube replied. Clean-shaven and a decade younger, he watched as the first man ran through a process he'd performed many times.

The tube, twenty feet in length, rested inside a semicircular channel that, to the untrained eye, might be mistaken for a piece of rain gutter. The channel was balanced on a fulcrum that allowed the tube to be pivoted and directed to a series of stands atop a shelf running the length of the lab. It took only a few minutes for an experienced hand to station the channel and the tube on top of the support stands.

Neumayer Station III was, as its name suggested, the third polar research station funded and operated by the Alfred-Wegener Institute. The station was the first of its kind, integrating research labs, operations, and staff accommodations under one roof. Normally staffed by a dozen scientists and graduate students, it could accommodate as many as forty people.

"Now you'll have something to keep you busy." The bearded man smiled, glancing at his younger colleague. He wiped his brow and removed his parka, folding it over a chair. "Post-docs have all the fun."

"Suits me just fine."

"Leave your gloves on for now. I'll push out the core for a look."

The bearded man grabbed a large plastic dowel, roughly three inches in diameter, and inserted it carefully into his end of the tube. He pushed slowly, and the ice core glided out into the channel.

"What was the depth for this one?" his assistant asked.

"Seventy meters or so."

"Gorgeous."

"Yep. It sure—*aahh,* what the hell?" The bearded man frowned. The pristine clarity of the core section that had just appeared was very obviously marred by a distinct discoloration—a thin, very dark ring with intermittent blotches of cream and yellow just below the outer surface of the drilled core.

"Maybe if I smooth the surface a bit?" the younger scientist suggested, gesturing with a gloved hand, unsure of protocol.

"Go ahead. You won't hurt anything."

The young man bent over and began gently rubbing the imperfection. After only a few strokes, he stopped, staring in disbelief.

"Good God!" his older colleague whispered, following his stare. "It can't be. There's *no way—*"

"I don't know about the black stuff," his assistant replied, his heart pounding as he got on one knee so he was eye-level with the core, "but I know a thumb when I see it."

3

No trumpets sound when the important decisions of our life are made. Destiny is made known silently.

—*Agnes de Mille*

The dark-skinned teenager kicked shut the door to his room, his hands filled with a sandwich and a cup of coffee. The room was illuminated by only the lamp on his desk, which was pushed tightly against his bed. He plopped down recklessly in front of the computer, spilling some coffee on the carpeted floor as he did so. He rolled his eyes, set his snack on the desk, and grabbed the shirt he'd worn yesterday from his bed to soak up the spill. *Good as new,* he thought, throwing the shirt into his closet.

He shook the mouse to stir his computer out of hibernation. His fingers flew effortlessly across the keyboard, logging into the network, then through the stacked layers of security or "gap management," as Madison referred to it. He finally arrived at the anonymous email program he used for communication with the outside world. His eyes widened as he read:

> *Silent One,*
>
> *Castel Gandolfo is beautiful this time of year. I sent you a good envelope today. Tell me what you think of it. God be with us all.*
>
> *Mantello*

Mantello. It had been weeks since he'd heard anything from him. His pulse quickened as he navigated another security gauntlet—one of his own designs—to retrieve the "envelope" Mantello had mailed him.

He had met the priest nearly a year ago online through an astronomy forum. He could scarcely believe his good fortune of meeting a high-level astronomer who worked at Castel Gandolfo, the Vatican observatory. He and Mantello soon became distant friends. He'd adopted the moniker "Silent One" since it best described someone like him who was incapable of speech. Plus, it sounded cooler than his real name: Kamran.

His self-esteem had skyrocketed when Mantello had begun to refer to him as his assistant. It didn't matter if the priest was stroking his ego just a bit. Kamran loved astronomy. He didn't know all the astrophysics and higher math, but he had a thorough grasp of stars and star-lore and could visually decipher the heavens like most kids his age could read HALO maps. Mantello had discerned this, and Kamran was grateful. Eventually the priest had introduced him to some new ideas. Some of these new ideas challenged his faith, but Mantello had been a patient guide.

Got them. Kamran's dark, deep-set eyes scanned the half-dozen images. To the untrained eye they were meaningless, mere computer representations of the night sky, cluttered with tiny white dots and scattered astronomical symbols and abbreviations. Kamran opened all the images simultaneously on his desktop, deftly tabbing through them in rapid succession, back and forth, then back again. He rearranged the order, finding new sequences. The only commentary was the date stamp in the upper right-hand corner of each image. There was no need for anything else.

Kamran swallowed nervously. *Is he serious?*

Present day, three months after the events of The Façade

4

Cruelty, like every other vice, requires no motive outside of itself; it only requires opportunity.

—*George Eliot*

Graham Neff stepped out of the helicopter, careful to keep his attention on what was ahead of him, not on his feet. His female bodyguard had already exited and was stationed at the bottom of the short stairway.

"Just keep your eyes on the jeep in the center," he directed as he stepped onto the hard, parched ground. "Stay on them until we're loaded."

The pair walked a short distance from their transport before stopping. Neff squinted through his sunglasses, adjusting his body armor, and assessed the situation. Five jeeps, one mounted with a machine gun, each loaded with Sudanese rebels. The rebels were disparately dressed in military fatigues and civilian clothing. Most wore head wraps. All were fully outfitted for combat. *A motley crew—and a deadly one at that,* Neff noted. A hundred yards beyond the jeeps, more troops—fifty or so, he guessed—were guarding four covered military trucks.

Neff was an experienced outdoorsman, and his toned body adjusted quickly to the oppressive heat. His face was slightly tanned from frequent weathering, and it was perfectly symmetrical. His square jawline and slightly prominent cheekbones betrayed a distant, now long-forgotten Native American heritage. Looking over the scene, he suppressed a smile. The flight had been long, but he could see it would be worth it.

Without a word, one of the soldiers hopped out of the center jeep and strode confidently toward them, stopping a few feet away.

"Identify yourself," the soldier demanded calmly in English. His accent was distinctively South African.

"Neff," he answered without expression.

"I am Commander Bahar," the soldier replied, equally expressionless. "I like your helicopter."

I'll bet, Neff thought. "Military surplus, an Mi-6," he said out loud. "Do you have the merchandise?"

The soldier glanced curiously at Neff's body guard. She was just a few inches over five feet tall, with immaculate, straight black hair that reached to the middle of her back, partially covering a small backpack. Her body armor did not completely conceal her elegantly curved body. The guard's smooth olive skin and deep dark eyes caught the soldier's eye momentarily, but her expression telegraphed nothing but hostility.

"A woman?" the soldier asked with a condescending tone.

"Absolutely," Neff replied, remaining motionless. "Israeli. Mossad, until I made her a better offer. She likes money. Do you?"

"Tavor?" the soldier asked, not about to be hurried. His men were alert behind him, eyeing the visitors suspiciously. The commander seemed more interested in the assault rifle than the woman holding it, its muzzle angled ever-so-slightly to the ground. He took note of the safety. It was off.

"Israeli TAR-21, forty-five millimeter, 800 rounds a minute," Neff answered, this time allowing a smirk to cross his face. "Positively breathtaking."

The soldier nodded. "Can you bring us some?"

"Maybe—assuming there's a next time."

Another nod.

"Since you're familiar with the TAR," Neff added, turning his head slightly in the direction of the helicopter, "you'll be able to identify this one, too."

The soldier's attention immediately fixed on the aircraft as a side door slid open to reveal an M1919 mobile machine gun and another woman at the ready. He glanced at the cockpit. The pilot was watching the scene intently.

"Mr. Neff, is this any way to meet a friend?"

"We're not friends."

The soldier looked squarely at his adversary, tight-lipped. After a few moments, he lifted his arm and waved, his eyes never departing from the foreigner. A soldier in the jeep immediately relayed the signal to the band behind them. Neff heard the trucks start and watched them begin to roll in their direction.

Suddenly a small, shoeless African boy leaped from under the covered side of one of the trucks. Shouting erupted from the foot soldiers watching the vehicles depart. Neff remained focused on the soldier in front of him, as did his bodyguard, knowing the scene unfolding before them might be a diversion. Two soldiers ran after the boy, catching him easily. One punched him hard in the face. The second dragged the dazed boy by the feet to the truck that had stopped, waiting for its lost cargo.

Neff waited for all the vehicles to arrive before speaking. "How many?"

"Sixty," the commander answered. "Forty-two girls."

"Virgins?"

"Twenty-four, counting the little ones."

"I specifically asked for at least thirty," Neff said, his irritation transparent.

"Some of the men were not informed. My sincere apologies. If you do not want the young ones, others will."

"Little girls are useful," he agreed. He gave a sly grin. "I have clients who have a special fondness for them. But short me next time, and you lose the TAR."

"Ah, so we *will* meet again." The commander smiled. "Now, where is the payment?"

Neff carefully removed the backpack from his bodyguard and handed it over to complete the transaction. The soldier unzipped it eagerly.

"One hundred thousand dollars in gold, as requested," Neff informed him.

The soldier sifted through the small gold bars with his fingers, then lifted the bag, testing the weight. "You cheat me," he accused angrily.

"Nope. There's sixty-three, single troy-ounce bars in there. Count them yourself. At today's value, that's a hundred grand. A month from now it may be more."

The soldier's expression softened slightly. He took one of the bars from the bag and bit it, then inspected his teeth marks. "Good."

The commander turned and barked some instructions in Bantu. A dozen of the men in the jeeps sprang into action, heading for the trucks. The rebels screamed at the human payload, pulling them from the trucks with determined speed. The sound of frightened weeping, punctuated by an occasional cry of pain from a soldier's slap, began to mix with the shouting.

Neff and his bodyguard watched the scene passively. The captive merchandise ranged from late teens to toddlers, all native Africans. Some were naked. The rebels pushed them along mercilessly toward the helicopter. The woman manning the machine gun, along with the pilot, waved pistols at them, motioning them inside the cargo hold. It was over in minutes.

"One more thing," Neff said as the commander turned to depart.

The soldier eyed the tanned white man quizzically as he unhooked his body armor and pulled it over his head. Neff handed it to the surprised commander, who beamed with delight, a spectacular white smile appearing on his creased black face.

"British Osprey, state of the art. *Now* we're friends."

***

Neff sat down in one of the available seats inside the helicopter. He closed his eyes. It had been a clean operation. The helicopter was safely airborne, so he could relax a bit. He was dozing off when his bodyguard touched his shoulder. He opened one eye.

"That was a risk back there," she said, her voice raised so she could be heard above the noise of the aircraft.

He read the concern on her face. He wrinkled his brow as if to ask what he'd done. He already knew what she'd say.

"Giving Bahar your body armor. Not a good idea. You were unprotected."

"It was good for business, you'll see. It's not the first time."

"I know, and I warned you those times. You're not a very good listener."

He smiled. "I have Nili Oren with me, the most lethal bodyguard on the planet. What's a little body armor?"

She wasn't amused.

"What's Madison doing?" he asked.

"Watching the payload. I think she's trying to tell them what's expected."

"She doesn't speak Bantu."

Nili looked back into the cargo hold of the plane. The other woman was making hand gestures. The captives' faces told her it was pointless. They were huddled together, quivering with fear, eyes darting about, completely bewildered. Some of the older girls wiped the tears from the faces of the little ones. Open mouths and pained expressions betrayed loud wailing, the sound of which was drowned out by the loud whirr of the rotors.

"Is she still armed?"

"Yes."

"Good—there's more of them than her. We don't want any problems. Bad for business."

Nili produced two pieces of paper from a pocket inside her body armor. She handed him the first. "This came from Tel Aviv. Ward printed it just before we landed.

Neff unfolded the paper and read it quickly.

"You think it's for real?" he asked.

"Yes. If they had nothing to say, they wouldn't bother. They have them both."

"Superb timing. We can divide up our passengers in Tel Aviv. Let our contacts know. Then we can take care of those two."

"Already done. And that's not all."

"What's in the second one?"

"You won't believe it," she said, handing him the message. "It's from Malone. He left this morning, so he's already on the ground and will have the necessary equipment. Madison showed it to me after we took off. She's convinced."

Neff read the note and shook his head in astonishment. "The same place?"

"The same place. Dress warmly."

5

Always remember that the future
comes one day at a time.

—Dean Acheson

"I can't look at another one," Melissa groaned, tilting her head back and closing her eyes. She moved her head from side to side to relieve the tension in her neck, her soft, dark red hair gently tossing with the motion. "Make it stop!"

Brian, seated a few feet from Melissa on the sofa, peered at her over the top of a book. He smiled at the sight of her stretching her legs, pointing her toes straight across the top of the ottoman. She was really starting to show. Brian did the math in his head. Almost twenty weeks now, based on what they had learned at her first ultrasound.

"How many yet to grade?"

"Why did I assign papers?" she moaned, eyes still closed. "You should have stopped me. I'd kill for some graduate students."

"Wasn't it Einstein who said that the supreme art of the teacher is to awaken joy in creative expression and knowledge?"

"What a blowhard."

Brian laughed and saw the smile form on Melissa's lips. It was good to see her like this, particularly given the stress of the past few months.

"You need to take me out," she said abruptly, looking over at him.

"It's eleven degrees out there, and we're a half hour away from anything that would be open."

"It's only seven thirty on a Friday night."

"Everything closed an hour ago. It's small-town North Dakota, not DC, remember?"

"*You betcha,*" she replied with a laugh, mimicking the native accent. "I'll get dressed. Let's go out for coffee."

"You know I don't drink coffee," Brian said, chuckling at the imitation.

"And you know I don't care. You're taking me out for a treat. It's what couples do—we're married now, remember?"

"You're just bored."

"I need a break. You're the one who gets bored."

"I'm not bored."

"Yes, you are," she insisted lightheartedly.

"It's nice and warm, I'm settled, I have a good book and good company. What more could I want?"

"You *must* be bored. I'll prove it. What are you reading?" she asked, tilting her head, trying to see the title.

Brian closed the book and set it down on his lap. "I know what you're up to."

"What is it?"

"You just want to mock me."

"If you don't tell me, I'm coming over there," she warned playfully.

Brian sighed and looked at the ceiling. He held up the book.

"Phoenician grammar? Seriously? How can you even be conscious?"

"Like I said, you just enjoy making fun of me."

"Really, let's go out," Melissa persisted. "We'll find something open in Fargo. You start training in two weeks, and when that happens, it'll be harder to get the free time. I'll be ready in ten minutes. Go get your shoes on—and change that shirt."

He watched her disappear into the hallway, then got up and headed downstairs. She was right. He'd finished what he'd promised Father Benedict three months ago that he would do—at least in the way he conceived it could be done. Now it was time to begin his own new life. He missed the priest desperately. *Where are you, Andrew?*

Brian changed quickly and came back upstairs. Melissa was waiting for him. He knew instantly her mood had changed.

"What is it?"

"Oh, just . . . this again," she muttered, putting her hand over her abdomen. "I shouldn't have looked at myself . . . and having to wear maternity jeans, and . . ." She let her voice trail off, her lip quivering.

Brian walked over and took her in his arms, holding her tightly.

"I'm sorry," she said, carefully wiping away a tear. "I've been trying not to think about all this . . . all the uncertainty . . . about Monday."

"Everything will be all right," Brian tried to assure her. "You'll be in and out of the doctor's office. The first ultrasound went fine. None of the tests detected anything unusual."

"All we learned from the first one is that it's alive—" she caught herself. "I mean, that he . . . or she . . . has a heartbeat. This time we're going to *see* something."

Brian heard the fear in her voice and hugged her again. "Look," he said gently, tilting her chin upward. "No matter what, we're going to get through this. We'll make the right decisions. You'll be safe."

The two of them left the house together in silence. Brian started the car and, after waiting a couple minutes to let the engine warm, pulled out of the driveway. All was quiet. The streets were empty.

Only the silent figure in the idling car two blocks away, watching the house through night-vision binoculars, noted their departure.

6

Take from the church the miraculous, the supernatural,
the incomprehensible, the unreasonable, the impossible,
the unknowable, and the absurd, and nothing but a vacuum remains.

—*Robert Green Ingersoll*

Beeeeeepppp! Beeeeeepppp! Beeeeeepppp!

The sonic burst from the medical alarm jolted the sleeping woman to consciousness. Her mind focused immediately. Pulling on the robe that was draped over a nearby chair, she bolted through her door, and down the short hallway into the center of a circular hub filled with furniture. She darted across the hub and into the corridor immediately opposite, cleanly bisecting the central living space with her path. The sprint took only seconds.

She pushed open the door and rushed toward the man lying on the bed. His CPAP face mask was secure, but his head jerked erratically from side to side, his shoulders shuddering in slight convulsions. She quickly scanned his vitals and then breathed a sigh of relief. Only a nightmare—again.

"Sabi," she said calmly as she removed his mask, her voice just over a whisper. She stroked the beads of sweat from his forehead with her hand, then patted his cheek. "Sabi, it's me. Wake up. You're okay."

His eyes fluttered open. His pulse and breathing slowed and soon returned to normal. A weak but apologetic smile creased his face. "So sorry," he whispered in the heavy eastern European accent that endeared him to his "family," as he referred to them.

"Quite all right." She dabbed his face with a soft towel. "Same dream?"

"Yes," he replied thoughtfully, "but this time . . . new things. I was moving toward a door—the same door as always. It was very dark, but small lights on the ceiling helped me see. The door opened for me—"

"And just like always, it's a room you've never seen, and it's very large—like a warehouse—and has lights and lots of equipment, boxes, and other things scattered everywhere?"

"Yes, but . . ." He closed his eyes in concentration. "But this time I hear voices . . . a woman. She is angry, but also frightened—*very* frightened. Some great evil is in the room as well. I smell . . . blood. It is the stench of blood. And *I can feel her terror.*"

He started to gasp. The woman peered at the monitor and saw that his readings were ascending rapidly. "It's okay," she comforted him, patting his shoulder. "Don't be afraid."

"I am not afraid," he said, recovering his voice. "*She* is so very afraid. In my dream I am calm, even as I hear her scream."

His caretaker frowned. "How is that? Why?"

The man's eyes gazed into the blackness of the room's ceiling, fixed on the scene running through his memory. "The presence of God is there . . . somewhere . . . everywhere." His eyes widened. "He bids me to—to defy the evil."

"But . . . how?" she asked, startled by his description.

"I do not know."

7

It is a mistake to look too far ahead.
Only one link of the chain of destiny can be handled at a time.

—*Sir Winston Churchill*

"Oh, that is *so* good." Melissa gingerly sipped her latte, holding the cup with both hands, inhaling the aroma rising in sinewy, steamy vapors from the cup. "You just don't know what you're missing," she said, diverting her attention to Brian, who was seated across from her at the strategically undersized table.

"Actually, I do," he replied, watching her contentedly. "I don't know how you can drink that stuff."

"Mormon," she teased. Brian laughed heartily.

Melissa took another sip and put down her cup. "Thanks for getting me out of the house," she said, stroking Brian's hand. His gaze moved from her mesmerizing green eyes down to their hands. He watched her fingers moving lightly across his own.

"You're doing so much better now in public," she congratulated him with a knowing smile. "You didn't even flinch that time."

"You're never going to let me forget about that dinner, are you?"

"Nope." She took the cup in her hands once more. "We can laugh at it now, but that was unbelievably awkward."

"It wasn't that bad, like everyone saw it or stared at us—for too long, anyway," Brian objected weakly. *Awkward* didn't even begin to describe it. The memory made him grin now, but he could still feel some of the sting of the moment.

"I felt like I was on TV."

"Oh, come on."

"No matter. I don't care if we ever go back to that restaurant anyway. We can always drive to Fargo if we want to go out."

"I'm sure there's another place in town."

"There's a McDonald's, the college dining hall, and a grill with a three-lane bowling alley. I already looked."

Brian laughed again. "Admit it—you're getting attached to the charm of small-town life."

"I'd use the word 'adapting.' "

"'Adapting' is good," he continued, inching his chair a bit closer to the table. "You were right about pretending to be married. It was a much better idea than the brother-and-sister routine. It deflects a lot of questions."

"But it'll create others if we're not in married mode."

"For sure."

"And speaking of marital bliss, let's do something else couples do," she said, pausing to catch his expression.

"Is this going where I think it's going?"

"Let's *talk*," she said, smiling. "There are things a husband and wife should know about each other. We don't want to get our wires crossed in a conversation with other people."

"Haven't we done this at least a half a dozen times?"

"Really?" Melissa feigned surprise. "You mean that in three months, we've cast five or ten minutes to the wind of personal details *six* times? That's really overkill."

"Okay, okay," he surrendered. "You know I'm not exactly skilled at this sort of thing."

"You're the only pretend husband I have, so you'll have to do."

"Okay, what do you want to talk about?"

Melissa took note of his body language. "If you feel uneasy now, wait until I make you start these discussions."

"Did you want to talk or just terrify me?"

"As much as I enjoy the latter," she laughed, "we have to be practical." She thought for a moment. "Tell me one thing that you've learned about me since we started living together that surprised you."

"That's easy—you can cook."

"You're right," Melissa replied. "You really aren't good at this."

"No, I mean you can *really* cook. I'm thoroughly impressed. You're amazing."

"Well, that's a little better." She smiled appreciatively. "And why was that a surprise?"

He paused for a moment, struggling to come up with a good explanation, "I think of you as a professional. I guess I didn't think that you'd be so . . . domestic."

Melissa sighed and rolled her eyes.

"What's the matter?"

"You should never tell a woman you can't picture her as domestic. Even if she wouldn't use the word herself, it's offensive."

"Why?"

"Because it is. You've been alone too long."

"Sorry."

"It's fine—I know where your heart is," she said, smiling. "Anyway, you have to remember, I was raised a good little Baptist girl. Women must be 'keepers at home,' you know," she added in a preachy twang.

"A profound piece of biblical wisdom."

"Sexist," she accused him lightheartedly.

"Well, you've got me all figured out," he chuckled. "You're turn now. What revelations about me have come to light?"

"Actually, not much," Melissa answered matter-of-factly. "That's something I aim to change."

Brian looked at her in uncertain silence.

"I've learned that you like routine," she began. "You basically do the same things every day, in the same way, and in the same order."

"Is there a problem with that?" he asked, feeling a bit defensive.

"Of course not. It's cute, actually. You also like to arrange your books by topic and height, left to right. You love football. You'll eat anything if I call it pizza. You like to rinse the dishes before putting them in the dishwasher. You actually enjoy shopping for groceries. You use only three fingers when you type. You—"

"Whoa, I thought you weren't learning anything about me!" he protested, amused. "I feel like a test subject."

"Well I'm *not* learning anything about *you,*" she replied, earnestly. "I'm just picking up on your habits. None of these things are personal."

"The habits are more interesting."

"Oh, stop it."

"You already know the important things, anyway," Brian insisted. "And I can't say I've learned a lot about you that's very personal, either."

"Have you ever *asked*?"

Brian sat back in his chair. Melissa raised her eyebrows, punctuating the question.

"You win," Brian said.

"I don't want to defeat you. I want to *know* you."

Suddenly, Brian and Melissa abruptly turned their heads in the same direction. They were seized by the sense that they were being watched. A young woman in jeans and a rumpled pullover fleece, her heavy winter coat draped over her arm, stood a short distance away staring at them. Her curly, light-brown hair looked as though it hadn't been washed in days. She wore no make-up. There was a small but noticeable infinity-loop tattoo on her neck. Her astonished expression—lips apart, eyes wide—unnerved them. They froze for a few eternal seconds.

"Can we help you?" Brian asked, breaking the silence.

The girl ignored him completely, her gaze fixed on Melissa, taking in every detail of her face. "I can't believe it. Dr. Kelley—Dr. Melissa Kelley," she said with alarming clarity. "What are you doing in North Dakota?"

Melissa's face was calm. Neither Brian nor her interrogator noticed her clasp her hands in her lap to prevent them from shaking. "I don't know how, but you have my first name correct," she bluffed. "But my full name is Melissa Carter. This is my husband, Brian."

"I don't care who *he* is," the girl persisted. "*You're* Melissa Kelley, from Georgetown University."

8

Coincidences are God's way of getting our attention.

—*Frederick Buechner*

"Who are you?" demanded Brian, startled. He moved his chair to position himself between the girl and Melissa.

"Why don't you ask your wife?" the girl replied defiantly, stepping to the side to speak to Melissa again. "You don't remember me, do you?"

"If you want to talk, have a seat." Brian stood up slowly, sensing that he needed to prevent this situation from escalating. He grabbed a chair from the adjacent table and positioned it for the young woman. Melissa said nothing.

The girl sat down without hesitating, still staring at Melissa, but she didn't repeat the question. The short break helped Melissa regain some composure. "I'm not sure why you're so convinced I'm this Melissa Kelley," she began, "but you're right about my not knowing who you are."

"Figures," the girl smirked, her voice trembling unexpectedly. She looked down at the table, then cupped her face in her hands and began to sob quietly. Brian and Melissa glanced at each other, mystified but still aghast at the sudden assault on their secret.

"Do you need help?" Brian asked.

"Yeah, I need help," she sniffed, looking at both of them. "I need a buttload of help, but I'm not going to find any. A few weeks ago it was all a thrill. In college we talked all the time about sticking it to the freakin' feds, but now I can't see any way out. At least Dr. Kelley would have understood why I did it."

"What kind of trouble are you in?" Melissa probed, carefully.

"I stole something. Actually, I took something my boyfriend gave me. He stole it, although it would be more correct to say he saved it. He's in jail now, but I got away with it—at least for now."

"Who are you running from?" Brian asked.

"The government, federal agents, FBI—who the hell knows?" She fretted with exasperation. "Do you have any idea what it's like to be on the run?" The girl's expression lapsed into distress as she fought back more tears.

Brian and Melissa avoided making eye contact. Both feared the same thing: that a shared connection might encourage the girl's suspicion. "Brian, why don't you get her something to drink?" Melissa suggested. "We can talk when she's ready."

The distraught girl nodded, and Brian left the table. He returned in a few minutes with her drink. The girl took it without a thank you and held it in her lap.

"Brian, this is Becky—Becky Leyden." Melissa was careful not to telegraph that there was something familiar about the name, though she couldn't place it. "Fargo is Becky's home town, but she hasn't been here for almost five years."

The girl nodded, and Melissa waited, prompting the girl to take over. "I moved to California after high school," the girl explained. "I was majoring in peace and conflict studies at Berkeley—you know, community activism, working for change, empower the 99 percent, 'screw capitalism,' and all that."

"Then what?" Brian prodded.

"After graduating I spent the next two years with Greenpeace. That's where I met my boyfriend. He was in a PhD program in environmental studies—global change ecology. He had a masters in polar studies from the UK. That's how he got to the Antarctic, where this whole mess erupted."

"What kind of trouble can you find in the Antarctic?" Brian asked.

"You wouldn't believe me if I told you."

"I might."

"I doubt it, though it's right up Dr. Kelley's alley." She glanced at Melissa, who knew she was deliberately referring to her by her actual name, as if probing for an advantage in a battle of wits. "Anyway, I applied to the graduate program in American studies a year ago at Georgetown. I wanted to study right-wing fascist movements in America. Not the normal ones like the Tea Party, though. I'm into—or *was* into—Nazi occult disciples, the Aryan Nation, the neo-pagan apocalyptic loons."

"I wanted to study under Melissa Kelley," she added, making direct eye contact again with Melissa, "since she's the best for that sort of thing."

Melissa stood her ground, trying not to let on that the brief recounting had jarred her memory. She now remembered voting to accept Becky's application into the program.

"But Dr. Kelley disappeared this past summer," Becky continued, scowling at Melissa. "All the dean would say is that she up and left the department to 'pursue personal interests.' So I quit. It was that simple. She was the reason I had applied."

She shook her head. "But as awful as that disappointment was, it was nothing compared to what followed after my boyfriend got home from his summer post-doc."

"Let me guess," Brian interrupted. "Your boyfriend brought government property back with him, and they were more or less waiting for him when he got to the States."

"Basically," she conceded. "He had barely been home a day when one of our friends called and told us federal agents had questioned them about him. The feds didn't know he was living with me; they'd gone to his old apartment.

"Some of the activist groups I hang with are ready for that sort of harassment, though. They got us out of DC in a car with some cash, but it only lasted a couple weeks. My boyfriend got desperate and tried to steal some money from a convenience store in Chicago, but he got caught. I was waiting for him in the car and took off when the cops arrived. He was still inside. That was our agreement, since I was carrying what they wanted. I had enough gas money left to get here. That was two days ago."

"I'm sure they know you're from North Dakota, so they'll guess you were heading here. Have you told your parents what's going on?" asked Brian.

"My parents moved to Mesa a couple years ago, so I've been staying with a friend from high school. It will make me harder to find, but it puts her at risk. They'll track me if I use a credit card, and I'm out of cash. It's looking like the end of the road . . ." Her voice cracked. "I really don't want to go to prison, but it was the right thing to do. The government is so freaking corrupt. We can't just let them fabricate history."

"What do you mean by that?" Melissa asked.

The girl took a deep breath and scanned the café for anyone who might be looking in her direction. "About six months ago, my boyfriend's scientific team in the Antarctic accidentally discovered plans for a Nazi base," she explained, eyeing Melissa carefully. "It was to be built in *Neuschwabenland*."

Melissa managed to suppress a gasp, but Becky saw the shock in her eyes.

"My boyfriend was at the station to study ice-core samples," she continued. "The first core he saw was contaminated. It had a human thumb in it, along with part of some sort of notebook. The core drill had bored right through it all. What are the odds?"

"That's . . ." Brian struggled for a response, amazed at the inconceivable circumstance.

"Freakin' incredible, I know," Becky finished his sentence. "Of course," she continued, now eyeing both of them carefully, "Antarctica has never been inhabited by humans. That fact, in addition to the notebook, immediately told everyone they had a modern anomaly. None of the researchers or their funding agencies knew of any missing-person report from the region or anywhere in Antarctica. In fact, only one agency—the one to whom my boyfriend was ultimately responsible for his funding—reacted."

"What agency was that?" Melissa asked.

"NASA."

"NASA?"

"They're involved in Antarctic research to study how life might evolve and sustain itself in extreme environments—ecosystems that are, in theory, similar to other planets. But that's just the official reason of interest. They have other, more obscure connections."

"Meaning what?" Brian asked, playing dumb. He and Melissa had an irresistible intuition of where this was going.

"The Nazis claimed the territory of Neuschwabenland during an expedition from December of 1938 until April of 1939. They wanted land in Antarctica for their whaling fleet, since the whaling industry supplied oil for food products as well as glycerin for creating nitroglycerine, used in explosives. The expedition also had secret military goals. On the return journey the expedition was supposed to check out some isolated islands off the coast of Brazil as potential landing places for the German Navy, especially U-boats."

"What did NASA say when they heard about the discovery?"

"They did what our beloved capitalistic superpower always does: asserted complete ownership and command of the situation. They decreed that all materials related to the discovery were to be impounded and returned to them. No one was to handle them, and the news was to be considered classified."

"So what happened?"

"All the scientists at the station had a look at them," she said with a satisfied grin. "They were too late in issuing the warning about not contacting the outside world about the news. My boyfriend had already emailed me about it. He knew I was into Nazis and World War II, and he'd seen the notebook fragments before the find was reported. He told me about a word he found in the notebook, but I didn't learn anything more until he came home. That first email was followed by news of NASA's orders. Further outside contact was strictly monitored, so we had to avoid the subject. We had no time to work out a code for communicating."

"What was the word he sent you?" Brian asked.

"Belastung."

"It means 'elevator,'" Melissa said thoughtfully, her mind running through the implications.

Becky noticed Melissa's slip and quickly seized the opening. "Do you remember," she asked, looking at Melissa, "the lecture you gave at Stanford a few years ago about neo-Nazi apocalyptic beliefs and Siegmeister's Hollow Earth ideas?"

"Yes," Melissa answered, her focus returning.

"Yeah, so do I, *Dr. Kelley.*"

"I—" Melissa stopped herself and closed her eyes. She'd blown it.

"Can we cut the alias crap now?" Becky asked.

Brian looked at her face. There was no hint of triumph on it, only relief mixed with resolve. It didn't help him feel any less exposed. "Look," he said, "we both know what it's like to be on the run. We're in a sort of witness-protection situation."

"Hey, I'm not looking to put either of you in danger."

"We're already in danger!" Melissa snapped, though she managed to keep her voice low. "We're not running from people who operate within the law like you are. The people who are after us are completely off the radar and report to no one. You have no idea."

"If you ever mention to anyone that you saw Dr. Kelley here," Brian said ominously, "you won't just be trying to avoid prison. You'll be looking to stay alive, like we are."

"He's not kidding," Melissa added. "Do you seriously think I'd leave a tenured position at Georgetown to come *here* if I wasn't forced to?"

"No, of course not."

"The best thing you can do is turn yourself in and return the fragments," Melissa continued. "It's your only chance for any leniency. Like I said, your pursuers function within the law—ours don't."

"You want me to give them what they want so they can just bury it?

Don't you want to see the fragments?"

"Of course I want to see them," said Melissa, keeping her voice low, "but you have to return them." She paused contemplatively. "I have an idea."

"What are you thinking?" Brian asked.

"We need to find some place to make copies of the fragments."

"Sounds simple," said Becky. "I feel sort of stupid that I didn't think of that. I guess all I've been thinking about is getting nabbed. The main library at North Dakota State here in Fargo is open until midnight. It's close."

"Melissa," Brian cautioned, "if we get caught with her, it's going to be very hard to maintain our identities here."

"We'll make up something. If the police are ready to grab her and we're there, we'll say she's a poor college student who asked for money for the holidays. It's a Catholic school, so acts of charity are believable. We're only in trouble if she gives away my identity."

"I won't do that," Becky promised. "I know what you're going through. Besides, I'd never get in bed with the police state."

Brian sighed. Becky's leftist rhetoric was irritating, though her mindset was probably helpful under the circumstances. Still, he was uneasy. "No offense, but we don't have anything beyond your assurances."

"Yes, we do," Melissa offered. "If we find out she's said anything—and no doubt, we would—I'll destroy the copies of the fragments. They aren't worth our lives. If she really cares about the truth being preserved, she'll turn herself in, return the fragments, and keep her mouth shut."

Melissa stood up and put on her coat. "It's time to choose. If you ever want these fragments to see the light of day, you'll follow the plan. Otherwise, we never saw you, and you're on your own. You'll get caught, and it will all be worth nothing."

"Let's go," Becky said, pushing her chair back from the table.

"Not so fast," said Brian. "We don't want to be seen leaving together. Melissa and I will leave and go to our car. Wait a few minutes, then meet us there. It's the burgundy Taurus at the end of the back parking lot. It will be idling."

"Got it."

Brian and Melissa left the table and headed outside. Becky waited dutifully, as instructed, before leaving.

That's right. Don't miss your ride, thought the balding man across the room. He calmly but quickly took out his ear buds and turned off his portable listening device, which was designed to appear, to the untrained eye, as a normal iPhone. He sipped the last of his mocha, watched the girl exit, then put on his coat and followed.

9

There is nothing like looking, if you want to find something.
You certainly usually find something, if you look,
but it is not always quite the something you were after.

—*J. R. R. Tolkien*, The Hobbit

"We should scan the photocopies as a backup," Brian said, removing his coat as he and Melissa walked through the door of their home.

"Good idea. I'll be right downstairs."

Brian opened the door off the main hallway that led down to their finished basement. The space was decorated to appear as a large family room, but it actually served as Brian's room—or, as Melissa like to refer to it, his cloister. Early on, he and Melissa had decided to make it look like the two of them shared her room, creating the environment any visitors would expect. Brian kept a few items of clothing downstairs in a small closet, along with his library and desk. Although the space had a small room that could have served as a bedroom, they had decided to use it for storage—again to conceal the fact that Brian slept downstairs on the couch.

Brian was at his desk waiting for his computer to boot up when Melissa came down the steps. She grabbed a pen from the desk and numbered each of the pages, handing them in turn to Brian, who fed them into the scanner.

"Make sure you give them some sort of innocuous file name."

"Right."

Once they had saved and backed up the files, they spread the sheets of paper across the available space of Brian's desktop. There were four pages in all. Each page held four or five circles that the core drill had cut from a notebook. In most cases the fragments held content on both sides. Some fragments had words on them that had been cut mid-sentence from their context; others had portions of what were apparently blueprints.

Melissa and Brian had no idea if the circles could be aligned in such a way as to match fronts with backs, since Becky had admitted she and her boyfriend had exercised no care in looking at the fragments in a specific order. The girl had also divulged that the material in her possession was not the entirety of the notebook content. Her boyfriend had pulled random circle fragments from the notebook material thinking that no one would notice if a few had been removed.

"There's the one with '*Belastung*'—that one, at the top," Melissa pointed. "The ink has blurred a bit, but you can make it out. And I'm guessing that drawing underneath is part of a diagram for the elevator."

Brian nodded.

"What do you make of these?" Brian asked. "Squares and triangles—are they part of an architectural drawing?"

"Maybe."

They continued to examine the images, particularly those that had words.

"Here's another legible one," Melissa said, pointing. "It might be '*Strahlturb*,' if that last word that's cut off is 'turbine.' Can you look up '*Strahlturbine*'? I don't know what the first part would mean."

"Yep." Brian quickly located a German-English dictionary on the web. "Got it. Get this: It means 'jet turbine.' "

"'Jet turbine'?" Melissa repeated, puzzled. "The German expedition was in the late 1930s. Was there anything like that then?"

"I don't know if they were used in jets," he replied, "but I recall reading about turbines for velocity that far back. It may be just a coincidence, but the source I read that in was about somebody we both know—Viktor Schauberger. He worked on turbine technology back in the early thirties."

"Good grief," she muttered, "the saucer geek. I feel like I'm back at Area 51."

Brian nodded. "I hear you. Most of Schauberger's research was destroyed when the Allies bombed Germany's top-secret rocket facility, Peenemünde, in 1943. Maybe the Nazis were thinking of using some of his work at an Antarctic base."

Melissa leaned on Brian's desk to survey the fragment copies. "This is pretty amazing. Up until this, the only potential info about a Nazi base in the Antarctic was pretty much assigned to propaganda status."

"But as fantastic as all this is," Brian said thoughtfully, "it doesn't prove the Nazis actually built such a base. At best, it only shows they intended such a project."

"True," Melissa said, her lips pursed in thought. "The human thumb proves only that someone was there—which we already knew. The polar expedition of 1938–1939 hasn't been a matter of dispute. But plans for an operational base? There's no documentation that I know of that the Nazis ever went back. War broke out in 1939, so it seems like they would have been pretty preoccupied."

"Still," Brian mused, "the British did set up base camps in the Antarctic during the war, including one in what the Germans claimed as Neuschwabenland."

"And then, of course, there's the notorious Operation Highjump, and Admiral Byrd's alleged battle with Nazi UFOs in the Antarctic right after the war. . ."

She looked at Brian, who said, "It still sounds funny—sort of."

"We can't let our imaginations run too far on this, Brian. The only thing we do know with a fairly high degree of certainty is that the UFO technology wasn't lost. We've lived that part."

"So, what should we do now," Brian asked, "other than hide this stuff and maybe do more research when we're bored? There's no way I'm posting this on the web as an addendum to what I've already put up there. I might as well send Colonel Ferguson a Christmas card."

"There's really nothing to do," Melissa said with a sigh as she gathered the papers.

"Maybe President Fitzgerald will have a suggestion," Brian offered.

"I don't think we should tell him."

"Why not? We know we can trust him."

"I don't doubt that, but he'll probably be upset that we've been exposed. I'm concerned that this new development may make him consider moving us. I could see Andrew going in that direction. I just don't want to move again."

"Neither do I. Okay, so for now we won't say anything."

"I suppose," she added, her mood lightening a bit, "you could hide all these in your secret desk drawer."

"Really?" He rolled his eyes. She suppressed a smile, but he could tell she had a point to make—again.

"I'm sorry it bothers you," he said, glancing at the only drawer in his desk that required a key. "I just have a few private things in there."

"I don't hide anything from you," she came back.

"Don't think of it as hiding. It's just a little personal space."

"Men and their secrets."

"Women and their curiosity."

"I'll figure out where to put the papers," she said, turning toward the stairs. "I might even tell you where."

10

When bad men combine, the good must associate;
else they will fall, one by one, an unpitied
sacrifice in a contemptible struggle.

—*Edmund Burke*

"And how are you this Monday morning—was it Molly?" the tall, sandy-haired man addressed the distracted co-ed seated at the desk.

"Oh, yes," she said glancing up from her keyboard. The man's sparkling blue eyes quickly chased work from her mind. "It's so nice that you remembered," she continued through a dreamy smile.

"Lovely faces are easy to remember," he said charmingly. "I'm sure Gloria will agree," he went on, glancing past the young girl to the secretary seated beyond her at another desk, near the doorway of his destination.

"Of course." Gloria smiled at him over her glasses. "Nice to see you again, Mr. Neff."

"Please, call me Graham, remember?"

"I guess I'm old school," she explained. "Board members deserve a little more formality."

"As you wish. I assume your assistant is doing a fine job," he said, turning his attention back to the younger woman with a smile.

"She's a big help, for sure. President Fitzgerald is expecting you. You can go on in."

"Wonderful." The man nodded appreciatively to the secretary and went into the office, closing the door behind him.

The girl's eyes followed him. "If you need to go out for some air," the older woman said, smirking playfully, "just let me know." The girl blushed.

Inside the office, the man took a seat in front of a white-haired, rotund priest whose face was creased with laughter lines. However, on this occasion his expression was serious. The office held a slight hint of the aroma of pipe tobacco. The priest rose abruptly from his seat and went to the door. The seated man heard him instruct his secretary to make sure they were not disturbed. The priest closed the door before returning to his desk.

"Now we can talk," he said, sighing and getting comfortable. "How was your trip, Graham?" the priest asked.

"Uneventful—and profitable," Neff replied. "The way I like them."

"Excellent. And Tel Aviv? Were there any problems?"

Neff shook his head. "The transaction went well. The cargo is in reasonable shape. There are some concerns, but my associates say they're nothing major."

"I presume you're staying on campus at the guest house?"

"Checked in before walking over here."

"How long will you be with us?"

"I'm not sure. I have some business in the area, so I'll be coming and going. You might see me here and there."

The priest became thoughtful. "How soon till we can all get together?"

"That's tied to the concerns my associates have expressed. I had expected a couple of weeks, but it depends on everyone being ready for travel. If that doesn't materialize, we'll bring whoever is ready."

"I understand. Two weeks would put us on the cusp of Thanksgiving break here. It would be good timing. Campus will be less active, as most of the students will be gone."

"I'll remember that," Neff replied casually. "And how are things with the college? Having a good term?"

"It's quiet. Enrollment is up slightly. We're plugging along."

"Good. I should add that the Tel Aviv arrangement was less expensive than I presumed it would be."

"My, that *is* a surprise."

"Yes. I thought I'd make another contribution with the savings. How does two million dollars sound?"

"Excellent," the priest beamed. "That's very generous."

"I'm sure you'll put it to good use. Take half a million and make sure our friends are taken care of—and keep everything anonymous. As always, I trust you'll be unfailingly cautious."

"Of course. The Lord does indeed work in mysterious ways," the priest said with a contented smile. "I look forward to seeing you around campus."

***

Graham Neff walked the short distance from the college president's office to the parking lot, where a four-door jeep was idling. The burly, balding man inside hit the unlock button as he approached.

"Good morning, Malone."

"Mornin'," the man responded. "Have some coffee."

"Thanks." Neff reached into his coat pocket and produced a baggie with some pills. He emptied the contents into the palm of his hand and popped them into his mouth, swallowing them with a careful sip of coffee.

"You might need something more potent once we talk."

"Tel Aviv?"

"Yep."

"What happened?"

Malone gazed into his own coffee, watching the vapors rise from its heat. He took a sip. "One of them wasn't clean. Nili got rid of the problem. Everyone got stateside okay, though."

"Interesting. Anything else?"

"Nili said it was messy, to put it mildly. She decided to call in Clarise once they were airborne. She must have thought it was serious. Clarise flew herself."

Neff shook his head. "I just told Aloysius everything was going fine."

"I wouldn't tell him any of this—not yet anyway. And if you think we stepped in it with Tel Aviv, wait till you hear what I learned last night."

Neff eyed him curiously.

"For one thing, our target is married."

"That doesn't sound like such a challenge," Neff replied.

"*Challenge* doesn't even begin to describe the situation. You won't believe the rest. I followed the two of them into a coffee shop. I couldn't get set up right away, so I only caught about half of the conversation, but just wait till you hear the recording."

"Do we need backup?"

"I hope not. We're a little short on that right now."

Neff sat back in his chair and rubbed his eyes.

"At the very least," Malone continued, "we'll need to rethink the plan. This is going to take longer than expected. And no matter what we come up with, discretion will be more essential than ever. We can't leave the slightest whiff of a trail or we'll be out of business, and then some."

11

There are no hopeless situations;
there are only men who have grown hopeless about them.

—Clare Boothe Luce

"How are we feeling this morning, Mrs. Carter?" the doctor asked, gently lifting Melissa's top to expose her abdomen.

"Nauseous. It really hit me hard for the first time."

"Well, that's not uncommon. Maybe it's a bit of anxiety, too," he suggested. "This is your first, after all."

"Right," Melissa replied weakly. Her mouth was already beginning to dry. She turned her head to look at Brian, who reached out, took her hand, and forced a smile. He couldn't completely hide his own apprehension.

"It's okay to be a little anxious," the doctor reassured her as he watched her blood pressure and heart rate slowly rising. "Just breathe in and out, slowly. Everything's just fine."

The doctor pulled on a pair of gloves. "This will feel a little cold," he cautioned as he began smearing Melissa's abdomen with the lubricant for the ultrasound. He reached for the transducer. "You can watch on the screen to my right. In case you don't recall, we're checking to make sure everything looks as it should, and, if we're lucky, we'll learn the sex of the baby—presuming you want to know that."

"Sure," Melissa responded, maintaining eye contact with Brian. Her mind started to race. The thought of seeing what was in her womb paralyzed her. She had imagined the likeness of the malformed, freakish thing hundreds of times. She couldn't push the face of Adam from her mind.

Melissa and Brian had tried to recollect the conversation they'd had about Adam with Father Benedict and Lieutenant Sheppard that last day on the base, but they couldn't be certain their recollections were accurate—not when every word was critical. Was Adam a real extraterrestrial? Was he a manufactured entity with enough consciousness to go through the motions the Group had contrived?

Melissa remembered Sheppard telling her that the Grays he knew of were dumb and useless, created by the Group to perpetuate an ET mythology. But she also recalled his uncertainty about the mind scans. He'd insisted the Grays—whatever they were—did not have that ability. She'd read a lot about so-called alien abduction, about how many researchers had concluded that mind scans were some sort of electrically stimulated effect that, along with a screen memory placed in a person's brain, amounted to mental conditioning—again to perpetuate the myth in alien visitation for whatever grander agenda.

She'd been content with all that until she discovered she was somehow pregnant. True, medical science could make women pregnant these days without intercourse, but the context of their bizarre experiences and the trauma of all that went on in the places she'd seen deep underground spurred her imagination in all the wrong ways. What about the pages Neil had given Brian? It hadn't taken long to figure out they were part of a DNA sequence. And why were parts of it circled? *What did they do to me*? Her pulse began to soar on the monitor.

"Mrs. Carter," said the doctor, hesitating, surprised by the spike, "calm down. Breathe slowly. You don't want to stress the baby." He looked curiously at Brian.

"She's had some friends whose ultrasounds revealed some unfortunate things," Brian lied, doing his best to explain Melissa's behavior. "This is a big step for her. I'll be her eyes."

"I'm sorry to hear that. I'll try to be brief, then. Just do what you can to keep her calm."

Brian nodded.

The doctor placed the transducer on Melissa's abdomen. Brian watched the monitor, fascinated by the sight. The grainy visual was an unfamiliar medium and initially disorienting. As his eyes adjusted to the fuzziness of the image and the doctor's movements, he was able to discern a small form.

"Have you felt any movement?" the doctor asked.

"A couple times," Melissa managed to reply.

"Okay, let's see. We have a slight side profile; the face is turned away from view—that's why we're only seeing one arm now. The crown of the skull looks good. Let me get some measurements."

Melissa opened her eyes to read Brian's face. She saw his concentration, but no alarm. She began to breathe more naturally.

The doctor held the transducer still and stared at the screen.

"Hmm . . ." He began to move the instrument to different positions on Melissa's abdomen, at times maintaining contact with her flesh, at other times lifting it to reposition it. Brian's attention alternated between the screen and the doctor's expression. He seemed perplexed and was far too quiet.

"Well, this is unexpected," the doctor finally said.

Melissa froze. In seconds, her face contorted in anguished panic. Her pulse raced again.

"No reason to worry, Mrs. Carter," the doctor said reassuringly, having seen Melissa's body tighten out of the corner of his eye. "You're fine."

Brian stroked her forehead. "Everything I'm seeing looks normal," he reassured her. "What is it?" Brian asked, turning to the doctor.

"Take a look. Here, I think I can get her to move just a bit."

"Her?" Brian wondered aloud.

"Yep. See the vertical lines there between the legs? You have a girl."

"Yes, I see them. So it's a girl," Brian said, looking at Melissa and smiling. Her eyes were still closed.

"But that's not the surprise," the doctor continued. "Take another look. I think I can get her to adjust her position again just a bit." He began gliding the transducer to different positions.

Melissa opened her eyes to watch Brian's expression carefully. He squinted and tilted his head back and forth, intently studying the screen.

"No way . . ." Brian said absently. He was still transfixed by the view, his intense expression shifting to one of amazement. He felt Melissa's hand suddenly tighten in alarm in his own. He patted her hand while he watched, shaking his head. Then he smiled.

"Twins," he said with a bewildered smile, turning to Melissa.

"*What*?" Melissa finally spoke, astonishment evident in her voice.

"Twins," the doctor confirmed. "Congratulations!"

"How can that be?" Melissa demanded. "There was only one heartbeat at the first ultrasound."

"I know, Mrs. Carter. I was there, remember?" he teased. "This really isn't uncommon. Sometimes we only get one heartbeat because the heartbeats of both babies are beating in unison. I've known cases where women were pregnant six months and had three or four ultrasounds before anyone knew there were twins. It's a cramped space in there, and the baby we see can prevent the other from coming into view. You're thirty-three, and women over thirty who have delayed pregnancy are more likely to have twins. And you for sure are having twins—twin girls, to be more precise."

"Shouldn't my wife be . . . bigger?" Brian asked awkwardly.

"Yes, for twins she should be showing more. It might be because of the abortion she had when she was nineteen. Statistically, there's a link between abortion and lower birthweight in a subsequent pregnancy. You should also know there's a link between previous abortion and later premature birth. But I'd say that, unless she doesn't start to show in a more pronounced way in the next month, things are progressing fine, and there's no cause for concern."

"What . . . what do they look like?" Melissa asked hesitantly.

Brian could sense the dread in her voice. He felt it, too. "Is there any way to get a glimpse of the faces?" he asked.

"We can try." The doctor busied himself with the transducer, looking for a workable angle. "Maybe if you turned over a bit on your side, Mrs. Carter."

Melissa complied, still refusing to look at the screen.

"There we go," he said, holding the device steady. He quickly pushed a button to capture a still image. "Now, bear in mind that you're only at twenty weeks. Lots of babies on ultrasounds at this point look like little aliens, but that's normal."

Melissa exploded with a wail and started to cry. Brian quickly leaned over and held her face in his hands as gently as he could. Her body shook with terror. With a jerk, she brought her knees to her chest to roll off the table, nearly smashing the doctor on the chin. She had turned toward Brian, whose body blocked her from escaping from the table.

"Melissa, it's okay," Brian said as he pressed his cheek to hers and whispered in her ear. "It's okay. They're beautiful—really. Everything's normal."

He felt her arms and chest relax under his own. She let go of the sides of the table and draped her weary arms around his shoulders, still sobbing. Brian waited for a moment, then stood up, glaring at the doctor. "Pretty poor choice of words."

"I'm so sorry," the doctor apologized, genuinely mortified. "Most patients find it humorous."

"Are we done here?" Brian replied coldly.

"There's no need to—"

"Are we done?"

"Certainly. Let's get a 4-D view of that snapshot; it's the latest thing, and the results are stunning," he said, touching the console. "Perhaps that will put your wife's mind at ease. We'll naturally be running more blood tests, but so far as I can see, everything here is completely normal. You have two lovely little girls. I'll leave the two of you alone for a moment. Again, my apologies."

Still fuming, Brian watched the doctor exit the room. He looked at the new image on the monitor. "Wow," he said softly, his calm returning. He looked down at Melissa. She was still catching her breath, but her eyes were open, looking up at him. "I'll understand if you decide not to," he said, "but you should look at this 4-D. What a wonder."

Melissa closed her eyes, steadying herself, and then turned her head. She stared at the two faces on the screen, tightly huddled together side-by-side, so delicate, so detailed, so . . . human.

"Thank God," she whispered, and closed her eyes.

12

Security is mostly a superstition. It does not exist in nature, nor do the children of men as a whole experience it. Avoiding danger is no safer in the long run than outright exposure. Life is either a daring adventure, or nothing.

—*Helen Keller*

"Mr. Carter, could we have a word with you, please?"

Brian glanced over his shoulder, then put the stack of books he was carrying into the library cart. Instinctively he plucked the two books from the row facing the wrong way and corrected the disorder before turning around.

"Who are you?" he asked politely, not offering a handshake.

"My name is Graham Neff," the speaker answered. "This is my friend, Doug Malone. We're from out of town."

Brian eyed them suspiciously. Neff was about six feet tall, a few inches shorter than he was, and lighter, but trim and athletic. Brian guessed he was in his forties. The other man was short and stocky, a balding fireplug of about sixty with a bushy, gray-white mustache that needed some grooming. Brian had been in North Dakota for almost four months now, and this was the first time anyone outside the college library staff where he volunteered had introduced themselves to him. Given the disturbing surprise at the coffee shop less than a week ago, he couldn't assume this overture was a casual synchronicity.

"Now's really not a good time," he answered. "I have a lot to do."

"You can do it tomorrow," Neff replied. "You get off work in less than five minutes. We've been waiting. We know you volunteer here a couple days a week."

"Yeah, I guess you're right," Brian replied, more annoyed than flustered. "I have to pick up my wife. Sorry."

"Your wife's class just started," Malone said quietly. "We know her schedule, too. We'll be done before she's finished."

"Okay. Let me be honest, then," Brian said. "I'm not in the mood."

"I appreciate your candor," Neff said, becoming serious. He glanced around to make sure they had no audience, then lowered his voice to a whisper. "I have no doubt you mean what you've said, *Dr. Scott.*" He watched Brian's expression carefully. Brian made no move and said nothing.

"We don't mean any harm," Neff continued. "We know who you are, and that's why we're here. We need information."

"My name is Brian Carter, and unless I'm mistaken, you know where I live. Whoever this Dr. Scott is, he isn't me." Brian moved to walk away, but Malone grabbed him by the arm. His grip was firm but not menacing. Brian's eyes flashed with anger, but he stayed under control. In his periphery he noticed they had drawn the attention of some students sitting at a nearby table.

"I should tell you," Malone added as he released Brian's arm, "that I followed you and your wife to the coffee shop last Friday night and caught the end of your conversation—the one about the Antarctic discovery."

"And just how did you do that?"

"One of these," Malone said, reaching into his pocket and producing what looked like an iPhone. "A portable listening device. It has a pretty sophisticated antennae. All I need to do is point it—"

"At whoever you feel like spying on. Nice."

"We aren't a threat," Neff explained. "Would Malone tell you he's been trailing you if we wanted trouble? Would we meet you in a public place if we had any intention of exposing you or your wife?"

"Maybe you're just trying to be clever."

"This is hardly clever," Neff said with a forced smile, hoping to convince onlookers that the conversation was a friendly one.

"Who are you guys? Let's see some ID."

"Let's go upstairs to the board room after you're done with your shift," Neff suggested. "We'll tell you what we can."

"The board room is locked and off limits to patrons. You don't just walk in there."

"You do if you have the key," Neff replied. He produced a set of keys from his coat pocket and flipped his way to a distinctively shaped silver key. Brian recognized it. He couldn't conceal his confounded expression.

"Graham's on the college's Board of Trustees," Malone explained, anticipating Brian's question. "He paid for the remodel in there, too."

Brian clocked out, grabbed his coat and his backpack from behind the desk, and went upstairs with the two strangers, dismayed by the brief exchange. He had hardly felt secure in their circumstances, but now it seemed as though the façade he and Melissa had been so careful to erect was crumbling right before his eyes. Neff opened the door and gestured for the other two to enter. He locked the door behind them. They took off their coats and took seats at one end of a long, polished mahogany table.

"So who are you?" Brian demanded.

"That's a bit more difficult to explain than you might imagine, Dr. Scott," Neff replied thoughtfully, folding his hands. "We can't actually tell you much about ourselves and what we do."

"Hardly seems like a fair exchange."

"I know, but we can only speak in generalities. The one thing I can be up front about is that we need your help."

"My help? If you guys have been following me around, you know I'm unemployed at the moment. I come here a couple days to week to volunteer in order to beat the boredom. I can't tell you anything you'd need to know except where the restrooms are."

"Actually," Malone droned though a knowing stare, "based on what I heard last Friday night, I'd say you volunteer here to be close to your wife. It's a good idea."

"Thanks, dad."

Malone's cheeks flushed red. "Being a wise guy isn't going to help you or us. We know you're either going to be at home or here—especially since the job you thought you had dried up this morning."

Brian couldn't hide his surprise, but his shocked expression quickly turned angry. "I'm guessing the police won't believe me when I tell them my phone is being tapped by Wilford Brimley, but I'll give it a try."

"You're good at pushing buttons, aren't—"

"Take it easy, Doug," Neff intervened. "He's doing what we'd do. He's exposed." He turned to Brian. "We haven't tapped your phone. We followed you this morning when you stopped by the real estate office, then went in and talked to them after you left."

"Are you the good cop?" Brian asked, smirking.

"Let me explain how we found you," Neff continued, ignoring Brian's sarcasm. He reached into his coat and took out a folded mass of paper. Brian could see it was a map of the United States. Neff spread it out on the table and turned it in Brian's direction.

"Here's Fargo, roughly our location. The five circles on the map are the places you drove to in order to upload your material to the Internet. They were all locations with secured Wi-Fi—hotels, libraries, coffee shops. You didn't store your content in the cloud; you had it on a flash. You created anonymous email addresses and free FTP programs with trial subscriptions to upload the information to a list of three or four UFO and conspiracy forums each time—and never the same ones, I might add. Some of my associates frequent a couple of the forums you used, which is where we first saw your stuff."

He looked at Brian, who returned his gaze and said nothing.

"The content was so compelling that we took an interest," Malone explained, now composed. "But we had no idea who you were or where you lived. Sure, we could find the locations where the upload occurred through the IP addresses, but that was about it. You did a good job of covering your tracks. The places where you got online had no relationship. When we drew lines between them, we could see there was no logical center—the locations were not equidistant from any one point, so we couldn't assume you were in the center.

"We therefore had no guess as to your point of origin. You never used any names, geographical points of interest, dates—nothing. You didn't even space the uploads in any consistent chronology. There are no cellphones traceable to your name or your wife's name. That takes some research."

"Is there a point to this?"

"We value secrecy in what we do as well," Neff explained. "Malone's just trying to tell you he admires the thought you put into this."

"Whatever," Brian said wistfully.

"The content only drew our interest because of other information we have," Neff added, "information that has a lot of resonance with what you were saying—about how all this UFO stuff is a façade for something much bigger and more sinister, how there's an evil intelligence using the idea as part of a fascist agenda."

"If you guys want to recruit me for some cult, the conversation is over."

"You misunderstand," said Neff. "We're involved with . . . a range of international business interests. The world is moving rapidly in very dark directions, toward a collective tyranny. We operate alongside, hidden in plain sight."

"Oh, everything's clear now."

"Let me try to explain." Neff paused as he searched for words.

"We can see hell from here," Malone offered bluntly. "But when the power-hungry set up their utopian Gulag on earth, they'll need the masses to believe in the cause. We think you're onto something that'll make people believe that when their leaders enslave the planet and need to eliminate the riff-raff, they'll be doing what's best for humanity. We could only see bits of it before; there was no narrative logic. You're framing things in a way that makes sense—but we need you to help us think through it in detail and plan accordingly."

"Plan accordingly? Are you guys some sort of militia group?"

"No."

"Mercenaries? NSA refugees? Pinkerton dropouts?"

"No, no, and no. We're not paramilitary and don't work for any government agency."

"I'm done guessing. Who are you?"

"I can only give you our names—and they're our real names."

"Sure. Look, I'm not your guy. Besides, you already have my thoughts."

"We suspect that what you posted is the tip of the iceberg—especially after discovering who you really are and where your real expertise lies. Once we knew that, we made it a point to find you. We're in serious need of a scholar with your training."

Brian looked at the table, tapping it nervously. He longed for the anonymity he had held the last few months.

"I know it's easy for us to say," Neff said, "but you shouldn't be alarmed that we found you."

"You're right—that's easy for you to say."

"We understand you have something very real to fear," Malone cut in, continuing Neff's thought, "though we don't know what it is—and we don't need to know. But you shouldn't think you were easy to find. You're not vulnerable so long as you keep doing what you're doing. We wouldn't have found you if it weren't for an unbelievable . . . coincidence."

"Such as?"

"One of our associates had read through your forum material a dozen times when she became convinced she'd seen your writing before," Neff explained.

"I've never written anything like what I've been posting."

"We know. We're talking about unconscious patterns in your writing. We have someone in our group trained in cryptography. Part of her training was in forensic linguistics. She thought she recognized some of your syntax patterns—how you use prepositions and conjunctions, that sort of thing. It has nothing to do with vocabulary and subject matter. The focus is on the words that *always* get used in writing—the little ones."

"You're kidding."

"Not at all," Malone assured him. "She sent off samples of both your Internet material and some pages of what she suspected would linguistically align with it to a friend of hers who is an expert in a field called authorship attribution. When her friend's data came back, we had solid matches between your Internet material and the item our associate had read before—your dissertation. Her guess that the authors were the same was correct. That gave us a name."

"Then we plugged 'Brian Scott' into some journal databases," Neff continued, "and found that you had published an article about whether Christianity could cope with an extraterrestrial reality. There was no way that was random. We looked for more, but that was the only published item we could find that bore your name other than your dissertation."

"I haven't exactly been prolific."

"We actually found a couple of other things you wrote, but—"

"I haven't published anything else."

"The other material wasn't published. Our web searches turned up two audio files, a sermon and a Bible lesson you gave in graduate school at some sort of student meeting. We downloaded them and had them transcribed. Haven't you ever searched the Web for yourself?"

"I'm not a narcissist, and I never uploaded anything like that."

"Someone did. People do that when they like something. Personally, I found the material fascinating. At any rate, we gave the published article to our authorship expert to run another set of tests, and that produced another confirmation match."

"Okay, so that gave you my identity, but how did you find my address? I've never had a job in my field or anything remotely related to it. How did you pull that one off?"

"We had our web-security expert look for your name and degree at any addresses with the domain name 'edu.' We tried church websites next. We spent over a week on it but always hit a dead."

"Then we made an educated guess," Malone added. "One of our associates figured that someone with a PhD in Hebrew and Semitic languages would always stay interested in their field. They'd want to keep up with the latest books—"

"And buy them with the money he wasn't earning?"

"Like I said, it was a guess," Malone said defensively. "Besides, she was right."

"We thought we might have to hack into Amazon's purchasing traffic," Neff began, "but—"

"Hack into Amazon? Are you kidding? That's illegal."

"It is," he conceded, "but we have the personnel and equipment to do that sort of thing. But we didn't have to. We found a good low-tech solution."

"What was that?"

"We made a list of publishers that specialize in your fields of expertise, especially the languages you're into. It wasn't long."

"Go on," Brian said, annoyed at the slight.

"We called them up and pretended to be you, convinced them you couldn't remember if you had put in the correct address for an order. Some places wanted credit-card information, but we finally found one who felt he was going the extra mile in customer service by just answering the question. It only took an hour."

"International businessmen, huh?"

"I should tell you, though," Neff continued, "that we don't know much of anything about your wife."

"And we aren't prying," followed Malone. "We're interested in you, not her."

"That's right. The point of all this, Dr. Scott, is that no one is going to find you unless they happen to have read what you've published before and think about it like a forensic computational linguist and hit some pretty wild guesses. That's a pretty rare set of circumstances."

"Is this where I breathe a big sigh of relief?"

"Please give our proposal some consideration. We'll pay you fifty thousand dollars for a week or two of your time."

"The only currency I'm interested in is security—especially for my wife. If you can't give us that, I'll have to start collecting cardboard boxes for another move."

Malone looked at Neff. "Told you so."

13

I imagine the only reason would have been concern
for broadening awareness of its existence.

—Dr. Sydney Gottlieb, Chief, Medical Staff, Technical Services Division of the CIA (1950s–1960s), remarking on why the details of the use of LSD on unwitting mind-control subjects under Project MK-ULTRA was kept secret from other CIA personnel

"The prisoner's in here, sir," said the MP, saluting as he opened the door.

The senior officer returned the salute and entered the room. His bright blue eyes scanned the small cell. Aside from the prisoner seated on the edge of her cot, the cell held only a sink and a commode. There were no windows. The walls were painted a dull gray that matched the linoleum on the floor.

"That's all. Take your post," he ordered. The MP closed the door behind him and took a position a few feet away in the hall.

The prisoner watched him enter and then looked away. The officer took note of the infinity-loop tattoo on her neck and then positioned himself where his frame could block the vertical window slit in the door. He removed his cap from his close-cropped blond hair and put it under his arm, exchanging it with the slender notebook he had brought into the room. He began skimming the contents.

"Comfortable, Ms. Leyden?" he asked dispassionately as he turned a page.

"Where am I?"

"You're at Minot Air Force Base in North Dakota."

"I turned myself in. I should be in jail talking to my lawyer. What am I doing on an Air Force base?"

"You're here because I want you here," he replied coldly, turning another page. "The charges against you are very serious."

"Federal jurisdiction doesn't mean Air Force," she replied. "I'm not stupid."

"That depends," he stated, closing the notebook. "Your case would normally be handled by the FBI, but—unfortunately for you—you've endangered national security. You and your boyfriend took something that is of personal interest to me. How smart you are is directly related to whether you decide to be useful."

"Go to hell! How does stealing a few pieces of mostly indecipherable notes and blueprints endanger national security?"

"That's for me to decide."

"I want to see a lawyer."

"I'm afraid not. And if things get as far as a trial, it will be by military tribunal."

"What are you talking about? I'm not some terrorist."

"You're apparently not familiar with the way the military and Homeland Security define 'terrorist.' We're working together nowadays. It's a wonderful world of mutual cooperation that enables us to detain 'domestic extremists' like yourself."

"What a pile of crap."

"My report says you think my employer is a police state. Are you saying you wouldn't fight us over that quaint piece of paper we call the Constitution?"

"Damn right."

"Well, there you are. In the eyes of the Justice Department, you're an extremist. They were forward-thinking enough to include people like you in the guide they published to assist the military and Homeland Security in identifying who we could potentially detain indefinitely under the National Defense Authorization Act. Thanks for making my job easy."

"Creep. What are you going to do, torture me?" she mocked.

"Perhaps some other time. I'd enjoy that, but I'm in a hurry today," he said casually, in an almost bored tone. She felt a chill.

"The truth is, after we're done here, I'll decide whether to let you go or commit you to an asylum for the rest of your life. A few months in some of the places I could send you would make you wish for a lethal injection."

Becky stared at him, her mouth open in stunned silence.

"Let me give you some clarity, Ms. Leyden. You're thinking that the Fargo police or perhaps the FBI know your whereabouts. They don't. Those two fine institutions of law and order know that the military has taken jurisdiction here. The two FBI agents who transported you from Fargo to the airport believed they were delivering you to a flight to DC. But unbeknownst to them, you wound up on a different plane. They have no idea where you are—and even if they did, they'd know that you can be held in any number of prisons without charges or trial for a very long time once you're classified an extremist. They'd know it could be years before anyone ever saw you again. Plus, they have their own bloated caseloads to worry about. So you're already well off the radar."

"*Who the hell are you*?" Becky said, her teeth clenched in rage as she tried to keep her wits.

"I'm Colonel Vernon Ferguson, United States Air Force. But perhaps you're really wondering why I've threatened you so transparently?"

Becky said nothing, her chest heaving, her mind overwhelmed with anxiety. Her eyes began to tear up.

"I thought so," the Colonel taunted her. "Well, between you and me, it's because you won't remember any of this conversation an hour from now." He looked at his watch.

"I'm telling you, I don't know anything else!" she pleaded.

"There's always something new to learn. Remember, it would be in your best interest to be cooperative."

The Colonel opened his notebook again and withdrew several items. He stepped toward the girl.

"While your escapades with the Antarctic documents would be enough to make me eager to chat with you, I'm interested in you for other reasons—three, to be precise. First, my associate, who's due to arrive here in a few minutes, noticed the particular tattoo on your neck. Second, your file indicates that your father and grandfather both served in the military. These two observations make me suspect you're one of ours."

"W-what does that—"

"In a moment. The third reason I'm interested in you concerns where you applied to graduate school. We may have a mutual acquaintance at Georgetown."

"So *what*?" she spat, trying to be brave.

"So we'd best get started. Pay attention, please," the Colonel said condescendingly. "I have three photographs in my hand. Please look at each one carefully."

Colonel Ferguson held up the first photograph, a black and white portrait of a man in a tweed suit. Becky gazed at it. A slightly dazed expression appeared on her face.

"Now this one." He slid the first photo behind the others, revealing another black and white photograph. She stared at the image of a World War II German officer in full uniform. Her eyes began to water. Saliva dripped from her mouth.

"And finally . . ." The last photograph was of a civilian man wearing a white lab coat. Becky wretched violently. The Colonel jumped backward toward the door to avoid the ejections of vomit that spewed from her throat and splattered onto the cold, hard floor. Becky's torso heaved in rhythmic spasms as her stomach emptied, timed to gurgling, frightened gasps. Becky dropped to her knees but quickly lost her balance. Her hands shot out in front of her, slapping down into the warm, chunky muck, to break her fall.

"Excellent," the Colonel mused aloud, putting the pictures back into the folder. "We're making progress. Now, one more thing, quickly."

Still on all fours, Becky's body quivered, her eyes closed. She slowly sat back to a kneeling position and gazed up submissively at him.

"I'm going to scan your brain now," he explained, smiling insincerely. "It's just something I do."

The girl's body instantly became taut. Her eyes rolled back into her head. The Colonel heard no sound; there were no words. Instead, he saw a kaleidoscope of images from all stages of her life, everything the girl had ever seen—people, places, objects, events. The chronology was uneven, as images stored in the human brain must be retrieved by other brain functions for sorting, but everything was here.

Hmmm, Melissa Kelley—what a small world. He continued tunneling through Becky's mind, seeing the girl's boyfriend, the fragments. He stopped abruptly. *Now this is indeed a surprise. My, my, the plot thickens. It's implausible, but not impossible.*

He released her, and Becky collapsed into the pool of her own vomit and groaned. The Colonel folded his arms behind his back, his chin resting on his chest, deep in thought. *She would speak under duress—her pain threshold is low—but at best she may only know a city or town. I can do better. She can do better.*

He heard a feeble whimper and glanced down at the shaken girl, who was struggling again to right herself. "Well, Ms. Leyden, thank you for your cooperation. You will indeed be of use to me."

The lock on the door clicked. The Colonel turned to acknowledge the expected visitation. "Good morning, Becker."

The new arrival nodded. He was dressed in an impeccably-tailored business suit and had an equally stylish winter overcoat draped over his arm. He looked disdainfully at the floor, which was still awash with the acrid contents of the girl's stomach. "We have a candidate," he observed dispassionately.

"Yes," the Colonel replied and handed him the folder. "Your guess was correct. You have a keen eye, Becker."

"Thank you, sir."

"She'll be useful in several ways, but I'll need your assessment."

"That may take a while."

"Understood, but make it a priority."

"Certainly."

Colonel Ferguson placed his cap on his head. "Get her cleaned up and give her the usual screen memory. Tell the MP she's ill. She's to be kept here under normal security—nothing unusual that would draw attention. There's no need for undue caution. We'll talk about her after your evaluation."

"Yes, sir."

The Colonel turned toward the door and grabbed the knob, then paused, momentarily seized by a thought. *Yes, what a delightful idea. A difficult challenge—something dramatic.* A demented smile creased his face. *How . . . providential.* He turned the knob and left the room.

14

It is better to be violent, if there is violence in our hearts, than to put on the cloak of nonviolence to cover impotence.

—*Mahatma Gandhi*

"It's Nili—apparently there was a setback," Neff said, looking down at the text message.

"You gonna call her?" Malone asked as he accelerated past a car on the interstate.

"Yeah," Neff answered, dialing. "I'll put her on speaker."

The phone rang only once. "I'll make it quick," said Nili's voice, reverberating inside the car. "We got here and nothing looked like it was supposed to—no hard drives, no boxed files, nothing. There was food still in the refrigerator. They took only what we came for."

"You're sure it was the right location?"

"Yes. The sleep chamber was in an attic accessible only through the second-floor crawl space, just like we were told. They left enough in there so we'd be able to tell we'd found it. They wanted us to know we'd failed."

Neff looked at Malone, who shook his head and said nothing.

"What happened then?"

"We had visitors."

"Who?"

"Muscle—two men, lightly armed, plain clothes. Totally unexpected."

"Were they a problem?"

"No. We took care of them. They didn't know we were inside since we parked a few hundred yards away. They're in a storage shed in the backyard. What do you want to do with the place?"

"You're certain there were no survivors?"

"Absolutely."

"Torch the house and get out of there."

"Are you coming back to Miqlat soon?"

"Not for a while. We may make some progress this evening."

"I'll update everyone. So long."

Neff turned off the phone and gazed at the road. "Let's hope dinner goes better than that did."

15

It's not enough that we do our best;
sometimes we have to do what's required.

—*Sir Winston Churchill*

"Are you sure this is a good idea?" Melissa asked, watching the snowflakes streak across the headlights, propelled by a strong crosswind.

"Nope," Brian answered, "but I can't say it feels like a bad one, either—at least if we're careful."

The two of them fell into silence as Brian drove toward Fargo. The last few days had been a strain. Brian's episode with the two strangers in the library had been a shock. They were both certain that the two men could not be trusted.

"I just can't shake the feeling that our encounter with Becky might have something to do with these two guys," Melissa said, breaking the silence. "The two things seem so unrelated, but my intuition says otherwise. I can't see a link, but there must be one."

"I admit, it bugs me, too—the lack of a connection, that is."

"We don't have the luxury of believing in coincidences."

"No, we don't," Brian agreed, making a turn.

"So why are we meeting them for dinner?"

"It was my turn to cook," Brian quipped, smiling at her as he stopped at a light.

"Good answer. I'm—we're hungry." She smiled back, patting her stomach. "I hope I don't make a spectacle of myself."

"How do you feel?" he asked, squeezing her hand.

"Pretty good. I won't ask you how I look, though."

"I think you just did. Nothing's changed. You're still adorable."

"I can't believe you just used the word 'adorable.' "

"'Radiant' would have been too much of a blow to my manhood."

"Thanks for sparing me."

Brian started moving through the light. "We're almost there."

"Honestly, though, why *are* we doing this?"

"I'm not sure. I don't like the circumstances, but I also have this sense that maybe the reason we sense a link is because there is one—but not a bad one."

"What do you mean?"

"Maybe it's providence. I mean, think about the last six months. We've seen a lot of awful things and had some terribly close calls, but those things are at the forefront of our minds because they were so traumatic. We filter our feelings now through the fear those events generated."

"Sounds like survival instinct to me."

"I wouldn't disagree, but it's one-sided. What gets lost are the unspectacular things—the small convergences of circumstance that accrue to our good. Maybe we're *supposed* to be there tonight."

"I guess that's possible, but we still have to be cautious."

"We will."

"We need to keep the conversation about you," she added, "since it was you who brought them here. They know about Becky and her discovery—at least the gist of it—but not much else, unless they're being coy."

"I'm thinking if they had more to say to me, they would have said it. I didn't get any indication that they know more than who I am, what I posted online, and what they caught from our conversation with Becky. They don't know where we were last summer, and if they don't believe we're really married, they've disguised their suspicions very well."

"There it is on the right," Melissa alerted him.

Brian pulled the car into the lot and shut off the ignition. He didn't open the door. "One guess as to what's creeping me out," he said to Melissa, peering through the windshield at the restaurant.

Melissa looked around at the outside of the property. "The lot's almost empty. It should be full on a Saturday night."

"Bingo."

"There are lights on inside," Melissa said, straining her eyes, "but I can't really see anyone."

The two of them sat quietly in the car, unsure of what to do.

"Why do I have the feeling that the place is going to be crawling with Special Forces any minute now?" Brian quipped.

"Don't say that," Melissa scolded. "That's nothing to joke about."

Brian started the car. "I don't like it. If they want to talk to us, they know where to find us." He began to pull out.

"Wait," Melissa said suddenly, putting her hand on his shoulder.

Brian followed her gaze. The front door of the restaurant opened, and a young waitress dressed in dark slacks, a long-sleeved white shirt, and a fresh apron left the building.

"I know that girl," Melissa said, surprised.

The waitress hurried toward the car on Melissa's side. Brian lowered the passenger-side window.

"Hi, Dr. Carter!" the waitress said cheerily. "Nice to see you again! This is where I work on the weekends. Come on inside. We're expecting you and your husband. My supervisor sent me out to get you when he saw the lights go back on."

"Hi, Amy. It didn't look like the place was open."

"Technically, we're not," Amy explained, shivering in the cold. "There are two men inside waiting for you. They bought out the restaurant tonight, so the four of you have it all to yourselves. Must be a special occasion—it's the first time I've gotten a tip before I even did anything!"

"Thanks for letting us know," Melissa said, smiling. "Go back in before you freeze. We'll be right there."

They watched the girl disappear back into the building.

"There's no way we'd be going in there if you hadn't known her," Brian said, still watching the restaurant door.

"You've got that right."

"Seems like—"

"Just hold that thought."

16

A ship is safe in harbor, but that's not what ships are for.

—*William G. T. Shedd*

"Thank you for dinner, Mr. Neff," Melissa said as she watched the waitress clearing the dishes. "The circumstances were a bit unusual, but it was worth the time."

"I'm glad you enjoyed it. And call me, Graham, please," Neff replied. "I hope after tonight we can be less formal."

"I'm not sure how much we'll be seeing you. Aren't you going to be returning to . . . where was it again?"

"Montana."

"I'm sure you have a lot of business to attend to—whatever it is that you can't tell us you do."

"Yes, we're busy," he answered, ignoring Melissa's obvious dissatisfaction over the secrecy he'd maintained over dinner. "I should tell you that we're not going to give up on getting help from your husband."

"I just don't see what more I can do for you," Brian said. "You've asked some good questions tonight, but they're the sorts of questions that would take hours or days to unpack and really address. They're just beyond sound bites."

"That's precisely our point. We need to pick your brain—however long that takes."

"But why? What's the context?" Brian insisted. "What would you do with the information? It can't be just to satisfy your curiosity."

"Why isn't it enough to know you're helping us out? You obviously felt burdened to get your thoughts out to as many people as possible. All we're asking for is more. Does that seem unreasonable?"

"I did it anonymously. Let's just say the last few time I said what I thought about this stuff, it didn't work out very well."

"We're not asking you to go public. You won't be exposed."

"I'm just not sure of that. You know a lot more about us than we know about you. Besides, even though I don't have a job to lose this time, I have to think of Melissa's safety."

"Which is why you brought a gun tonight?"

"How . . . ?" Brian couldn't hide his surprise.

"We knew as soon as you came in," Malone explained blandly. "We brought one of these," he went on, pulling a small, square device with a screen from a satchel next to him in the booth. "It actually couldn't detect your weapon now. You'd have to put your coat back on. It's a scanner that uses a sort of reverse infrared mapping.

"See, everyone's body emits energy. This device tells us if there's something on a person's body that's obstructing the emission. Works great inside twenty feet. We saw the shape of the handgun on your body as soon as you walked in."

"You must have a gadget for everything," said Brian, visibly annoyed.

"Pretty much."

"And to answer your question, yes, I brought it just in case. And I'd use it if I had to. *Nothing* is more important to me than her."

"Of that I have no doubt, but it seems a bit extreme under the circumstances."

"You have no idea what extreme looks like," Brian said, staring him down. "We do."

Melissa was a bit taken back by the exchange, but she didn't let on. Brian was always so steady and congenial in her presence. This was different. She'd seen Brian's look of unflinching resolve on her behalf before, back on the tarmac at Area 51 when Neil Bandstra had engineered the first attempt on her life.

Her mind drifted back to that event, remembering how the two of them had run toward the jeep for cover from the attack dogs, how she hadn't been able to keep up. The look she saw now was the same one Brian had worn when he'd turned around and run past her, throwing himself into the beasts to give her time to get under the jeep. She shuddered unconsciously and closed her eyes, trying to block out the images of the horrific aftermath.

"Are you all right, Dr. Kelley?" Neff asked from across the table.

"Oh . . . yes," she answered, opening her eyes. "Just a bit of a flutter inside."

"So what can I do to convince you we're sincere?" Neff asked. "What do you need?"

"Peace of mind," Brian answered. "Money can't buy that."

"Brian," Melissa intervened, "that was a little rude."

"No offense taken," Neff said, folding his hands on the table. "Having a lot of money can buy you excellent security. But at the end of the day, it can't change your state of mind."

"No, Melissa's right," Brian acknowledged, "I was out of line."

"Over and done. Now what—"

Neff's cellphone went off, interrupting the conversation. He took it from his belt and glanced at the number. "Do you mind if I take this call?"

Brian and Melissa shook their heads.

"Hello? Yes . . . *oh, no.*" Neff's expression became serious and drawn. The others saw immediately that something was terribly wrong. "Tell me what you need," he continued. "You know we'll do anything to help. . . . No, don't reserve a flight. I can take you there tonight in the Lear, you'll get there much faster. . . . All right, I'll have Malone call the airport right away and have them prepare the plane. . . . Understood . . ."

Brian looked over at Malone, who was already dialing. His familiar, detached expression had been replaced by one of focused concentration. He got up and walked a few feet away from the booth to talk.

"And Aloysius," they heard Neff say, "I'm deeply sorry to hear this. I know the two of you were close. I'll pick you up at your house in about two hours."

Brian and Melissa exchanged startled glances. Neff put away his phone and let out a deep breath. He looked over at Malone, who was still on the phone.

"My apologies to both of you, but we'll have to cut the evening short," he explained. "A bit of an emergency—a tragedy, really."

"Pardon," said Melissa, "but did I hear you call the man you were talking to Aloysius?"

"Yes."

"You were talking to President Fitzgerald?"

"That's correct. You don't often meet someone named Aloysius, do you?"

"What happened?" Melissa urged, now visibly concerned. "Why would he call you in an emergency?"

"My relationship with Aloysius goes beyond my membership on the Board of Trustees. We've been good friends for almost ten years. But tonight he got news that he's lost an even older and dearer friend—someone esteemed at the college, in fact."

"They'll have the plane ready," Malone said, returning to the table, "and the coffee. I can fly this time, if you like."

Neff nodded and looked again at Melissa. "We have to get President

Fitzgerald to Nevada tonight. His friend had no next of kin, so he needs to fly out there to set his final affairs in order. He wants to bring the remains back here for a memorial service on campus. If we can get things done quickly, that can happen before Thanksgiving break begins."

"His 'remains'?" asked Malone, eyebrows raised.

"Aloysius doesn't have many details, but this will be a closed-casket affair. His friend was found in Death Valley National Park. Apparently he got lost, which isn't that uncommon, sadly. The investigators are guessing his body was exposed a month or so, maybe longer. A ranger found him. We'll know more once we get there."

17

Earth has no sorrow that heaven cannot heal.

—*Thomas Moore*

Melissa stared at the icon for her campus email account on her computer's desktop. Brian, seated next to her at her desk, squeezed her hand. "We have to look."

"I just can't," she sighed.

"I know."

The two of them had heard rumors on campus earlier that morning that classes on Thursday might be canceled for a special memorial service. Melissa had waited for Brian to arrive at her office before reading her email.

It had taken only minutes for a sickening suspicion to gnaw its way into their consciousness after their dinner with Neff and Malone the night before. Neither wanted to utter the horrible, haunting intuition. Their silence was only broken at breakfast, when they each confessed to having spent nearly an hour online the previous evening searching for details about the ghastly discovery Neff had described.

Stories about the tragedy were easy to find, but details were sparse. No name had been released to the public. There were only vague lines about how the authorities were working on an identification. But there was really no need for all that. Somehow they both knew it was Andrew. The only question was how he had wound up over a hundred miles from Las Vegas, where they had last seen him, and nowhere near his intended destination when they had parted. Assuming he'd made it back to Area 51, the fact that his body was found in an isolated, inhospitable desert could mean only one thing: It had been dumped there.

Melissa closed her eyes and steadied herself. She clicked on the icon and then silently logged in. She opened the all-campus message from President Fitzgerald.

> *President Fitzgerald, along with the administration, faculty, and the Board of Trustees, wish to express their profound sorrow at the passing of a beloved friend to the family of St. Ignatius College and its alumni. Father Andrew Malachi Benedict, Jesuit scholar and servant of his heavenly Father and Lord Jesus Christ, has passed from this life to the next. The entire college family is invited to attend a service of remembrance and celebration of this life, so faithfully lived, on Thursday, November 15, two o'clock p.m., in Martin Chapel. All classes scheduled to meet on Thursday have been canceled. A funeral Mass will be held on Friday, ten o'clock a.m., at Transfiguration Catholic Church. Father Benedict will be interred on campus at Cedar Grove Cemetery following the funeral Mass.*

Brian and Melissa sat silently, staring at the message with a feeling of helplessness. Although they had both anticipated the words, the deep ache that now throbbed inside them at the confirmation of their fears hit with full force. They held hands and cried, both out of their own pain and for Andrew, whom they felt with certainty had died dreadfully.

"I want to know what happened," Brian said after a few minutes, wiping his eyes and gaining some composure.

"Are you sure that's a good idea?" Melissa asked after a moment.

"I can't say I care," he answered, then stood up.

"If there's evidence that he didn't just wander out there, the police will do all they can to get to the bottom of it."

"We both know who's responsible, and he won't be answering to a local police department."

"He won't be answering to you, either, Brian."

"Ferguson can't be untouchable," he replied, pacing the small office.

"He lives at Area 51. I'd say that qualifies him as untouchable."

"And yet here we are," he contested. "You never know."

"And we want to *stay* here, don't we? Out of sight, out of mind . . ."

Brian put his hands in his pockets and looked down at Melissa. The hint of anxiety in her eyes set his mind right. He couldn't let any harm come to her, and he'd reached the point where he couldn't bear to think of life without her. As captivating as she was, he was bound to her by something much deeper. With Father Benedict gone, as his own parents and Neil Bandstra before him, she was all he had—his sole friend, his confidante, his connection to life. She was all that mattered and all he wanted.

He silently reminded himself, as he'd done so many times already, to keep his feelings buried. He wanted to say more, but that would only turn what they had into something awkward and, ultimately, futile.

"Yes, absolutely," he assured her. "We'll ask President Fitzgerald about it after the memorial service. Beyond that, I won't pry. I'll let it go."

"Thanks," she replied, her expression lightening. "Let's go home."

18

Don't let what you cannot do interfere with what you can do.

—John Wooden

Brian and Melissa paused at the bottom of the concrete steps and looked back at the chapel. Hundreds of people streamed from its several exits.

"I had no idea there were so many people on campus," Melissa said as she watched the crowd. "I guess I'm too cloistered."

"We'll never spot President Fitzgerald here," Brian said, scanning the crowd.

"I saw him head for the exit behind the stage," Melissa noted. "I'm sure he got out before we did. Let's just head over to his office. His secretary, Gloria, left me a text message just before the service saying that he'd meet us there afterward."

Brian nodded.

"Although, at the rate I travel," she sighed, "it might take us the rest of the afternoon—unless you roll me there."

Brian smiled and took her hand, helping her negotiate a small patch of ice. "I'm sure he'll wait."

The two of them made their way slowly across campus to the administration building, a majestic late nineteenth-century, Victorian-style structure built of red sandstone. Brian had never taken the time to really take in the campus. The medley of orange, yellow, and brown hues, flecked with scattered trees that glistened with the remnant of a light snowfall earlier in the week, produced a rugged yet beautiful landscape. A mixture of modern and period-style buildings, all meticulously maintained, punctuated the scene.

It was the sort of place he'd have enjoyed as a professor—a small student body, colleagues more focused on teaching than research, a community with some unified sense of purpose. None of that was ever going to materialize now, but he was glad to be here. He'd have to try harder to make friends and fit in. Preoccupation with Melissa, their circumstances, and fulfilling his promise to Andrew had pushed mundane realities aside. It only hit him now that he needed to start planning for the future.

"Why so quiet?" Melissa asked.

"Just thinking."

"I can see that."

He nodded.

"This is the part where you tell me what's on your mind," she coaxed.

"Sorry, I'm just wondering about what to do next—you know, finding work . . ."

"You wouldn't have liked real estate anyway. And we have plenty of money right now."

"Sure, right now. But I need to start contributing."

"Are you sure you just don't want to get out of the house?"

He gave her a perplexed look.

"You know, I was hired with an agreement for a paid sabbatical for maternity leave next semester. Winters are long here. We're going to be stuck together in the house for months. You might be looking for some time away."

Brian eyed her curiously. He assumed she was teasing him, but there was something in her expression that made him unsure. "That's the last thing I'm looking for."

"Really?" She stopped and looked up at him earnestly.

"Absolutely."

"Are you reconsidering putting the babies up for adoption?" Brian asked as they resumed their journey.

"No, I'm still planning on it. It's not like they're mine . . ."

"But . . . ?"

"When I was young, there were a lot of couples at church who were foster parents. I remember thinking I'd enjoy that. But that was a lifetime ago."

"Well, no matter what," he said, "I'll do whatever you need me to do. You won't be alone. You know that, don't you?"

She stopped again and turned to him. "Absolutely," she replied, imitating his familiar answer, the corner of her mouth easing into a demure smile.

"Good. And one more thing."

"What's that?"

"You're still young."

A few minutes later they reached their destination. The door leading into the small reception area outside the president's office was open. Melissa peeked inside. Gloria was at her desk, busily typing.

"Might as well answer some email while I'm here," Gloria sighed pleasantly, noticing Melissa. "Lord knows it never ends. Dr. Fitzgerald will be available in a moment, dear. He has some out of town company, but he assured me you two wouldn't have to wait long. Please have a seat."

Brian took Melissa's coat. They turned toward the chairs adjacent to the president's office, but, as if on cue, his door swung open. Brian and Melissa gasped in unison as a lanky African-American man emerged. He stopped in mid-step, stunned into silence at the sight of them. The three of them stood staring at each other in a moment of bewildered disbelief before they all broke into a joyous grins.

"*Malcolm!*" Brian exclaimed and rushed toward him, grabbing him by the shoulders before pulling him into a bear hug. A delighted Melissa beamed at the unexpected reunion.

"Whoa, dude," Malcolm said with a laugh, jolted by the embrace. "You're gonna break something!"

Brian released him and took a step back. "I can't believe it!"

Malcolm moved to hug Melissa but stopped, taken again by surprise. "You're pregnant?" he asked, lowering his voice.

"That's kind of obvious, don't you think?" Melissa answered. She glanced back at Gloria, who was still seated at her desk and smiling approvingly at the threesome. Melissa reached for Malcolm's neck. Malcolm embraced her and listened as Melissa whispered into his ear, "We're pretending to be married here. We'll explain later. Same first names, but our last name is Carter."

Malcolm broke the embrace with a smile, but she saw unmistakable concern in his soft brown eyes. He looked at Brian, who read the logical question on his face. Brian glanced at Gloria, whose attention had returned to her computer screen. He looked again at Malcolm and quickly shook his head just enough for him to catch the gesture. Malcolm's face filled with anxiety as he turned to Melissa. Her helpless eyes gave him the answer. His lips tightened in a thin, hard line.

"We've got to find a private place to talk," Brian whispered after taking a step closer to him.

"For sure," Malcolm agreed. "I need to talk to you both, too. Something's going on, and I don't like it."

"Where's Dee?" Melissa asked softly. "Did you get her out?"

Malcolm hesitated. "We never made it."

"*What?* Then how—?"

The door to President Fitzgerald's office opened again. Graham

Neff exited and turned toward Gloria to say something, but he stopped abruptly at the sight of the three figures huddled together in hushed conversation.

"You all *know* each other?" Neff asked, shocked.

"Malcolm, how do you know *this* guy?" Brian asked incredulously in the same instant.

"It's a long story," Malcolm answered slowly, searching for words that wouldn't reveal too much information. "Graham . . . got us out . . . of our last arrangement."

"'Us'? Where's Dee?" Melissa asked again, eyeing Neff with a mixture of suspicion and wonder.

"You know *her*, too?" Neff asked.

"Yes," Melissa answered, studying his startled expression.

"She's with President Fitzgerald and Malone," Neff answered. "She should be out any minute. I'll let everyone know you're here," he added and went back into the office.

"Both of you, listen," Malcolm said in a hushed tone after Neff was gone. There was an uncharacteristic tone of uncertainty in his voice. "I really don't know who this guy is or what he's about, but he got us out of Area 51 and away from Colonel Ferguson. He doesn't actually know that's where we were, though. We've been out for a couple weeks. He told us about Andrew a couple days ago, and we insisted on coming for the memorial."

"But—" Brian began to interject.

"Not now," Malcolm stopped him. "Like I said, we got caught. I can tell you everything when we get a chance. Right now, you just need to know that when we were released, it was the first time I'd seen Dee since the day we tried to escape. She's . . . had a rough time."

"What does that mean?" Melissa asked in a distressed whisper.

"It's complicated—even more now," he added, looking at her. "Let's just say that if I had my way, we wouldn't be meeting right now—not like this, anyway, with you being pregnant."

"*Why not*?" Melissa demanded, barely maintaining her hushed tone.

Their attention was diverted by office door opened again. Neff and Malone appeared first, then Dee, followed by President Fitzgerald. Dee broke into a relieved smile when she saw Brian but immediately froze at the sight of Melissa.

"Oh, my God!" Dee gasped.

Melissa cupped her mouth with her hand in stunned disbelief.

Dee was pregnant.

19

If you're going through hell, keep going.

—*Sir Winston Churchill*

"I'm sorry about how things went down back there," Dee apologized, relaxing in a chair in Melissa's office.

"Don't say another word about it," Melissa reassured her, patting her knee. She walked around behind her desk and sat down. "The fact that you're here is all that matters. And if you and Malcolm want to stay with us, you're certainly welcome."

"I appreciate that, but I owe you an explanation—at least what I can give you."

The black woman's drawn face betrayed her condition. The mischievous eyes and sassy air Melissa had come to enjoy last summer had been dimmed and subdued by whatever events had assaulted Dee's spirit. Still, Melissa could see that the fight hadn't entirely departed.

"Dee, please don't take this the wrong way, but it looks like you've been through hell," Melissa said.

"I have. The last couple weeks back in the free world have helped clear my head, but I never expected to see you—especially pregnant. And I know the feeling is mutual."

Melissa nodded. "I was—oh, looks like they're back." The door to Melissa's office swung open. Brian and Malcolm carried two extra chairs and some pizza inside. Malcolm closed the door with a bony elbow.

"It's the only thing we could find open on campus," Malcolm said as Melissa cleared room on her desk for the food. "Everything's shutting down for Thanksgiving break."

"Malcolm and I were speculating about what Malone and Neff must be thinking," Brian said, shutting the door. "You could tell they didn't like being excluded."

"And we didn't exactly conceal the fact that we all had a history together," Melissa lamented, stating the obvious.

"They're just going to have to deal with it," Dee stated in the matter-of-fact manner Brian remembered of her.

"There's no way any of us were leaving campus without some time to talk," Malcolm observed.

"Yeah, it's not like we're going anywhere," Dee smirked. "A black couple isn't exactly gonna blend in and disappear in these parts."

"Do you two trust them?" Melissa asked. Brian carried a chair and set it down next to Melissa.

Malcolm shrugged. "All I can say is that we've been treated well. I'm not sure what they did to get us away from the Colonel, but it worked."

"I can't believe Ferguson would ever let it happen," Brian said, handing Melissa a paper plate. "Neff and his friends have to be extremely well connected to pull that off."

"They're really tight-lipped about who they are and what they do," noted Dee. "And from what we've seen so far, they have serious money."

"Dee's right," Malcolm said. "I don't know where the cash is coming from, but they've got planes, boats, weapons, communications, food storage, all sorts of gadgets you could only get from the military—it's amazing. The safe house they took us to was well stocked. Whatever they're up to, they'll be ready for it and then some."

"Interesting," Melissa said thoughtfully. "I've been studying fringe apocalyptic groups for years. Let's hope we're not going to get a closer view of one than we'd like. They don't act like they're in some survivalist cult, but that's no guarantee."

"When we were back at the base," Dee said, looking at Brian, "Malcolm told me how Father Benedict planned to get you two off the base. But what about the situation now? Melissa told me what's happened in the last couple of weeks while we were waiting."

"I think Neff and Malone are being honest with us," Brian answered, "at least about not having any attachment to anyone who'd be tracking us down for the government. But like Melissa said, we really don't know what to think about them. The coffee-shop thing was just so random, but I can't shake the feeling it's related."

"What was the girl's name again?" Dee asked.

"Becky."

"We'll have to trust that our little threat about destroying the fragment copies is enough motivation for her to keep quiet," Melissa said. "She has no reason to want us in harm's way, and plenty of reasons to want to see the government embarrassed."

"So tell us what happened back at Area 51 with you guys," said Brian. "How did you get out?"

"Well," Malcolm began, "while you two and Andrew were doing your thing with the Colonel, I went and got Dee out of her room and told her what was happening. I had two override cards and uniforms for us to wear—we even had helmets with reflectors and weapons to avoid facial recognition. The plan was to follow you topside and blend into the action, then take a jeep off the base, assuming the jeep was where Andrew said it would be.

"We took the elevator about twenty minutes after you guys took off with Andrew, but as soon as we used the override cards, it shut down. The Colonel had already changed the code. The cards essentially told security where we were. We didn't get far at all."

"What did Ferguson do when he found you?" Melissa asked.

"He was pretty cocky—acted like he knew what was going on. It really unnerved me, to be honest. I wasn't sure what had happened to you two, or Andrew, and he wasn't about to put my mind at ease. We all know he likes playin' with people."

"He has a superiority complex," Dee broke in. "And put that down as a professional opinion."

"The Colonel split us up after we got caught," Malcolm went on. "We were both in solitary. I'll let Dee tell you her story," he finished, eyeing her sympathetically.

All eyes turned toward Dee, who took a deep breath. She choked up before she could begin.

"She doesn't need to do this now," Melissa objected.

"I'll be okay," Dee sniffed, wiping a tear. "I'm the psychologist, remember?" She sniffed, trying to smile. "It's good for me to talk it out."

The three of them waited for her to collect herself.

"After the Colonel separated us," Dee began, "I spent a couple days in a cell, and then some MPs and a doctor paid me a visit. The doctor wanted urine and blood samples—gave me some bull about why. I knew the MPs were there in case I wasn't cooperative, so I gave him what he wanted. I saw him only once more."

"How strange."

"Oh, it gets weirder. After that visit, everything was normal, even tolerable. They moved me back to my old room, brought me menus to order meals, gave me research to do—mostly light busywork, nothing challenging or important. I did it to beat the boredom. The only thing new was that they installed video cameras in every room of my living space—and I was never allowed out of it."

"They did the same busywork thing to me, eventually," added Malcolm. "Piddly stuff—things that any grad student could have done. I'm not sure what the point was."

"I demanded to speak to the Colonel," Dee continued, "but that never happened. They wouldn't tell me what they'd done with Malcolm. I didn't know if he was dead or alive."

"What happened next?" Brian asked.

Melissa saw the apprehensive look on Malcolm's face as he watched Dee. "Well, I'm guessing I was in my cell for a few weeks when I began to suspect I was pregnant."

Brian and Melissa exchanged anxious glances. The time frame approximated Melissa's own circumstance.

"I'd missed my period the previous month, but I attributed that to the stress of our last month at the base. When I missed again, I was scared—really scared. I thought maybe they put something in my food that was causing problems internally. There was no way it was pregnancy. I hadn't been with a man for over a year. But when I started to show, there was no denying it. Whatever the creeps did to me, they did it while we were all there. I don't know how," Dee struggled to compose herself, "but there I was, pregnant. When I saw you . . . it just freaked me out."

"Pretty understandable," Brian offered.

"I guess so. I know you two have sort of started a new life here, but I'm just not . . . I don't know what to think. My head's just not right."

"Malcolm . . ."

"I haven't had a chance to tell her," Malcolm stopped Melissa, anticipating what was coming.

"Tell me what?"

Melissa looked at Brian, then turned to Dee. "I don't know how I'm pregnant, either," Melissa replied.

"What?"

"Brian and I haven't been intimate. We're pretending to be married here. No one knows otherwise—not even President Fitzgerald, Andrew's contact. He just assumed we were a married couple when Andrew gave us the same last names for my position here at the college."

"Good God, girl!" Dee said, exasperated. "Why didn't you get an abortion?"

"Well, for starters, I'm on faculty at a Catholic college."

"That wouldn't stop me. When I found out, that was the first thing I tried to do—and I'm still planning on it."

"And that's why they had you out like a light the rest of the time you were at the base," Malcolm interrupted.

"Well, they aren't clueless. I'd have tried again." She looked at Melissa. "I hit myself in the abdomen a few times after I was sure I was pregnant, but that wasn't going to work. It had to come out. The only thing I had in my room were coat hangers. I was desperate. But I forgot they'd turned my room into a film set. Security busted in before I could go through with it. They must have sent the guards as soon I started pounding myself. That doctor who'd visited me earlier came in a few minutes later and gave me a shot. That was the last thing I remember clearly until I woke up in Maine."

"They kept you sedated for almost three months?"

"We think it was probably some sort of induced coma," Malcolm suggested. "Given their concern over protecting the child Dee was carrying, drugs in the blood stream would seem too risky. I'm sure that bunch had other ways to put her out. Once we were stateside, Neff's people took good care of her. She was underweight, but otherwise healthy. The Colonel obviously wanted the baby safe, and he wasn't trusting Dee."

"What was in Maine?" Brian asked.

"Our first stop—after Tel Aviv, anyway. A safe house."

"Tel Aviv?"

"We're getting a little ahead of ourselves. We need to back up."

"Before you do that," Melissa interjected, steered the conversation back to their earlier topic, "why haven't you had the abortion yet, Dee?"

"Father Bradley here has done everything he can think of to prevent it," Dee answered with a smirk.

"You told her you were a priest?" Brian asked Malcolm.

"Yeah, at the safe house. I thought it was time to put everything on the table."

"Neff's doctor wouldn't do it, either," Dee replied with irritation. "I'm too far along to do anything myself. Too risky. I don't have access to any services yet, and I can't go anywhere by myself. It's like I'm still under house arrest."

"That's a little over the top," Malcolm protested.

"Is it?"

"I'd say so. You've got no place to go, to be honest. And I'm in the same boat."

"Take a good look at me and say that again," she quipped.

"So you think you'd be safer out on your own? We need to lie low, and you know it."

"Bottom line—once I'm on my own again, it's comin' out."

"All the tests Neff's people ran say the baby is normal," Malcolm said, avoiding Dee's gaze. "No surprise that I'm opposed to the abortion. If it wasn't human, then—"

"It isn't *mine!*" Dee protested, raising her voice. There was an awkward silence. She looked at Melissa for support. "You're crazy if you have that baby, Melissa. I don't care what the tests say. There's no telling what it is. You saw the unholy crap they have on that base—you know what they're capable of."

Melissa closed her eyes, trying to stay calm. Brian could see her fear returning. "I know you mean well," he said to Dee, "but we've had Melissa and the babies tested several times, including ultrasound. Everything's normal."

"Except how it got there," Dee retorted.

"'Babies'?" Malcolm interjected.

"Twin girls."

"I thought about abortion," Melissa explained to Dee, now looking more calm, "but aside from my status at the college, one is enough for me. As Brian knows, I had an abortion in my first year at college. I didn't think it was right even back then, but I was forced to do it. This time we decided that was only an option if there was something . . . abnormal."

"Just say it," Dee said bluntly. "You mean if it was *alien*. Let's not mince any words."

"Okay, it would be an option if they weren't human, but they are. I can't explain how, but every test we've done says I'm carrying normal girls. There's nothing amiss. I'm going to give them up for adoption, but I don't want to go through with another abortion. I don't want to relive that part of my past."

As he listened to Melissa, Brian's mind drifted back to the first time he'd heard her story and felt her pain and rage. He couldn't explain it, but knowing her at such a level was what had captured his heart. He'd wanted to heal her pain, to restore her lost faith, to fill the breach of her betrayal. He remembered her brokenness; it was the moment their bond had been formed.

"You're doing the right thing," Malcolm assured her.

"But they *can't* be normal," Dee insisted.

"They actually can—artificial reproduction is routine. I think it's obvious the Colonel had us implanted," Melissa retorted. "The only question is why. Maybe he did it for the same reason he used the nanotechnology back at the base to create fake bodies in our beds, or inject Brian's arm—just to show us what he could do. It suits the arrogant creep."

"I don't know . . ." Dee wasn't persuaded.

"It could be that simple," Brian said. "You two weren't there, but just before Andrew came to us with his escape plan, we were being held at gunpoint in my room by a mole in the Group—a Major Sheppard. He told us in no uncertain terms that the Group made Gray aliens using nanotechnology. He said the episode where Melissa and I both woke up on the same morning with each other—the artificial bodies in our respective beds—was a demonstration of that technology."

"That's right," Melissa recalled. "Sheppard said the Colonel and the Group could fake Armageddon if they wanted to. But I also remember he wasn't sure about Adam."

"I think we can conclude that Sheppard wasn't privy to that particular experiment, not that he thought Adam was a real alien."

"I don't know about that. What spooked him was the mind scans," Melissa reminded Brian. "And I know you remember his theory for that."

"Yeah."

"What was that?" Dee asked.

"Sheppard said he'd seen . . . an entity—some creature—that was very tall and not human. He told us he saw it kill Kevin back on the base."

"But I thought—"

"The Colonel's explanation for Kevin's death was a lie. Sheppard didn't know what killed him, but it wasn't a Gray. Without going into the details, his description sounded to me like what some ancient Jewish texts call a Watcher."

"I remember you using that term back at the base. What is it again?"

"In simplest terms, it's sort of an evil spirit that can take physical form, but not an extraterrestrial in the literal, scientific sense. Andrew said he'd seen one once. Sheppard speculated it might have made Adam and given him the power to read minds since the Group's technology couldn't pull that off. He didn't have any proof, though— and I think he'd have laid it out if he had it. He knew he wasn't going to see the next day."

"So you believe him?"

"I believe that an evil intelligence is behind what's been passed off as an extraterrestrial mythology, or religion, and that there are divine beings who can interact with us in physical form. That's a pretty straightforward point in biblical theology. But I have no idea if Sheppard was anywhere close to being right about Adam. In one sense it doesn't matter."

"Why?" Dee asked, surprised. "Adam was inside my head—you

were there."

"Was he?"

"Hell yeah."

"I mean, was it *him* . . . or something else? Remember, I thought Adam healed my arm—and that happened right in front of us. But it turned out to be nanobots that had been injected into my arm a little before the event. They're still in my bloodstream. So, if Adam's power in my case was faked, there may be some other explanation for your experience."

"And more importantly," Melissa followed, "if Adam was a real extraterrestrial with genuine powers, there'd be no need to fake the healing."

"So Sheppard's idea of an evil entity is more plausible, but not certain," Brian reasoned.

"Great," Dee said, her voice rising. "That's comforting. Six months ago I'd have said you needed therapy if you believed stuff like that. Now I'm hoping the priest in the room is a frickin' exorcist."

"Look, we've been safe here for months," Melissa pointed out. "If something evil wanted to kill us, it would have shown up by now. We'd be dead—we'd all be dead. I think we need to give God a little credit here for watching out for us."

Malcolm raised his eyebrows. "Preach it, sister," he said, enjoying the irony. "That kind of talk is a far cry from what I remember coming out of you."

"Don't go there, Malcolm," Melissa said, trying unsuccessfully to sound annoyed. Brian shook his head, chuckling softly.

"Hey, I teach at a Catholic college and live with a Hebrew scholar," she said, folding her arms. "It rubs off."

"Getting back to how you got off the base," Brian said, looking at Malcolm. "If Dee was basically unconscious, what do you know about your release?"

"When we asked about how he pulled it off, Neff was evasive. All he said was that he'd negotiated our freedom. No kidding, right? The State Department people on the plane weren't any help, either."

"The State Department?" Brian asked.

"Yeah. The Air Force handed us over to State, and they flew us overseas to Tel Aviv. When we landed, some Israeli soldiers turned us over to two of Neff's people, who were waiting for us. One of them was Israeli, too."

"What's with the Israeli connection?"

"Beats me," Malcolm replied. "Neff's people didn't waste any time.

There was a guy named Ward. The Israeli was a woman named Nili. The soldiers handed us over to them in a medical room in the airport. Nili swept us for tracking devices."

"You're kidding," Melissa said and looked at Brian. "Who are these people?"

"I don't know, but she knew her business. Really professional. You could tell she'd done this sort of thing before. I was impressed."

"You mean you were smitten," Dee said matter-of-factly. "Some priest."

"She's exaggerating," he protested.

"Think Salma Hayek as paramilitary Barbie, and you get the picture."

"That's pretty accurate," Malcolm acknowledged with a grin. Dee rolled her eyes.

"Anyway, it's a good thing they thought of sweeping us for bugs. Nili found something on Dee."

"You mean *in* me," Dee corrected him with a look of disgust on her face.

Brian and Melissa looked questioningly at her.

"I'll let Malcolm tell it. He was the one awake, not me, thank God."

Malcolm shifted uncomfortably in his seat. Brian and Melissa exchanged a curious glance.

"I might as well be direct," he said. "Dee had some sort of implant in her rectum."

"Good night," Brian gasped.

"It gets stranger. I expected Nili to call a doctor when she found it. Instead, she took it out herself with no anesthetic. I guess she didn't need it since Dee was out, but it took me by surprise. She and her partner, the guy named Ward, huddled up to make the decision, and then she just cut it out. It was close to the surface, so it wasn't complicated, but it was just weird. They obviously didn't want anyone to know what they'd found or what they decided to do about it."

"I'll say it again," said Melissa, "who are these people?"

"On the flight, Dee had some bleeding. She was in and out of consciousness. They had some over-the-counter medication on board that they managed to get Dee to swallow. Nili eventually made contact with a doctor, who met us in the US. Dee wasn't in any real trouble, but I think Nili thought she might be in over her head."

"What did she do with the implant?"

"This is sweet," Dee said, mustering a smile. "I was fine with my sore butt when I heard the Colonel would be ticked off."

Malcolm laughed and flashed a wide smile. "Yeah, it was pretty funny. Before we took off, Nili took the implant and put it in a wad of chewing gum. When we went outside to get on their jet, she stuck it to a baggage cart."

"I love it," Melissa grinned.

"So for some reason the Colonel couldn't prevent you from leaving, but he was determined to follow you," Brian said.

"I'd say that's certain. He's probably wondering by now why we're wandering in circles in the Tel Aviv airport."

"So it's pretty obvious that the Colonel is behind my pregnancy," Dee interjected. "And that's the only reason I need to get rid of it. The first safe path I see for that, it's a done deal."

"It's still hard to believe the Colonel didn't prevent you from leaving," Melissa wondered aloud, "especially if he has an interest in the pregnancy. Why not tell whoever was pressuring him that you were too ill to travel, or fake your death—something?"

"He isn't God," Malcolm said. "I'm guessing he didn't feel either of those ideas would be worth the risk."

"What do you mean?" she asked.

"Once the State Department made a demand, he couldn't really do anything but agree without prompting a demand for justification, and maybe an inquiry. Whoever was making the demand above him wouldn't settle for any refusal without a verifiable reason. The Colonel may have figured he didn't have time to come up with something foolproof. It's not like he was expecting any of this. Who in the world would even know where Dee was? Getting asked about her whereabouts must have caught him completely by surprise."

"That seems reasonable," Brian said thoughtfully. "And you raise a good question—how did Neff's people ever find the two of you? If they really don't know exactly where you were located, they must have asked somebody at a high level of authority about you—someone who at least knew you both had been drafted into a project by the Air Force."

"Sounds logical, but only Neff can explain all that."

"So when you got to the States, Neff's people took you to the house in Maine?" Brian asked. "Then what?"

"We were met there by another woman—the doctor Nili had contacted," Malcolm answered. "Her name was Clarise. She gave Dee a thorough checking. It was a good thing she was there, since Dee needed attention and some nursing back to health. After about a week we flew to another house in Michigan, and we've been there ever since. We overheard Neff talking about Andrew, and we insisted on coming. That's how we got here."

Brian sat quietly, looking at the floor, his arms on his knees, hands clasped. "Andrew ... How many times have we mentioned him?" He looked up at the faces of his friends. "I wish he were here."

"We all do, man," Malcolm said, placing his hand firmly on Brian's shoulder.

"He'd know how to proceed."

"I'll bet he would, but we'll know, too. God will make it clear when it needs to be clear. We just have to have our eyes and hearts ready and open."

"No doubt. There are just so many questions that still need answering."

"Neff could no doubt help there," Malcolm answered, "but don't expect much. When we were in Father Fitzgerald's office we didn't learn much. Father Fitzgerald said that he had gotten worried about Andrew when he hadn't heard from him for almost two months. His attempts to find information about Andrew somehow led to me, but I'm still fuzzy on the details. He didn't lay it all out. And I don't know how Dee got into the picture. We only had a few minutes in the office. I'm positive that even though Neff got us off the base, he doesn't know where we actually came from."

"So what do you think he *does* know?" Brian asked.

"That we were somewhere in the Southwest. He told us he suspected we were being held against our will but wasn't completely sure until they found out about Dee."

"I obviously don't know what you've shared with Neff," Dee interrupted, glancing first at Brian and then Melissa, "but it's certain he's going to suspect your circumstances are connected to ours."

"You know," said Melissa, voicing a realization that had just occurred to her, "judging by Neff's reaction when he saw that we all knew each other, it seems certain President Fitzgerald hasn't said anything to Neff about our circumstances. He wouldn't have been so surprised if Father Fitzgerald had given him information about us."

"That makes sense," replied Malcolm. "But despite that, I think the only people we *know* we can trust are right here in this room."

They exchanged glances, nodding. They knew instinctively that Malcolm was right.

"But Neff's smart," Brian noted after a moment, with some apprehension. "He's going to be suspicious."

"And our sense of urgency about meeting right away today will only feed that suspicion," Malcolm guessed, "despite not knowing the details."

"For sure," Melissa added, feeling a bit more exposed.

"So what's our story?" Malcolm asked. "Time for some Jesuit ethics."

Brian couldn't help laughing. "No matter what the situation, you're on your game, Malcolm. I wish Andrew were here to have heard that."

"Oh, he'd probably laugh, then launch into a sermon reminding us of how the order and most of the Church is spiritually corrupt—that we have to be the guardians. If there was a pulpit in the room, he'd pound it a few times to make the point."

"That sounds true to form."

"But you know what I'm talkin' about, man. God used deception in the Bible to preserve life and His people. Until we know who we're dealing with, we're all at genuine risk. Don't tell me you don't agree—you're the one pretending to be married, here."

"I know, I know . . ."

"So what does he know *for sure* about the two of you?" Melissa asked.

Malcolm looked at Dee, unsure of the precise answer.

"He knows I'm a psychologist and that Malcolm is a scientist," she answered.

"He might know I'm a priest, too, given his relationship to Father Fitzgerald," Malcolm mused. "Andrew and I worked together a lot over the past few years. Like I told you, my name came up in that connection, but I'm not sure about details. I'm betting he's done background checks on all of us—you with your new names, of course—so he probably knows where we went to school and our work history, that sort of stuff."

"We're making this too hard," Melissa observed. "Let's tell him the truth—at least part of it. We'll tell him we were part of a group working this summer to study the religious and psychological impact of various crises caused by global warming. We'll tell him we left after a couple of weeks because Brian and I were being pursued. That puts us all together for a little time and fits with what he knows about us already. All we need to do is find an event in the Southwest that'll match the cover story. It shouldn't be that hard—someone's always getting paid to spend a summer talking about global warming."

"Missy, I love it when you're cynical," Malcolm joked. "That's perfect."

"Thanks," she replied, smiling, then added, "And I thought I told you last summer to never call me Missy."

Malcolm laughed. "You remembered!"

"One more thing," Dee said seriously, looking at Melissa. "You both need to get examined for implants."

"She's right," Malcolm agreed. "Around here, X-rays are the easiest way."

"But we haven't had any problems here. I don't think—"

"I'm dead serious, honey," Dee cut Melissa off. "I know you're about to say that if you were being tracked, they'd have already come for you. But let me ask you: How do you know that? What if they're just biding their time?"

"That doesn't seem logical," Melissa tried to counter.

"Yeah, I know—kind of like the last six months of our lives."

20

To erase or "de-pattern" personality traits, Cameron gave his subjects megadoses of LSD, subjected them to drug-induced "sleep therapy" for up to 65 consecutive days, and applied electroshock therapy at 75 times the usual intensity. To shape new behavior, Cameron forced them to listen to repeated recorded messages for 16-hour intervals, a technique known as "psychic driving."

—Washington Post, *July 28, 1985, quoting the* Congressional Record *of the Senate, 99th Congress, 1st Session, Volume 131, No. 106, Part 2, p. 131, in regard to the mind-control work of psychiatrist Dr. Ewen Cameron, former President of the Canadian, American and World Psychiatric Associations, while in the employ of the CIA*

"How are things proceeding, Becker?" Colonel Ferguson asked, gazing through the two-way glass.

"Wonderfully," came the assured answer. Dr. Becker fastidiously surveyed the settings of the equipment panel before which he was seated. "Once we were able to locate her history, the programming path was clear."

"How long yet?" the Colonel asked.

"A few more days. We didn't have to produce another alter. Just needed to take her driving for a couple weeks."

"Good."

"The task you've assigned her is straightforward. If there are any other directions, now would be the time to implant them."

"I don't need anything else from her. All the details are in place. The media will be led to the right conclusions." The Colonel turned to leave.

"Have a good Thanksgiving, Vernon," Dr. Becker said, reaching for a knob on the panel. "I presume you'll take in the football game—I won't be paying for dinner this year."

"Oh, I'll be . . . watching," the Colonel said, not bothering to turn around so he could conceal his amusement at his choice of words. "We'll see."

Dr. Becker watched the secured door close behind the Air Force officer. He adjusted his glasses and then flipped a switch on the panel, signaling his assistant on the other side of the glass to reinsert the bite guard into the prone girl's mouth. The assistant stepped back, and the bespectacled psychiatrist calmly turned the knob. Becky's body jerked to rigidity as the electrical impulse surged through the electrodes and into her brain.

"Such a good patient."

21

Actions are the seed of fate; deeds grow into destiny.

—*Harry S. Truman*

"Why would you ask if I could arrange X-rays for you and your husband?" Neff inquired, wearing a perplexed expression. He scanned the four faces before him. He, Malcolm, Dee, Melissa, Brian, and Malone were now seated in the lounge of the campus guest house, the agreed upon point of rendezvous after the impromptu meeting in Melissa's office.

Malcolm took the initiative to answer. "We told them all about Dee's implant."

"Why would Dr. Harper's ... unusual circumstances ... be a concern?" Neff asked.

"Maybe I'm being paranoid," Melissa replied, searching for a workable answer, "and I didn't pry, but Dee thinks the intelligence community or military had something to do with what was put in her. Our own problems," she added, glancing at Brian, "are connected to an intelligence agency as well."

"Fascinating," Neff said thoughtfully, looking from Melissa to Brian, then back again.

"I don't want to say more," Melissa continued. "I just don't like the coincidence."

"Coincidences can be unnerving," Neff replied as he studied her face.

"Well?" Brian asked.

"I'm not sure if an X-ray is wise, Melissa, since you're pregnant. Have you considered that?"

"I did a little research on that in my office before we had to leave. Everything I read said it wouldn't cause any harm," Melissa countered.

"I'd need to ask our own doctor about that," Neff responded. "I'd trust her opinion. But I'm not sure if we could arrange it anyway."

"You don't have your own machine?" Malcolm asked. Neff looked at him, his face showing some irritation. "Sorry, I guess that was a little out of line," Malcolm apologized. "It's just that you guys seem to have, well, everything."

"To satisfy your curiosity, Dr. Bradley, yes, we have our own X-ray machine. But it's at home." Neff didn't say it, but the implication was clear: They weren't invited to headquarters.

"Have you really thought this through?" Malone joined the conversation. "A hospital or clinic will want a good reason to give a pregnant woman an X-ray. They might agree that the danger is minimal, but they'll still ask questions. You can't just tell them you want to know if you're carrying a tracking implant. You'd wind up under psychiatric observation."

"Well, to be honest, I hadn't considered that," Melissa said, wistfully. "I guess I was hoping it could be arranged with someone who wouldn't ask questions."

"They'd have to, if for no other reasons than liability. The only way you'd avoid the questions is to find a friend who can do it."

"Yes," Neff said, a look of satisfaction appearing on his face. "You'd have to trust someone—namely, us, presuming we could arrange it. But the two of you have had a difficult time with that. Wouldn't you consider getting on a plane with Malone and me taking a serious risk?" His sarcasm was light, but clear.

Brian and Melissa didn't protest—they couldn't. The lounge fell silent for a few uncomfortable moments.

"I'll see what I can do," Neff finally said, knowing he'd won the exchange. "Our doctor, Clarise, has a lot of contacts, some of whom have done business with us before. Perhaps she can call in a favor with someone who can get access to a machine. But there's one other consideration."

"Go on," Melissa asked.

"What if they find something?"

"Then I'd want it removed . . . by your Clarise."

"That's not what I'm talking about. What if you were targeted like Dr. Harper? The fact that someone did that to her suggests she and the baby have some importance."

"And what about staying in North Dakota?" asked Malone. "Dr. Harper's implant was obviously for tracking. If we were to find an implant, we'd have to assume that whoever you're running from and whoever implanted Dr. Harper were the same people."

Melissa fell silent. Brian knew she was thinking she'd made a mistake by bringing up the X-ray—that they'd exposed too much about themselves.

"Look," Brian said, thinking quickly, realizing that the connection Malone wanted to make was one for which he had no real information. "We know who's looking for us. The trouble we're in started before we met Malcolm and Dee this summer. If something was implanted in Melissa, we can add that to our list of problems whether there's a connection or not. We'd decide what to do about the pregnancy if that was the case."

"If you can do this," Melissa said, feeling somewhat relieved at Brian's response, "we'd be in your debt."

"You already know what I want," Neff said. "I want your husband's time. We need information from him about what he's been posting."

Malcolm and Dee simultaneously gave Brian a mystified look.

"I'll explain later," he told them, then turned to Neff. "We didn't have time to get into all that. I suppose you have a deal."

Neff's reply took Brian and Melissa by surprise. "Dr. Scott, I don't want your help if it comes only out of a sense of obligation. I want you to help us because you trust us. I'll give Clarise a call and see what she can do."

22

A person often meets his destiny on the road he took to avoid it.

—Jean de La Fontaine

"Ready for show and tell?"

"Yes—and take your time," Melissa replied. "If there's anything to notice, I don't want you to miss it."

"I won't. Nobody's going to interrupt us on a Sunday, unless somebody in town finds a body."

"A body?"

"The guy whose office we're borrowing—his name is Cal—is a pathologist, as well as the local coroner. He's got some corpses stored away down the hall. We just don't want to have him bringing in any new ones."

"I see," Melissa replied uneasily.

"Are you queasy?"

"No, just a bit on edge."

"I don't expect this to take long."

Melissa watched the tall, striking woman attaching her X-rays to the lighted viewers. She appeared to be her own age, roughly mid-thirties. Her long, tight curls of light brown hair shifted wispily as she looked back and forth from image to image. Melissa started to dress as Clarise silently moved down the row, intermittently positioning and then removing the narrow, dark-rimmed glasses that hung from a delicate chain around her neck. It was the perfect look—studious yet stylish.

"Congratulations on the twins, by the way," Clarise said, turning to her with a sincere smile.

"Thank you."

"Any problems with the pregnancy so far?"

Melissa hesitated, taking note that Clarise had asked the question while inspecting the X-ray of her abdomen. "No, none at all."

"Good. Everything looks fine here, at least in terms of what can be seen in an X-ray."

Clarise moved to the next image, continuing her inspection. The images provided a complete head-to-toe view. Melissa noticed her lingering over several. "Anything out of place?" she asked apprehensively.

"Not yet," Clarise replied, leaning in on the images of Melissa's feet. "I don't do a lot of this sort of thing, but I've read a good bit about implant technology. Usually the best place to hide something is the digits—between toes and fingers, that sort of thing—and teeth, of course."

"Teeth?" Melissa asked incredulously.

"Teeth."

"How much of that sort of thing *really* happens?"

"Hard to know, but happen it does. Obviously there isn't a truckload of published work on this sort of thing. I wish I'd seen your friend's implant before Nili ditched it, but they obviously couldn't bring it along. Some of the patents I've seen are fairly exotic. Since hers was military, it may have been especially interesting."

"Patents?"

"There are lots of tracking implant devices. The government knows about this sort of research and naturally funds and develops some of it. All implants are supposed to be registered with the federal government in the National Medical Device Registry. I'm betting your friend's wasn't."

Melissa looked at her, dumbfounded.

"I know, you have better things to read than healthcare laws and medical patents," Clarise continued. "The legislation doesn't specifically mention things like tracking whereabouts—something like RFID—but it doesn't rule it out, either. It just describes implants that might contribute to gathering medical information and 'patient safety,'" she added with wry smile.

Melissa remained speechless.

"But you don't have to worry about that," Clarise said, removing her glasses. "You're clean, just like your husband."

Melissa sat down on the edge of the examining bed, visibly relieved. "Thank you so much. And tell your friend how much we appreciate him letting us use his office."

"I'll do that—although this didn't come without a cost."

"You mean whatever it was that he asked in return?" Melissa asked, recalling the brief exchange she and Brian had overheard between Neff and Malone on the plane.

"Right."

"I know it's awfully forward to ask, but—"

"I don't know what he wanted," Clarise interrupted her. "And if I did, I'm not sure I could tell you."

"I understand. It's just that Mr. Neff seemed agitated about coming here without knowing specifically what was expected in return."

"He was," Clarise admitted, grabbing the doorknob and opening it for Melissa. "But Graham wanted to do it. He believes you were worth the risk."

Melissa looked at her uncertainly.

"Graham likes to help people. It's a deep character flaw," she explained, grinning. "So does my friend Cal, but he had something specific in mind when he lent us his office for the day. We'll find out soon enough whether it was a Faustian bargain."

The two of them left the examining room and walked the short distance to the waiting room to rejoin the others.

"Find anything?" Neff asked as soon as they appeared.

"She's clean," Clarise announced, "just like him."

"Good," he answered, looking at Brian.

"Thanks again," Brian responded. "We really do appreciate this."

"You're welcome," Neff replied. "Now we need to discuss what's expected of us in return."

"Shouldn't we do that without them?" Clarise asked, glancing first at Neff and then Malone.

"They can be here," Neff replied. "If we end up agreeing to this—and, frankly, we don't have much choice—it looks like they're going to be caught in the middle."

Brian saw an immediate change in Clarise's expression. She made no attempt to hide her alarm. Then he looked quickly at Malcolm and could tell he'd picked up the change as well.

"What does Cal want?" Clarise asked. "We've worked with him before. Is it . . . the same sort of business?"

"Yes, and no," Malone answered. "Same kind of cargo, but an unusual situation. Since we haven't had the chance to do any pre-planning, it's less predictable than usual—and therefore possibly dangerous."

"What kind of 'business' are you talking about?" Malcolm broke in, asking the question for the rest of the outsiders.

Neff waved his hand. "Not now. If my partners and I are on the same page, you'll see. But Malone's right—certain elements make this task dangerous."

"How many are we talking about?" Clarise asked.

"Thirty," Neff replied. He paced a few steps to look out the window.

"We need the Hook for that," she responded. "What's the timetable? Can we get one of them here?"

"Dawn tomorrow," Malone replied, "so we have enough time. We've proposed a location about 120 miles northeast of Duluth just stateside of the Canadian border. A chopper can be there in time, even though it would have to refuel twice. From where we're at now in International Falls, we're less than an hour away if we take the Lear. There's an abandoned airport a mile or so from the airport where we'd actually land. That would be the site."

"But the Hook is in for maintenance," Neff interjected, still gazing out the window.

"The Puma won't hold thirty," Clarise replied. "It's not the kind of helicopter that can pull this off."

"I know. That's one of the reasons it's complicated."

"Can we take the rest in the Lear?"

"We can't fly into the active local airport because we'd never get the cargo out," Malone explained. "The abandoned airport's runway was originally only 2,800 feet. It would be unbelievably risky to try to land and take off with the Lear on something that short—and you can bet the runway now is even shorter and in disrepair. And it'll be covered with snow. We'd probably either crash or get stranded."

"I think I know what's coming next," Clarise said in an apprehensive tone. "Is this really *that* important? Can't we pay Cal back another way?"

"We'll have to have both Pumas from Miqlat," Neff said, finally turning toward them and rejoining the small group. "Three of our pilots are right here in the room, which means—"

"Which means the other two have to either fly without co-pilots or with co-pilots who aren't fully trained . . . and Kamran can't use the radio. This is sounding too dicey by the minute."

Malone chimed in, making no attempt to contradict her. "One Puma has the LRAD on it; the other has the prototype EMP cannon. They'll transport weapons since we can't take anything in the Lear through airport security."

"Pardon me," Dee interrupted in an insincere tone, "but I'm not liking the sound of all this."

"Did you just say '*EMP cannon*'?" Malcolm asked incredulously, nearly speaking over her.

"That's understandable, Dr. Harper," Neff acknowledged, ignoring Malcolm, "but irrelevant."

"And just why is that?" she demanded. "Why can't you just do what you need to do and leave us here?"

"We *can* leave you here, in a manner of speaking. In fact, I'd recommend that you and Dr. Kelley stay behind at the hangar where we leave the Lear, given your circumstances. But—well, we need Dr. Bradley and Dr. Scott with us. They'll improve our chances for success."

"Graham—"

"This is starting to sound like some private war," Dee shot back angrily, cutting off Clarise. "I say we get our own tickets and head back to North Dakota."

"With what?" Neff asked, his voice piercing. The retort stung, as intended.

"We can buy plane tickets," Brian replied in her defense. "We can all get back to North Dakota."

"Yes, I suppose you could do that . . ." Neff's voice trailed off and his gaze fell to the floor as he collected his thoughts. "But if you do that, you'll miss your chance to see what we do. You and your wife have wanted to know that from the beginning.

"I admit, I'm less than enthusiastic about the idea of you learning about our business, but we don't have much choice. To be honest, we're short-handed. I'd feel better if you and Dr. Bradley were there . . . in case something goes wrong. We may need assistance. We usually plan these sorts of things weeks in advance. This is completely unscripted."

"Man, you're gonna have to level with us about this 'business' before we agree to anything," Malcolm said, his face hardened with conviction. "And I don't like the idea of leaving Dee anywhere—and I'm certain Brian feels the same way about Melissa."

"It's not going to happen," Brian confirmed without hesitation. "And that means I want to know the risks up front."

"I've already said it's dangerous."

"I heard you. But there's no way I'm leaving Melissa alone. If someone is watching us, leaving her alone would present an easy opportunity for them to try to take her. If we ever meet up with our problem, I at least want to make it difficult for them to get what they want. We're staying together." He looked at Melissa for confirmation, and she nodded.

"That's acceptable."

"I didn't agree yet," Brian quickly followed. "I want to know this isn't something I'll be ashamed of later. Laugh if you want, but I try to do what's right in God's eyes with the information I have. I don't have much to show for it, but that's who I am."

"Ditto," Malcolm agreed.

Neff eyed both of them thoughtfully. A trace of a smile, barely perceptible, appeared on his face. "I'm grateful to hear that."

"Graham," Clarise interrupted gently, "you haven't really answered my question yet. We've never done this before with outsiders. Is this really worth the risk? I mean, can't it be done another time?"

"There's one other thing you should know about the payload," Malone responded for Neff, watching Clarise's expression. "The Filipinos are in this lot." He raised his eyebrows to accentuate his point.

"You're kidding."

"Nope. Cal has confirmation, and it's convincing."

"That's unbelievable."

"Is it?" Neff asked slowly, a faint expression of irony on his face. "We don't believe in coincidences, remember?"

"How did he pull that off? That had to be absolutely—"

"Reckless?" Neff mused, completing her thought.

"Yeah."

Neff shrugged. "That's his middle name, remember? He thinks the people he pissed off a little over two weeks ago are still looking for their property. Cal's kept the lot together. He brought them across the border in a two-seater, one trip a night, flying under the radar—literally. The last was yesterday. They have to move now."

"Have you asked Miqlat about this?"

"A few minutes ago," Malone answered.

"And?"

"Everybody thinks it's the right thing to do."

She shook her head. "Okay then." Then, in a more confident tone, her expression strangely relaxing, she went on, "The timing is certainly ideal."

"Wait a minute," Melissa burst in, her rage building. "Your friend Cal 'brought *them* across the border'? Your business is human trafficking? What's wrong with you people?"

"You're right, Melissa," Neff answered calmly. "We buy and transport people, among other ventures. But you won't be turning us in to law enforcement."

"The hell we won't!" Dee seethed.

"No, you won't, Dr. Harper," he smiled. "You of all people will appreciate what we do, the risks we take. Remember the Underground Railroad? It's alive and well today—and you're about to get a glimpse of how it works."

23

Better to fight for something than live for nothing.

—*General George S. Patton, Jr.*

"When we get to the site," Neff instructed as he drove, "I want all of you to get into the helicopter right away."

Brian, who was riding shotgun, nodded. His head was throbbing from the flight. He hated flying.

"One of the Pumas is already there, according to my watch. The other one will touch down about a half hour from now. That'll put us about forty-five minutes until the rendezvous. It should be enough time for Clarise and me to show you and Dr. Bradley the setup and explain the plan."

After landing at the small airport, the seven of them had piled into a rented SUV for the short drive to the pick-up site, a little over a mile to the south. Brian glanced out the window. The trees lining the heavily-wooded two-lane road glistened with snow. The break of dawn produced the sort of picturesque scenery you'd see on a postcard. The natural beauty manifesting before Brian's eyes clashed with the anxiety churning inside him. Even on a ride this brief, he'd expected to see at least a handful of cars on the roads, but there hadn't been any. The location felt terribly remote.

As they came to an intersection, Brian spotted a clearing straight ahead. It didn't test his powers of deduction to discern that this was their destination. The snow wasn't deep enough to obscure the roadways, which were subtly revealed by tall shoots of underbrush visible in scattered tufts on the otherwise flat surfaces on either side of the now defunct entryway. He shook his head at the road signs, which announced they were approaching Airport and Devil Track Roads.

The abandoned runway came into full view in less than fifty yards after they crossed the road. The Puma, not visible from the intersection, was positioned off to the left, its nose pointed perpendicular to the runway toward the entrance so that its side doors faced both ends of the runway. Its engine was off. Neff parked the SUV a short distance away and off the entry road as the Puma's pilot emerged.

While Neff, Malone, and the pilot conversed, Brian and the rest did as they'd been told and boarded the helicopter under Clarise's direction. They passed what looked to be a large, round speaker, perhaps four feet across, covered with a metal mesh and mounted on a sturdy cast-iron roller. It was strategically positioned so that it could be swiveled and pointed out of the large side doors at either side of the helicopter.

Brian counted a dozen or so upright seats, two across on one side and a single-seat row on the other, with a small aisle between them. A visible arm and hand flipping toggle switches in the cockpit informed them that someone else was on board, though they couldn't see who. Clarise took the opportunity to give them a sort of orientation.

"This is one of our two Puma helicopters," she began, "at least from our main base of operations. We have a few others on the coasts and locations scattered here and there in other countries. It has room enough for about twenty seats, though we've removed a few for the LRAD—the long range acoustic device. It's the device set up in the center of the Puma."

"The round thing?" Brian asked.

"Yes," she answered. "It's designed for long-range verbal communication up to a mile and a half. It can also disable people with sound."

"So it's a headache machine?" Malcolm surmised.

"Yes, or an eardrum shattering machine, depending on the setting and the range. It's non-lethal, but you don't want to be in its transmission path. Graham will explain more since one of you may have to handle it today—hopefully not, though."

Brian and Malcolm looked at each other uncertainly.

"Who's the pilot?" Melissa asked, leaning to get glimpse of the two men conversing.

"Ward," she answered. "Your friends have already met him on the trip from Tel Aviv." Ward Bennett was in his early forties. He was trim, athletic, and—from what Brian could see—all business.

"Military?" Melissa asked.

Clarise smiled. "No, though he looks the part. Ward has never spent a day in the service. He has a background in international finance. He spent most of his career in venture capital and economic development in foreign countries. He speaks Spanish and Russian fluently—

Spanish because of a grandmother, and Russian because of his career."

"Sounds impressive."

"He wouldn't describe it that way. If you asked him what he did in his old life, he'd call himself a glorified mobster. His career was all legal and legit, but it amounted to putting poor countries into crushing debt relationships with his employer and the US government so they could control the country's natural resources and leverage the geography for the military."

"So he's out of that now?" Dee asked.

Clarise nodded.

"What does he do now—besides fly helicopters?"

"He keeps track of all our businesses, investments, expenses—everything financial that concerns us. We have to hide our money and cash flow all over the world. I should mention that he's also my husband."

"So Mr. Right Stuff is a full-time accountant?" Malcolm asked, trying to pry a little more out of Clarise about their operation.

"Sort of," she agreed, chuckling at the reference. "I think we need to get back to what we'll be doing here."

The four of them listened attentively.

"We'll be picking up thirty people, nearly all of them girls. They'll be anywhere from preteens to young adults. Roughly half will be Filipino; they'll all speak a little English, some better than others."

"How do you know that already?" Melissa inquired.

"We run almost a hundred orphanages around the world, most of them in the poorest places on the planet. We finance another fifty or so mercy projects in the US. We've also created an international network to move all sorts of victims to safe locations—mostly battered women and kids. But our orphanages are the priority. They focus on the young people we rescue from slavery, sex trafficking, violent revolutions—all the vile crap you never want to think about.

"We make trips to Africa, Asia, and the Americas and pose as slave traders and sex traffickers to buy people—mostly kids—all year round. Our operations are off the radar and separate from any funding we report to the IRS under the name of non-profits we've created solely for that purpose. It has to be that way since we bend or break international law when we must to rescue kids. We don't hold meetings with politicians or the UN—we get people out."

"So one of those orphanages is in the Philippines," Malcolm concluded.

"Right. Almost three months ago, a dozen kids were kidnapped from one of our orphanages. Our network has been hunting for them ever since. We heard they had wound up in Canada, but we had no idea where until two days ago. They're together, but only because they were all put to work in a new brothel."

Clarise stopped to gaze at their faces, which were filled with horror, disgust, and outrage. She waited, but no one said anything.

"What you'll see here won't be pretty. Some of them will be recovering from being heavily drugged. Some might be injured from beatings and rapes—who knows? But the task is simple: get everyone into the helicopters and head out as fast as possible. It shouldn't take more than ten or fifteen minutes."

"Does Neff know if the people who were holding them know where they are now?" Melissa asked anxiously.

"No. We don't know anything about how our contact, Cal, got them out or who the creeps are that pimped them. We don't even know where the kids are hiding—only that they're being brought here. So far, everybody has been safe, but Cal is convinced there are people in the area tracking them."

"Where do you want us?" asked Dee.

"I want you and Melissa to sit in the last two seats in the rear. You'll have a walkie-talkie. Keep an eye out the windows on both sides of the helicopter. The kids will be in three vehicles, all arriving at the same time. If you see any other vehicle at any time after the cargo gets here, let us know immediately. Any surprises mean trouble, and we'll have to act fast."

Neff climbed inside the helicopter and joined the small group.

"Ward has Nili about ten minutes out," he said to Clarise. "When she lands, she's going to point her Puma perpendicular to the runway from the other side, about fifty yards to the left of this one. Malone is going to take her place piloting that craft. Ward will pilot this one. They'll sit in the cockpit with the rotors running, ready for takeoff. You and Madison will leave in this one when we have our people. Nili and Kamran will go with Malone." He looked toward the cockpit. "I'll let Madison know; she probably needs help with the weapons. Be back in a minute."

Clarise nodded approvingly and turned to the others. "We always try to have two experienced pilots on every flight in case one can't fly for some reason. Madison—the girl in the cockpit—can fly, but she's not very experienced. Our other associate, Kamran, is the same. He's logged a lot of hours for only being eighteen, but we like to group people with the most experience, especially with human cargo on board.

He'd only fly if it was an absolute emergency."

"What about the flight home?" Brian asked.

"Graham will have to solo that. We need everyone on the other end to process the people we're picking up. Don't worry," she reassured him, grinning, "he can fly just about anything."

Neff and Madison emerged from the cockpit together. The others watched as they removed several snub-nosed assault rifles, hand guns, and body armor from a secured bin. Neff motioned the group to move closer to the center of the plane, where he and Madison were crouched.

Brian estimated that Madison was in her mid to late twenties. Her thick, strawberry-blonde hair was neatly tied back into a pony tail. The cold air circulating through the open helicopter doors caused her smooth white cheeks to turn rosy, an effect that accentuated her sparkling blue eyes. She expertly picked up one of the assault rifles, checked the action and the sight, and handed it to Clarise, then grabbed another to repeat the process. Her perfectly incongruent look was completed by a camouflage parka, torso body armor, and army-green shoulder bag stocked with clip rounds for the assault rifles. She noticed Brian watching her and smiled cheerfully.

"Are you Dr. Scott?" she asked, extending her free hand.

"Yes," he said, returning the gesture.

Madison looked at Clarise with a delighted grin. "Sweet! Nili's going to be *so* jealous." She turned to Brian and laughed at his perplexed face. "I'm just sayin'," she added, observing Melissa's tell-me-more expression.

"There are three entrances into our location," Neff interrupted, making eye contact with each of them. "There's the one we came in, the far east end of the runway, and a road to the south of us that runs parallel to the runway. That road is accessible only from the east end and comes out about a hundred yards from our location. Unwelcome company could come from any of these entrances."

"Who gets the walkie-talkie?" Madison asked.

Clarise took it from her and handed it to Melissa.

"Do you think Cal—?" Madison started to ask.

"No—no time for that," Clarise interrupted, shutting her down with a wry smile.

"No harm in asking," the younger girl replied with a grin before heading back toward the cockpit.

"Madison has a thing for Cal," Clarise explained.

"Okay, we have three TARs," Neff continued, this time speaking directly to Clarise. "One for you, one for Madison, and one for me. Nili has her own. We have two extra sets of body armor. I recommend the ladies wear them," he added, looking at Melissa and Dee.

"Seriously?" Dee complained.

"They're just an extra precaution," he assured them. "You won't have to wear them long."

"Hand 'em over," Dee yielded, rolling her eyes. She turned to Melissa. "I'll bet we're the only people on earth that could turn getting an X-ray into a black-op with army rangers."

Clarise helped Melissa and Dee return to the rear of the plane and put on the armor. Neff watched them move toward the back of the Puma out of earshot, and then turned to Brian and Malcolm. "Dr. Scott made it clear to us earlier that he's handled a gun before, but what about you, Dr. Bradley?"

"A few times." He looked curiously at Brian, who shrugged.

"Good. We have Glocks for both of you. Madison's getting them. She'll load them and show you the safety basics, which are pretty simple: don't handle the weapon unless you're going to use it. I'm sure they won't be necessary—all of this weaponry is purely precautionary."

"Sure," Brian replied, doubting him more with each reminder.

"Do you both see the logic in the way I described the position the Pumas will take?"

Malcolm looked Neff in the eye. "You can aim that sound weapon down either end of the runway and at the road we took to get here. The third road comes out adjacent to our helicopter a hundred yards away, so we have that angle covered, too. When the other helicopter lands, it'll be able to do the same. The positions allow for either a crossfire—I remember you said the other Puma had an EMP cannon—or a clear line of sight to all three entry points."

"Excellent. Did you learn that in graduate school?" he asked with a friendly smirk.

"Military Channel," Malcolm answered coyly.

"Of course," Neff smirked good-naturedly.

"So what's the EMP cannon do?" Brian asked.

"It's just—"

"I know—it's a precaution," he cut him off. "How do you plan on using it?"

"Kamran, our associate in the second helicopter, will use it if a hostile vehicle approaches. The EMP cannon will instantly disable a vehicle.

At that point, we'll demand the occupants surrender. We can communicate with them at a distance through the LRAD."

"And if they don't surrender?"

"Then we use the LRAD as a weapon. A good dose of high frequency and they'll be eager to give in—assuming they can speak, that is. We'll have ear protection; they won't."

"What if the hostile vehicle is old and doesn't have microprocessors controlling its electrical system?"

"You're becoming more fascinating all the time, Dr. Bradley. I'm truly impressed that you know how the EMP cannon works—and when it won't."

"I'm a scientist. So what's plan B if we need it? You know that anyone coming our way who isn't on our side is going to be armed and pissed."

"We can't allow a hostile vehicle to approach the Pumas. That'll turn the rescue into a fire-fight. If the EMP cannon doesn't work, Nili will have to destroy the car."

"With what?" Brian asked.

"She'll use the Spike she's bringing along. . . . Do you know what that is as well, Dr. Bradley?"

"That'll kill everyone inside the car." He looked at Brian apprehensively. "A Spike is an anti-tank guided missile that can be fired by one person. It's Israeli."

"Correct. Who says there's nothing good on TV?" Neff said, casting another skeptical look in Malcolm's direction. "And yes, to be sure, it would kill everyone instantly. We've never had to use the Spike or anything like it, and I hope we won't. We normally don't have to use any weapons, much less lethal force, but that's because we spend weeks planning our missions. We've never operated like this before."

He hesitated before continuing. "If it comes to the Spike, we'll have no choice but to save our lives and the lives of the people we're here to rescue. Do you agree, Dr. Bradley?"

Malcolm looked at him grimly. "Yeah, I do."

24

I would rather have a good plan today than
a perfect plan two weeks from now.

—*General George S. Patton, Jr.*

Brian looked over at Malcolm nervously. The two of them knelt on either side of the LRAD, handguns tucked into their belts under their coats, the cold wind chilling them as it blew through the helicopter. On the surface, the job was simple. Neff had shown them both how to adjust the intensity of the sonic beam, as well as how to use it as either a weapon or for communication. Composed of some dials and a switch, it would be easy to handle—unless they had to improvise.

Nili's helicopter had landed thirty minutes ago. Brian and Malcolm had watched from a distance as she unloaded more gear, chatted with Neff briefly, and then suited up. Once she was ready, she had helped a thin, dark-skinned young man position the EMP cannon. It took up more space than the LRAD but, despite its bulk, it swiveled easily on its stand. Then came the Spike. Nili unpacked and readied it in no time at all. Smooth and efficient.

Just precautions.

Outside on the ground, midway in the fifty-yard space between the Pumas, Neff, Nili, and Clarise stood waiting, each of them armed with a TAR and wearing protective headgear around their necks. All three had their eyes trained on the entrance through which their rented SUV had come. Madison stood outside the open door a few feet from Brian and Malcolm.

Brian looked back at the second Puma to his left, its blades rotating lightly in the same manner as their own craft. He could just see the nose of the EMP cannon in the open doorway. He glanced at the rear of their helicopter. Melissa and Dee were huddled together for warmth, trying not to look frightened. It wasn't working.

Neff looked at his watch. As if on cue, a windowless gray van drove into view. The three sentinels raised their weapons but quickly lowered them when two more vehicles appeared, a large passenger van and a four-door covered jeep. At first Brian couldn't see anyone through the windows of the second and third vehicles. Once all three pulled in between the Pumas, though, some faces began to pop up from below window level. In unified, choreographed response, the blades on both helicopters accelerated, their whining pitch elevating in preparation for take-off.

All three vehicles burst into activity as soon as they came to a halt. The drivers quickly exited and opened the side and rear doors. The passengers filed out, looking somewhat bewildered as they listened to the verbal commands being shouted over the noise of the choppers. About half had coats, the others were draped in blankets that were inadequate for the cold. None of them had boots, but all wore some sort of footwear in various colors.

Brian estimated that the kids ranged in age from about nine through the late teens. The Filipinos were easy to spot by their dark faces and black hair. The rest were a mix of races. At first they seemed apprehensive, hesitant to move toward the armed people who were urging them to get into the helicopters. But it only took a moment for some of them to recognize their liberators. Some shouted for joy; others began to cry, their terror giving way to a torrent of relief. Three girls bolted toward Neff and threw their arms around his waist. He hugged each one quickly and motioned for them to get on board. The rest hurried toward the craft, some hobbling with limps, but all with eager resolve.

Madison ran a few paces toward the line that Clarise had funneled in her direction. Malcolm and Brian directed traffic inside their helicopter, helping to get the kids seated. Malcolm glanced through a side window and noticed that some of the kids needed help getting into the other helicopter. Kamran had been ordered to not leave the controls of the cannon, and Nili had no one to assist.

"I'll be back in a minute."

Brian nodded.

Malcolm jumped out and ran to the second Puma, hurriedly helping everyone inside in as orderly a manner as he could manage.

Brian looked back at the vans. Two had already pulled out and were heading away from the runway. Neff and the remaining driver were each carrying blanket-draped girls who couldn't walk to the helicopter, Clarise close behind. Brian knelt at the edge of the chopper and took the first girl from Neff. She wore a thin dress underneath the blanket, and Brian could see that her legs were badly bruised. She was semiconscious. Clarise had been right. The sight was unforgettably ugly.

"Make sure she's buckled in tight," Clarise said, hopping into the Puma. They quickly slid the girl into a seat. Malcolm suddenly reappeared and took the second girl, who was in similar condition but also had a swollen black eye and broken lip. Brian watched the final driver run back to his vehicle, get inside, and make his getaway.

"We've got trouble!" Dee shouted from the back, her eyes wide with fear. Melissa was already relaying what they'd spotted to the others via the walkie-talkie. A slate gray SUV was speeding toward them from the east end of the runway.

Neff quickly put on his ear protection and motioned for the others to do the same. He looked at Brian, who quickly got behind the LRAD. Nili waved at Kamran and pointed toward the vehicle, which was now about 100 yards from the nearest Puma. Brian looked back at the second craft and watched the cannon pivot. A blue glow suddenly coursed through the barrel. There was no sound. He turned toward the speeding car and saw arms with handguns protruding out the lowered windows, preparing to fire.

For a moment Brian thought the cannon had failed, but then the SUV noticeably lost speed. It rolled silently to a halt about fifty yards away. The occupants' confusion was visible through the windshield. Neff, Madison, and Nili quickly took crouching positions, their assault rifles trained on the vehicle.

Brian flipped the switch on the LRAD and spoke into its microphone as he'd been instructed. *"Throw your weapons out the windows, then get out of the car with your hands in the air. No one will get hurt."*

Brian could see the men in the car arguing. He could hear some of the younger kids crying behind him, but he kept his concentration. Clarise, Dee, and Melissa did what they could to keep everyone calm.

"Last chance," Brian warned.

Still no compliance.

Neff raised his hand, and Brian hit the button that Neff had shown him earlier. Brian could hear a loud hum. There was no visible emission from the LRAD, but the effect was immediate. Brian watched in fascination as the SUV began to rock—not because of the sonic beam, but because of the occupants' agony.

Neff had told him that the device could give a severe headache to anyone caught in the beam's diagonal coverage 1,000 feet out; it would cause debilitating pain to anyone under 300 feet away. He hadn't exaggerated. The passengers grimaced and clutched their ears and faces wildly. In less than a minute, the chaos inside the SUV subsided, as everyone inside appeared to either be unconscious or numbed into submission. The vehicle stood absolutely still. As directed, Brian kept the beam active but reduced the intensity.

Neff, Nili, and Madison ran toward the SUV. Neff first opened the driver's side door and pulled the inert form out of his seat, while Madison and Nili kept their weapons at the ready. They emptied the car of three assailants in total, stripped them of weapons, and dragged them by the ankles through the snow a short distance away. Madison took a roll of duct tape out of her bag and, with Neff, began binding their hands and legs and taping their mouths.

Brian turned off the LRAD at Neff's signal once everything was secure. Nili slipped off her headgear and strode toward the car. She let loose with the TAR and obliterated a tire, reducing the radial to a mass of black and gray spaghetti. Neff smiled at her and said something. She turned and jogged toward her Puma, rifle on her back. Madison and Neff did the same, heading in Brian's direction. The whole incident had taken less than ten minutes.

Brian turned toward Malcolm, who was looking at the second Puma. He followed his gaze and watched Nili hop into the helicopter. She and her partner hurried to quickly secure the cannon and their gear. They took the hint: It was time to leave.

"Close the far door while I get a head count," Madison shouted with urgency.

"Brian!" Melissa screamed from the back of the helicopter. "The entrance!"

Brian, Malcolm, and Madison whirled in the direction of the van, which was parked about thirty yards beyond their location and to the left, just off the turn in the road where it had entered. A black Hummer was a few yards inside the runway area and headed straight for their Puma. Brian saw a rifle and a head jutting out the passenger window. A shot rang out and hit the Puma broadside, the marksman's aim thrown off by the potholes and ruts in the damaged runway hidden under the snow.

Wails of terror erupted from inside the helicopter from the young passengers. "Turn on the LRAD! Hit 'em with it!" Malcolm hollered at Brian. Knowing Nili and Kamran were packing up, he had guessed correctly that the EMP cannon couldn't be positioned in time.

Malcolm jumped out of the Puma and motioned wildly for Nili to put on her headgear, pointing at his own. The gunfire had fixed her gaze on the road, but the motion quickly caught her attention. She discerned the intent immediately and obeyed, then pulled her weapon from her back and sprinted for the van.

Madison jumped from the Puma, ready for the LRAD burst. She caught Nili's form out of the corner of her eye and took off for the van as well. Neff was already there, pointing his TAR out over its blunted hood at the oncoming vehicle. He squeezed the trigger, and a hail of gunfire peppered the car's grill and front wheels. It lurched forward violently at the loss of the front tires, but it kept coming, its enraged driver struggling to keep it on course.

His heart pounding frantically, Brian flailed at the controls of the LRAD. His target in line, he spun the dials up in a rush and hit the button. In seconds the windshields of both vehicles exploded. Tiny shards of glass sprayed in all directions. Incredibly, he could hear screams from the men inside the Hummer despite the thunder of the Pumas. The now unguided vehicle rushed on, completely out of control, veering in the direction of the van—and Neff.

Brian watched in dismay. Neff, knocked to his knees by the hail of glass from the van's windshield, was rolling on the ground in pain, holding his ears, his headgear knocked askew by his fall. For a horrible moment he feared Neff would roll into the path of the oncoming car. The deflated wheels of the Hummer hit an unseen depression in the decrepit runway with startling force, jolting the rear of its heavy frame into the air. The car's grill dug into the ground, and it came to a sliding, scraping halt about ten yards from where Neff lay.

Brian waited breathlessly, unsure of what to do next. Madison and Nili crouched a few feet away from the motionless hulk, which had smoke billowing from its grill. Seeing Neff in pain, Nili turned and signaled to Brian, who cut the LRAD.

After a few moments Nili approached the Hummer, crouching in readiness, but there was no need. The two passengers were alive but only semiconscious. Their faces were pocked with tiny slits and gashes from the shower of windshield glass. Blood flowed from their mouths as the pain from the unexpected sonic blast had clamped their teeth onto their tongues and lips. Madison and Nili moved quickly, unfazed by the ghastly scene. They pulled the victims out, taking their weapons as they had done earlier.

"Graham needs help!" The two women stood up and saw Clarise a few feet away, kneeling next to Neff's stricken form. They rushed to join her.

Malcolm and Brian looked on as Neff attempted to roll over to get on his knees, but Clarise held him down. Brian tried to read her lips as she shouted to Madison and Nili, both of whom appeared to argue with her for a moment. Madison relented first and ran back to the Puma.

"Time to close up shop and get out of here," she shouted.

"What about Neff?"

"He'll be okay. We've got to get these kids out of here."

"Can he fly?"

"Clarise thinks so—maybe in a few hours. Any more than a few seconds of that thing, and he'd be in worse trouble."

Suddenly Malcolm pulled out his handgun and fired it into the air. Nili and Clarise whirled in his direction. Malcolm pointed urgently at the Hummer. Nili turned and saw one of the men struggling to his knees, clumsily trying to gain balance while reaching for his pant leg. In their rush to check Neff, they had neglected to bind the two assailants.

Nili bolted toward the man and was on him in just a few strides. In one blinding, fluid motion she kicked his hand away from what she now saw was an ankle holster and, gathering momentum from the turn of her body, smashed the butt end of her rifle into the man's face from the opposite direction. Blood streamed from his broken nose as he writhed on the ground in agony, gasping in pain. Madison quickly joined her and helped her tape the two securely.

Brian moved to the back of the helicopter to retrieve Melissa and Dee. Clarise and Madison met them at the door in a few minutes. They watched the other Puma rise into the air behind them.

"Neff's in the van. One of you needs to drive," Madison said loudly into Brian's ear as she handed him the keys. "There's no window glass, so it's too cold to be in it for long. Get him somewhere warm and wait till he can fly. And leave your weapons here—we're sticking with the plan."

25

The heart has its reasons, of which reason knows nothing.

—*Blaise Pascal*

"Just look at this," Brian said as he brought the car to a standstill in the parking lot.

Melissa took a moment to watch the delicate flakes of snow land on the windshield, each one silently melting away on the heated surface. Here and there they could see the students left on campus walking hurriedly to take their final exams or to their cars to head home for the holiday break. She sighed. A picturesque ode to life in a tranquil, small town, nestling in for Christmas. *The only thing missing is Nat King Cole over the radio . . . and a dose of reality,* she mused.

"Doesn't it seem surreal?"

"It does," she agreed. "Three weeks ago we were at our own little war zone on the Canadian border worried about living to see Thanksgiving, and today I'm conducting my last final, looking forward to getting comfortable in front of the fireplace and having you wait on me all weekend." She looked at him with a wry smile, and he laughed.

"And six months ago we were having lunch at Area 51, riding in UFOs, and—" He stopped, seized by a recollection.

"And what?" she asked with concern, already sensing what had caused the shift in tone.

"And watching friends die," he finished, his voice trailing off. The lightheartedness of the moment was disappearing as fast as it had come.

"I take it back," Melissa said, finally returning to the scene outside the windows. "Surreal doesn't even begin to describe it."

"I still don't quite know what to think about the last few weeks, either," Brian confessed, returning to the present. Both of them had expressed this uncertainty several times since the harrowing experience with Neff and his team.

"Any second thoughts about our decision to just let it be, to not tell anyone?" Melissa asked.

"No. My head tells me we broke more than a few laws out there, but my conscience tells me it was the right thing to do. I keep seeing those kids, and thinking about what they went through. It just makes my blood boil. Any member of Neff's team could have killed those thugs easily, and arguably with no sense of regret, but they didn't. As violent as it was, they showed amazing restraint. It was all about saving lives, not payback."

"I know. I kept waiting for one of them to do what I would have done to the lowlifes."

"I know exactly what you mean."

"And all that money!" she said incredulously. "Graham must spend millions out of his own pocket every year to keep everything afloat."

Brian nodded silently. Something about her wording sounded odd. He quickly realized he'd never heard her refer to Neff by his first name before.

"And you know there's more to it than the orphanages," she continued. "What he and his people do is noble, even heroic," she added thoughtfully. "We were completely wrong about them—though I'd still like to know where his money comes from."

"Me too," Brian responded thoughtfully. "Now that I've been able to spend time with him and Malone, I can see that they're solid guys, strong Christians with a mature faith, sure that they're serving God in what they do."

"They have a clear sense of mission," Melissa added, a hint of approval in her voice.

"I still feel like a jerk for how I talked to them."

"You didn't know," she said, patting his hand where it rested on the console between them. "Besides, you were just being protective. Anyway, the three of you appear to have hit it off this week since Malone got back."

"I guess so. Maybe they just have an appetite for the odd. I seem to be the go-to guy for that."

Melissa chuckled, but Brian just turned the key to read the time on the car's clock. "We should get going. You have just enough time to drop off your sabbatical paperwork at Father Fitzgerald's office before I take you to your classroom and go meet Neff and Malone again."

The two of them walked carefully, hand-in-hand, through the falling snow toward the administration building, navigating small patches of ice. Once inside they walked the familiar path to President Fitzgerald's office. Melissa excused herself to use the restroom just outside the entrance. Brian went inside and, turning to the left, greeted the president's secretary and her assistant. He sat down in the waiting area, closing his eyes to collect his thoughts.

He'd been meeting with Neff and Malone for almost a week. It had been an interesting exercise, to say the least. They'd gone through his published article paragraph by paragraph, and then his series of posts, insisting on digitally recording every word. He'd been careful not to divulge his involvement at Area 51 or their true identities. Neither was necessary for what they wanted. Still, he had begun to sense that they suspected he hadn't posted about several issues about which he must have strong opinions. If so, they were right on the mark. He'd been struggling over whether to bring up certain topics. He'd settled on only answering the questions that they asked.

He opened an eye, distracted by the sound of laughter. A conversation between Father Fitzgerald's secretary and her young assistant had grown more animated since he'd come in. He listened to their co-ed concerns over a boyfriend and plans for Christmas vacation. Innocent but childish. He closed his eyes again. He'd be cutting his meeting with Neff and Malone short. He had other things to think about today—a surprise for Melissa he'd been planning for weeks. She had no idea. He smiled at the thought.

"I saw that smirk on your face, Mr. Carter." He opened his eyes again and looked in the direction of the two women.

"What?"

"You're laughing at us," Gloria accused, an amused look on her face.

"No, I wasn't—really," he said apologetically. "I was thinking about something else."

"A likely story. A pity, since you can probably set Molly's mind right."

Brian hesitated. *Great. Get drawn in, or say nothing and come across as a disinterested jerk.* He marveled at how women could so easily produce an internal crisis with just one sentence.

"What's the problem?" he asked, hoping for the best.

"Molly's sister suspects that her boyfriend may propose over the break. She's having trouble with her feelings—you know, whether she really loves him—so she asked Molly's advice. We were just talking about it."

"Why do you think I'll be able to help? I wouldn't say men are authorities on feelings. I know I'm not."

"But you're happily married to a strikingly beautiful woman. I've never been married, so you're the best resource in the room. Surely

Dr. Carter drew the attention of a lot of men, and yet you pursued her and won her love. How did you know she was the one?"

She did it again. He'd managed to avoid just this kind of opportunity to get tongue-tied since they'd arrived in North Dakota, and now he was trapped on the last day of the semester, on what would have been his last trip to campus for months. His heart raced. He could feel the perspiration under his shirt. *Stay calm*.

"Well . . ." He hesitated, alarmed by the rapt attention of the two women. He took a breath, and his mind cleared. "Well, from my perspective, I think you know that you love someone when you're consumed with the thought of making them happy—when there's no question they matter more to you than yourself—and when the thought of anyone else making them happy just kills you inside."

The two women stared blankly at him for a moment, saying nothing. Brian cleared his throat, a self-conscious expression on his face. "I know that wasn't very lyrical, but—"

"It was perfect," Molly said with a grateful smile. "That's what I'm going to tell my sister. Thank you so much."

"You're welcome," Brian said, relieved.

"Yes, that was a wonderful answer," Gloria echoed. "Wouldn't you agree, Dr. Carter?"

Brian turned his head sharply over his left shoulder. Melissa stood in the doorway a few feet behind him, holding her leather portfolio in front of her tummy with both hands, a feigned inattentive look on her face.

"I certainly would," she answered cheerfully. "You'll have to tell me all about your conversation on the way to class," she said to Brian with a beguiling smile. "Sorry to be in a hurry, Gloria. I just wanted to drop off my paperwork."

"Off course, dear. I'll make sure it's taken care of."

Melissa turned and offered her hand to Brian. He took it and followed her out. They walked back to the car in silence. Neither said a word on the short drive to the classroom building.

"I'll pick you up at five thirty," he finally spoke, pulling into the parking lot.

"I'll be ready."

"Bye, then."

"Not so fast."

"Don't you have an exam?"

"It doesn't start until I get there. The victims will be grateful for a few extra minutes to cram. Besides, you have to walk me to the building, remember?"

"How much did you hear?" he asked, reaching for the door.

"Enough."

"Isn't that spying?"

"It is," she replied blankly. "What of it?"

"Well . . . you could have helped. It was pretty uncomfortable."

"You pulled yourself together nicely. I do have a question, though."

"What's that?" he asked, trying not to look her in the eye.

"Have you ever felt that way about anyone, *ever*?"

Brian looked past Melissa out the window, then awkwardly at the dash. He sighed, opened his door, and exited the car. He walked around the rear of the car and then opened Melissa's door.

"You don't have to answer," she said quietly as he reached for her hand.

"No, I think I do," he contradicted her. "There's nothing wrong with the question. If I can't trust you, who can I trust?"

They stepped carefully onto the sidewalk and headed for the building. Brian opened the door and walked the short distance to her classroom. He reached for the classroom door, but didn't turn the handle.

"Yes," he said, finally opening the door, "I have felt that way about someone."

"Thank you," she said wistfully, forcing a smile. "I'll see you later."

26

In politics, nothing happens by accident.
If it happened, you can bet it was planned that way.

—*Franklin D. Roosevelt*

"Thanks for breakfast," Brian said appreciatively.

"Thank the dining staff," Neff responded, smiling. "They always do a great job."

"I will."

"We only have an hour or so this morning," Neff informed him. "We have to get ready for a trip."

"That's fine. I have some run-around stuff to do, too. Do you have another . . . mission? I don't know if that's the right word."

"Yes," Neff answered, "but not like the other. We're visiting one of our stateside orphanages. We'll only be gone a day or two, then we can spend another few days here before we head home for the holidays."

"What about the snow?"

"That's why we need to get moving," Malone explained. "It's coming down pretty steady now, and it's supposed to get worse."

"Will Malcolm and Dee be leaving with you?"

"Not tonight. But when it comes to the holidays or anything long term, they'll be coming with us. Otherwise, I feel like I'd be abandoning them."

"What do you mean?"

"I just don't feel they're safe yet. No specific reason, but in light of what it took to get them out . . . well, call it a hunch."

"I read through your material again last night," Malone interjected, pouring himself another cup of coffee.

"How many times does that make?" Brian asked, standing next to him, working on a cup of tea.

"I'm almost in double digits now," he responded, smiling.

"Is there something that isn't clear?" Brian asked, taking a seat in front of a small coffee table.

"As a matter of fact," Neff answered, taking a seat next to Malone, "that is indeed the problem."

Brian gave him a curious glance and waited for an explanation.

Neff took a sip. "Don't get me wrong, you've been clear in one respect during our conversations over the last few days," he began. "We know that, on the one hand, you have no trouble as a Christian and biblical scholar with the idea of intelligent extraterrestrial life. Your article lays all that out coherently."

"But on the other hand," Malone chimed in while Neff took another sip of coffee, "your Internet postings are very negative about anything to do with alien life—conspiratorial, even."

"And we find those essays persuasive as well," Neff noted. "We'd agree with your suspicions that both academic and pop-culture fodder about aliens are planting the suggestion in people all over the world that extraterrestrials—were there ever any proof of their existence, even without contact—would be deified by both the religious and the atheist. They would be transcendent in every way. Any such revelation would have believers in every tradition racing to rearticulate or accommodate their sacred books to the extraterrestrial reality. It would propel a paradigm shift."

"I don't see the conflict. I wouldn't want that paradigm shift to happen, mainly because I don't think it's at all intellectually or theologically necessary," Brian replied. "But it would happen."

"Agreed—but that isn't the tension we feel. Those ideas dovetail, as you suggest. But Malone and I both suspect there's more to it. From breadcrumbs you've dropped here and there in the ways you've answered our questions, we get the sense that you think something related to all this is being orchestrated *right now*—that there's some sort of deliberate, intelligent plot being hatched to quicken the pace of this shift. Do you?"

Brian shifted in his seat and played with his tea bag for a moment. "Well, as long as we're being open about gaps in the discussion, I should say that it isn't really clear to me why you guys are interested in all this. It seems absolutely unrelated to what you do."

"It's true we haven't said much on that," Malone answered, "but we did say we'd get to it."

He glanced over at Neff, who tilted his head in a nonchalant gesture. "Fire away."

"I'll tell you what we see," Malone said, leaning forward in Brian's direction. "And mind you, this isn't what we *think*. We're not guessing. Everything I'll mention has a clear paper trail that we've studied, and a reality that we've experienced all over the world—including here in the United States. We don't care for speculative conspiracy stuff. We're about hard data and real people. It's one of the reasons we appreciated your work. You grounded it in things we could check—at least what you were willing to say."

Brian said nothing, eyeing Malone. He was staring at Brian with just a hint of mischief, but not enough to diminish the seriousness of what he'd said. "Go on."

"The free world is changing," Malone began, his voice clear and assured. "Western democracy is lurching toward fascism—from both political directions. The political categories of left and right in this country are window dressing. People in both parties have been more than willing to advance an agenda that grows the state and curtails freedom. The West seems bent on diminishing the liberty of its citizens—and a lot of the citizenry *wants* it."

He went on, "Everywhere we look, people seem willing to trade freedom for the comfort of what's being marketed to them as a fair and good life bestowed by an all-benevolent state. They're willing to accept the promise that they'll have everything they need if they just comply. And big media—especially in the US—keeps everyone entertained instead of thinking. It's like the population is in a cognitive stupor, numbed by some sort of collective historical amnesia while they amuse themselves into submission."

"People have been seduced by the myth of utopianism before," Brian offered.

"But it's much worse than that," Malone continued in earnest. "I'd admit that political leaders have cloaked themselves in democracy before to gain power, but the *extent* is new. Leaders of free nations around the world have calculated strategies in place that can only result in the surrender of their own sovereignty to global interests—a global power structure over which they have no final say."

"Malone's right," Neff agreed, "What's happening now really is different. It's not the blindness, but the scale of it all. We're not seeing ruling elites striving to solidify their power to settle old historic nationalistic scores or expand their borders. We're seeing people in various positions intelligently steering the masses to embrace the erosion of the very institutions that have given them freedom—and not so they can be *regional* kings. They want *global* power and influence."

Malone broke in again. "We have contacts all over the world who are highly placed in governments, scientific organizations, and the military and intelligence communities. We couldn't do what we do and have access to the equipment we have without them. We have plenty of cash, but it isn't just a matter of money. We have to operate under the radar—operate like a terrorist cell, in some respects, using the techniques the bad guys use to avoid detection. And sometimes we need help, like in the case of getting your two friends out of wherever they were."

Brian stopped him for a moment. "I'd still love to know how you did that, especially since your gut tells you they're not in the clear."

"We'll give you—and them—all the details when we get back. I promise. We know we can trust you."

"Fair enough."

"Anyway, since there are lines we won't or can't cross, we need insiders, people who are like-minded—who not only believe in what we do, but share our concerns. We hear and see things that lend weight to what we're saying. And we protect and help these insiders in return when it's in our power to do that."

"Assuming you're correct, what makes you think," asked Brian, "that this is even workable? The impulse for freedom is basic to humanity. It's part of our nature as imagers of God."

"True," Neff replied, "but to answer your question in one word: *technology*. Technology makes it workable. The global overlords have technology at their disposal that is unlike that of any other time in world history. The populations of the world can be effectively controlled—even downsized. And I'm not speaking only about bloodshed and war. The people who want this to happen have the technology to reduce populations, create shifts in demographics, manipulate national economies, dictate a country's international financial standing, control the food supply, and spy on their citizens—even within their own homes. More importantly, leaders within democracies have shown the will to use all of those technologies."

"Do you remember Ward, one of the chopper pilots?" Malone asked.

Brian nodded.

"Before he joined our cause, he was what people in global finance call an economic hit man. His job was manipulating undeveloped countries into what they thought were deals to develop their countries. The end result was debt-slavery to US companies, who then turned around and forced their compliance via US military interests in the region, whether it was about tactical advantage or access to resources, like oil. The military and corporate worlds have been married since World War II."

He continued, "In your online stuff you mentioned your belief that a lot of UFOs were really man-made craft being used to reinforce the myth of alien visitation. That's dead on. I've actually spent some time researching that. I ended up looking for information on something called Operation Paperclip. Ever heard of it?"

"Yeah, I know a little about it—what it was," Brian answered, taking a sip of tea. He'd been careful to avoid including anything in his posts that might make people presume the anonymous author had experience inside the black-op world. He'd deliberately stayed clear of Paperclip, focusing instead on popular media and religious themes.

"It's amazing stuff," Malone continued. "But it wasn't about wingless craft and nuts and bolts. There's a whole side of it that deals with psychological warfare, even brainwashing. Back in the seventies, when my wife was getting her credentials to be a psychologist, she worked under someone who'd been part of all that.

"What I've read about Paperclip scares me. The program produced a military industrial complex that had access to exotic technology that was easily weaponized, along with world-class expertise in propaganda and psychological warfare. And when I know what Ward used to do for a living, how easy it is for a small group of insiders in that military industrial complex to assert their will on countries—controlling things like the food supply, water, wages, you name it—it just scares me. In theory, the only thing standing in the way of that happening to our own population is to create an alert population. But the population is being distracted and numbed every day."

"You mention food supply. How could anyone control the global food supply?" Brian asked skeptically.

"It's easy," Malone answered. "It requires only that you take away the right or ability to produce your own food. And that's already being done in Western countries through legislation and, when they can't get laws passed, through regulation—writing rules that relate to enforcement of existing laws. Once that's done, the population becomes dependent on what the state can or will supply. Other nations dependent on trade will have to give what's required or do without."

"I'd say we're a long way from that."

"You'd think so, but it's closer than people realize. Transference of the food supply to the state is already happening through things like zoning and safety laws, under the label of 'sustainability.' Few people really pay attention to what their city, county, and township governments do. They're silently enacting globalist agenda items as we speak, whether the people passing the laws realize it or not."

"Can you give me some real examples?" Brian asked skeptically.

"Sure. In the United States, the process involves putting all food production—even down to small plots in your own yard—under the regulations of the FDA. Over the past couple of years, the number of instances where family farms have been driven out of business through regulation has increased dramatically. The FDA can claim jurisdiction on any number of things a family farm needs to stay in business and then fine violators exorbitant amounts.

"Think of it like the IRS. No one—not even professional CPAs or IRS agents themselves—really have exhaustive command of all the tax laws. It's millions of words, and the laws grow and change all the time. The only reason every individual and business isn't audited every year is logistics. The IRS goes after who they want to, or whoever provokes them. But they could actually nail everyone. The amount of regulation is just overwhelming."

"My personal favorite," Neff interrupted with a smirk, "is noncompliance to federal rules for manure management."

"Talk about a back-door approach," Malone chuckled. "But the idea of crippling family farms by putting kids who work on the farms under child-labor laws is more recent."

"Child labor?"

"Lots of small family farms—and other family businesses—have their kids contribute by doing chores and such. The federal government wanted to undermine that. Family farms would have had to hire replacement labor, which would create more expense. And that doesn't count potential fines.

"Now, neither of those examples would wipe out a farm," he explained. "It's a strategy of attrition. They just chip away from dozens of angles to undermine a business' ability to function. There are the tens of thousands of pages of regulation covering production, processing, packaging, and moving food. It would be very easy for the federal government to run individual companies out of business or take control over industries—to pick the winners and losers. They'd only have to keep bringing federal lawsuits to bear whenever and wherever something was amiss."

"It's important to catch what Malone is saying," Neff interrupted. "We're not saying this is all currently happening or will go into effect tomorrow. The point is that a lot of it is *in place*, just waiting for the switch to be flipped. And this is just regulatory control *within* the country. The next level is to hand over national authority to global power-holders. Have you ever heard of Codex Alimentarius?"

"No. What's that?"

"The phrase is Latin for 'Book of Food.' The term refers to an internationally recognized set of guidelines relating to food production and food safety."

"What's wrong with that?" Brian asked.

"Do you want the United Nations determining how many calories you can eat per day, or what percent of a particular vitamin you can or must have in your diet?"

"Of course not—that's absurd."

"That's Codex Alimentarius," Malone countered. "A commission of the same name established the guidelines in 1961. That commission was created by the Food and Agriculture Organization of the United Nations. The World Health Organization has partnered with the commission since 1962. In fact, the World Trade Organization already recognizes the Codex Alimentarius Commission as having international oversight for resolving disputes lodged by countries who sign on to their standards."

"How about Agenda 21? Ever heard of that?" Neff fired another question at Brian.

"A little. I don't spend my time researching this kind of thing," he said apologetically, feeling a bit defensive.

"Most people don't. They're naturally absorbed with the day-to-day concerns of their lives," Malone offered, sensing Brian's discomfort.

"Agenda 21 is the global environmentalist equivalent of the Patriot Act," Neff clarified. "The United Nations created it in 1992. It's the UN action plan for the nations of the world when it comes to sustainable development. In so many words, it seeks to co-opt privately held land under the guise of ensuring its sustainability—with the approval of the governments of member nations, of course."

"What does that mean, exactly?"

"It means that the UN has come up with a way to market the man-made global warming myth to strong-arm nations all over the world into giving them control over land in the name of sustainability. I presume you've at least followed the global warming scam?"

"Actually, that one I'm familiar with," Brian replied. "The media called it Climategate, right? It was the release of all those hacked emails from . . . where was it?"

"The Climate Research Unit of East Anglia University," Malone answered.

"Right. They showed that the science was completely politicized. That was enough for me. But isn't Agenda 21 dependent on government approval? I don't recall hearing that the US has bought into it yet."

"That's correct. The US hasn't surrendered its sovereignty to it yet," Neff replied. "But that isn't a rebuttal of the threat. It's true that governments have to approve it. What's happening is that local city and county laws and regulations are implementing the goals and policies of Agenda 21. Basically, there isn't a local governing body in the United States that hasn't passed some part of Agenda 21's sustainability program. But you're right, it's not federal law—yet."

"Agenda 21 also claims all the oceans under its sustainability program," Malone added. "It even lays out plans for what it calls 'population control' in the name of saving the environment. The language is too Orwellian for my taste."

"The eugenics angle is real, too," Neff explained. "Overt eugenics is too offensive, though many in the globalist community love the idea. Anyone who has studied the Nazis knows they were deeply influenced by eugenics thinkers and writers in Europe and the United States well before taking power in Germany. Clarise has a very detailed knowledge of the history of eugenic thought. But what we really need is to find an expert on the Aryan mythology—the occult or quasi-religious beliefs that fueled it." Neff looked up at Brian. "You don't seem surprised or alarmed."

"Eugenics is actually something I'm interested in," he replied. Brian didn't want to add anything. He knew Neff was on target since everything he'd mentioned was part of Melissa's scholarly expertise. "I even know that one of the World Bank's leading demographers—now retired—has admitted that some of today's vaccination campaigns are part of global population reduction goals."

"That's right," Malone confirmed. "That was John May. I'm impressed."

"But do all these goals and ideas converge the way you suspect they do?" Brian asked. "Maybe you're misreading connections."

"Do you believe in coincidences on such a grand scale?" asked Malone. "I thought you believed in intelligent evil—and providence."

"I do, on both counts, but that doesn't address the question of whether these agenda items are really motivated by intent."

"We're not saying everyone—or even most people—who hold power in these areas are involved," Malone went on. "We're saying that there are enough people in important positions of power who are committed to these ideas that it matters. We don't believe in conspiracy theories like an Illuminati running everything. Even if one exists, you don't need it. All you need is enough people of power and wealth to believe in a set of ideas, along with enough arrogance to think that they should be part of a global ruling class. I'd say that's quite theologically consistent with both human nature and intelligent evil."

"Well, put that way, I can't really disagree. It's just hard to believe."

"Because you don't *want* to believe it," Neff said. "We understand that feeling all too well. You need to read the CIA's National Intelligence Council report called 'Global Governance 2025.' It's on the flash drive. It was written in 2010. I printed off the preface, since I figured we'd get to this point in the conversation." Neff handed Brian a single piece of paper.

> *The United States' National Intelligence Council (NIC) and the European Union's Institute for Security Studies (EUISS) have joined forces to produce this assessment of the long-term prospects for global governance frameworks . . . The US and the EU do not always see eye to eye on every issue on the international agenda, but they share fundamental values and strategic interests to an extent not matched by any other partners in the world. Transatlantic agreement is no longer enough to effectively manage global challenges. Doing so will require renewed efforts to address governance gaps and strengthen multilateralism, in partnership with other pivotal centers of power and with the international community at large.*

"Does that sound like there's no intent behind global governance?"

"Well . . . no."

Neff looked at his watch. "We could go on and on with other examples. We deal with this stuff with disturbing regularity. We have an associate who devotes her full time to researching all of it and archiving resources. We live with it."

"Well, I promise to read through as much of what's on the flash as I can over the next few weeks. I can see some relationship . . ." He hesitated.

Neff and Malone immediately heightened their attention. "Such as?" Neff asked cautiously, trying to gain a sense of what Brian was thinking.

"Well, the US intelligence community has a long history of using its resources to manipulate thought—to frame peoples' perception of reality. UFOs and the alien question have historically been a part of that."

"You mean things like Operation Mockingbird? COINTELPRO?" Malone asked.

"No, I'm not familiar with those. What were they?"

"Mockingbird was a CIA program used in the fifties to manipulate members of the mass media. The 1976 Senate Report on it is on the flash drive. COINTELPRO had different aims, like infiltrating and disrupting political groups—basically to interfere with the democratic process. The program used psychological warfare and illegal activities—stuff like burglary and vandalism, all the way up to discussing assassination."

"Anything on the flash about that?" Brian asked.

"Yeah, the final report of the Church Committee. That was 1976, too," Malone replied.

"So what were you thinking about?" Neff pressed.

"Several things. ECM Research, Project PALLADIUM . . ."

"What's ECM?"

"Electronic Counter Measures. Basically, it's technology that the CIA used to create false radar readings. It goes back to the fifties as well. Dr. Leon Davidson—who had worked on the Manhattan Project—said publicly that the CIA had used this technology to create phony flying saucer sightings. They could put phantom saucers of any size, going at crazy speeds, on radar—but it was all contrived. But to me, what Wernher von Braun said was scarier."

"What did he say?"

"What I'm thinking of comes through his former spokesperson, Dr. Carol Rosin. She was a missile defense consultant to several agencies in the intelligence community. Back in the seventies, she was the corporate manager at something called Fairchild Industries, an aircraft company. That's where she met von Braun, who was dying of cancer at the time. Rosin testified that she and von Braun talked about aliens—what he called 'off planet cultures'—several times. But there's more than one way to take what he told her. If you have a second, I'll show you what I'm talking about."

"Sure," Malone said, turning his open laptop toward him. Brian quickly navigated to a search engine and produced a transcript of UFO witness testimony given by Rosin. "Here." Malone and Neff looked at the screen and read Rosin's words:

> *What was most interesting to me was a repetitive sentence that von Braun said to me over and over again during the approximately four years that I had the opportunity to work*

> *with him. He said the strategy that was being used to educate the public and decision makers was to use scare tactics. . . . That was how we identify an enemy.*
>
> *The strategy that Werner von Braun taught me was that first the Russians are going to be considered the enemy.*
>
> *Then terrorists would be identified, and that was soon to follow. . . . Then we were going to identify third-world country "crazies." We now call them "nations of concern." But he said that would be the third enemy against whom we would build space-based weapons.*
>
> *The next enemy was asteroids. Now, at this point, he kind of chuckled the first time he said it. Asteroids—against asteroids we are going to build space-based weapons.*
>
> *And the funniest one of all was what he called aliens, extraterrestrials. That would be the final scare. And over and over during the four years that I knew him and was giving speeches for him, he would bring up that last card. "And remember, Carol, the last card is the alien card. We are going to have to build space-based weapons against aliens, and all of it is a lie."*

"This is the kind of thing that troubles me," Brian explained, again being careful to cloak the depth of his personal attachment to the issue. "People who want to believe there are aliens will assume the lie von Braun refers to is that the aliens are hostile. But what if the lie is that there are aliens *at all*? Von Braun is suggesting that the military-industrial complex will use all these points of fear to justify militarizing space and producing all sorts of exotic technology in the name of defense."

"Which would then, in turn, be used against its own citizens—like drones are now," Malone followed. "All of the ways the government collects information on us and spies on citizens. You think the alien idea would be useful to erect a police state."

"Well, that's one application," Brian said, choosing his words carefully, "but there's nothing in the public arena to really prove that something like that is in operation. I just see how it *could* work. Frankly, something that paradigm stretching could be used to make people believe almost anything."

27

I do not believe in a fate that falls on men however they act;
but I do believe in a fate that falls on them unless they act.

—*G. K. Chesterton*

"All done with the end-of-semester death march?" Dee asked, looking over her glasses at Melissa with a friendly, knowing smirk as they sat in the cafeteria.

"I'm done with everything I have to do here, anyway," Melissa said, opening the plastic lid of her salad. "I still have a little grading to do. I just didn't want to take committee work home. Skipped lunch to get it all done. Brian will be here in an hour, but I just have to eat something now. I'm famished."

"You sure?" asked Malcolm. "Your salad looks like it's been sitting a while. The place is all but cleared out."

"I'll nibble on the croutons if I have to."

"Why not come with us tonight? We're out of here in less than an hour."

"What's tonight?"

"The Christmas reception for faculty and administration?" he answered. "Did you forget?"

"Oh, *that.* I'm really not into receptions and parties. How would you know about that anyway?"

"Neff and Malone are going, now that they've been grounded. They insisted we tag along. He assumed you and Brian were going. We told them we'd see if you were still in your office and that we'd meet them here in the cafeteria."

"Grounded?"

"They were going to visit one of their orphanages," Dee informed her, "but the airport is closed down because of the snow. Are you sure Brian can get here? It's getting nasty out there. I heard we've got a foot on the ground already, and from the look outside, it's not slowing down."

Melissa looked out through one of the windows. "I didn't even notice. There are no windows in my office. But Brian will be here. He'd come even if he had to walk to tell me we're stranded."

"Why don't the two of you just hang with us then?" asked Malcolm.

"I just want to stretch out and relax, especially in my condition."

"I hear that," Dee followed. "Pregnancy takes a lot out of you."

"Besides, Brian would rather wait on me at home than do anything social." When Malcolm and Dee laughed, Melissa continued. "I'm not kidding," she said, picking through her salad, chuckling at her own words. "He's a homebody zealot. I hardly have to do anything. He does the cleaning and the laundry, loads the dishes, takes out the trash—really he does everything except cook. He'd starve without frozen pizza and macaroni and cheese."

"Sounds like you have it pretty good," Dee suggested, glancing at Malcolm while Melissa was distracted by a tomato. He caught her drift.

"Brian has a lot of laudable character traits, but 'fun-loving' isn't one of them—trust me. Honestly, though, it suits me. I'm not really one to hit the town, either. And we've had to be cautious."

"So what's it been like?" Malcolm asked.

"What?"

"You know, living with Brian. What's it been like?"

Melissa sat back, an amused look on her face, eyeing both of them. She started to laugh and shook her head.

"What is it?" asked Malcolm mischievously.

"Some of the stuff he's done, you'd think I was making it up." She laughed again. "I shouldn't talk about him, though."

"But you want to," Dee teased, grinning.

"Absolutely."

"So dish, honey."

"We're all friends," Malcolm added, putting on his most sincere expression. "You know he'd laugh too if he were here."

Melissa nodded agreeably. "He's so socially awkward, but it's actually endearing, most of the time. He can be like a teenager."

"I can see that," Dee agreed, smiling and leaning forward.

"When we moved here, we obviously had nothing, so we had to do a lot of shopping. Buying clothes for him was an exercise in patience, let me tell you. It was like he had no concept of the sort of thing a married man in his thirties should be wearing."

"He probably doesn't. He's been alone since leaving for college," said Dee. "There's never been a woman in his life. You can't expect much."

"I didn't, but I was still unprepared for it. He told me one day he was going to Walmart to shop for clothing, but I threatened him with divorce if he did it."

"Excellent!" Malcolm laughed.

"Then, when we did go shopping, it was all blue jeans, sneakers, underwear, football jerseys—you get the idea."

"So how did you win the argument?" Dee asked, enjoying the description. "He looks just fine, so I know you did."

"I told him that if he didn't dress well enough, no one would believe I'd married him. That buried every objection," she explained with a satisfied smile.

"No doubt," Dee said. "I remember some of our conversations back at the base. He's got some self-esteem issues."

"He's getting better. He's had to in order to make our little façade believable." She started chuckling to herself again.

"What now?"

"I was just thinking of our first 'married date.' It was unforgettable, but in all the wrong ways. We went out for dinner at the only nice restaurant in town. Right as we were finishing our meal, he leaned over in a panic to tell me he left his wallet in the car. I told him I had my purse, but he was embarrassed at the thought that someone would see the woman paying for the dinner."

"Did you have a fight?"

"No. That may have been better, though."

"This oughta be good," Dee cracked, glancing at Malcolm.

"He got up to go out to the car but didn't look behind him. He elbowed a plate right out of a waitress's hand. Most of what was on it wound up on the floor, but some landed in a customer's lap."

Malcolm hooted, clapping his hands. "Did you get any video?"

"I'm not through—or I should say, *he* wasn't through," she added over their laughter. "The waitress and the manager had to talk him out of helping to clean up the mess. This is in front of a dozen or so people, mind you. After he sat down, I tried to hold his hand and tell him it was okay, and he flinched like a bug had crawled on him. He told me later he just didn't expect it. Needless to say, we got out as soon as we could."

The table shook as Malcolm slapped it, laughing hysterically. Melissa tried to return to her salad, but she couldn't from the sight of Dee, who was laughing so hard that tears filled her eyes.

"We're making a scene," Melissa finally warned, gaining her composure.

"Oh, who cares?" Dee said with a sniff.

"Man, that's sweet!" Malcolm exclaimed. "I'm sure that's just the tip of the iceberg."

"Trust me, it is," Melissa agreed. "It feels good to laugh, though, even if it's at his expense."

"Well, despite his misadventures in other areas, Brian sure has good taste in diamonds," Dee said, looking at Melissa's hand. "Or did you pick out that rock?"

Melissa held up her hand, gazing at the gem for a few moments. "We picked out the bands together, to keep up with appearances," she said, "but he bought the engagement ring himself. I'll admit, it's fabulous." She turned her hand, looking at the ring once more. "He spent too much, though," she added. "He paid for it out of his own money and wouldn't tell me what it cost." She showed it to Malcolm.

"I don't think I would have, either," Malcolm said, eyebrows raised, taking a good look. "The other night when we were at your place, I remember hearing how he gave you most of the money that Neil and Father Benedict had given him. He must have blown it all on this. It's huge."

"I don't know what he has left," Melissa said wistfully. "We use a joint checking account to help maintain our married identity, but he won't touch it. He insists it's mine and refuses to buy anything personal with it. I know he bought a laptop and a lot of books besides the ring, so he might not have a dime left of his own. He won't tell me."

Malcolm and Dee looked at each other again, then at Melissa.

"What is it?" she asked.

"Melissa," Dee said in a serious tone, "what we really want to know is how you are with your situation . . . with Brian."

Melissa's eyes dropped to the table. She sat thoughtfully for a few moments. "I'm okay. Life with him is, well . . ."

"You're happy," Dee supplied the term with a knowing look. "And you don't really know how to process it."

Melissa paused again, but this time only for a second. "You know," she acknowledged, "you're right. That's a good way to describe it. As odd as it sounds, I've been happy—except, of course, for the circumstances that put me here. I never would have expected it. I'm living in the middle of nowhere, teaching undergrads who scarcely know why they're here or what they want to do with their lives, but every time my mind isn't seized with terror at the thought of getting caught, I feel . . . content."

"You know that wouldn't be the case if Brian hadn't come with you."

"I know," she said. "I—" She stopped short. Dee and Malcolm could see the misty look in her eyes. "Shrink," Melissa said good-naturedly, wiping her eyes with a paper napkin. The other two chuckled.

"That's what I do, honey. If you weren't happy, we'd *all* know. We remember the angry Melissa."

"I made sure of that, didn't I?"

"You sure did," Malcolm agreed. "But the old things have passed away."

"It's strange," Melissa mused, "I have a lot of things to be angry about now, but I'm not. I'm scared, but I don't have the edge any more. The rage is missing. And every time I think about what Brian did . . . well . . . he didn't have to come here. It was a crazy decision."

"Not for him," Malcolm said.

"What do you mean?"

"You *know* what I mean."

"No, really, what—"

"Come on, Melissa. Brian loves you. And I'm not talking about being smitten or some infatuation. He loves you more than his own life."

Melissa sat silently, looking from Malcolm to Dee.

"As much as I relish contradicting Malcolm any chance I get," Dee said, "I have to agree with him. This one doesn't need a diagnosis—it's obvious. We saw it already back at the base."

"I'm not so sure," Melissa replied faintly.

"Why?" asked Malcolm.

"He's never said anything like that. Frankly, he says almost nothing about what he thinks or feels. I don't go fishing—too much, anyway. But there have been opportunities for him to open up, and he just won't."

"Why do you care?" Dee wondered, looking her in the eye.

"I . . . I just want to know where things stand," she answered calmly, straightening herself in the chair, returning Dee's gaze. "After all, we live together. I'm grateful he's here and that I'm not alone. It's just good to know."

Dee eyed her carefully, studying her expression and body language. "So let's hear what you think is the problem."

"We're not as different as you might suppose," she said thoughtfully.

"How's that?" asked Dee.

"I've been alone since I started college, at least emotionally. We've both been pretty isolated, but for very different reasons."

"Now we're getting' somewhere," Dee said, paying close attention. "Go on."

"Well, he was something of a social and emotional misfit, and he still carries some of that. I had lots of attention through high school, but the one person who told me he loved me turned into my rapist. Then my spiritually counterfeit parents forced me to have an abortion. After that, it was all about revenge. I wanted to throw their phony faith in their faces every chance I got. I did what I wanted with whomever I wanted. I've had lots of men, but none of it was about love. I started targeting guys who reminded me of the hypocrisy I hated. They got what they wanted, and I got to ruin their reputation. Nothing like that even crosses my mind anymore. I want something real."

"So where is Brian in all this?" Dee asked with a knowing look.

"A lot has changed, to say the least. We talk a lot about faith, about real Christianity, how people play church. I've thrown everything at him—all the questions I'd learned and internalized to justify how much I hated Christians like my parents and the guy who raped me."

"And that's been good for you," concluded Malcolm.

"It has. Honestly, it's been like therapy. Brian is never preachy, but he doesn't flinch about what he believes. He just doesn't care about pleasing anyone if it means he can't be honest with them."

"That's honorable, and it'll get you into trouble, too," Malcolm said. "I learned that from Andrew."

"Brian has definitely paid a price for telling it as he sees it. You two know he lost a job at a Christian college for some of his thoughts, but that isn't all. Last summer he'd planned to go to seminary, but he's told me he knew he wouldn't last in any denominational environment. He enrolled in seminary because he didn't know what else to do."

"He didn't want to just throw it all away even if he believed he had no future," Malcolm said, nodding.

"Right. None of that has made him leave it all behind, but he has a fairly low tolerance for most of what goes on in Christianity—the trendiness and sappy theology. He says he isn't a Christian because of Christians. He once told me that if Jesus were to apply for a divorce from the Church on the grounds of adultery and desertion, he'd get one."

"That's pretty brutal," Malcolm noted, nodding, "but hard to disagree with."

Melissa continued. "Being with him has convinced me I need to approach things the same way. I want what he has. It was something I thought I had a long time ago. He's just helped me detach it from the phoniness—to frame it differently."

"So how has all this affected your feelings for him?" Dee prodded.

Melissa looked down again at the table for a moment, collecting her thoughts. "Honestly, he has the character of the man I wanted when I was younger. That seems like a lifetime ago. It's just, I trust him completely. It's hard to imagine life without him. . . ." Her voice trailed off.

"What's wrong, then?" Malcolm pressed gently.

"I'll be blunt," she sighed. "I can't escape the feeling that when he looks at me, he sees used goods."

"Melissa," Malcolm said sympathetically, placing his hand on hers, "that isn't true. You're not reading him clearly. He knew about your past long before you got here. You were the one who told him. Why would you think it matters now?"

"I'm just not sure," she answered. "What if our circumstances were different? And if I'm wrong, why won't he say something? He's impenetrable when it comes to what's really going on inside."

"He's scared out of his wits, honey," Dee said matter-of-factly.

Melissa looked at her dubiously.

"He's terrified. Trust me."

"I don't follow."

"He's afraid of what might happen if he told you how he feels."

"What do you mean 'what might happen'?"

"You might not feel the same way," she replied. "It's a thought he can't bear. And knowing him, he can't imagine any other outcome. You know his story. He'd rather be with you the way things are than lose what he has by making the relationship awkward. He can't imagine it would turn out any other way if he told you how he feels, so he ain't touchin' it. It's simple, from where I'm sitting."

"That seems . . . I've never thought of it that way."

"You wouldn't. You've been in control of all your relationships—except the abusive one, of course. He's never been in that position. He's emotionally locked down. But don't think for a minute he doesn't love you."

Melissa looked at Malcolm. He nodded firmly.

"That means," Dee said, her eyes narrowing, "the real question is how you feel about him."

Melissa looked at each of them earnestly, then averted her attention to the snow falling against the dark sky, illumined by the lights shining on the sidewalk outside.

"If you really can't imagine yourself with someone else—"

"Folks," Malcolm interrupted in a low voice, "it's time to change the subject."

They looked over at him and saw him wave. Following his line of attention, they turned and saw Neff and Malone approaching.

"Hello, everyone," Neff greeted them. "Are we ready to head over? I assume you talked to Melissa," he added, smiling in her direction.

"They did," replied Melissa. "I think I'm going to pass. Brian is supposed to pick me up in about a half hour."

"He could join us—if he's able to even get to campus. What kind of car do you have?"

"Just a sedan."

"He'll never get here," Malone countered. "We rented the biggest SUV they had at the airport and barely made it. Interstates are passable, but the roads in town are in bad shape. Some of them haven't been touched by plows yet."

"If you'll pardon me for saying," Neff continued, "I think you should let me take you home this evening. We can get you there. It will probably be easier later on, too, even though it's still snowing. It'll give the road crews time to plow in town. I'd take you now but I might not make it back in time. Once I told President Fitzgerald I was coming tonight, he insisted I say a few words at the beginning—board member stuff," he explained, smiling again.

"Sounds like good advice, Melissa," Malcolm suggested. "It'll just cost you a few hours. You don't want to get stranded. It's not just the snow; it's the cold."

"Real cold," Malone followed. "It's almost single digits."

"I'd also consider it a personal favor," Neff added. "I'm going to talk about how pleased I am with the performance of the new faculty member occupying the position I funded."

"Do you mean to say—?"

"Yes," he grinned. "That would be you, Melissa. Aloysius didn't tell me anything about the faculty member who'd be hired with the gift. He just said there was an urgent need, and that the person needed protection and was highly qualified. Once I heard Father Benedict had made the request, there was nothing to debate. I didn't know Benedict personally, only by reputation, and that was enough. That the beneficiary turned out to be you was a happy . . . coincidence," he explained pleasantly.

"I thought you didn't believe in coincidences."

"I don't. Please, I'd appreciate it if you were there tonight."

"Well, all right," she agreed.

"Good. I'm sure it won't get too late. You'd best call Brian and tell him."

***

"Hello?" Brian answered, sticking the phone between his ear and cheek while he put on his coat.

"Brian, it's me."

"I was just getting ready to leave. Is everything okay?"

"Just fine. You don't need to pick me up."

"Why? If you need to stay a little longer I can come over and keep you company. I don't like the idea of you being there after hours by yourself."

"Graham and Malone are here, and so are Malcolm and Dee. Graham's talked me into going to the Christmas reception tonight. He said he'll bring me home."

There was a moment of silence.

"Brian? Are you still there?" Melissa asked.

"Yeah."

"I wish you could be here."

"What are Neff and Malone doing there? They told me this morning they were flying out this afternoon."

"They were, but the airport's closed. They said the snowstorm is terrible."

"I shoveled the driveway an hour ago. It didn't look that bad."

"They just got here and said the roads in town aren't passable. They're not plowed yet. They figure they'll be more clear in a few hours, and they have the kind of vehicle it'll take to get me home if it stays bad."

"Hmm, okay," he surrendered unenthusiastically.

Melissa sensed the melancholy in his voice. "Is everything all right?"

"I guess so."

"Please don't worry. It won't be too late. I promise."

"I won't worry. I know you're in good hands. Have fun."

"I'll try. Wait up for me, okay?"

"Sure. Bye."

"Bye."

Brian slipped the phone into his pocket and stood silently at the door leading to the garage. After a few moments he turned and slowly walked into the kitchen, turning off the oven and then the lights. A few steps later he found himself in the dining room, where he pulled out a chair and sat down, hands in his lap.

The house was dark now, save for the light from the delicate rays of two solitary candles on the table. He watched the random shadows mingle on the walls with the beamed reflections thrown from two Corsair wine glasses. They shivered with every vibration of the flames.

He looked out over the settings, arranged neatly atop the pressed white tablecloth. Everything was in perfect order. He'd followed the instructions to the letter, then checked and rechecked them. A small, rectangular, elegantly-wrapped gift rested on Melissa's empty plate. He sighed.

What were you thinking?

28

The risk of a wrong decision is preferable to the terror of indecision.

—Maimonides

Melissa closed the door and silently watched Neff trudge through the snow back to the SUV. He'd dropped Malone, Malcolm, and Dee off at the guest house after the reception. His guess had been on target. Though it was still snowing, the trip to the house had presented no difficulty.

After rearming the security system, she shook the snow from the edge of her coat and took off her shoes. The cold white powder clung to her pant legs. She bent over as best she could and took a few seconds to brush them off. Standing up, she removed her coat and draped it over her arm and the purse already hanging there. She looked around, her eyes adjusting quickly to the dimness. A faint light emanated from the dining room.

"Brian?"

No answer.

"Brian, where are you?" she asked, raising her volume a bit.

Still no answer.

She cautiously walked toward the dining room, stopping momentarily at the threshold, then crossed into the room. She gasped.

Melissa stood motionless, mouth agape, staring at the unexpected sight of an elegantly prepared table set for two. Every piece was unfamiliar, having been purchased for the occasion she now knew that her absence had ruined. The only discernible imperfection was the wax from the unattended candles, which had trickled down the high, slender tapers onto their holders.

She detected a faint aroma and looked into the adjoining kitchen, which was completely dark. She walked the length of the table toward the opening but stopped, her attention arrested by a slender, rectangular box, stylishly wrapped, positioned atop one of the plates.

Her curiosity piqued, she picked it up, finding it to be heavier than she'd anticipated.

Returning the box to its resting place, she turned and went into the kitchen, flicking on the light. The sink and counters were strewn with an array of utensils and ingredient containers. The oven door was room temperature. She opened it and saw something covered with foil. She didn't know what it was, but it smelled delectable. She closed the oven, wistfully. *You blew this big time, Melissa, whatever it was.*

Melissa shut off the light, retrieved the gift, and snuffed out the candles. A faint vertical crack of light helped her navigate her way to the basement. She approached the door and opened it, but hesitated, uncertainty welling up inside her. Her mind drifted back to the conversation with Dee and Malcolm earlier in the day.

She sighed and carefully descended the steps. The basement was dimly lit. The low light of the fireplace and the small lamp sitting atop Brian's desk to her left provided just enough of a glow for her to make out his sleeping form on the couch. He was facing inward, a light blanket drawn over him, his jean-covered leg sticking out at an angle.

The desk was uncharacteristically disheveled. She walked over to it and picked up several of the papers scattered across the desktop. *Recipes.* She couldn't help smiling as she flipped the pages, noting the highlighting and notes scribbled here and there. Trying to cook something was completely out of character for him, but this fit. Just like everything else he did, he'd made a study of it.

She quietly returned the pages and laid her purse and coat on the desktop. Her heart skipped a beat. *The drawer.* She'd playfully poked fun at his secrecy, making a game of guessing its contents every time she came downstairs. It appeared unlocked. She was sure of it. She'd memorized its appearance, and now her eye had detected something amiss. The flat surface of the top edge of the drawer was just barely visible, not even a quarter of an inch.

She sat down at the desk. The chair made a loud creak. She stiffened and held her breath for a moment, but there was no stir from the couch. She took hold of the handle and gingerly pulled. It gave way. A pang of conscience rippled through her. She desperately wanted to know what he'd been hiding since they'd moved into the house. She squinted vainly into the darkness of the crack her tug had produced. She closed her eyes. *He'll forgive me.* She slowly pulled it open and peered inside.

"Oh, my," Melissa whispered, stunned by the sight. Her eyes moved quickly to the couch, then back again. She carefully withdrew a clear plastic page protector, its top taped shut. Inside was a single piece of pale blue construction paper, to which was affixed a solitary, withered, white carnation, faintly yellowed by time, its stem bent in two places. She recognized it instantly.

Her mind raced back to Area 51, the day she'd visited Brian after he'd nearly died in surgery—after he'd put his life on the line to save her from the charging attack dogs. She remembered plucking the carnation out of a vase in the cafeteria and giving it to him the day of her first visit, overwhelmed with guilt for all that she'd done to him. She'd played the conversation over in her heart dozens of times. He'd forgiven her without reservation.

How did he get this out? No sooner had the question surfaced in her mind than the answer came. Images from their last day on the base suddenly rushed into her mind. There in Brian's room, Father Benedict had laid out his plan. She'd had to remove Lieutenant Sheppard's right hand and eye to enable their escape through the biometric security. She recalled wrapping the grisly items in a towel and putting them in Brian's backpack. Then she'd gone into the bathroom to wash her hands. When she'd emerged, she'd noticed Brian closing his desk drawer, then standing to slip the backup on. *I can't believe it.* He'd left everything he owned in that room. Of all the things he could have kept, he'd gone back for *this*.

She looked down at the dehydrated, fragile blossom. The plastic had been pressed tight in an awkward attempt at preservation, but it had shriveled and come apart. Her lip quivered. Melissa closed her eyes, pressing the clumsy keepsake to her breast, and began to cry. Tears streamed down her cheeks as she sobbed, struggling to keep quiet.

After a few minutes she regained her composure. She took the sheet and reached toward the drawer to return it. The glow of the desk lamp penetrated the plastic, revealing that something had been scrawled on the back. She gently turned it over and stared in fascination. He'd penciled several rows of Egyptian hieroglyphs onto the reverse side.

Suddenly, Brian turned in his sleep on the couch. She gave a start and watched him closely. Stillness returned after a few seconds. She stood up, wiping the tears from her face with her finger. With the page in one hand and the gift from upstairs in the other, she made her way to where he lay. Once there, she knelt by the couch, carefully sliding the plastic sleeve underneath. She watched the slow, rhythmic movement of his chest as he breathed, laying on his side, facing her. She lightly touched his hair, letting her fingers course through it. He stirred, opening his eyes. The two of them watched each other for a moment.

"Hi," he whispered, blinking.

"You didn't wait up for me," she said, taking his glasses from the end table next to the couch.

"Sorry, I guess I was tired." He took his glasses from her hand and put them on, propping himself up on an elbow.

"Understandable. After all, you had a busy day, didn't you?" She rocked back on her knees to watch his expression.

"Not real—oh, yeah. I guess I did."

"I'm sorry about tonight," she apologized. "Upstairs, it's beautiful. I can't tell you how surprised I was. You put so much work into everything."

"It's okay. You didn't know. I did my best to keep it a secret."

"Mission accomplished," she said, pursing her lips into a thoughtful pout. "I had absolutely no idea—and still don't. What's this all about?"

He looked at her kneeling alongside the couch, his eyes now fully adjusted, transfixed by every feature of her face and the deep orange glow of the edges of her hair against the fire's light. "I wanted you to feel special."

"I do," she replied with a soft smile. "But what's the occasion?"

A sly expression creased his face. "It's your birthday."

"No, it's not." She cocked her head to one side, taken by a sudden realization. "It's not Melissa Carter's birthday, but you're right, today is my real birthday. How did you know that? I'm sure I've never told you."

"I have my ways," he answered, grinning with satisfaction.

"I want to know how you found out," she insisted, trying unsuccessfully to look annoyed.

"It's called research."

"Don't give me that," she replied, trying not to laugh.

"I know your real name and where you're from. I found your name with your picture in an old issue of your local newspaper, something about kids from your high school serving a meal around Christmas time. It was dated and happened to mention the meal was on your birthday."

"A picture? From high school? I bet my hair was ghastly."

"It wasn't as nice as it is now, but I liked it."

"Well, two can play this game," she said in mock defiance. "I'm going to discover yours, along with some unflattering information."

"You'll never find it. You might see my name in a box score or something, but otherwise I'm invisible."

"Then tell me."

"There's no way I'm telling you my birthday."

"Why not?"

"It's embarrassing. I still have *some* dignity left."

"Were you born on Hitler's birthday or something?"

"No, it's worse than that," he joked.

"Come on!" She laughed.

"Forget it. I'd only tell you if I knew I was dying. Then the humiliation wouldn't matter."

"We'll see about that."

"Are you threatening me?"

"I'm considering it."

"Get used to disappointment." He stopped. Melissa could see that the word moved the evening's circumstances back into his thoughts.

He sighed. "I'm glad you're home safely. Did you have fun?"

"Actually, yes. I didn't expect to, but I did. But I don't want to talk about that. I want to talk about what you were up to. Whatever you made up there smells wonderful, but you can barely boil water—unless you've been feigning incompetence all this time."

"No, my ineptitude is real," he answered, enjoying her astonishment. "What you missed tonight is now the one thing I can make. It's Martha Stewart's spicy coconut chicken casserole. She and I hooked up on YouTube. I've been practicing the recipe."

"Martha Stewart?" she exclaimed with a laugh. "You've been secretly watching Martha Stewart videos down here in the bunker? Wait till Malcolm hears this."

"He's never going to know."

"He's going to know *tomorrow*—unless you tell me your birth date."

"Do what you must."

She laughed again. "How did you pull it off? If you've been practicing, what did you do with all the food?"

"I'd make it in the morning right after you left, then have some and take the rest to one of the guys' dorms. I'm a big hit over there."

"I can't believe you could be so deceptive," she said, pretending to be shocked.

"Believe it."

"Oh!" Melissa touched her tummy. "Just some movement in there," she explained before he could ask.

He took the cue and sat up. "Plenty of room up here," he offered, patting the space next to him and taking her hand.

She got up slowly and joined him on the couch. "Now," she said, settling again. "What's this?" She held up the gift box.

"That's for you."

"I know it's for me," she said, rolling her eyes. "I want to know what it is."

"You'd know that if you opened it. It won't harm you."

"I'm more interested in how much it damaged your bank account," she replied with a hint of sternness in her voice.

"The bank account's dead. It died happy."

"*Brian*, you—"

"Open it," he interrupted her.

Melissa eyed him suspiciously and began to remove the wrapping. She stopped as soon as she saw the name on the box. "Tiffany's? Are you serious? That better be just for effect."

Brian answered only with a sheepish raise of his eyebrows.

She opened the box. "Oh my gosh," she exclaimed breathlessly. The contents gleamed blistering white as the box tilted toward the fire's light.

"It's a necklace," he said in order to puncture the awkward silence. "And that's not silver," he added, "it's platinum. I wanted something different. I liked the shine. And I asked for the emeralds. They match your eyes."

Melissa stared at the contents, speechless. She slowly removed the dazzling piece. It was a woven, geometric necklace about the width of her finger that had two small ovular emeralds attached to a much larger, square-cut stone in a Y-shaped structural design.

"Hold it up so I can see what it looks like on you."

She hesitated, but then complied.

Brian stared, captivated by the symmetry of Melissa's face, the glow of her auburn, shoulder-length, bobbed hair. Even in the dim light he could make out her deep green eyes, matched by the gems. "Wow, it's just perfect."

"Well, at least I can still feel attractive from the neck up."

"*Please*. You're amazing."

"Sure," she said gratefully, but with a whiff of skepticism. "And 'amazed' is the right word," she said, eyebrows raised in a mild scolding. "Brian, this is really too much. I don't even know where I'd wear this."

"Wear it around the house if you think it's too flashy."

"You don't wear something like this around the house, Brian. A state dinner, maybe."

"Do you like it?"

"Of course. It's breathtaking. It's just—you're too good to me." She smiled appreciatively, returning the necklace to the box. "Now how much did it cost?"

"If I tell you, will you ask me to return it?"

"Probably."

"Too late. I already burned the receipt," he replied, nodding in the direction of the fire.

"I'm serious, Brian. This must have cost a small fortune. You shouldn't have spent all that money on me."

"Melissa," he said, becoming serious, "you have to understand something. It was a few thousand dollars, but—"

"You spent a few *thousand* dollars on a necklace? Brian—"

"Let me finish," he said. "It's been four years since I celebrated Christmas with anyone. The necklace is for your birthday and Christmas too. I wanted to give you something exceptional—something that would make you think of me whenever you saw it. I may never have the money or the opportunity again. I needed to do this while I could."

"What do you mean you may never have the opportunity again—and that it'll make me think of you?" she asked, alarm rising in her voice. "What are saying? You sound like you're leaving."

"I'm not leaving," he responded, smiling reassuringly. "I'd never leave you—" He stopped as if needing to catch his breath.

"What is it?" she urged.

"I'm not planning on going anywhere, but I know the day will come when you'll need me to go."

"Brian, if I must say it, what the hell are you talking about?" she demanded, her eyes flaring.

He looked at her. She saw the anguish in his eyes and didn't press.

"The last few months here with you," he began, "have been the best months of my life. I wouldn't trade them for anything. But I've come to realize that my being here has made you a prisoner. And tonight sort of reinforced the point."

"What? How?"

"Don't you see? The babies will be here and then gone in a few more months. You'll be able to start over. At some point you'll apply for another teaching position somewhere else. We can move together to maintain appearances here, but you'll have a chance at a new beginning—the chance to meet someone and get married and have a good life. But you can't do that the way things are now. I'm in the way."

"What if I'm happy here?"

"I didn't say you weren't, but you need the freedom to make choices. You don't have that now. You're going to meet someone and fall for them, someone who can give you the kind of life you deserve—someone life Neff."

"*Neff*? I see the problem now. Why are you threatened by Graham?"

"Seriously? He's rich, good looking, and has clear direction in life. Other than that, we're like twins. I just can't give you those things. The truth is," he stammered, "I have nothing to offer you. You just can't see it now, but I see it—clearly."

She turned to face him squarely. The light of the fire glistened off his moistened eyes. "You're right," she said, locking eye contact. "As usual, your analysis is very logical, but your argument isn't compelling. You've overlooked something—something that's fatal to your thesis."

"What's that?" he asked, surprised.

"He's not you."

"I think that's exactly my point," he protested.

"Malcolm and Dee were right," she said thoughtfully, studying his expression. "You really can't imagine this being your real life."

"Malcolm and Dee? Right about what?" he asked anxiously.

"I had a little talk with them earlier today, about you . . . and us."

"What does *that* mean?"

"It means they were right—at least about one thing. But I need to hear it." She forced a smile, her own disquiet creeping into her heart.

"What did they say?" he asked, trying not to sound too defensive.

"I'll tell you, but first I need to say something."

Brian eyed her apprehensively.

"I'm thrilled with the necklace," she said. "And I won't question your judgment again about the money. But you need to know that it won't be the thing I remember about tonight for the rest of my life. It won't be the dinner, either."

Brian looked into her eyes, trying to divine her thoughts. They drew him in but weren't giving anything away. "And what's that?" he asked cautiously.

"This," she said, reaching down to the floor and under the couch. She brought out the plastic sleeve, never breaking her gaze. His eyes looked down at her hand and then closed tightly.

"Melissa," he groaned. "You shouldn't—how could I be so *careless*?" he berated himself, then fell silent.

She put down the page and took his hand, squeezing it affectionately. "Do you love me?" she whispered in earnest, undeterred by the anguish on his face.

"Melissa, don't . . ."

"I *need* to know," she whispered again. She released his hand and took hold of his arm, then rested her head on his shoulder.

"Please . . ." His voice cracked. A tear trickled down his cheek.

"I want the truth, one way or the other."

He was trembling, fighting for control. She waited patiently. She tried not to measure the silence. Her awareness drifted back to her conversation with Malcolm and Dee. There was nothing she could do but wait and fight the anxiety slowly invading her heart. Her mind clouded with regret. Suddenly she felt him relax.

Brian sniffed and cleared his throat. "It's true." His voice broke again, but he managed to keep going. "It's true. You're my first thought every day, and my last thought every night. I've really tried hard not to let it happen. . . . I'm sorry."

Melissa sighed quietly, reaching across his chest and pulling herself closer. He put his arm around her. A wave of relief swept over her. "Thank you—and there's no need to apologize."

"I don't want things to change," he replied haltingly.

"I do."

"Why? Things are so good now, despite the danger."

"I don't think you understand," she replied, sitting up. "I love you, too."

"Don't say that, please."

"It's true," she said, repeating his own answer with a smile, wiping a tear from his face. "I know you're afraid that I don't mean it, or that I'll change my mind, but I won't." She looked him in the eye. "I know what I'm saying. I feel the same way you do."

"That makes no sense," he objected.

"Of course it doesn't," she challenged wryly. "If love made sense, it would be predictable. It doesn't follow a formula. If it did, it would always happen the same way for the same reasons. It's not about logic, so let's put that to rest."

He looked at her, a dazed expression on his face. "You just destroyed everything I've been thinking for months in a couple of seconds. That's a little intimidating," he said, a faint smile appearing.

"Intimidating? I'm not done with you yet," she warned airily, reaching again for the slipcover. "What does it say on the back?"

"It's Egyptian."

"I can see that. That wasn't my question. I want to hear what it says."

"No one really knows exactly what spoken Egyptian sounded like, but—"

"You're stalling—and you're wonderfully bad at it. Let's have the translation."

"It's a poem."

"Fascinating. Now what does it say?" She was grinning, enjoying the joust.

"It's a New Kingdom text from the Chester Beatty papyrus."

"Class is over, professor."

He grinned. "It's a love poem . . . and it's a little embarrassing."

"That just makes me want to hear it even *more*," she said, laughing. "If you need a dictionary, I'll get you one from your shelf."

He took her hand in both of his, caressing her fingers. "I don't need a dictionary. I know it by heart." He recited the words:

One alone is my sister, having no peer;
more gracious than all other women.
Behold, she is like the rising morning star;
at the beginning of a good year.
Shining brightly, fair of skin;
lovely is the look of her eyes.
Sweet is the speech of her lips;
she utters no excess of words.
Sloping is her neck, fair are her breasts;
her hair is true lapis lazuli.
Her arms surpass gold;
her fingers are like lotuses

"Mmm, I like it. Is that all?"

"No, but I should probably stop there."

"Oh, really. Why's that?"

"It gets a little . . . racy."

"Oh, that's even better," she cooed warmly, leaning in close to him. "I hope you never learn how to extricate yourself from a conversation."

Brian looked into her eyes. His eyes fell to her mouth. He ran his hands over her arms, then her shoulders, and then to her bare neck, feeling the warmth of her soft skin. She turned her head and kissed his hand. He gently turned her face toward his.

The phone rang loudly, piercing the silence. Neither of them flinched, their full attention still on each other, inches apart.

The phone rang again, insistently.

"I'd better get that," Brian said in a low, parched voice.

"It's *my* phone," Melissa replied, her words barely audible.

A third ring.

Melissa pressed her cheek against his and nibbled playfully on his ear. "Hold that thought," she insisted in a whisper filled with promise. She pulled back slowly and slid off the couch, then headed toward the desk and found her phone in her coat pocket.

"Hello?" she answered.

"Melissa, it's Graham. I'm sorry to bother you so late this evening, but something terrible has happened."

"What's wrong?" Brian heard the alarm in Melissa's voice as she returned to the couch.

"Well, when I got back to the guest house tonight, Malone had a disturbing report. He was watching a rebroadcast of tonight's news and saw that girl's face on TV, the one who confronted you at the coffee house."

"Becky?"

"Right."

Melissa shot a bewildered glance at Brian, who was watching her intently.

"Is she all right?"

"I don't know. The report wasn't about her. It was about her boyfriend, the one who got arrested in Chicago. He's dead."

"What? How can that be? He should be in jail awaiting trial."

"Our thoughts exactly. Apparently he made bail a few days ago and was shot tonight outside a bar. The only reason it was on the news here was the local connection with Becky. There was no word on where she is."

"I can't believe it."

"I don't like it," Neff said ominously. "There's just something not right about it. I can feel it. Malone and I are going to watch your house tonight in the car. We'll take turns. We're used to that sort of thing. I just wanted to let you know."

"Thank you," Melissa replied, her heart pounding.

"Make sure Brian knows. We'll talk tomorrow morning."

"I will. He's right here." She stared at Brian, her eyes wide with fear. "I'll tell him everything."

29

Many evil things there are that your strong walls and bright swords do not stay.

—*J. R. R. Tolkien,* The Fellowship of the Ring

"Is this the place where you two met that Becky girl?" Dee asked Melissa, surveying the eclectic mélange of patrons in the small café who were sheltering themselves from the bitter Fargo winter over their favorite hot treat. There couldn't have been more than a dozen people scattered here and there at the tables. Most had Christmas packages tucked near their feet, making the cozy space feel cramped and confined.

"No," she answered, "this is a new place. A lot smaller, but as long as the coffee is good, I don't care."

"It beats Mayberry," Dee quipped. "Fargo has been worth the drive already."

"I know exactly what you mean. It's nice to get out."

Melissa fiddled with her coat while she watched Brian and Malcolm chatting in the line. Doing as she'd been told, she studiously avoided eye contact with Neff and Malone, who were each sitting alone a few tables apart on the other side of the shop. Neff had insisted that they not leave town alone in the wake of the previous evening's troubling news. Once they'd arrived at their destination, he'd laid out strict rules of no contact between the foursome and the two of them.

"Were you nervous about coming here tonight?" Dee asked, lowering her voice.

"Not really. If Becky had run into the Colonel and said something about us, we would have found out the hard way weeks ago. I admit, the news about her boyfriend last week scared me, but once I read about what happened, Neff's concern seemed a bit overblown. Anybody can have too much to drink and get in a fight, especially in Chicago. Besides, we're just assuming the Colonel would be involved just because NASA is in the picture. But that's a huge leap."

"I think we can all forgive ourselves for being predisposed to some paranoia after what we saw last summer. If the Colonel was involved in what happened, the blue-eyed thug would have been on your doorstep in a heartbeat."

"And Becky would have had to tell him what our new names are in order for him to find us," Melissa added. "We never told her where I was teaching or what town we were in. For all she knows, we're living here in Fargo."

"Batman and Robin didn't seem to think any of that mattered."

Melissa chuckled at the caricature of Neff and Malone. "I know. I don't get why they insisted on coming in here first. I'm not sure what they were on the lookout for, especially since they don't know anything about Colonel Ferguson. They don't even have his name, so it's not like they'd know what he looks like."

"I didn't follow, either," agreed Dee. "But we might as well let them do their thing. No harm in that, right?" Dee stopped, troubled by the change in Melissa's expression. "Melissa?"

She turned, following Melissa's stare. Through the windowpane adjacent to the front entrance, the view partially obscured by streaks of frost, she saw a young girl wearing a dark, olive green, goose-down jacket gazing into the window, wisps of curly brown hair protruding from under a black beanie. A hint of a nervous smile creased her face as she shifted the backpack she was wearing and waved cautiously in their direction.

"I don't believe it," Melissa breathed through a forced smile.

"You've got to be kidding," Dee said, turning back to her.

"I wish I were," she added, half-heartedly acknowledging the girl's signal. "She's coming in."

Dee broke protocol and looked in Neff's direction, but her view was quickly blocked by someone looking for a seat. She quietly slid an unclaimed chair from the adjacent table in their direction.

"Thanks," Becky said appreciatively, looking at Melissa. She sat down at the end of the table between the two women, whose backs were to the corner walls. "It's hard to get a seat in here sometimes," she followed, sheepishly, opening her coat and setting her backpack on the floor.

"Well, Becky," Melissa said, not bothering to conceal her surprise. "Pardon me if I'm a little stunned. This is Deidre, by the way."

Becky nodded to Dee. "Sorry to intrude, but I saw you through the window—again. Weird, huh?"

"For sure," Melissa said, taking a brief look around, trying not to betray her anxiety.

"Have we met before?" Dee asked, her brow furrowed in concentration.

"I don't think so," Becky answered. "I would have remembered you. North Dakota isn't exactly a melting pot of diversity."

"You've got that right," Dee replied, satisfied.

Brian and Malcolm had made it to the cash register, but their backs were still to the table. Across the room she saw Neff reading something on his phone. Malone was nowhere in sight. "It feels awkward to ask," Melissa began, "but how are you here and not . . . you know . . ."

"In jail?" Becky blithely finished Melissa's thought, glancing at Dee.

"Right. And it's okay to talk. Dee here is a psychologist. She's used to keeping secrets."

"Well, I don't have any of those anymore," Becky said ruefully. "I surrendered to the police, just like you advised, and gave them what they wanted. There wasn't much to interrogate me about after that, other than where we'd gone while we were on the run, but they knew most of that."

"Of course."

"They more or less just let me sit in a cell for a few weeks. They told me they thought about turning my case back to the state authorities, but then they let me out—with an ankle bracelet, mind you. I'm wearing it now."

"Well, I guess that's good news," Melissa continued the small talk, having already decided she'd let Becky steer the conversation.

"I was surprised, believe me. I'm not going to try anything, either. I'm staying with my friend from high school again. It's just nice to be out."

"I don't need to know any details," Dee said, "but you were in federal custody?"

"Yeah. Why do you ask?"

"Based on your story, they seem too nice." She shrugged. "I've had a few run-ins with the feds myself. Your situation seems atypical."

"Maybe it is," Becky offered. "It's my first time. Who knows?"

"Here we go," Malcolm said, arriving at the table with their drinks. "Can you introduce me?" he asked Melissa. His eyes told her he already knew.

"This is Becky," Melissa replied. "Fargo is her hometown."

"Nice to meet you," Malcolm said pleasantly. "Can I get you anything?"

"I was just about to ask the same," Brian said, now standing in front of the seated women next to Malcolm. He handed Melissa her drink. They read the anxiety in each other's eyes. "So, would you like some coffee?" he asked, turning toward Becky.

Becky's expression instantly changed. Her body became rigid. She stared straight ahead with a blank, fish-eyed gaze, then looked down at the table. "Do they have coffee here?" she asked slowly, still looking at the surface of the table.

Brian's eyes darted quickly to the faces in their group, where he saw a mixture of alarm and bafflement.

"Yes," he answered. Her question was disturbingly obvious. "They have coffee here. It's a café."

Becky raised her head and looked at each of them for a moment, moving left to right, then back again. She locked onto Brian's face.

"So nice to see you again," she said in a detached monotone, staring into space.

"What?" Brian asked.

"You are Dr. Brian Scott," she went on, her expression unchanged. "Dr. Brian Scott, PhD, University of Chicago. AWOL for several months."

"Oh God, no!" whispered Melissa, panic surging through her. Brian and Malcolm were blocking her view of Neff and Malone. She fought the urge to try to alert them by shifting her position.

"I have a message for you, Dr. Scott," Becky intoned firmly in the same voice, which by now had taken on a robotic drone. After a few moments of silence, she looked up at the ceiling, then resumed her fixed stare straight ahead.

"What do you want?" Brian decided to ask.

"1-1-3-6-1-9 . . . H-G . . ." She chanted in a slow, deliberate cadence, then paused momentarily. Malcolm hurriedly reached into his pocket for a pen and began writing on a napkin. "W-E-S-T-O-N . . . 8-0-5-0-3." She stopped and stared straight ahead.

"What the—"

"1-1-3-6-1-9 . . . H-G-W-E—" Becky began to chant the sequence again.

"I suggest we all get up calmly," Malcolm whispered cautiously, shoving the napkin into his pocket, "and just leave quietly. The others will notice and follow."

Brian nodded, reaching for Melissa.

"One more thing . . ." Becky said lightly, almost musically, after finishing the series.

The four of them stopped and watched in transfixed curiosity as Becky methodically turned her attention to the backpack between her feet on the floor. She slowly unzipped the top and reached inside. Then, in a sure, startlingly swift motion, she pulled out a handgun and pointed it at her own head.

Brian instinctively pulled Melissa off her chair and onto the floor, quickly crouching in front of her. Several customers heard the commotion. Heads turned toward them in unison. The sight of the gun immediately jolted several people into panic. Some turned and ran for the entrance, shouting for patrons to get out. Others stood up, craning to see what was causing the unfolding chaos. A woman screamed. The loud banging of wooden chairs knocked over or flung out of the way rattled through the small café.

"Put it down, Becky," Brian said breathlessly. Malcolm and Dee slowly backed away.

"Stay busy . . . busy, busy, busy . . . merry Christmas . . . happy birthday to baby Jesus . . ." She smiled broadly, then pulled the trigger.

30

The shifts of Fortune test the reliability of friends.

—*Cicero*

"Let me through!"

The shout rose above the clamor of screaming and shouting, jolting Brian from his shocked stupor. He stood helplessly over Becky's lifeless body, her eyes still wide open, looking up at the ceiling in the same catatonic stare that had riveted him just moments ago. Only seconds had passed, but already a sizeable pool of blood and cranial fluid had oozed from the girl's shattered skull. Bits of bone and brain tissue floated like flotsam and jetsam amid strands of hair in the sickening puddle.

"Let me through—I'm a doctor!"

Brian heard the voice more clearly now over the wails echoing through the formerly calm cafe.

Neff pushed his way past a few onlookers and knelt beside Becky's body. "You'd better see to your wife," he said, not looking at him as he passed. Neff put his fingers to the girl's neck, checking for the pulse he knew wouldn't register. He was just trying to perpetuate the charade.

Malone appeared, having pushed his way past more gawkers. He looked at the body and began ushering people away. "Let the doc do what he can. The police will be here soon. Please, let's go outside and wait for them."

As soon as people began complying, Malone turned toward Neff and watched him gently close the girl's eyes, turning her head to hide the largest of the two gruesome wounds as best he could. "I was a medic in Vietnam," he said, loud enough for the remnants of an audience to hear. "Anything I can do?"

Brian watched as the two spoke, still stunned by the violence. For a moment his mind flashed back to Neil's death. He shuddered at the memory of his friend's head exploding before his eyes. Malone got up and hurried to the now abandoned service counter, shuffling over the countertop. The motion brought Brian back to the present. He watched as the older man returned with an apron and a towel and handed them to Neff, who covered Becky's head.

"Brian," a voice beckoned weakly from below and behind him. He turned and looked down at Melissa. He quickly knelt next to her and helped her to her feet, pulling her close, trying to quell her trembling. Malcolm was crouched next to Dee, who sat awkwardly on the floor, legs apart, leaning against an overturned chair.

"You! Hey, buddy!" Brian heard a voice behind him and turned back toward Neff and Malone. Malone was motioning to him. He whispered to Melissa, who gave a quick nod, and joined the twosome.

"You've got get out of here *now,*" Neff said in a low, ominous hush as soon as he arrived.

"We can't just leave a crime scene in front of all these people," Brian objected. "We were witnesses. Someone will say something to the police."

"You don't want to hang around for the police. You'll be detained—and then handed over to whoever arranged this."

"How—"

"Listen closely," Neff interrupted. His voice was calm but firm. "This girl was being monitored."

"I know," he replied. "She said the police made her wear an ankle bracelet."

"That's no security bracelet she's wearing." Neff motioned with his eyes to the girl's foot. Brian looked. "That's a sophisticated vital-signs monitor. It's Israeli. We've seen them before. My guess is that whoever gave it to her knows she's dead and is already on his way here. You've got to get out of here *now.*"

"Dr. Harper doesn't look right," Malone added, drawing Neff's attention, "but that may not be enough. We'll need to improvise."

"Enough for what?"

"Malone is going to get you all out—front, back, wherever," Neff explained with urgency. "Follow his lead. He'll make it as natural as possible. It would help if one of the women went into labor in the next sixty seconds—and it needs to be convincing. Now go!"

Without a word, Brian stood up and rejoined the others.

"I'll handle things here," Neff whispered to Malone. "Text me in fifteen minutes."

"Got it."

Malone stood up and moved slowly toward Brian and the group. Dozens of people were now pressing up against the windows to get a glimpse of the carnage. He helped Malcolm get Dee to her feet.

"She's in shock," Malone said, looking at Malcolm, again speaking loud enough for anyone within earshot to hear. "I think there's an employee break room in the back," he added, gesturing toward a door behind the counter. "Have her lie down there. The police will be here soon."

The couple made their way slowly to the opening. "There's an exit in the back," Malone whispered to them, touching the slender black man's arm and directing him forward. "Get out, make a left down the alley, and wait for us where it comes out." Malcolm and Dee disappeared through doorway.

Malone turned his attention to Brian and Melissa. Melissa groaned and grabbed her abdomen. Her knees buckled. Brian held onto her.

"Make way, folks," Malone said sternly. "She's started labor. We've got to get her outside." He'd no sooner mouthed the words than the distant sound of sirens drifted into their hearing. Melissa groaned again, this time more loudly. She clutched at Brian's sleeve and doubled over in feigned agony. "Keep moving," Malone motioned to Brian as they headed to the entrance. The crowd began to part. "We'll get her out and find some help. Just stay calm."

Once outside, the three of them turned left in the direction of where they'd parked along the street. The car was parked perpendicular, with the driver's side facing the crowd, roughly fifty feet away. Malone turned his head slightly, noting that a few onlookers were following their movements. After stepping between the parked cars, he discreetly slipped Brian the keys. "Follow me to the passenger's side with Melissa, then go back around and get in the driver's seat."

The two men acted out the ruse, helping Melissa around the rear of the SUV and into the passenger's door. Her genuine shakiness made the scene believable. Malone instructed her to sit behind the driver's seat. Malone held the side door open. The wail of the approaching sirens reached a crescendo.

"Now what?" Brian asked.

"Just wait."

Brian did as he was told. Seconds later, two squad cars shot into view around the corner to their left, passing their vehicle at the rear before coming to a screeching halt. An ambulance appeared from the opposite direction. Brian watched as the officers bolted from the car, hands covering their weapons. Neff appeared through the crowd and waved them in. They disappeared into the building. All heads were turned toward the action.

Malone jumped into the SUV and shut the door, crouching as best he could behind the front passenger seat. "The windows are tinted, but I'm not taking any chances of someone seeing me with you guys. Get moving, make it natural. Take the street on your left just before where the police cars stopped. Take it to the next intersection and make a left. I'll direct you from there."

"What about Malcolm and Dee?"

"I'll tell you as soon as you give it some gas."

Brian pulled out of the space quickly but smoothly and followed Malone's directions. Melissa could see that they were making a circuitous path around the opposite side and rear of the coffee house. It took less than five minutes for them to circle far enough to where they could see Malcolm and Dee waiting at the corner of a parking lot. The two of them quickly got inside.

"Thanks," Malcolm said as he closed the door.

"Where to now?" Brian asked.

"Keep going straight ahead past the street the coffee shop is on. Take the second left and then head into the parking lot farthest removed from the shop. Park as far back as you can. Then move back here into this seat. I'll have to squeeze in the back row with Malcolm and Dee. We don't want anyone visible through the front.

"He's going to find us," Dee said suddenly in a low, frightened voice.

"We have to wait for Neff," Malcolm said gently. "We're safe here."

"Like hell we are," she grumbled. Brian was relieved to hear that she sounded like herself, but he shared her dread. He positioned the car in the last row about a hundred yards away and shut off the ignition.

"We also want to learn what we can," Malone said, wedging himself into the back row and then reaching under the seat in front of him. He drew out a small case and produced a pair of binoculars, which he peered through toward the café.

"Brian," Melissa asked, "what are we going to do? He knows we're here." The desperation in her voice cut through him.

"He knew we'd show up in Fargo, so Becky must have let something slip. But we don't *live* in Fargo."

"Don't try to make me feel better," she said with panicked irritation. "He's behind this. He *knows*, and even if he doesn't have our address, he'll get it. We're not safe. We're—" She stopped and put her hand over her mouth, trying in vain to keep herself from crying. Brian reached across the aisle separating the seats and tried to console her.

"Why now?" she raged through her tears.

Malcolm reached forward and put his hand on her shoulder. "You're gonna be all right. He's not God."

Malone had put down the binoculars, his attention drawn to the exchange. He glanced at his watch, then quickly grabbed his phone and began texting furiously. Malcolm watched closely as the mustachioed man deftly alternated between several apps and fired off three or four texts in succession. "Mind if I ask what you're sending Neff?" he asked.

"It's his ticket out of there. Some instructions—including where we parked."

"There's no way they're done questioning him," Malcolm said doubtfully. "You know that somebody is going to mention the missing witnesses."

"And the fat, balding guy with the mustache," Malone added, but he didn't laugh. "Don't worry. They won't have a choice but to let him go."

Malcolm eyed him dubiously.

"If you're bored, you can keep an eye on things and tell me if you see anything interesting." Malone handed him the binoculars.

Malcolm held the field glasses up to his own spectacles and adjusted the lenses. He scanned the crowd, which was still as thick as before, only now it was dotted with a few more squad cars and emergency personnel. He held his breath as he searched for the face none of them wanted to see.

"A couple of cops just came out," Malcolm narrated. "They're headed down the street in opposite directions."

"They're looking for us, naturally," Malone replied stoically.

"There he is," Malcolm said.

"The Colonel?" Malone asked.

"No, no. It's Neff. He's talking to one of the officers taking notes. Now they're shaking hands. . . . He's on his way."

"Never in doubt," Malone replied. The two men made eye contact. A wave of comprehension swept through Malcolm as he returned the binoculars. He'd been had.

"Nicely played," he whispered.

Malone looked down at his phone and texted another message. "It's what we do."

31

Choices are the hinges of destiny.

—*Pythagoras*

"So the girl was completely normal until you two guys walked up to the table?" Neff asked, startled by what he was hearing.

"Totally," answered Malcolm. "We engaged her a bit, and then she seemed to just go into a trance."

"And the numbers and letters—they don't mean anything to any of you?" Neff continued to drive, being careful to stay within the speed limit.

"I have no idea what the point was," Brian said, choosing his words carefully.

"What do you think?" Neff asked Malone, who had migrated to the front passenger seat after they'd pulled out.

"I think you already know."

"You mean what Fern's going to say."

"Yep."

"We'll see."

"Who's Fern?" Brian asked.

"Before we go down that path," Neff said, speaking again to the passengers, momentarily deflecting the question, "I need to ask if any of you knew whether Becky had any unusual marks on her body—maybe a tattoo? I didn't do any checking in there. Had I known what happened, I'd have made a point of it."

"Come to think of it," Melissa recollected, "she did. She had a tattoo on her neck. It wasn't unusual, though. It was an infinity symbol. You see them a lot."

Neff looked uneasily at Malone, whose expression seemed to shout "I told you so."

"Fern's gonna hit the roof."

"Again—who's Fern?" Brian asked, more impatiently this time. "And could you guys tell us what you think is going on?"

"Fern is my wife," said Malone. "She studies this sort of thing."

"What sort of thing?"

Malone remained silent, watching the road. He caught Neff looking at him in the rearview mirror. "Fern used to be a psychologist," Malone finally said. "We met in 1977. She was fresh out of law school and paging for a federal judge in DC. I was a hippie."

He paused, gauging the incredulous expression on Brian's face. "Hard to believe, I know. Anyway, we met at a protest. It was the last place in the world she'd ever expected to meet her husband—or to *be*, for that matter. But then again, she never expected to look at her father and see an enemy of the state, either. Her dad worked in the CIA for a man named Richard Helms." He turned his head toward Dee. "Given your field of expertise, Dr. Harper, I suspect you know who Richard Helms was?"

Dee eyed him cautiously. "Yes."

"And do you know what happened in 1977? Or maybe 1973 will ring a bell."

Dee hesitated a moment, as though remembering something unpleasant. "I do."

"How about the rest of you?"

They shook their heads.

"Richard Helms was the Director of the CIA," Dee elaborated. "In 1973 he ordered that all government files associated with MK-ULTRA be destroyed, which they were—at least most of them."

"Right," Malone confirmed. "MK-ULTRA was one of the CIA projects aimed at what's popularly known as mind control—programming people for intelligence and military applications."

Brian looked at Dee, eyebrows raised in recognition, then at the others. No one offered any comment.

Malone turned and continued, eyeing them carefully. "What Helms did became widespread knowledge in 1977 when the Senate investigated MK-ULTRA as a result of a Freedom of Information Act request that turned up 20,000 pages of documents that had been missed in his purge. Fern's father sided with his boss on the issue. It destroyed her whole world—what the country was supposed to stand for, the man she thought her father was. It was a crisis of conscience, to say the least. She became obsessed with the investigation and wound up going into psychology."

"So your wife is going to think Becky was programmed?" Melissa asked.

"Absolutely. I'd bet my wife knows more about these research programs than just about anyone, except for the criminals who were and still are directly engaged in it. It's something of a crusade with her. Becky's behavior is textbook programming, and the tattoo is significant. People who have been subjected to the sort of trauma or drugs involved in this 'research' are often marked for identification. The infinity symbol is one of the more common ones."

He scanned their faces again. The silence was punctuated only by the hum of traffic. "I'm just dying to know why you all look like you've heard this sort of stuff before."

Brian spoke up. "Let's just say we're familiar with people like Sidney Gottlieb and MK-ULTRA." He turned to Melissa. "We just can't seem to get away from Operation PAPERCLIP, can we?"

"Did you hear that, Graham?" Malone asked, turning in Neff's direction.

"I did," he answered. He put on his turn signal and turned into a dimly-lit parking area for what appeared to be some sort of sports complex.

"Why are we stopping?" Brian asked.

"It's time we had a heart-to-heart chat." Neff turned off the lights but let the car idle. "It's time to be honest."

"What do you mean?"

"He means you need to come clean," Malone said. "There's no way all of this is coincidental. We come to nowhere, North Dakota, to talk to some biblical scholar trying to hide his identity while putting conspiratorial UFO stuff on the Internet that we know isn't crazy. That guy turns out to be married to a woman who got hired with Neff's money at the college where he's a board member.

"Then we bring Dr. Harper and Dr. Bradley along to Father Benedict's funeral, and that same couple just happens to know them—which is really odd since none of us, Father Fitzgerald included, knew either Malcolm or Dee from Adam and Eve. They only appeared on the radar after Father Fitzgerald became concerned about Father Benedict—who the same North Dakota couple also turns out to know."

"And *now*," he continued, pointing at Brian, "a girl kills herself in public at the orders of some psychopath, and all four of you think it's the same guy—some *Colonel*. The four of you did more than meet this past summer. It took everything we could muster to get Malcolm and Dee out of wherever they were. I suspect that's the same place you two were."

"We *really* don't believe in coincidences," Neff added, smirking.

"I think you're making some assumptions there," Brian protested.

"Brian, forget it, man," Malcolm butted in. "They know. I slipped while we were waiting for Neff. I blew it."

Brian looked at him and sighed.

"We have some decisions to make," Neff went on, not waiting for more argument, "and they can't wait. As I see it, if the police solicit information from the public about what happened tonight, or if some do-good citizen tells them they saw either of you at the scene, and someone knows your names, you'd be lucky to last a week before this *Colonel* catches up to you. As it stands now, you have a small window of time to act. The fact that the guy didn't show up at the scene tells me he was content to let the police get the information he needed. Then he'd move in, assert federal authority, and have all the information necessary to find you himself. He didn't get that, but the net's getting smaller."

"How do we even know you're not part of all this, just settin' us up?" Dee shot back angrily.

"Come on, Dee," Malcolm groaned.

"Well how did he get out of there so fast? How did he pull that off? And we still don't know just how he pulled strings to get us out. Why? Because he won't tell us."

Neff closed his eyes and shook his head. "This needs to stop. I can see that this fellow has all of you on edge, but you've got to start thinking clearly—and trusting us. We'll tell you everything, but we can't get sidetracked now. As for tonight, we're trained for situations like this, and we rely on that training. As frightening as it all was, it wasn't difficult to navigate—at least to this point. But we're running out of time."

"Graham and I went into the café ahead of you for a reason," Malone explained. "Given what's happened over the last few days and all the odd convergences of the last few months, we felt that caution was justified. We checked out the building to see if it had security cameras, which it didn't. That was a plus since it would help prevent you from being identified if anything were to happen in there. We felt safe with the location, so we went in. After we were settled, I took a restroom break to confirm the place had a rear entrance."

"We're trained to sit separately so that we can always pretend we don't know each other if a scenario develops," Neff explained. "It's easier to reveal a relationship later than deny one. That came in handy tonight. We were able to assume control of the situation. We each have several aliases, complete with the best fake IDs that money can buy. We use them when they're needed."

"While you folks were talking," Malone continued, "we were busy checking out the area surrounding the building on our phones. We look for hotels, streets, hospitals, and other landmarks. We know how to use that information to manipulate circumstances or get out of situations like tonight."

"I'll ask it again," Melissa said in amazement, "who are you people?"

"You know who we are," Neff said. "This sort of thing needs to be second nature for what we do. The woman you saw at the border, Nili, is a former Mossad agent. She trains us, and she knows spycraft exceedingly well."

"So what did you text Neff to get him out of the building?" Malcolm asked.

"Malone sent me the location of the car, the nearest hospital, and the name of a hotel between the café and that hospital. They were all less than a half mile from each other. Once I got the message, I told the officer that I was a surgeon from the west coast who was in North Dakota to conduct a heart and lung transplant. I told him I'd just stepped out for some coffee while I waited for the call."

"And you told him the text message was the transplant alert," Malcolm reasoned.

"Precisely. I told the officer that I was staying at a hotel two blocks away and was on call at the hospital—it's a surgical center—on the other side of the hotel. Without that information, he'd be suspicious that an out-of-towner didn't have a car or would have offered me a ride to a place I had no intention of going. I gave him bogus contact information, then I jogged away in the correct direction—knowing Malone had stationed the car along that route. "

"Pretty impressive," Brian said.

"Was all that necessary?" Malcolm asked. "Police can't legally compel you to give them information as a witness. People walk away or clam up all the time in those situations."

"That's true, but once I inserted myself into the incident, I had to come up with something believable. If you all hadn't been directly involved, we'd have just walked out of the café and been done with it. I had to know what happened. It's a good thing I did. One of you probably would have felt obligated to give the police your contact information. I think it's pretty clear this *Colonel* would have gotten that information in short order and used it. He basically programmed this girl to kill herself in an attempt to find you."

"Did anyone else on the scene report that they saw what had happened?"

"I heard a few folks sharing what they saw. It's a clear suicide, and of course the ballistics will back that up, so I'm not worried about any of us being the subject of any manhunt. The law enforcement officials I know wouldn't bother with the time and effort it would take in an open and shut case. My concern is different, though."

"What's that?"

"Come tomorrow or Monday, your faces could be in the news. I assume the Colonel will read the papers and watch the news."

"I thought you said the café had no cameras?" Melissa said, alarmed at the possibility.

"It didn't, but there's always a chance that someone could have snapped a photo with their phone, or some camera outside on the street could have caught your image. And if that's the case, someone—maybe someone from your sleepy little town who came to Fargo tonight for Christmas shopping—might recognize either of you if the police ask the public for more information. There's no way to be sure that won't happen."

"And so," Neff continued, "we'd be very wise to be out of North Dakota in less than twenty-four hours. Our plane's here in Fargo. We can drive back to your place and collect some belongings—laptops, some books, clothing, whatever you can box in a few minutes. Then we need to get back here and take off."

"But I can't just leave the school hanging," Melissa protested, disconcerted. "I have responsibilities—and a job I need to keep."

"I'll tell President Fitzgerald what's going on. He'll want things to play out like you're on sabbatical—maybe you're spending time with family, or some such scenario. You'll be able to communicate with him securely through our methods. We'll do everything we can to keep the disruption minimal for the school, but I don't expect you'll ever be able to return. I'll let him know. He'll understand."

"Shouldn't we worry about airport security?" Brian asked.

"That won't be a problem."

"How's that?"

"We're our own security. One of the companies I own is a private flight security firm. It's fully registered with the FAA and TSA. We're the owners and credentialed experts. If we say you belong on our plane, you belong."

"You guys are unbelievable," Malcolm said, a smile finally breaking through.

"We put a lot of careful thought into all these kinds of things before we ever decided to devote ourselves to our cause," Malone informed them. "We spent a couple years laying the groundwork for what we do. But no amount of preparation is foolproof. Something unforeseen can always happen—like tonight. We need to leave."

"And leaving forces us to make a decision about where to take you," Neff said.

"Meaning?" asked Dee.

"We've never taken outsiders to our headquarters. We use safe houses for people we help. Those would only be adequate in the short term in this situation. My gut tells me we need something more secure."

"I'm not sure it's a good idea," Brian confessed. "You'd be putting yourself at a terrible risk."

"We take risks all the time."

"I think it's a safe conclusion that you've never run into anyone with the clout and resources of Colonel Ferguson. He's NSA and Above Top Secret."

"Hmpf," Malone grunted. "You get more interesting with every conversation."

"I'm not going to pretend to know this guy or how much of a threat he is," Neff said, "but we're still a step ahead of him. We'll put all our cards on the table. But we need you to promise that you'll tell us your real story. We need to know *exactly* what we're dealing with."

"We also need permission from home," Malone interjected.

"Permission?" Melissa asked.

"We don't make any decisions this big without unanimous consent from our whole team," Malone explained, pulling his phone from his coat pocket. "I'll call Miqlat," he said to Neff, who nodded. Malone turned back toward the front of the car to dial.

"So what's it going to be?" Neff asked. "Are we done playing charades?"

The four friends looked at each other.

"Dee and I don't have anywhere to go anyway," said Malcolm. "I just assumed you guys would put us somewhere at some point."

"We had plans for that, but taking you to our nerve center wasn't in the picture until now."

"Any place where the Colonel isn't is home enough for me," Dee deadpanned.

"We're in then," Malcolm continued. "But we can't very well give you the full picture without Brian and Melissa being on board."

"Understood. So what about you two?"

Brian looked at Melissa apprehensively. He didn't see a realistic alternative, but the thought of surrendering their carefully crafted world paralyzed him. He could tell she was struggling, too.

"I know this turns everything you've protected upside down," Neff admitted. "Your life here is a basically a wash. Whatever you had in the bank is essentially gone, too. We could move the money for you electronically, but if this Ferguson discovered your location, he'd trace the money trail, and that puts our money-laundering network at risk. I can't allow that."

Melissa's expression hardened. "It sounds irrational, but I just can't bear the thought of leaving everything behind again," she said, exasperated. "Although it's not like there's any real choice."

"We did it once, and we can do it again," Brian said.

"But we had something to start on. I at least had a job."

"I know," he said somberly.

"Listen to the two of you," Neff scolded. "You still can't trust anyone but the friends who lived your trauma with you. I can replace everything you'll leave behind, but you're blind to it. Is it too fantastic to believe that God would providentially have our paths converge and give us the resources to help you? Do you believe God has a purpose for your lives, or not?"

Brian and Melissa sat in stunned silence, the sting of the rebuke tempered only by the magnanimous gesture. Brian nodded, unable to speak. "Thank you," Melissa said haltingly. "If your team accepts us, we'll go."

Malone turned toward the back. "Let's get moving. Everyone gave it an instant thumbs-up on the other end, even Summit."

"What did Sabi say?" Neff asked as he put the car in drive.

"Nothing—just that 'God is up to something' laugh of his."

32

Justice is truth in action.

—*Benjamin Disraeli*

"Get any shut-eye on the plane, doc?"

Brian turned to look in the direction of the voice. He recognized its source from the skirmish at the Canadian border.

"Ward Bennett," the man said as he approached with a smile, extending a hand, his bright blue eyes concealed behind reflective sunglasses. The wool-lined collar of his leather jacket was pulled up to guard his face, but his cheeks were already turning pink. The early morning sun promised a beautiful day, but it did little to take the edge off the cold outside.

"A little," Brian said, shaking his hand, a bit surprised at the power in his grip. "But mostly I just got a headache. I'm not one for flying. And please, call me Brian. Thanks so much for your help."

Ward's trim, muscular build, sunglasses, and flight jacket fit what Brian recalled from Clarise's brief description of her husband's background weeks ago, all except for his role as the financial manager of Neff's enterprise and his jovial manner. He was no desk jockey.

"I've got some aspirin in the car. It's a pleasure to actually meet you, and you as well, Dr. Carter," Ward added, taking Melissa's hand as she emerged from the plane to help her down the short stepladder. "It's terrible what happened, but we're thrilled to have you."

"Thank you," she said with a heartfelt smile, adjusting her coat. "We're grateful. And please, call me Melissa."

"Have a seat inside the car; it's still warm," he said. "It's over there," he clarified, pointing to a hulking Ford Expedition about fifty yards away. "We'll be on our way in no time."

Brian watched Ward chat with Malcolm and Dee as he helped Melissa into the SUV. The pair joined them a moment later. Neff, Malone, and Ward retrieved two suitcases and four cardboard boxes from the plane parked inside the private hangar. Brian was reminded again of how little they'd been able to bring, but he felt blessed to be where he was.

"Thanks for the lift." Neff patted Ward on the shoulder as he took a seat behind him. "I know how you like to sleep in."

"Right," he laughed, starting the van. "This was the perfect chance to avoid Kamran's cooking. It's his turn this morning."

"That was quick thinking."

"It's a gift," he said, smiling wider. "Got you some coffee inside while I waited," he added, handing Neff a tall Styrofoam cup with a small plastic baggie containing several pills. "Take 'em now. Clarise will ask."

"Thanks," he replied.

"We'll try to be quiet on the way," Ward joked loudly, slapping Malone on the arm as he tried to find a position in the front passenger seat for a nap on the way.

"You do that," the stocky, older man grunted, closing his eyes and snuggling up against the door. "Somebody had to get us here."

"Took you long enough."

"Maybe if I'd had a better flight instructor."

Ward laughed again and pulled out.

"Actually," Neff said, turning toward their passengers, "this is a good time to explain the situation with Dr. Bradley and Dr. Harper. It'll help pass the time."

"How long of a drive do we have?" Brian asked.

"Several hours," he replied and took a sip of coffee. "We're out in the boondocks."

"By all means, then. I'm dying to hear about it."

"So are we," Dee reminded everyone.

"Well, the story actually starts months ago, near the beginning of last summer. One of our associates—his first name is Kamran—had struck up a friendship in an online astronomy forum with an astronomer whom we later discovered was a priest at Castel Gandolfo."

"The pope's summer home," Malcolm observed.

"Yes—also home to the Vatican Observatory. Have you all heard of that as well?"

"Yeah," Brian acknowledged. "Father Benedict told me about it once."

"I'm guessing the two of you talked a few times about your published article?"

"More than a few."

Neff nodded. "Kamran will have to relate the specifics, but he and one of the astronomer priests got involved in a discussion about astronomical religious symbolism. It's a favorite subject of Kamran's, one that none of us can really follow. He's very young—he just turned eighteen—but he's something of a prodigy."

"What was the priest's name?" Malcolm asked, looking at Brian.

"Why don't you ask it the way you mean to ask it," Brian said, anticipating the response. Neff looked puzzled.

"Yeah, might as well. Was the priest's name . . . Mantello?"

Neff's expression shifted to amazement. "How did you know that?"

"We were all with Father Benedict this summer, as you deduced, and that name came up. Andrew discovered that a friend of his had suddenly and suspiciously died. He told us the story and noted that he worked at Castel Gandolfo. I thought I'd take a shot at the name."

"Fascinating," Neff said thoughtfully. "Kamran never got the name of his friend directly. The two of them used aliases online. That's part of our security protocol. I'm not sure why Father Mantello chose to do it, though. Anyway, the two of them exchanged notes and image files regularly in a secured drop box that we use, but that all stopped without any notification. Kamran was mystified. Weeks went by. He eventually paid a visit to the observatory's website and found a press release about the death of Father Mantello. He had died the evening of what turned out to be the last communication between Kamran and his mystery colleague. The conclusion was evident."

"How did Kamran take the discovery?" Malcolm asked.

"He was terribly upset. When you meet him, you'll learn that Kamran can't actually speak, but he communicates well enough. We use sign language and texting with him. He, of course, hears just fine and has a good command of English."

"Why can't he speak?" asked Melissa.

"He has no tongue," Neff said. He couldn't completely hide his grim tone. "Kamran is an orphan. His father had been a Christian pastor in Afghanistan, but was murdered, along with his mother, by the Taliban. When Kamran refused to renounce his faith, they cut out his tongue."

"How awful."

"It was. I found him about six months after he was orphaned on a trip to Pakistan. From what I could learn, he'd been taken there by some relief workers after American soldiers had driven the Taliban out of his home region. That was about six years ago. When we met, he didn't know English, and I didn't know sign language, but I felt compelled to take him in. You'll find that everyone at Miqlat has a history. None of us has led an uncomplicated life. We all know tragedy, but that's part of what makes us a family."

"So how did that involve Malcolm and Dee?" Melissa asked.

"Kamran wasn't only emotionally stricken by what happened," Neff explained. "He'd found—and now lost—a mentor. Like I said, what Kamran is interested in is way over our heads. He felt lost without Father Mantello. Apparently he'd set Kamran on some kind of trail that he didn't feel competent to pursue without help. I'm still not sure why or what it was. One day Kamran was going through their old messages and came across Father Benedict's name. I had, of course, heard that name before from Father Fitzgerald. Kamran wanted to make contact, hoping Father Benedict would be able to help him in his research. I contacted Father Fitzgerald about making that happen—and that's really where things started to veer in the direction of you two," he noted, looking first at Dee, then Malcolm.

"You found out that Father Benedict was nowhere to be found," guessed Dee.

"Exactly. Father Fitzgerald and Father Benedict were, as we all know, fellow travelers. I'm not privy to all of what they did or got themselves into over the years, but I knew from experience they were both entirely trustworthy. I regularly give money to Father Fitzgerald, both for the college and for his own projects and the people they involve. Father Benedict was involved in several, but I just knew him by name and reputation."

"So what happened when you couldn't contact Andrew?" Brian asked.

"Father Fitzgerald told me it wasn't unusual—that Andrew would be incommunicado for weeks at a time. So I had to drop it and tell Kamran to be patient. Two months later Father Fitzgerald contacted me that he'd heard from Andrew, but the brief communication had him out of sorts."

"Why?"

"Andrew confessed that his present mission—he didn't say specifically what it was—had turned out to be far riskier than he'd anticipated. He mentioned you specifically, Dr. Bradley."

"What did he say?" Malcolm asked.

"He was worried about your future. He wondered if you were, to quote him, 'going to succeed.' "

"Do you know where that email came from?" Brian asked. He turned to Malcolm. "It's hard to believe that security would have ever let him send that from the base. The timeline feels like it would have come just before Andrew helped us escape."

"I know."

"It came from his office at the University of Arizona," Neff replied.

"Where he'd been teaching as an adjunct professor," Brian recalled.

"Right. What base were you at? And you say you *escaped*?"

"We were at a couple different locations," Malcolm answered. "We'll give you the whole story tonight—trust me, it'd be a distraction now. Brian and Melissa made it out, but Dee and I didn't."

"I suppose Andrew could have been allowed off the base," Brian reasoned. "He was part of the Group. He could have made it to his office."

"*The Group*?" asked Neff.

Malcolm shook his head.

"Okay, we'll save that for later," Neff sighed. "At any rate, Malcolm, neither of us presumed from the email that you were actually *with* Father Benedict. We assumed Andrew had sent you on some important errand. Father Fitzgerald had told me you were a priest and a scientist, and that you and Father Benedict had a history. We found your MIT email address in the Bcc: field of an email sent to Dr. Fitzgerald a year or so earlier."

"Aren't those invisible?" Dee asked.

"Not for someone who knows how to get into the stored information. Madison—the young woman you met briefly at the rescue—managed that pretty easily. She's in charge of all our IT systems and computer hardware. She's an experienced hacker."

"So when you tried to find Malcolm, what happened?" Melissa asked.

"We found out he was on a classified government project—and also that his initial commitment to that project had been unexpectedly extended."

"'Extended,'" Malcolm repeated, smirking. "That's a nice way of putting it."

"We pressed your department manager at MIT to contact you. We told her it was an emergency. She stonewalled for a week before admitting that the government agency claiming authority over you would be using your services indefinitely. That was just too suspicious for us."

"So how did you find me?"

"On the strength of Father Benedict's reputation, we decided to treat the situation as an involuntary detention. We brought Nili into the problem at that point. Her background, of course, means she has extensive contacts within Mossad. One of her family members works for Israel's version of the state department, and that person agreed to inquire about your whereabouts. After a week or so of persistence, that individual produced an interesting reply—that 'Dr. Bradley and his associate Dr. Harper were fine and hard at work.'"

"Why would they mention me?" Dee asked. "That's kind of odd."

"We thought so, too. People in that line of work are supposed to say nothing with as few words as possible. Our best guess is that it was an error—and a very providential one." He looked again at Malcolm. "We think whoever replied made the mistake of trying to make your situation sound normal by putting you with some company."

"What did Nili think?"

"She suggested right away that if we ever broke through to whoever was detaining you, we'd try to get Dr. Harper as well."

"But how in the world did you pull it off?" Brian marveled.

"We got Mossad and the Israeli government directly involved," Neff revealed. "We decided to make a trade, even though it made us feel a little exposed. It was the only way."

"What do you mean?" asked Malcolm.

"To make a pretty convoluted story brief, in exchange for the two of you being brought to Israel, I offered to put up some ransom money for some Israeli soldiers and share some cyber intelligence on Hamas that Madison has gathered in the course of our own work. We told them that we suspected certain elements within the US intelligence community were holding you against your will."

"I get the money and the intel angle," said Malcolm, "but why would Mossad play hero when they knew they'd piss off their US counterparts if they succeeded?"

"In a nutshell, it was about settling a score," Neff informed them. "Back in 2010, some people within US intelligence called Mossad our worst intelligence ally and accused the Israelis of stealing secrets. It really insulted them."

"Was it true?" Dee asked.

"Maybe—that's what intelligence communities do. But that didn't matter. It was the public nature of the accusation that irked them. Add a string of other insults Washington has tossed in their direction in recent years, like kissing up to the Muslim Brotherhood and warming to the Palestinian cause, and a little payback project like ours didn't need extraordinary persuasion."

"People are people," Malcolm mused.

"That they are—and it's a good thing. The Israelis were able to identify Dr. Harper, though we're not sure exactly how, and that helped them concoct a scenario that had the Israeli government requiring research services from both of you in Israel for a few weeks. It was all a ruse, of course, and the Israelis knew neither of you would be staying in the country. They didn't care if you went AWOL after work some afternoon."

"That's incredibly risky," Melissa interjected. "They had to know there'd be hell to pay if it worked."

"Of course. To protect themselves, the Israelis planned to apply some pressure on a few key senators if and when Malcolm and Dee went missing and whoever was holding you demanded action. Israeli intelligence has dirt on hundreds of members of Congress and other people in the DC establishment. Lord knows some of them make that sort of thing painfully easy when they travel overseas and otherwise behave corruptly. Presumably the Israelis carried through. Once we got you out of the country, we didn't care."

"Now, I have a question for our biblical scholar," Neff said, looking at Brian with a hint of mischief in his eye. "Did we do the right thing?"

Brian didn't hesitate. "I'd have done it. I can't say for sure Malcolm and Dee were in a life-threatening situation, but knowing their context, that's a distinct possibility. I don't believe for a minute Father Benedict wandered out into the desert on his own—and he was part of the whole situation involving Dee and Malcolm. They could have been next."

"Yes—we'll have to chat about poor Andrew later as well. I don't think his death was accidental either."

Brian and Melissa exchanged a pained glance. "But beyond that," Brian continued, "God uses you and your team to bless thousands. I wouldn't lose any sleep if God decided to use you as an instrument to punish wicked people now and then. They sow what they reap. 'Their sin will found them out,' to use the biblical phrase."

"Well said," Neff acknowledged. "It's clear you've thought about such things."

"We haven't had much choice," Brian replied with a sigh.

"We appreciate all the effort," Malcolm said gratefully, "and the risk."

"We certainly do," echoed Dee. "And if you ask me, we *were* going to be next. I think we all know by now that once the Colonel is finished with you, you're expendable."

Melissa unconsciously touched her mid-section.

"I don't know what they did to me," Dee added, discreetly avoiding eye contact with Melissa, "but it's a good bet that when it came time to get what they wanted, I'd have been an inconvenience that needed fixing."

33

Affliction is often that thing that prepares
an ordinary person for an extraordinary destiny.

—*C. S. Lewis*

"Man, this place is sure tucked away," Malcolm said through a yawn. He and some of the others had nodded off to sleep after their conversation. He checked his watch. It had been three hours since they'd left the airport hangar. His ear caught the faint sound of crunching ice and snow under the tires. He wasn't sure how long it had been, but they were no longer on paved road. Peering through the windshield, he could see they were navigating their way on a winding road through a heavily-forested enclave. The pathway was wide enough for two cars and packed solid from earlier snows and plowing.

"This is magnificent," Melissa said, admiring the thick tree lines, a mixture of bare but majestic timbers and rows of towering dark green pines glistening with snow. "I had no idea Montana was so beautiful."

"We love it," Neff said, opening his eyes and shielding them from the sun.

The car came to a slow halt. Melissa could see a metal gate blocking their way. She watched as Ward waved a card out the window in front of a small screen fixed to a metal pole. The gate swung open.

"That lets everyone know we've hit the property. Another minute or so till we're at the house. We have about 140 acres out here. It's remote, but that's what we want. We have a house in town near the airport that we sometimes use if we know we'll be doing a lot of flying. Otherwise we take a helicopter from home to the airport if we need to get there quickly. Honestly, though, I love the drive—at least when I'm awake for it."

"So what *do* you keep out here?" Melissa asked.

"Lots of things," he replied with a playful grin. "You'll see."

Melissa eyed him thoughtfully, but not with suspicion. "I take it that the name Miqlat stands for something. What does it mean?"

"It's Hebrew. It means 'haven' or 'refuge.' "

"Sounds perfect."

"Pretty close," he said, straightening himself in his seat. "I suspect you'll agree."

The van broke through the tree line. Melissa surveyed the stunning landscape that exploded into view. A large, picturesque log home was nestled on a wide, sloping hill in the direct center of a clearing. The clear-cut area surrounding the house sprawled about a hundred yards in all directions, ending at a densely-wooded forest. Melissa saw two helicopters off to one side of the house, about half the distance to the edge of the forest. Beyond them, situated within the tree line, was a building that had the appearance of an oversized garage. Despite being surrounded by the rising pines, the view was breathtaking, dominated as it was by the towering, snow-capped mountain range straight ahead from their vantage point.

The vehicle rolled to a stop in front of a wide, three-car garage door. "Rise and shine, everybody," Ward said. "Get the defibrillator for Malone."

"Someday you'll get that wish," Malone replied with a yawn.

Brian blinked out of his slumber and then raised his hand to shield his eyes from the sun's rays, which were streaking across the horizon, breathing life into the wintry panorama. He turned his head to get a look at their new home and stopped cold. Without a word he quickly unbuckled himself, opened the door, and got out. He stood for a moment gazing at the house and then started to run away from it, down the snow-covered path over which they'd just come.

"What the—what's up with him?" Malcolm exclaimed, turning to Melissa. Her own perplexed expression added to the confusion.

They exited the car as quickly as they could. Ward and Neff were already out, looking in Brian's direction, equally astonished. The small group watched as Brian stopped and turned in the direction of the house. He stood motionless for a minute and then dropped to his knees.

"Something's wrong!" Melissa urged. The four men in the company quickly ran out to Brian's location. They slowed their pace, taking note of his thunderstruck expression.

"What's up, man?" Malcolm asked as he knelt beside Brian, his hand on his shoulder. Brian turned, uncertain of how to answer.

"I don't know how," his voice trembled with astonishment, "but I know this place. . . . I've seen it before."

"That's not possible," Neff said. "We only finished building it three years ago. No one besides us has ever lived here. There was nothing here before."

"But . . . I've seen it before," Brian repeated, staggering to his feet. "The door opens to a foyer." He closed his eyes in concentration. "To the right there's a huge sunken den with a big stone fireplace. The wall of the foyer hides another open family room that adjoins to a kitchen, and the kitchen has a passageway that leads into a pantry that's really large."

"That's right," Neff confirmed slowly, looking at his companions, who were at a complete loss for words.

"I've seen this place . . . in some dreams," Brian continued, gesturing toward the log home. "I used to have this dream when I was a kid—I'd be in front of *this* house, right about at this distance. I'd walk up and go in, and I'd look around. Nothing spectacular. When I got older, I stopped having it—until a couple days after my parents were murdered."

The three men exchanged uneasy glances. "Brian's had some pretty severe personal tragedies," Malcolm offered.

Brian looked at Malcolm. "I've had the dream once more since then—last summer, after Neil was killed. I don't know what it means, but I *know* this house."

"Well," said Neff, giving no indication of skepticism, "maybe we'll learn something else inside. Let's go in."

Brian nodded, and the five of them walked back to the vehicle. Brian and Malcolm explained what had happened to Melissa and Dee before they retrieved their belongings and headed inside.

"You're probably surprised to see the place empty," Neff began after they'd set everything down on the floor and he'd locked the front door.

"Now that you mention it, yeah. Where is everybody?" Dee asked.

"The house is used quite a bit. We're up here a lot. There are five bedrooms, some large living spaces, a modern kitchen, three baths—all the sorts of things you'd expect."

"I sense a 'but' coming," Malcolm said, his hands on his hips.

"But," Neff continued, smiling, "it's really just a façade."

"What did you mean by 'up here'?" Melissa asked apprehensively.

Ward broke in. "Miqlat is underneath. Forty feet, to be exact."

"Are you telling me Miqlat is an underground bunker?" Melissa asked with a pained expression.

"It's much more than a bunker," Neff answered. "It spans almost six square acres. It has everything we need and want—accommodations, a research library, a theatre, an infirmary with two fully-functional emergency rooms, a chapel, an armory, a pistol range, exercise rooms, hot tubs, our own Internet servers and telecommunications. We even have vehicles stored underground. If we had a real chef, it would be a five-star hotel."

"But it's underground," Melissa said, more to herself than anyone else.

"Miqlat is completely self-sufficient," Ward added quickly. "Everything is powered through state of the art solar energy, with several layers of redundancy. It has its own heating, central air, plumbing, ventilation, water supply—you name it."

"The whole enterprise cost almost twenty-five million dollars," Neff noted. "We have two more like it under construction, one in Belize that's basically finished and another that just got underway in South Africa. They're both bigger than this one. The dollar goes a lot farther in those places."

"But it's *underground,*" Melissa repeated with a groan.

"Miqlat isn't a dungeon," Malone replied. "Honestly, you have to see it to believe it."

"I guess so," she sighed. "It's just that we've all had experience with living underground, most of which we'd like to forget."

Ward tried to diffuse the tension. "Trust me, you'll be impressed. It's not like you're moving into Area 51 or something." He chuckled at his own punchline, but their humorless, stony expressions stopped him cold.

"Can you believe that?" Dee cracked, looking at the others. "Hello, Dreamland. Is Adam home?"

"*Dee . . .*" Malcolm reproached, scowling.

"What did I say?" Ward asked, concerned.

"Forget it. No harm done," Brian replied.

"Well . . . sorry just the same," Ward said sincerely. "You all can spend as a much time as you want up here. We only insist that you never tell anyone what you're going to see underneath. This is ground zero for what we do, and no one can ever know it's here."

"No worries there," Brian assured him.

"Follow me." Neff led them through a hallway that ran behind the foyer wall. The floor plan conformed precisely to Brian's description, and in a few seconds they found themselves standing in the pantry, a room as large as a single-car garage.

"This is the only entrance into Miqlat from within the house," Neff informed them. "There are six tunnel passageways that lead from within Miqlat to the outside, all of them beyond the tree line except for the one that leads to the chopper shed. Each exit within the forest is camouflaged in some way and blocked by a door that requires biometric identification. Two of the passages are large enough for our ATVs. We have a small, off-site facility about a half mile from here at our private weapons range. You'll learn the locations of all the tunnels soon enough. The main entry from within here is voice activated. We say our first and last name, then give the password."

"Didn't you say Kamran couldn't speak?" Melissa recalled.

Neff laid his hand on a tool chest sitting atop the bench next to where he was standing. "We have a backup biometric passkey. That's what Kamran uses. This toolbox has a false bottom. Once you remove that, you'll find a metal slide that will expose a small screen. You have to press your thumb to that screen and hold it for a few seconds. The system will recognize any of our thumbprints. Yours will be added once you're settled in. Remember to replace the slide and the false bottom if you use the biometric.

"Once the system accepts your voice activation or thumbprint, the entire floor of this room will descend—it's actually a freight elevator made to look like a large pantry. All the cabinetry lining the walls and this bench are bolted to the floor, which drops about forty feet to a concrete landing that leads to a door. Miqlat is on the other side."

Neff paused and took out his phone.

"What's up?" asked Malone. "They know we're in the pantry."

"Cameras?" Brian asked.

"Not inside the house, just outside. Motion detectors, too. When anybody gets near the tree line we have visual alarms in various places on the inside that let us know someone is on site."

"Sabi asked me to call when we were ready to come down," Neff explained, answering Malone's question. "I'm not sure why." Neff hit the speed dial button and waited. It rang once.

"Graham!" a cheerful male voice sounded from the phone, "so *wonderful* that you are finally here!" Brian took note of the heavy eastern European accent and its enthusiastic tone. "We are so eager to meet our guests. Everyone is greatly excited!"

Neff smiled, his affection for the man on the other side transparent. "We are, too. Why did you want me to call first?"

"This is a special day," Sabi explained with a deliberate cadence, his earnestness evident, "a very special day for all of us—especially one."

Neff's brow wrinkled. He glanced at Malone and then Ward, who shrugged. "What do you mean?"

"Today we are all reminded that there is a God in heaven who guides our lives, never forgets us, and loves us deeply. But one of your number needs this fixed in his heart more firmly, needs to feel it in a powerful, personal way—and so it will be, this day. Professor Scott, what is the password, please?"

All eyes immediately turned to Brian. Melissa felt a spasm of panic as she caught sight of his startled expression. She gave Neff a quick glance, but saw instantly that he, along with the others, was dumbstruck. She turned back to Brian, whose head was bowed, either in defeat or a silent prayer, she couldn't tell.

"Just a moment, Sabi," Neff said calmly into the phone, watching Brian, the anticipating building. "He's thinking."

"No. He is *not* thinking," the voice replied. "He is *believing*. Professor Scott knew the password the moment I asked. The Most High gave it to him years ago. We used the voice recordings of your meetings with him to add his voice to the system."

"But—"

"He's right," Brian interrupted softly and looked up. He turned to Melissa and took her hand, squeezing it tightly, choking back the emotion. "He's right." His chin quivered. "I know it."

The room fell silent. Brian looked at their amazed faces, then around the room, and finally upward toward the ceiling. He cleared his throat. "Brian Scott," he said firmly, "*I am my brother's keeper.*"

A low hum instantly vibrated through the room, and the floor began its descent. Melissa looked up into Brian's face and saw his eyes welling up with tears. Out of the corner of her eye she saw Ward silently mouth an incredulous, "*How did Sabi know?*" Neff shook his head, his lip slightly upturned in a barely discernible smile.

"Welcome home, Dr. Scott," Sabi's reassuring voice reverberated from Neff's phone. "Welcome home."

34

Length of days with an evil heart is only length of misery.

—*C. S. Lewis*

"Any progress today, detective?"

The man at the desk turned from his computer screen toward the voice. Two men stood before him. One was FBI, the same suit he'd debriefed yesterday. He looked past the federal ID that was thrust unnecessarily at his face.

The question had come from the second man, who'd extended neither hand nor identification. He stood stiffly erect, hands clasped behind his back. Tiny bristles of close-cropped, blond-white hair were faintly visible on the thin line of skin between his ear and the rim of his cap. His two piercing eyes of topaz blue gazed from under the cap's brim. His square jawline, rigid yet elegant, was held perfectly motionless. Lines of colored ribbons, indecipherable to the civilian eye, decorated the left breast of the navy blue Air Force uniform just under the familiar wing lapel pin. The blue tie was perfectly straight. The creases in the pants looked sharp enough to draw blood. By both age and demeanor, he was obviously in charge and accustomed to the status. There was only one reason the soldier would opt for dress blues instead of the daily fatigues: Intimidation.

The detective's blood rose. "Who the hell are you?"

"Colonel Vernon Ferguson," he said calmly, offering no gesture of goodwill, much less camaraderie. "My associate tells me that when he phoned you this morning, you let on that you'd come across an important piece of evidence, but you weren't predisposed to share that. I thought I'd pay a visit and ask if there was a problem. Is there?"

The detective stared at him coldly. "Yeah," he said defiantly, "there is."

"Please enlighten me."

"I know how you guys work. The feds want to avoid responsibility for this girl being out on the street. I've played the game before—you come in, take jurisdiction, screw up, and then blame the locals. It ain't happenin' this time."

"Did my associate say something to give you that impression?" the Colonel asked, turning toward the agent, who remained silent and avoided the officer's gaze. The detective took note of the body language.

"Well, no—not exactly. I don't need it."

"Then what exactly leads you to distrust our intentions?"

"Experience."

"Yes, you did say 'this time.' I presume that unfortunate incident involving two men from the 119th is what's going through your mind. What was it, seven years ago? It's too bad that cost you a promotion."

"Forget the spy game, Colonel. I know that one, too—and it's all the proof I need to justify not trusting any of you. You'll get what I have when I get some official assurance that you boys are going to own your own decision this time. You're the ones who let that girl out on the street, nobody else."

"Quite right, detective. I believe we can come to an agreement."

"You apparently didn't hear me."

"Oh, but I did—it's you who hasn't heard me." The Colonel turned to the FBI agent. "Could you excuse us for a moment?"

"Of course." He turned and left the detective's office. The two remaining men watched him close the door. Another detective in the outer office glanced curiously through the blinds but quickly returned to his own desk work.

"We can do this one of two ways," the Colonel said confidently, reaching into his lapel pocket. He removed two pieces of paper and proceeded to unfold one of them and spread it on the detective's desk. It was a type-written letter on the Colonel's personal stationery.

"I've taken a recent interest in your career, detective. This is a letter of commendation from me on your behalf," the Colonel explained. "You'll notice in the second paragraph that the occasion of the commendation is a reassessment of the incident that has stymied your journey up the law enforcement ladder in this charming piece of tundra. The reassessment in turn was occasioned by a new piece of evidence—a participant in the . . . altercation . . . has changed his story."

The detective eyed the officer suspiciously but picked up the letter. He read it quickly, confirming the content.

"Those guys were in lockstep against my version of events—the real version. They were buddies. There's no way either of them would flip on the other."

"Buddies die, detective. Sadly, one of the men in question was killed in action in Afghanistan a few weeks ago. The other wants out of the hellhole—and his change of heart prompting this letter is his ticket. I spoke to him myself earlier this morning. Now, I can sign this for you, or I can pursue a different path."

The Colonel unfolded the second piece of paper. "I believe you've seen a cellphone record before," he said, sliding it toward him. "The first highlighted number is yours," he said, pointing with his finger. "The second is that of a very attractive woman who lives here in town who isn't your wife."

"*How the hell*—" The detective stood up, seething.

"Oh, come now," the Colonel cut him off, pulling back the second document. "You can't possibly be surprised, given what you know about federal information gathering—and that would be the tip of the iceberg, truth be told. This is trivial. And let's not hear any nonsense about needing a warrant. You know as well as I do that this isn't a legal matter, and that I could concoct one if such a need arose."

The detective sat down slowly and took a deep breath.

"Now, what's it going to be? Do you want a promotion or a tawdry divorce? I'm ready to sign that letter and leave it with you—in exchange for what you've got, of course. Or I can leave now and call a reporter."

The beaten man sighed, then pulled open a filing drawer. He flipped quickly through the row of folders, opened one, and pulled out a sheet of paper. "Here."

The Colonel took the page and looked at it carefully. "A bit grainy—reminds me of one of those silly UFO pictures we get asked about," he smirked.

"Camera phone images are rarely crisp," the detective replied, "especially when enlarged. You can clearly see the victim with the gun to her own head and make out some other faces."

"Yes," the Colonel agreed in a low voice. "This does appear quite useful. Do you have any information on any of these people?"

"Yeah, we do."

35

All changes, even the most longed for, have their melancholy;
for what we leave behind us is a part of ourselves;
we must die to one life before we can enter another.

—*Anatole France*

"Don't try to step off until you hear the hum stop," Malone warned, moving carefully toward the area of the descending platform that had been blocked by the back wall of the pantry. The entire elevator was rimmed with the cabinetry, which—bolted as it was to the floor—formed a haphazard, oak-paneled guardrail. The descent was surprisingly fast given the lack of a completely enclosed foot space. The half-wall perimeter had been designed as an ingenious camouflage that took precedence over safety. "When the hum stops, we're on the bottom."

The elevator shaft had been dimly lit by the ambient light emanating from the house above. Brian noticed that as soon as the blackness seemed to engulf them, the soft glow of a different light source from below reached their position. A few more seconds elapsed, and an open space underneath the elevator became faintly visible. Near the bottom, Brian was able to discern that the area was about the width of a driveway for a two-car garage. They felt a light touchdown, synchronized with the cessation of the hum.

Malone took a step off and extended a hand first to Melissa, and then to Dee. "It's only a couple inches, but trust me, you can still stumble off the thing." The others followed.

Neff lingered a moment. "Hit this light switch to send the lift back up," he explained, demonstrating from inside the faux pantry room. "The switch won't do anything upstairs; it only works when the unit is in this position." He flipped the switch and quickly stepped off. The elevator began its ascent. "We can call it back down from inside Miqlat."

The area was illuminated by a series of unstylish floodlights on the walls. A short distance from where they stood was a solitary door of burnished metal, embedded into the frozen, rocky earth. To Brian, it gave every impression of impregnable design, something akin to the door of a bank vault, though much plainer.

"Opening the door requires your thumbprint," Ward said as they approached, pointing to the small screen affixed to where one would expect a knob.

"We're all familiar with those," Dee said matter-of-factly.

"There's a manual lever a few feet to the right as backup, but it's held into its current position by an old-fashioned combination lock. We'll, of course, make sure you memorize that."

"The biometrics aren't new, but *that's* different," Malcolm said, grinning and pointing to their feet. A small rectangular doormat greeted them with the message, *There's no place like 127.0.0.1.* "I don't know what it means, but I'm sure there's some fun behind it."

"That was Summit's idea," Neff explained, chuckling. "She's—well—unique, as you'll all find out. 127.0.0.1 is what's known as a loopback address—it's the address of the local host for a website."

"It's how geeks say 'home,' " Malcolm laughed. "I love it."

"Exactly."

Neff moved to press his thumb onto the reader but stopped. He looked at Brian. "I should tell you that you're something of a celebrity here," he said with a humored air. Brian looked at him skeptically. "I'm just saying. And what happened upstairs is bound to add fuel to the fire."

Neff pressed his thumb to the reader. A loud click echoed through the small subterranean chamber; the door popped ajar. "Please," Neff said pleasantly to Brian, gesturing toward the entrance. Brian took Melissa's hand. Her face was still lightly etched with apprehension.

"Anywhere with you is the right place to be," he told her softly.

She looked up at him appreciatively. "I'll be fine."

Brian led the others through the doorway. The contrast to the dark, bleak underground scenery they'd left on the other side was overwhelming. He heard Dee gasp behind him. He turned toward Malcolm, whose brilliant, toothy grin captured his own feelings perfectly. Melissa stood speechless, her hand on her chest, eyes wide at the unexpected sumptuousness before her.

The entrance opened into a round, spectacularly spacious living area. Brian estimated that the area had to be at least a hundred feet round. A high, domed cathedral ceiling composed entirely of oak was sectioned off by dark, sturdy beams. Lights at regular intervals gave the entire circumference a warm, understated, radiant glow. Directly across the expanse was an enormous fireplace, its tall, wooden-overlaid column extended from a gray base of variegated stone. It was currently decorated with an enormous Christmas wreath.

Brian's eyes drifted downward to where they stood. The circular space had an outer perimeter of deep brown hardwood flooring. Various points of exit and entry dotted the pathway, each open lintel decorated for Christmas. A full quarter of the wall space to their right was taken up by a modern, exquisitely equipped kitchen.

The lion's share of the living space was taken up by a sunken inner circle, accessed by several ramps and short stairways. Portions of the inner space were carpeted and furnished with luxuriant leather sectionals. Brian could see a large viewing screen on one wall, which an array of reclining theatre seats and loungers faced. A popcorn machine was positioned against the wall adjacent to the screen. At the very center was a rustic, U-shaped oak table. Its two protruding limbs were disproportionately long, giving it the appearance of a massive wooden tuning fork. A small welcoming committee stood inside the inner depression at the end of a wide ramp that sloped downward from where the visitors stood.

"Didn't I tell you that you just had to see it?" Malone said, reading their stunned expressions, his thick mustache obscuring a satisfied grin.

A beaming, strawberry-blonde girl in skinny jeans and a simple red-and-navy checked shirt clapped. It took a few seconds for Brian to recognize her without her fatigues, pulled-back hair, and automatic rifle. "Safe and sound!" Madison whooped as she ran up the ramp. She embraced Ward tightly, then Malone and Neff. The others followed behind.

Clarise's familiar face, framed by her mass of long brown curls, was the first to greet Brian. "Welcome to Miqlat," she said as she reached out to hug him, holding the embrace longer than he expected. She repeated the gesture to Melissa. Others in the group were likewise welcoming Malcolm and Dee, along with their colleagues.

"This is our little ritual," Clarise explained, releasing Melissa. "We see so much evil—so much of what's wrong with the world—that we make it a point to always let everyone who enters Miqlat know that they're wanted and secure. It may seem a little odd, but it keeps us close. We're the only family each of us has."

"Not odd at all," Brian said softly. "We know just what you mean."

"Good," she laughed, "because the more people we get down here, the longer it takes!"

The greetings continued, the murmur of enthusiastic, friendly voices reverberating through the domed chamber. Suddenly, a shout of joy pierced the air. Heads turned toward three people emerging from an opening next to the kitchen. Brian recognized one as Nili, her shoulder-length jet-black hair parted in the middle, resting atop a simple white collared shirt tucked into her jeans. The girl next to her was much younger, an expressionless teenager with long, tussled pink hair, wearing a pair of oversize square black glasses. She was holding a cat. Between them sat a thin, bearded man with dark brown, shoulder-length hair in a wheelchair, who was beaming from ear-to-ear. He raised his arms a few inches and shouted again. Nili smiled down at him and pushed him forward toward the group.

Neff broke through the mix and stood next to Brian and Melissa. "That's Sabi," he said, smiling toward the approaching wheelchair, "but I'm sure you guessed as much."

"We did," he replied.

"While it's true that my money is behind all this," Neff continued seriously, "if we have a leader, it's Sabi."

They looked at him, unable to conceal their surprise.

"Don't be fooled by his appearance. Sabi is special."

"How?" asked Melissa.

"Well . . . there's really no other way to say it, even though it's so cliché—and there's no awkward pun intended. Sabi walks with God. It's as simple as that. We do nothing without his blessing."

Brian watched as Nili stopped a few feet away. With what seemed considerable effort, the impaired man slowly lifted his right arm from his lap to the rail grip of his wheelchair, then slid his hand toward a protruding knob. At his touch the chair moved the rest of the distance toward where they stood.

"Professor Scott," Sabi greeted him in his now familiar accent, "what a pleasure to meet you face-to-face. I cannot stand to embrace you and your lovely wife," he apologized, still smiling broadly, "but would you do me the honor?"

"Absolutely," Brian said with a smile, bending over and hugging his frail shoulders lightly but firmly. Melissa did the same.

"I really have to know how you knew I'd be able to give the password," Brian said.

"The Lord tells me such things," Sabi said sincerely with a broad smile, "when I need to know."

Brian didn't know what to say.

"You must learn not to doubt," Sabi warned good-naturedly. "We have much to talk about and much time to share our stories. God will show us what he is doing. But now there are others who have waited much too long to meet you." Sabi turned his head to make sure the pathway was clear and backed up his wheelchair.

Nili took a few steps forward. To Brian's surprise, she was crying. Tears flowed from her soft brown eyes over the perfect olive skin of her cheeks.

"I'm sorry," she managed, trying to smile. She stepped forward and embraced him tightly around the chest, then pulled back slightly and looked at Melissa. "May I?" Melissa nodded, unsure to what she was agreeing.

Nili took Brian by the shoulders, raised herself on tiptoes, and kissed him lightly on the cheek. "Thank you so much," she said, releasing him, still weeping. "I will try to explain later. I'm sorry for crying like this," she added, wiping her cheeks.

"I look forward to hearing your explanation," he answered, hoping he wasn't blushing. "No need to apologize."

"Summit, would you like say hello to our guests?" Nili asked.

The pink-haired girl came closer and stopped a few feet away. She looked carefully at Brian and Melissa, studying their faces. "This is Squish," she said, looking down at the Siamese cat in her arms. "Do you like him?"

"Of course," said Melissa warmly. "May I pet him?"

"You can try."

Melissa reached out to the cat and stroked it on the head. It was alarmingly thin. Had it not been for the alertness in its eyes, she would have wondered if it was malnourished. Squish pressed up against Melissa's fingers, revealing a slightly crooked jaw. He began to purr loudly.

"Do you like Squish?" Summit asked dispassionately, having turned her attention to Brian. She watched him intently through her exaggerated eyewear. Brian noticed for the first time that the frames had no lenses.

"I do." He carefully scratched the feline behind one of its ears. The cat closed its eyes, enjoying the attention.

"Thanks for coming here."

With that, Summit turned and walked away down into the sunken den with Nili. Brian and Melissa looked at each other, then at Neff and Sabi. Brian caught a glimpse of Clarise approaching out of the corner of his eye.

"Well, it looks like you both passed the Squish test," Clarise said, rejoining the group.

"Are you sure?" Brian asked. "She left pretty abruptly."

"That's normal," she assured them. "We're not sure if Summit is autistic or if she has Asperger syndrome. It's one or the other. I'm her doctor now, but those conditions are a bit outside my expertise, so I've had to educate myself about them the best I can. In either case, social skills are a real challenge. We don't insist that Summit show affection, but we make sure to let her know how we feel about her. If Squish takes to you, you're accepted."

"Does Summit need any special care?" Brian asked.

Clarise shook her head. "Just patience. She's pretty high functioning other than the social issues. I'm guessing you won't be amazed when I tell you she's very eccentric."

"No kidding," they acknowledged simultaneously through a smile.

"Summit has been at Miqlat almost from the beginning, about three years. She's Nili's cousin. Nili is the closest relation that would take her after her parents were killed in a bus bombing in Jerusalem."

"The poor thing," Melissa said sympathetically, her expression turned to distress.

"Summit has suffered much," Sabi added. He'd been listening from his wheelchair. "The scars on her heart are deep, but she has a loving home now, as do we all. God gave her to us and us to her."

"Summit has a special talent," Clarise explained. "It's a unique gift. Apparently she's had it since early in childhood. She's sixteen now, though her maturity level is a few years behind that. I should warn you—she has absolutely no filter."

"What's her gift?" Brian asked, his curiosity piqued.

Clarise grinned. "I'll let you both discover that for yourselves. All I'll tell you now is that she's our librarian. I'm guessing you'll be spending time in the library pretty soon."

"Excuse us," came Malone's familiar voice from behind. Brian and Melissa turned in its direction. "This is Fern, my far better half," Malone said cheerfully.

Fern Malone was a few inches shorter than her husband, who stood a couple of inches under six feet. Her grayish blonde hair was cut precisely to chin length and perfectly styled. Brian and Melissa guessed she was in her early sixties, like Malone. Her slender figure and seasoned face gave the impression of formidable elegance, but her smile erased any pretense.

"Welcome to our home," she said eagerly and gave each of them a brief, friendly embrace. "I'm sorry it took so long to get over here. Dougie had to drag me away from Dr. Harper. She and I have a lot to talk about given the awful incident at the café. I'm so sorry you both had to see something like that. It's terrible."

"It was," Melissa acknowledged with a sigh. "It still makes me shudder a little."

"Well, if you need to talk about it, don't hesitate. I know you have your friend and, of course your husband, but I've dealt with a lot of people who've been traumatized—far too many, truth be told—and with dozens of victims like Becky, though the ones that awaken to what's been done to them prefer the term 'survivors.' I have a good set of ears," she went on, smiling again and giving Melissa's hand a little squeeze.

Fern turned to Brian. "We'll chat after we have lunch," she said, patting his arm.

"I'm sure you want to have a look around and get settled in."

"Thanks," Brian replied appreciatively.

Neff's phone suddenly beeped. He retrieved it from his shirt pocket and looked at it. "Kamran says it's his turn to meet them." He looked up and saw the teenager watching him a short distance away. Neff waved him over. "Kamran can hear just fine," Neff reminded them. "And he's quite talkative, even for someone who can't speak."

The dark-skinned young man smiled enthusiastically at them, shaking hands with both of them and then embracing them. He was a few inches shorter than Neff, with black hair and a brilliant white smile, accented by a stubbly goatee. He turned to Neff and signed a question.

"We've all learned sign language fairly well for Kamran," Neff explained. "We thought it was a wise skill for everyone to acquire in case there's no digital means of communication. We occasionally have to maintain device silence on missions. Kamran wants to know if Brian has ever studied the biblical magi."

"A little bit," Brian answered.

Kamran quickly signed to Neff again.

"How about Psalm 19?" Neff translated.

"I'm more up to speed, there," Brian replied. "I wrote a paper on it in graduate school for a textual criticism class. Can you tell me where it's quoted in the New Testament?"

Kamran smiled knowingly. This time he texted his answer to Neff.

"Romans 10:18?" Neff offered.

"Correct. It says, 'their voice'—the voice of the stars, in context—'has gone out to all the earth, and their words to the ends of the world.' It's fascinating because it clearly uses the language of communication for the stars. The quotation is Paul's answer to the question of whether all people had heard the good news about the coming of the Messiah."

"Really?" said Neff. "I don't recall seeing that. How could I have missed that?"

Brian explained, "Paul is quoting the Septuagint there—the Greek translation of the Old Testament." He glanced at Kamran. "The Hebrew text has a different wording."

Kamran signed quickly to Neff, who appeared confused. Kamran repeated the signs.

"He just said 'their line,'" Neff offered. "Does that mean anything? I'm sure I have it right, but I don't get it."

"He's right, and it certainly does," Brian replied, his interest rising. "That's the Hebrew reading in the Masoretic Text. Most scholars think that refers to the horizon."

Kamran shook his head emphatically and, in seconds, texted another reply to Neff.

"He says it refers to the line of the ecliptic, the path of the zodiac," Neff said, raising his eyebrows.

Brian stood silently, pondering the interpretation. Kamran seized the lull in the exchange and feverishly went to work on his phone. After nearly a minute of typing, he sent it on its way and looked at Neff eagerly.

"Whoa, this is new," Neff said with some uncertainty and looked at Kamran.

"What is it?" Brian asked.

"Well, first he wants to know if *you* know that the Gospel of Matthew never quotes Numbers 24:17, the prophecy about a star coming out of Jacob, when describing what the magi saw."

Brian hesitated. The young man's questions had more than confirmed Neff's earlier description. This was no casual interest, and Kamran was no casual student. "Yes, that's true. . . . Matthew never cited that passage—even though you'd think it would have been obvious for him to do so in that episode. What else?"

Neff pursed his lips and glanced at Kamran. "For real?" he asked.

Kamran nodded.

"Okay, then. He wants to know if you understand the ramifications of all this, especially—how it might relate to what you've been posting online."

36

Whatever our souls are made of, his and mine are the same.

—*Emily Brontë*

"I don't know about you, but I'm exhausted," Melissa groaned, stretching out on the couch and placing her bare feet on Brian's lap. She adjusted the pillow under her head and closed her eyes.

"Me, too," he agreed, kicking off his shoes. "The trip's really hitting me now that I've had something to eat." He began to massage her feet.

"Oh, that feels wonderful . . ."

"The doctor told you to expect the swelling. You should stay off your feet as much as possible."

"That's kind of hard when you're running for your life—and the extra half ton I'm carrying doesn't help."

"Oh, stop it," he scolded with a grin. "You'll get more pampering now. I'm up for it."

She sighed and closed her eyes. "That was the plan, anyway—curl up by the fire and relax. I miss our house," she added wistfully.

"Well, this isn't bad, and the shared space out there is nothing short of spectacular."

"I agree. As far as underground bunkers go, the place is pretty nice. What did they call our little subterranean bungalow again?"

"Our living pod," he reminded her.

"How quaint." She opened her eyes.

The two of them looked around at what would be their home for the foreseeable future. The space, they had been told, was forty feet long and twenty feet wide. It had the look of a moderately-sized modular home. The entrance opened into a small living area, roughly fifty percent of the pod's length, complete with a sofa, an under-sized desk, flat-screen television, a recliner, and a small ottoman. A queen-size bed and full bathroom consumed the other half-length. The bedroom and bathroom took up about two-thirds of the width, allowing for foot traffic between the two halves. The wall space running parallel to the bedroom served as closet space, though it could be converted to bunk beds.

"It serves the purpose," Brian replied. "Like Fern said, it's just for sleeping. Everything we could want is somewhere else at Miqlat."

"I guess so," she acknowledged and closed her eyes again.

"We have a few hours before the big get-to-know-each-other pow-wow tonight," he yawned. "We can grab some sleep and then decide if we're going to tell all."

Melissa carefully opened one eye. She started to smile but bit her lip lightly to hide the expression. "So what's keeping you?"

"That ought to be obvious. You're on my bed."

"Change of plans."

"And just what does that mean?"

"You're taking a nap in the bedroom with me."

Brian stopped massaging her feet. He looked at her uncertainly.

"It'll be romantic—at least for the few minutes I'll be awake."

He started to reply but stopped, unsure of every word floating through his mind.

She started to laugh. "If you could just see the look on your face."

"No doubt," he managed to say with a nervous grin.

"Help me sit up."

Brian took her hands and pulled gently. Melissa sat up and then pivoted on the couch, laying her head in his lap. He looked down at her face, studying it again as he had hundreds of times before. His eyes surveyed every elegant contour, from the understated widow's peak in her thick, reddish-auburn hair, her electric green eyes, her soft cheekbones, the curves of her natural red lips, and the delicately blunted tip of her chin. He stroked her hair slowly, running it through his fingers, but said nothing.

"What are you thinking?" she asked, enjoying his touch.

He waited for a moment. "I'm wishing I had something more magical to say right now than 'you're beautiful.' It's inadequate, but safe. At least I can't mess it up."

"You're sweet." She smiled sincerely. "I know this is all new to you. Just relax. You don't need to be afraid of saying or doing the wrong thing. I know who you are."

"I don't want to irritate you."

"You won't—and so what if you do? I'm not going anywhere."

"Neither am I."

"I know. I'm glad."

"I just wish I felt like I knew what to do. I want to be sure I'm giving you what you need."

"Stop worrying about making mistakes. You've already given me what I need the most."

"What's that?"

"Forgiveness—back at the base. Loyalty, honesty, emotional security—all the things that were taken from me years ago. You give me a reason to believe in the things I used to believe in, rather than hating all of it. It sounds like a cliché, but you make me happy. You gave me my life back—literally, and in all those other ways."

"Best thing I ever did," he whispered.

"I believe you. But do you believe I'd do the same?"

He looked into her eyes, again unsure of what to say. The thought of such a sacrifice pierced him with guilt.

"You're the only person I'd risk myself for," she said softly. "You need to believe it. Do you *trust me*?"

"I don't even want to think about that. If something happened to you, it would crush me."

"Answer the question," she pressed gently, looking up into his eyes. "You and I have the same needs, but the reasons are different. You're my answer—and I want to be yours. Trust is hard for you, like it was for me." She paused, then asked again, "Do you trust me?"

Brian swallowed hard. "I do." He paused briefly. "I know you're telling me the truth."

Melissa smiled and stroked his arm, never breaking her gaze. "I'm yours. I can help you with your confidence, but I can't make you believe."

"I do."

"Good. So, is there anything else you'd like to communicate?" she asked mischievously, eyeing his expression.

"Hmm . . ."

"I can think of a thing or two," she interrupted, "but I like getting inside your head too much to volunteer."

"I've noticed," he replied.

"Well?"

"I look at you a lot," he said in an almost contrite tone that caught her ear, "especially when you don't know it."

"You don't need to be sneaky about it."

"Good to know, since it's a habit I can't break. I watch you all the time—when you're grading stuff at home, when you're thinking, even when you fall asleep reading. It's like I'm hypnotized when you're in the room."

"Tell me more," she prompted, grinning. "It does me good. I feel a lot of things these days, but attractive isn't one of them. *Rotund* is more like it."

"You're so wrong," he insisted, chuckling. "You're so stunning I can't remember what I just had for lunch."

"You didn't have anything. I ate yours."

Brian laughed heartily.

"Really," Melissa followed, enjoying his delight, "I'm flattered, especially with all the Bond girls running around down here."

"I hadn't noticed."

"You're a terrible liar."

"You have no competition—here or anywhere else."

"Show me," she said in a hushed tone, reaching for his neck.

He embraced her and pulled her close, but hesitated.

"The phone's not going to save you this time," she whispered beguilingly, their lips nearly touching. She pulled him in, her arms wrapped around his neck, and kissed him passionately. He gave in immediately. The two of them caught their breath for an instant and kept going, pressing against each other, mouth to mouth, locked in a heated embrace. He ran his hand down her side, feeling the curve of her hip. She relaxed and pulled back gently, looking into his eyes.

"More?" she teased breathlessly.

"What do you think? I didn't learn how to lie in the last few seconds."

Melissa tilted her head back and laughed. "I love it."

"But yeah, we need to cool it. It would change everything in all the wrong ways."

"That it would," she whispered. "This needs to be different. I want a clean break from my past."

"It will be."

"But it does seem obvious that Mr. and Mrs. Carter should get married," she smiled playfully. "I know a priest in the next pod who could do the job."

He grinned. "We'll add that to what we need to talk about before the meeting."

"Sounds like a plan," she agreed, and gave him a quick kiss. "Come on, we can catch a couple hours of sleep and then make some decisions."

"I might need some adult supervision," Brian added, smirking.

"I can manage that."

37

I love power. But it is as an artist that I love it. I love it as a musician loves his violin, to draw out its sounds and chords and harmonies.

—*Napoleon Bonaparte*

Father Fitzgerald opened the door to his study. Guided by the light from the hallway, he walked inside to his desk and turned on the small desk lamp. He sat down and turned on his computer. As he waited quietly for it to boot up, his troubled mind went over the unexpected events of the past forty-eight hours.

The news from Graham had shaken him, but he felt assured that the two charges Father Benedict had entrusted to him were by now somewhere safe. The problem of how to explain Dr. Carter's sudden absence was now compounded by the morning's visit from the FBI. He had had no idea of her whereabouts to begin with, but the visit would no doubt leak out, as would the picture the agents had shown him of his suddenly unavailable faculty member at the scene of a terrible, dramatic suicide. He needed to clear his head.

"Oh, Andrew," he sighed aloud, "what would you do if you were here?"

"What indeed?" a voice floated out of the darkness from the far corner of the office.

The space was large, as it housed the priest's considerable personal library. His heart pounded. He carefully slid open a desk drawer as he squinted at a faintly discernible form that was moving toward him.

"Who in God's name are you? And what right do you have breaking into my office?" he demanded.

He carefully brought both hands into view, but left the drawer open. He relaxed a bit when he saw his visitor was in military uniform, but he took note of an odd detail: He was wearing his white dress gloves.

"First," came the reply, "let me assure you that I'm not here in the name of your God or anyone else's."

The figure now stood in full view, facing the anxious, angry priest.

"Who are you?"

"I'm Colonel Vernon Ferguson, your nine o'clock appointment for tomorrow morning. I'll be keeping that appointment. Unfortunately, you won't."

"Are you threatening me?"

"How perceptive."

The priest quickly retrieved a gun from his desk drawer and pointed it at the Colonel. "Don't move. I'm calling the police." He reached for his phone.

"I hope one of them has a bullet," the Colonel snickered, "because you don't."

Father Fitzgerald hit the button for his speaker phone, but nothing happened. Without glancing at the mocking face peering at him, he tapped the button furiously, dread rising in him. He slammed the receiver down and popped open his revolver, staring through the empty chambers. He slowly put it down, a grim scowl creasing his face as he looked up at his adversary.

"I can't be sure what dear Andrew would do about now," the Colonel taunted, "but I can tell you he'd never let himself be caught without a plan. He was so intriguingly resourceful. I'm shocked he would ever bring you into his dealings."

The Colonel took note of the surprise on the priest's alarmed face. "Oh, please, your holiness," he said sarcastically, "you have to know that secretaries love to talk. Granted, you've not told her or, I presume, anyone else about what's really been going on here and who's been coming and going. For someone like myself who knows what he's looking for, it's not hard to ask the questions that will produce the information."

"What do you want?" Father Fitzgerald growled.

"I want to know where they are."

"I don't know, and even if I did, I'd never tell you."

"Now you're sounding like Andrew—faithful until the end."

"Who—*you're* the one responsible for his death!"

"Your analytical powers are impressive."

"I'm warning you," the priest seethed, "you may kill me, but I'll make sure to do enough damage that the police will find you."

The rotund man stood up, expecting the Colonel to pull out a weapon or assault him. Instead the Colonel turned and casually walked back to the dark corner of the study from which he'd emerged. Father Fitzgerald's eyes darted to the door and the hallway beyond, and then back to the Colonel. He turned to run, but his body seized and stiffened.

A wave of panic swept through him.

"Ah, ah," the Colonel's voice drifted from the far end of the office. "Have a seat, old man."

The priest's body was violently jerked backward into the chair at his desk.

"We're just getting started."

38

The friend in my adversity I shall always cherish most.
I can better trust those who helped to relieve the gloom of my
dark hours than those who are so ready to enjoy with me
the sunshine of my prosperity.

—*Ulysses S. Grant*

"How are all of you feeling?" Fern asked pleasantly, setting a serving tray filled with baked goodies on the coffee table in front of them. Brian, Melissa, Malcolm and Dee were seated on the broad side of one of the leather sectionals in the "Pit," as the sunken focal point of Miqlat was known as.

"Much better, thank you," Melissa answered.

"Good. Let me know what you'd like to drink—coffee, tea, or whatever—before we get started. And let me know what you'd like in it."

Each of them did as requested, along with the rest of the group. . . .few of Miqlat's residents had gathered together, sitting on the floor or a random piece of the furniture that had been rearranged for the discussion. Once everyone had ordered something, Fern and Summit left for the kitchen.

"So, Melissa, how far along are you again?" asked Clarise, who was seated next to Ward. "I don't quite recall from when we examined you at Cal's office."

"It'll be twenty-seven weeks next week, right around Christmas."

"Very close to Deidre, then" she observed.

"That's in the ballpark," Dee replied stoically. "I can't say I'm doin' the math."

Brian looked across the area toward the kitchen where Fern and Summit were busy preparing the beverages. "We're likely going to get into some adult discussion tonight," he said, looking at their faces and finally focusing on Nili. "Is that going to be okay for Summit?"

"It should be," Nili answered. "Just use discretion. We'll pick up on what you're getting at. The only thing that would be a concern is anything violent or frightening."

"Understood."

"Don't worry if Summit appears distracted or disinterested," she continued. "That's not a problem. We'll know if she's troubled."

The six of them chatted while they waited for the others to arrive. Summit returned after a few minutes, carefully carrying a tray with four cups. Madison and Kamran had taken seats next to each other on the floor, and they quickly moved to make a path. Summit placed the tray in front of the four newcomers and then walked off without saying a word.

"The drinks should be arranged in the order you're seated in," Clarise told them with a wry smile.

"Something to do with Summit's gift?" Melissa asked, taking her cup.

"In a way," Neff replied. He and Malone had each pulled chairs onto the periphery after wheeling Sabi in to join the group.

"Summit has a gift?" Dee asked.

"So we've heard," Brian answered. "Clarise told us earlier, but she didn't tell us what it was. She said we'd find out soon enough."

"Finally—a *fun* mystery instead of all this other conspiracy cloak-and-dagger."

Summit and Fern brought the rest of the drinks. Fern took a seat next to her husband, and Summit squatted down on the floor. Squish suddenly appeared from nowhere and climbed up on the girl's lap, seeking some attention.

"I guess we can start with us," Neff said after everyone was comfortable. "I'll go around and summarize what everyone's focus is and let people chime in with any personal history they'd like to add."

He began, "Our operation began roughly eight years ago with me, Clarise, and Ward. I'd been an entrepreneur in several businesses, all of them with an international reach. I'd amassed a lot of money but, to make a long story short, I had a spiritual crisis that caused me to want to do something else—something that had eternal value. I'd led a wicked life before I met the Lord—which happened through Clarise and her sister—and wanted the rest of my time here to matter.

"I really didn't know what to do with all my money. I had about four hundred million dollars. I started giving it away. Clarise introduced me to Ward a year or so after my turnaround, and that gave me some direction. They'd just gotten married and were thinking about their own future, and our destinies just sort of meshed. I think Ward can explain better."

Ward nodded. "About two years before I met Clarise, I'd had my own awakening. I was what's called in the world of crony capitalism an economic hit man. The job was just like it sounds, but instead of targeting people, I targeted developing countries. My job was to represent my employer's interests—which had ties to US intelligence agencies and the military—by convincing a country's political and financial leaders to accept huge development loans from large private companies like mine, or international lending bodies like the Word Bank. If the money came from a private company, the deal would usually sound like we were going to develop the country's infrastructure or help it capitalize on untapped natural resources. Supposedly our involvement would help the country industrialize and make a lot of people wealthy while raising the standard of living for everyone. I had to make it sound like they'd be saying no to a modernized Utopia."

"I take it you were successful?" Malcolm asked.

"Unfortunately, I was good at it. The goal was to saddle these countries with debt they could never repay so that the US could later pressure them in a variety of ways—either directly or through the investment company that employed me. The debt would neutralize a country politically so that, in return for not calling in the unpayable loan, that country would vote as we desired at the UN or do something else we wanted—say, allowing the US to build a base somewhere in their country.

"The really sinister part of it was that once we developed an industry to take advantage of a region's resources, the only people who got wealthy were the parent companies and political leaders who saw things our way. The average person got a job if they wanted one, but it was like our own industrial revolution in this country—it created a huge class of working poor. Granted, the working poor in those countries had enough to eat and a roof over their heads, but they were essentially wage slaves. That wasn't how the idea was presented. I was essentially getting wealthy by putting people in deep poverty or keeping them there."

"So what turned you around?" asked Dee.

Melissa could see the conversation had touched a nerve.

"My first wife died of ovarian cancer. We thought we had everything life could offer and then discovered that none of it really mattered. We moved to a cancer-treatment center in the South, which I assumed would eventually fix the problem. I should have just quit my job and stayed with her. We certainly had the money. But quitting meant leaving even more cash on the table. Ultimately, the doctors weren't able to help her. But I like to say that even though my wife died, the move saved her life."

"Why?" Melissa asked.

"She met a Christian there—a real one. He was a retiree who'd gone back to work part-time as a janitor to make ends meet for himself and his wife. He loved to chat with the patients, including my wife. She and I used to make fun of Christians like they were uncultured simpletons or gun-toting trailer trash, but here was this guy who kept my wife company and gave her comfort. He wasn't even close to us when it came to money or status, but he showed my wife what life was really about and who Jesus was. I saw her die happy—and not only happy, but full of hope and anticipation at meeting the Lord. The whole experience was a jolt in so many ways." He paused. "It's hard to explain."

"I think I understand," Melissa replied.

"Anyway, I started searching, and eventually, through Clarise and her sister, I found the faith my wife died with. I quit my job shortly after my wife died. My conscience wouldn't let me continue there, but I knew I didn't want to just play golf. I was too young and wanted to do something that mattered. Clarise and I met at a bookstore, but she wouldn't go out with me. There wasn't a thing I could do or say to impress her. I'd never been shut down like that before."

Clarise laughed at the recollection. "I knew the type."

"Eventually she let me know loud and clear that her issues were spiritual ones, but that was just what I needed. She was able to answer a lot of my questions. We got married about a year and a half later."

"What about your sister?" Brian asked Clarise. "Where is she now?"

"She's gone," Clarise answered. "She passed away from an illness just before we got married. She was young when she died, but she had a tremendous impact on Ward, Graham, and me."

"So, roughly six years ago, the three of you had the idea to do what you do now?"

"That's the simplest version," Neff said. "I met Ward just after he and Clarise were married. I had known Clarise earlier. He was a godsend. His background in finance and the developing world was just what I needed to turn my wealth into something honorable. We spent a couple years laying the foundation for what we do now before going full bore at it."

"Rather than just running through money," Ward explained, "Graham needed to be more forward-thinking. We could build things and buy stuff, but he had enough money that, if properly invested, it could just keep paying for everything year after year."

"So how do you guys finance all this?" Brian asked.

"It took about seventy million dollars to get everything in place," Neff explained. "We bought properties here and outside the country for safe houses, acquired all sorts of equipment—trucks, boats, planes, helicopters, the big things. But to really understand what we do, you have to know that we essentially operate in two worlds. On one hand, we directly finance dozens of homeless shelters, teen pregnancy centers, abortion alternatives, orphanages, and mission agencies that we believe make the gospel central to what they do."

"Yeah," Malone interrupted. "We do lots of service things like building churches, schools, infrastructure—all that sort of stuff. But we know firsthand that if that's all you're doing, you're basically building a Marxist day camp. We have no time or money for that."

Neff jumped back in. "We hand-pick ministries because we want to be the sole source of their funding to avoid government interference. They're all set up as non-profits, so each entity can and does take donations, but we devote a specific yearly amount regardless of the donations. They really aren't that expensive, to be honest, and because of Ward's genius, the interest on our investments covers all those annual costs."

"Is all the money invested? What about risk?" asked Dee.

"We have about a hundred million dollars in low-risk savings in off-shore accounts, stable foreign currencies, and Swiss bank accounts. For each safe house we have about fifty thousand dollars in gold in a safe deposit box in a local bank, and another fifty thousand in cash inside the house in a secure safe. Cash is always preferable when we're trying to move people around. Other operations have their own discretionary spending accounts. What we do personally doesn't require us to do much spending—we're in and out. If we need money on the fly, the safe-house cash is adequate and leaves no electronic trail. The whole time in North Dakota we never used a credit card."

"What about the rental car in Canada?" Brian asked.

"We use a card linked to one of our businesses," Ward answered.

"To finish answering Dee's question," Neff said, "aside from low-risk savings, we've got about two hundred million spread out in various ways at different levels of investment strategy. That generates a lot of income every year."

"What about personal expenses?" Dee asked. "You have to just want something from time to time. How do you do that and protect your identity?"

"We have a central discretionary spending account that all of us can draw on, but we only keep a couple hundred thousand in that. We take mail in town at our businesses, but we only pick it up twice a month unless we have to go to town unscheduled. Anyone here can buy what they need."

"We should hit the other side of what we do," Ward said, steering the conversation. "The other half of our operation concerns the network we've created to do the kind of work you saw up close—getting women and kids out of the human-trafficking industry. That operates under the radar of law enforcement, political bodies, and, of course, the bad guys. The weapons we have and take outside would draw a lot of unwanted attention, but our posture is defensive."

"We gathered as much after the border experience," Melissa noted.

"You could've killed them all," Dee recalled. "I'm not sure I'd have cared after learning what they'd done."

"We know how you feel, but we're not about settling scores or starting revolutions," Ward responded. "We want to prevent harm, not participate in it."

"Tell me more about the safe houses," Dee asked. "Are they all like the one we were in?"

"To some degree," Clarise answered. "We have fifteen safe houses in the US now and twenty more scattered in other countries. Each one of those is run by someone hand-picked by us. We train them in the security protocols we use, make sure they know first aid and CPR, that sort of thing. We pay them well, and they know we'll meet any material need they have. We look for people who can competently manage operations and who are absolutely in line with the cause. Loyalty is essential."

"The safe houses focus on women and children in crisis," Neff added. "We try to keep foreign victims in locations out of the United States since there's less scrutiny. We finance about a hundred orphanages outside the country. The kids learn English, get an education, and learn about Jesus. We've had a few kids who wanted to train for ministry, so we set that up as well.

"We hide the funding sources through a combination of front companies and real businesses, along with the sorts of tricks that drug lords and Arab sheikhs use to hide their activity. The dollar goes a long way in those places, so it's quite manageable. The bigger problem is staffing, but we're blessed that a lot of the people we save want to stay to help somewhere in the network."

"Wow," Malcolm said, shaking his head in awe. "That's amazing."

"Just so we're clear," Neff continued, "we aren't anti-Church. I think it's more accurate to say we're ambivalent toward them. We're glad when God's work gets done where it gets done, but we aren't waiting for large organizations to plod through committee decisions. We despise bureaucracy."

"We also trust ourselves more than organized Christianity," Ward chimed in. "To be blunt about it, we've come to doubt the character of the Church at large. We think it's worldly. Christians, especially in this country, seem to equate popularity with excellence or God's blessing. More energy goes into appearance than permanence. We're just done with that."

"It is unfortunate," Sabi offered sadly, "but we feel that many believers are focused on social connection but not devotion. I enjoy friendships and desperately need everyone here, but they cannot replace the inner life."

"Our mission is simple," he continued with an open, gentle smile. "We devote ourselves to Jesus with the affection of our hearts; we enjoy His love and forgiveness; we love and enjoy each other; we spend ourselves helping those who are suffering the most. It is a full life."

"And as long as we're talking about what we're not," Malone added, "we also want to be clear that we're not survivalists. It's true we're prepared for just about anything and could live off the grid for years, but we live this way because it gives us the maximum freedom for our own ministries. When the Lord comes back, we don't want Him to just find a lot of freeze-dried food; we want Him to find faith."

"Thanks for that," Brian replied with a chuckle. "Melissa and I have had some long discussions about our place—or lack thereof—in the normal church situation today. Once you get to know our circumstances, you'll understand why."

"I suspected so," Neff said appreciatively.

"Even without the danger, that's no surprise given what you write," Nili surmised.

"Yeah," Madison agreed. "You won't hear that stuff in church."

Neff broke in again. "Keep in mind that all of what we've described is just a sketch. We naturally have to equip the safe houses with vehicles, food, clothing, and medical supplies. We've got a dozen planes and almost that many helicopters stationed in different parts of the country. All of them need regular maintenance and storage. Then there's the fuel

. . . It's a logistic challenge, to say the least."

"You got that right," Malone agreed.

"Doug and Fern are in charge of tracking all the logistics and supplies for our stateside safe houses," Neff said, "along with all the maintenance. Kamran helps them out when he's not busy with his own area of responsibility—the foreign safe houses. All three of them know firsthand what it takes to make all this work. Doug, Ward, and I also keep an eye on our businesses and travel. We try to visit every operation we finance at least once a year. And we all participate in missions, subject to Nili's planning."

"You mentioned 'real businesses.' Can you describe those?" Brian asked.

"Well, let's use Miqlat as an example," Malone said. "The safe houses are sort of smaller versions of Miqlat, so some of what I'll describe applies to them. We run two businesses in Bozeman that we use to generate income and to disguise our own transactions. We're essentially upper management.

"Day-to-day operations are run by folks we've recruited and hired. One store sells outdoor supplies and sporting goods. We use that to order things like our long-term food storage, small arms, ammunition, outdoor wear—basically any sort of camping or preparedness item we need. If we want anything more exotic, Neff and Nili handle procuring those sorts of things.

"The other store sells medical supplies. We use that to supply our infirmary and meet any needs Clarise has for research. And we naturally arrange for safe-house personnel to order what they need online from those businesses. We've duplicated this model in a couple of the towns where it makes sense."

"What kind of research do you do?" Malcolm asked Clarise.

"I'm an MD but also have the credit equivalent of a graduate degree in genetics. Neff knew we'd need our own doctor, so after we started this little operation, he sent me to medical school. I finished my residency a year ago. Along the way I took every course I could in genetics. I dabble in it, but sometimes we need to do forensic work."

"We should let Doug and Fern fill in a little more about their backgrounds," Neff resumed. "They're colorful, to say the least."

"They know we were hippies," Malone said to his wife, "and recent events led to telling them a little about your interest in MK-ULTRA. Maybe you can add a little to that."

She nodded.

"As for me," Malone continued, "I used to be a weatherman."

"Like on television?" Dee asked in surprise.

"No, not like on television," he said in an amused tone. "Like in domestic terrorist."

"A domestic terrorist? *You*?" Malcolm exclaimed incredulously.

"Yeah, I was part of the Weather Underground. I was an anarchist."

"Man, that's crazy. You just don't look the part."

"What exactly does a leftist radical look like?" he asked, chuckling.

"Not you," Malcolm said with a laugh.

Malone shrugged and looked at the others. "In case you've not heard of the Weathermen, it disbanded in 1973 after the Vietnam War ended, the same year that I met Fern. After those events, Fern and I drifted in and out of community organizing groups devoted to the sorts of causes you'd associate with the political left—abortion, global warming, overpopulation, communism, the works. So, while Ward worked firsthand for the corruption and imperialism that right-wing crony capitalism is infamous for, we did the same for liberal fascism. Fern eventually did something useful and got licensed as a psychologist. I just screwed around and lived off grant money."

"Have you kept up on these sorts of movements?" Melissa asked. "Brian told me a bit about your concerns about global governance and such."

"The global governance problem is easy to track since it's decades old, and that's where most of our knowledge and experience comes from. We try to follow how the ideas are reborn and repackaged today, especially in American pop culture. But it's honestly hard to wrap your head around the utopian weirdness. Granted, it has roots in our time, but a lot of it is so pagan—all this esoteric, neo-Nazi, fascist religious stuff about root races and occult bloodlines. We have no skills for sifting the wheat from the chaff in what we read there. It makes your head spin."

Brian looked at Melissa with raised eyebrows. She held her expression.

"Want to add anything, Fern?" Malone asked.

"We should mention that sometimes our safe houses and network get used to protect survivors."

Malone nodded.

"You mean people who claim to be victims of mind control or trauma-produced mental dissociation—what used to be called multiple personalities?" Dee asked.

"Yes, and most of what we deal with goes well beyond claims."

"How do you know? I've done a lot of research on that, and it's controversial to say the least."

"It is, but we rarely deal with referrals from psychologists or psychiatrists—for precisely that reason. We follow the human traffic—the network of current experimental abuse."

"Are you saying you know this is still going on and who is doing it?"

"We've had dealings with several operations, and we have circumstantial evidence for the existence of a few others. Are you familiar with the 2004 Goodwin case?"

"No, never heard of it."

"It's Canadian. The courts there gave 250 victims the legal right to seek compensation . . . for unwillingly being subjected to mind-control programming. Trauma-based mind control is, unfortunately, real," she added softly, "and your Becky is testimony that the interest isn't purely academic."

39

We shall see that at which dogs howl in the dark,
and that at which cats prick up their ears after midnight.

—*H. P. Lovecraft*

"You have an impressive library, father," the Colonel mused. "I took the liberty of browsing while I waited. Some of the volumes inspired me with an idea in case you were uncooperative."

"I don't know where they are!" the priest blurted out, discovering he could still speak.

"I believe you. You may be a little slower than Andrew, but deniability is fundamental to what you—and I—do."

"Then why not just let me go—and why can't I move? How are you—"

Father Fitzgerald suddenly fell silent, but this time of his own volition. His mind filled with terror. He closed his eyes and began to pray silently.

"Fool," the Colonel growled, watching the movement of the priest's lips. "Your prayers are useless."

"Only a demon could do this," the priest said grimly, opening his eyes, steeling himself.

"A demon? It isn't wise to insult me."

"Demon!"

The Colonel sighed condescendingly. "You might have been in league with Benedict, but you share little of his insight."

The Colonel placed the stack of books on the desk and leaned in close toward the priest's face, his expression turning hostile. "Demons are like puppies," he hissed. "They come when summoned. I do what I please."

The Colonel straightened himself and turned his attention back to the stack of books. He methodically adjusted each title so that the spines all faced the same direction. He looked over at the priest and then walked slowly around the desk. The priest felt his chair begin to rotate. It came to a stop when he was facing the officer. Father Fitzgerald felt a chill run through him as he looked into the cold blue eyes.

"I'm not going to kill you—yet," the Colonel mocked, "but rest assured, this will be very painful. The good news is that I've decided to put you to sleep. You're so fat, your heart would probably give out."

Colonel Ferguson watched in smug amusement as the terrified priest tried and failed to shout. He put his hand over the priest's eyes, and Father Fitzgerald fainted away into unconsciousness.

The Colonel took out a radio and walked to the lone window in the study. He pulled back the curtain a few inches and smiled. The priest's house was situated on the outer edge of the small town, in virtual isolation. An expansive wheat field rolled on for what seemed like miles. The location was perfect.

"Ferguson here. Uncloak."

He looked up into the dark sky. A large, round blackness slowly blotted out the stars in the dark winter sky.

"Be in position for transport in five minutes. I have a passenger. He needs immediate medical attention."

40

He that takes truth for his guide, and duty for his end, may safely trust to God's providence to lead him aright.

—*Blaise Pascal*

"Trauma-based mind control—today?" Dee asked skeptically.

"Very much so," Fern replied. "You know the evidence goes back to just after World War II and of course includes MK-ULTRA. The victims were subjected to electroshock treatment and mind-altering drugs. For the rest of you, if you've read the MK-ULTRA material or seen the movie *Conspiracy Theory*, you'll have an idea what was done to them."

"I'd like to read the court documents. Do you have them?"

"I do; I'll get them to you tomorrow," Fern promised. "You'll find that the testimony produced names of universities and their faculty who were part of the experimentation. Once you have that sort of information, you can find out who the graduate students were, what grants were received, and where the money went."

"But since all of that's public, it would be insane for professionals and universities to keep going with the research."

"It would, which is why this sort of thing typically surfaces in private practices nowadays. Most of the time we engage professionals doing the research for someone else, like the military, for example. They target runaways or drifters, but they're not above using extended family members. We've been fortunate to have people who care about the abuse and its implications on the inside who have occasionally been able to give us names and places where the research is being conducted. We treat that situation like we would any other human trafficking. Sometimes we find victims; other times we fail. It's less successful since we're not buying people."

Malone jumped back in, addressing Brian. "The thoughts you posted online about alien abduction syndrome and its similarities to this sort of stuff really caught our attention. It sounded like you'd had some firsthand exposure to mind-control trauma."

"We have," Brian acknowledged. "We ran into it at the base where we were confined."

"Before we get further into that," Neff interrupted, "let's continue our introductions. Madison is next. She's in charge of all our information technology and communications security."

"I've been wondering how you keep all that secret," Brian said. "Melissa and I use cellphones, but only to call each other, and we didn't use our names for those. For everything else we use prepaid phonecards."

"Did you bring some?" Neff asked, looking at her.

"Yep," Madison replied. She turned and pulled a backpack from behind a chair. She opened it and retrieved four electronic devices that were larger than a typical smartphone. Brian recognized them, having seen Neff and Malone handle them.

"These are secure phones," Neff said as he handed one to each of them. "Madison can explain."

"These devices are NSA approved for secure phone calling, emailing, web browsing, and anything else you'd use a PDA or wireless phone for."

"Isn't this what the president uses?" Malcolm asked, admiring the piece of technology.

"Same technology, different model."

"Madison used to work at NSA," Clarise added.

"Wow," said Brian. "Really?"

"Just for a year," she said, enjoying the recognition.

"Why did you quit?"

"I got a degree in computer science in college and then I had to decide what to do next. I thought about grad school but took a one-year internship at NSA instead. It was interesting, but kind of dull, actually. I wanted something more stimulating."

"You mean you found hacking more of a rush," Ward teased.

"I won't deny it," she said slyly. "Once mom and Ward told me about what they were doing here, I wanted in."

"Mom?" Melissa asked, looking at Clarise.

"I had Madison when I was fifteen. I wasn't married, so she has my maiden name, Sims. She's twenty-nine, but she's still my baby."

"You must have gotten into technology awfully young," Malcolm observed.

"I did," Madison confirmed, looking whimsically at Clarise.

"How did that happen?" Malcom asked.

"Go ahead," said Clarise, rolling her eyes.

"Let's just say, mom had an unscrupulous boyfriend at one point of my childhood who got me into it. I saw the movie *The Net* when I was eleven, and he showed me how the woman in the movie did what she did. I was hooked. He taught me to do all sorts of illegal stuff and not get caught. It was awesome."

"Really, I didn't intend to raise a criminal," Clarise said, shaking her head.

"I use my powers for good now," Madison said, smiling mischievously before adding, "mostly."

"'Mostly'?"

Everyone laughed as Madison continued. "Outside Miqlat we don't use email or any text messaging on any device but these. Inside Miqlat we have a little more flexibility, though we have several layers of encrypted defense on every computer. We have to guard against anything that could be downloaded invisibly to capture key strokes or surfing history, not to mention viruses. And webcams are disabled. They can be taken over remotely."

"That's comforting," Dee said with a smirk.

Neff then turned his attention to Nili, explaining, "Nili handles all our security and tactical planning."

"No way," Malcolm feigned surprise.

Everyone laughed again.

"For real," Neff continued, enjoying Malcolm's sense of humor. "Nili trains us in weapons use and self-defense. She's also the point person for planning missions and leads debriefing afterward. We go over what we did to learn whether we could have done something better or whether something could have gone wrong."

"We have our own small-arms pistol range underground," Nili told them, "and an outdoor firing range for high-powered and military-grade weapons."

"Like the LRAD and the EMP cannon?" Brian asked.

"Correct. The goal is that anyone who might go outside on a mission is completely comfortable with any weapon we might have to use."

Brian turned to address Nili. "So you're ex-military?"

"I served in the Israeli army full-time for seven years before transferring to Mossad. I'm still informally connected to the agency."

"I met Nili on a trip to Israel five years ago," Neff explained. "She was considering leaving Mossad and coming to the United States for some personal reasons, which she can share if she wants."

Nili nodded. "It's a long story, one that ended for the better a few months ago. Your work played an important part," she said, looking at Brian. "It was a blessing from Yeshua to discover it."

"I can't think of anything I'd have done that would have been useful to you."

"You were the difference between heaven and hell for my father," she said earnestly.

Brian could see the emotion in her eyes.

Neff continued, "We're fortunate that circumstances developed where Nili could both work for me and maintain some attachment to Mossad. It's been invaluable."

"I have an uncle who is very highly placed in the agency," Nili explained. "He knows we have the logistics to help if he needs my services outside the country. And occasionally we spy for them or exchange information. Graham also has the resources to provide things outside Mossad's funding."

"Graham hinted that was part of the process for helping Malcolm and Dee," said Melissa.

"That's right. Occasionally Madison—how do you say it?"

"'Lurks'—'trolls'—for data," the girl offered some vocabulary.

"Yes, *trolls*," Nili said, knowing it sounded odd with her accent. "We have scripting and robot technology that flags keywords in Arabic, and then I read the results to see if it's important."

"So you speak Hebrew and Arabic?" Brian asked.

"Yes," she replied, smiling demurely and observing he was impressed. "It's very useful for what we do. In this case, it provided valuable intelligence to trade."

At that point, Neff jumped in to continue the introductions. "I've already shared your story with them, Kamran," he said, "and Clarise has introduced Summit to everyone."

"I like sushi," Summit interjected. "So does Squish."

"I love it, too," Malcolm answered, enjoying her quirky manner. Summit didn't look at him, but contented herself by stroking the cat.

"Sabi, what about you?" Neff asked. "Could you share a bit of your story?"

"Of course," he said quietly. He sat silently in his wheelchair for a few moments, collecting his thoughts. Then he said, smiling, "I am Georgian. You can tell from my accent."

The others laughed with him.

"Really, though, I am Georgian—just not your Georgia. My country is very small, between Russia and Armenia. My Georgia was still part of the Soviet Union when I was a boy. I am thirty-four years old now—a miracle."

He paused before resuming. "Georgia became independent from the Soviets in 1991. There was turmoil at the beginning. Several ethnic factions fought for control. The Russians sided with our rivals from Ossetia and Abkhazia. Many native Georgians were expelled from our homeland, including my family. We returned in the 1990s.

"My mother wanted a quiet life for me. We were Christian Orthodox, and she wanted me to be a priest. Instead, I joined the army. There was fighting off and on, but peace came in 2005. My mother tried to convince me to leave the army, but I resisted. It was a fateful decision.

"In 2008 war broke out again between us and the Russians and Ossetia. Both sides said the other started the fighting. It does not matter. I was stationed at the airfield near Marneuli. The Russians bombed it and I was injured—paralyzed."

Sabi became quiet once more. Madison reached out and patted him on the shoulder. He turned toward her and nodded appreciatively.

"At first my family tried to care for me, but my needs were too great. I was sent to an institution." He paused momentarily. "I will not call it a hospital. Those in the West have read about such places—places for orphans and the insane . . . and people like me," he added with resignation.

"It was a horrible place. Many times I was hungry or thirsty, living in my own filth. The few kind people there could do little; they were so burdened. I begged God to kill me. I am ashamed to say this, but it is true."

A tear trickled down Sabi's cheek and into his dark beard. Brian watched with his heart in his throat as Nili produced a soft handkerchief and gently dabbed his face. A silent thank you formed on his lips. He drew in his breath and continued.

"I grew very angry. I decided I would no longer eat or drink, and I asked the nurses to poison me. They refused, fearing trouble. I begged God to let me die, but He would not listen. I hated Him for that." He paused. "And then it happened."

Sabi stopped and made eye contact with Clarise before resuming. She began to tear up.

"One night I awoke and saw the form of a woman standing at the foot of my bed. It was dark, so I could not see her face. When she saw me looking at her, she came to me and sat on the edge of my bed. When the moonlight touched her face, I could see she was young and beautiful. I had never seen her before, and she was not dressed as a nurse. I said nothing, but waited, just looking up into her face, wondering who she was and why she had been watching me.

"Suddenly, she said, '*Sebastian, it is time. There is much to be done.*' She told me that God had sent her to tell me I would be leaving soon with two Americans who would know my name. And then she disappeared—she vanished before my eyes."

Sabi was smiling now. He looked at Ward, who took the cue.

"Sabi's story is part of our story," Ward explained. "After we got married, Clarise and I talked about adopting some children as part of our new life and purpose. We spent weeks going back and forth about it, praying about it. One night we were lying in bed when—honestly, I'm not kidding you with any of this—we heard a voice, just as clear as anyone here in this room. It said, 'His name is Sebastian.' We both heard it. It just freaked us out; we didn't get much sleep that night, let me tell you.

"Then, about a week later, it happened again, only this time in Russian. My extended family immigrated from Russia, so I speak the language pretty well. We both took it as a sign that God wanted us to adopt a child from eastern Europe from a Russian family." He looked at his wife.

"I think you can put the rest of the story together," Clarise, now composed, took up the narrative. "We wound up traveling to eastern Europe. Circumstances—some of them pretty odd, too—eventually put us in Sabi's institution. We had actually gotten lost trying to find an orphanage. We were trying to get directions from some staff people when we overheard someone mention that it was time to 'change Sebastian.' That set off an argument about seeing him, which we eventually won with a bribe."

"Needless to say," she continued, "we were shocked when we saw him. As soon as Sabi learned we were Americans, he told us his story. We couldn't deny our own experience, but we couldn't accept a paralyzed man was the point of it all. We just weren't ready for that."

"They did not truly believe," Sabi broke in, smiling broadly, "until I described the woman."

"It was my sister," Clarise said, wiping her cheek. "But she was dead—she'd died six months earlier. But it was her. His description was precise."

Brian couldn't contain a gasp. He watched as Ward put his arm around Clarise and looked at Brian and the rest of the newcomers.

"It actually wasn't that difficult to get Sabi out," Ward explained. "Adoptions are much harder. Once we had his family's permission and had paid off who we needed to, we took Sabi home with us. As soon as Neff heard the story, he jumped right in and made sure we had everything we needed. We didn't know what the point of it all was, but we didn't dare disobey something so clearly from God."

"That's awesome," Malcolm exclaimed, beaming. "I think we all need reminders like that—that God still does that sort of thing."

"It reminds me a little of Melissa's near-death experience back at Mount Weather," Brian said to Malcolm, who nodded.

"I was thinking that, too," Melissa added. "I'm still not sure about what that meant, but I think it's safe to say it was supernatural."

"Let's not talk about that place," Dee moaned.

"You're never going to see it again," Malcolm assured her. "And you can't let living underground remind you of it, either. Besides, look around—this is pretty sweet."

"Sure, it's nice—and we all agree that it has Area 51 beat by a mile—but you *know* that's not what I'm talking about."

"The Colonel isn't going to find us here," he insisted.

"It's not just the Colonel we need to be worried about," Dee said, sounding more agitated, "especially if Brian is right about what happened with Adam. *That's* why I don't like thinking about Mount Weather. What's worse, one of Brian's Watchers, or a little gray twerp that reads minds?"

"They have limitations," Brian said confidently. "Or we'd already be toast."

"Umm, Brian . . ."

He felt Melissa touch his arm and turned to her. Her eyes motioned away from the couch. He turned his head toward the dumbfounded audience listening to the argument, their expressions a spectrum of disbelief and apprehension.

"Did I really just hear you say 'Area 51'?" Ward asked through a dry mouth.

"'Little gray guys'?" Madison asked, her eyes wide.

Brian sighed. "I guess it's our turn now."

41

I have learned to use the word 'impossible' with the greatest caution.

—Wernher von Braun

"I'm speechless," Neff said, glancing at his watch. "I can't believe the four of you spent the summer at Area 51 and Mount Weather, riding in UFOs, experiencing HAARP in action, seeing alien bodies—not to mention the personal tragedies of having friends and colleagues killed. It's just mind-boggling."

"That's putting it mildly," Brian replied. "We were all shell-shocked last summer when we found out where we were. We knew the situation we were involved in was serious since we were put in there against our will, but we had no idea. I hope you understand now why I felt like your involvement with us was risky."

"Absolutely."

"I'm glad we decided to send Summit to her room," Nili added. "This would be too much for her."

"I'm not only amazed at *where* you all were," Ward added, "but that we actually got two of you out."

"Ditto," added Malcolm.

"So, if I'm following," Malone interjected, "you were taken to Area 51 and given a bogus environmental crisis as the reason for your 'recruitment.' Then later, the people in charge—this 'Group'—arranged a series of revelations to convince you that what was really in play was a government extraterrestrial disclosure?"

"Exactly," Melissa answered. "When the Group saw we weren't buying the first yarn, we allegedly got the truth from them about alien disclosure."

"But that turned out to be a misdirection as well?" Ward asked uncertainly.

"Yes, but that's something we had to deduce on our own. For sure the mole inside the Group filled in a lot of gaps, but we had our own suspicions before he spilled everything."

"You mean the Lieutenant Sheppard you told us about," Malone interrupted, "the one who was motivated by guilt by what he had done to you two in the past?"

"The one that Father Benedict shot?" Madison recalled.

"Yes," Brian confirmed. "When Sheppard revealed himself, it was an incredible shock. Of all the things that happened last summer, that was the most unexpected. It brought Melissa and me full circle and wound up helping us get off the base."

"What caused your initial suspicions about the alien-disclosure scenario?" Neff asked.

"Melissa was on to it first," Brian said, looking in her direction.

"I started to think we were being taken for another ride when we were shown the alien corpses—or what they presented to us as dead aliens. There were some features that I knew could have been alterations."

"Did you share your suspicions with any of your colleagues?" Nili asked.

"No, I didn't trust anyone there," Melissa answered. "At least, that's what I told myself. The truth is that I sort of knew Brian was honest, but I didn't care—all I felt when I saw him was contempt."

"Why?" Nili asked, wide-eyed with surprise. "How could you feel that way, especially now that you're together?"

"It wasn't him so much as what he stood for. It's hard to explain. Let's just say that Brian reminded me of people in my past who had ruined my life. All I could think about was getting revenge. He was a convenient target."

"What changed?"

Melissa looked at Brian warmly. "He saved my life. I treated him like garbage and did all I could to humiliate him, and he gave me my life in return—and almost got himself killed doing it."

Brian listened as Melissa recounted the dramatic twist of fate that had led to their reconciliation, the unexpected catalyst that had brought them to where they were now. Flashes of the powerful security dogs' vicious attack on the surface at Area 51 streaked across his memory. He closed his eyes and tried to tune out the details.

"Brian, are you okay?"

He opened his eyes and looked in the direction of the words he'd heard. It was Madison.

"Yeah," he assured her along with everyone else, as they had all turned their attention to him. "I just haven't thought much about it. I didn't think at all when it happened. I just knew what I had to do and did it."

"Combat is the same way," Nili said, "but the decision must still be made. You were very brave."

"I'd have died on the tarmac if it wasn't for Melissa's quick thinking. She saved me as well."

"Based on what I've heard just now, that's very likely," Neff said.

"You don't seem to have suffered any permanent damage," Clarise said in a transparently curious tone.

"I don't have any," Brian answered.

"How is that?"

"Well, this is where we get to the part about little gray guys—living ones, or so it seemed at the time."

The group listened with riveted fascination as Brian related their encounter with Adam and his healing. Malcolm and Dee added their own experience at Mount Weather with the spindly gray creature.

"I'll say it again," Nili spoke when they were finished, "Summit should not hear about these things. This would give her nightmares."

"Are you absolutely certain that you weren't really healed by Adam—that it was nanotechnology?" Clarise inquired.

"Absolutely," Malcolm answered her. "I saw it myself. I had enough experience with nanotech in my own PhD work to know that's what I was looking at under the electron microscope. His blood was swimming with nanobots, and they reassembled the destroyed tissues and nerves in no time. It was spectacular."

"Adam didn't inject me with anything," Brian added, "but the base doctor did, shortly before the meeting. I'm convinced the Group had staged the episode to make us believe. Lieutenant Sheppard also told us point-blank that the Group had the technology to create a conscious life form through nanotechnology. In effect, they have the blueprints and recipes for everything they need."

"I know it sounds macabre," Clarise continued, the fascination evident on her face, "but I've just got to see that for myself. I've read a lot about nanotechnology, and that sort of application and performance just isn't available today, at least in any public setting."

"If you want to draw some blood, that's fine," Brian said with a chuckle.

"I'll bet you can show everyone now," Malcolm said, looking at Brian with raised eyebrows.

"What do you mean?" Brian asked.

"Haven't you ever wondered if what's inside you is still active? No time like the present to find out."

"To answer your question, Malcolm, no, I haven't thought about what might still be inside me."

"No way."

"Way—and you've got that look on your face again."

"What look?" he asked with a knowing grin.

"The reckless one."

42

Never be afraid to trust an unknown future to a known God.

—*Corrie ten Boom*

"Come on, let's see what happens if you cut your finger or something. I bet it will heal in a couple minutes."

"Come on, Malcolm."

"Don't tell me that you wouldn't like to see."

"I can live without the suspense."

"Just a little nick. If it doesn't work, you can cut me, too. We'll be blood brothers." He laughed.

"Do you believe this?" Brian asked Melissa.

"Actually, I'm kind of curious about it now, too."

"Count me in," seconded Dee.

"The motion passes!" Madison said enthusiastically.

Brian rolled his eyes.

"I'll get a knife and some gauze," Clarise said, her own curiosity getting the better of her.

She returned a few moments later and handed the knife to Brian. Everyone watched as he lightly ran the edge of the knife against the underside of his ring finger. Clarise dabbed the blood and then wrapped his finger in gauze.

"If they're still in there working, it won't take long," Brian said with a sigh. "The whole arm was healed in less than an hour. Any more questions while we wait?"

Malone's phone went off. "Kamran asks, 'What about Adam and consciousness?' " he read aloud.

"Good question," Dee spoke up. "Mind you, I'd still like to believe the little freak was an alien, given the alternative, but to be honest, consciousness doesn't require that he was a real alien. It only requires a brain. The leap here is that a brain could be constructed from the ground up with nanotechnology, but if it was, it should do what a brain does."

"Would an artificial being have a soul?" Ward asked, incredulously.

"It would depend on how much terms like 'soul' and 'consciousness' really overlap," said Brian, "as well as what a soul actually is and where it comes from. Theologically speaking, the Bible isn't clear on that. Personally, I don't think the soul has a one-to-one correspondence with the brain, but like Dee said, a brain is required. After all, higher animals have consciousness—but it's dog or cat consciousness, for instance. Animals possess a consciousness that doesn't include sentience—self-awareness. Sentience may be a clue to whatever the soul is—that disembodied self-awareness that, according to the Bible, survives death."

"Some specialists in animal cognition think they have detected self-awareness in animals—say, birds—since they can communicate thoughts," Dee went on, "but that's still controversial since the communication must be interpreted. But aside from that, I'd agree sentience is not to be equated with consciousness. It transcends consciousness."

"So you're saying you suspect that Adam was manufactured through nanotechnology and had enough conscious awareness to move from person to person?" Madison asked. "But what about the thoughts in your head and the communication that went on?"

"That's the part we disagree on," Brian said.

"Only because what you think is worse," Dee reminded everyone.

"My viewpoint," Brian began, "is that if Adam were a genuine ET, why would they have needed to make it seem like he had healing powers?"

"Worship?" Sabi suggested.

"We've thought about that," said Melissa. "That might have been the Group's intent, but if it was, then our present knowledge that he didn't heal Brian argues against him being a true alien. If he's a real ET and just couldn't heal anyone, why didn't the Group tell us that Adam gave them nanotechnology for medical purposes or something? That would have shielded them from the problem. It would never have been an issue. But they didn't do that."

"By now you know my belief that the thoughts came from another source," Brian explained. "I don't think it was Adam in our heads. Remember, the voice told me to touch Melissa's hand. That prompting would demonstrate that my arm was repairing. But Adam wasn't, in fact, my healer—the nanobots prove that. That makes the whole thing seem orchestrated. Someone else had to be in on it. Getting a voice in my head was either another piece of technology or a non-human entity acting to deceive me. Father Benedict suspected it was beings referred to in the Bible and other Jewish texts as Watchers."

"Melissa," Fern asked, shifting the topic slightly, "your near-death experience has come up a few times. I presume that happened when Brian's friend—what was his name?"

"Neil Bandstra."

"Yes, Neil. Did you have your experience when he tried to kill you?"

"That's right," Melissa confirmed. "I left my body and was taken to a room at Mount Weather. Later, when I recovered, we retraced the path and found a room that had a Nazi occult symbol in it—a black sun. We also found a human tooth there."

"Creepy." Madison shuddered. "Do you have any idea what it meant?"

"Not really," Melissa confessed. "The black sun wasn't hard to recognize. Given the connections between the UFO technology we saw at Area 51 and the Nazi scientists brought into the US rocketry and aeronautics programs under Operation Paperclip, a Nazi occult symbol didn't seem out of place—at least in hindsight. We have no idea about the tooth."

"It has to mean more," Neff insisted. "We know now that the Colonel did indeed have an interest in Becky, and the only reason he'd have encountered her was by investigating what she and her boyfriend had on them—pieces of architectural plans for a Nazi base in the Antarctic. I didn't like the notion of coincidences before, but after meeting you and learning all that's happened, there's no way that what you saw or Becky showing up is random. What do you think, Sabi?"

"I agree," he said, concentration etched on his face. "God is up to something."

"How did you know what the black sun meant?" Malone asked Melissa.

"It's part of my field. I've read thousands of pages about Nazi occultism. In my life before Area 51, I wrote a book and several articles about that sort of thing."

"I thought your expertise was church history," Neff said in surprise.

"I've had a lot of graduate work there, but it isn't my PhD field."

"You know," Neff continued, "we actually don't know much about you, Melissa. We didn't ask about your identity before since we didn't have a reason to pry."

"And you wouldn't have gotten an answer anyway," Brian said matter-of-factly.

"No doubt," Neff noted, "and now we know precisely why. Malone and I assumed Melissa Carter wasn't your real name, but now I'm even more curious as to your background."

"My real name is Melissa Kelley. My PhD is in American studies, and my academic focus is apocalyptic religious cults, especially neo-Nazi groups."

Malone stared at her in disbelief. "Did she just say what I think she said?" he asked eagerly, looking around at Sabi and then the others.

"Yes," Melissa said, hesitating slightly. "I taught at Georgetown until this past summer. That's how Becky knew me. Is there a problem?"

"I didn't catch any of that on my recording," Malone said, turning to Neff. "I only got about half their conversation after I followed them to the coffee shop. Can you believe it?"

"In light of the last few weeks," Neff replied, grinning widely, "you bet. But it's still amazing."

"What is it?" Melissa asked.

"Most of us have read your book on right-wing Christian apocalyptic groups," Malone answered. "It's been a go-to resource for trying to understand some of the cultural shifts we keep running into. It has given us clarity on some fronts, but it has mostly produced a slew of breadcrumb trails to religious and occult ideas that we sense are important for what we're seeing in the world, but which we know nothing about. And here you are! It's like you just dropped right into our laps," he exclaimed.

Melissa had no response, taken aback by this additional intersection of their circumstances.

"Wow," said Ward. "The four of you are exactly who we need to help us think through everything we're trying to process. You cover all the bases."

"That's true," Sabi said, smiling faintly and enjoying the moment. "For the child of God, there is no such thing as an accident. What a blessing for our research."

"All of these details explain a lot about what you were posting online," Malone said to Brian. "And I assume now that you had input from Melissa, since some of it involved occult research."

"That's true," Brian answered. "Father Benedict thought it was important that I post my thoughts online. I felt I owed it to him to go through with it. Melissa is extremely knowledgeable in all the intellectual histories behind mainstream and fringe occult worldviews. There are an amazing number of intersections between all that and belief in aliens and UFO experiences, so we've had a lot to think about as we try to figure out the point of it all. We tried to be careful, though. I presumed that if the Colonel saw anything that only we would have seen or heard, he'd have known one of us was behind the posting and track us down."

"That's not exactly what I was thinking of, though," Malone noted. "I mean the tone. Like I told you back in North Dakota, I got a sense that you knew something was going on right now, but it was never clear."

"That's because we're still not sure how the pieces fit together. Andrew had his own views, but I'm not sure I agree with them. Neither does Melissa."

"Where are you at on Father Benedict's perspective, Malcolm?" Melissa asked.

"I'm inclined to trust Andrew's instincts that the plan is something big, like faking the second coming or something like that. I'm curious, though—why don't you agree with Andrew's thinking?"

"Well, I think all this *could* have something to do with convincing lots of people that they're seeing end-times events, and that aliens have something to do with that. But I'm bothered by a few things. For one, I don't see how Genesis 6 and the Nephilim have anything to do with little gray aliens, real or imagined. I don't see any congruence between the way they appear—weak and emaciated—and a warrior race. Plus, the Nephilim and other clans are consistently described as being unusually tall. It makes no sense."

"But if memory serves," Malcolm said, "didn't you say that the Greek word *titanos* can refer to the Titans of Greek mythology and also mean 'gray'?"

"I did," Brian admitted, "but that word is a homograph."

"A what?"

"Greek is like English in that you can have two words that are spelled exactly the same but are completely unrelated and have entirely different meanings. Take the word 'change,' for example. In the verb form it describes becoming different, but as a noun it can refer to loose coins. There's no relationship in meaning. In the case of *titanos*, there's more than one Greek word spelled that way. One means 'gray,' and the other means 'Titan,' but they're unrelated."

"Got it."

"But having said that," Brian continued, "it's also true that ancient biblical and non-canonical Jewish literature contains threads about giants, gods, and eschatology that intertwine. But I just don't see a role for the little gray alien in all that. It seems completely incongruent."

"We'll have to talk more."

Kamran, having waited for the exchange to play out, immediately began texting a message as rapidly as his thumbs could move. Malone's phone went off. He was sitting across from Brian. "Here," he said without looking at the phone, handing it to Brian. "It's for you again."

Brian looked at the message. "Kamran says his study of astral prophecy has produced some links back to Genesis 6, but he agrees with my take on things." Brian looked up at Kamran. "You and I really have to spend some time together," he said, and Kamran nodded enthusiastically.

"I have a question," Madison piped up. "I've heard the word 'Watcher' come up a couple times now. What is that?"

"It's a term from Jewish literature dating a few centuries before the New Testament era, books like *1 Enoch*. In some retellings of biblical stories—Genesis 6, for example—it replaces the phrase 'sons of God,'" Brian explained. "A Watcher is a divine being like the ones in that story. Some ancient texts suggest their normal physical appearance is serpentine but that they can change their appearance."

"No one ever knows who the Watchers are," a soft voice observed from the periphery of the assembly, "unless God reveals it."

Everyone's attention turned to Sabi.

"I am sorry to intrude," he said apologetically. "But this thing you must all know. The entity known to the four of you as Adam may have been a Watcher—disguising himself to be that which he wanted you to see and hold in awe. Or he may have been someone in the room, invading your thoughts to manipulate your belief." He paused. "Or he may have taken no form at all."

"You talk as though you have some familiarity with these . . . things," Dee said cautiously, visibly spooked by his words.

"Yes . . ."

"What do you mean, Sabi?" Clarise asked.

Brian could tell this was something new.

"When you are as I am, much of life is spent in prayer and meditation, in communion with God. God shows me things when He wishes to—allows me to see things of the unseen world, the spiritual realm. That is how I knew Professor Scott would have our password," he added, smiling gently at Brian. "God told me of his dreams. I cannot anticipate learning such things, but there is always a purpose when God acts in this way. At times I have been shown . . . presences . . . in the unseen world when God beckons my spirit to meet with Him."

Brian glanced around the group. There was no sign that anyone took Sabi's words lightly or considered them in any way misguided. His own experience with the frail man was evidently not unique for those in the room.

Sabi continued. "Scholars call such experiences . . . what is the phrase? 'Altered states of consciousness.' I do not know about such things. I only know that I have visited the divine realm, though never at my own bidding. Our sister Melissa knows about this. She left her body and was instructed by a guide—a presence. This is what I speak of. It is hard to explain to others, is it not?" he asked, looking at Melissa.

She nodded.

"I know such beings are part of the unseen world. They are very powerful, even if they are disloyal to God. Professor Scott knows what the Apostle Peter said about this."

Brian thought for a moment. "The 'glorious ones,'" he replied. "Second Peter 2 tells us that wicked people are foolish enough to blaspheme the glorious ones—something even angels won't do. The name comes from proximity to God's glory—His throne room."

"And so we must be like Michael, the archangel, when dealing with such beings, as Jude, the Lord's brother, told us."

"We let God rebuke such powers," Malcolm finished Sabi's thought.

"Yes, there is no other choice. They do not answer to us. God will deal with such powers in His own time. We must prepare our hearts and minds to see what is there when God exposes the darkness by His light."

"Now do you see why I'm hoping aliens are real?" Dee asked, scowling and peering over her glasses at Madison. "If it weren't for Brian's nanobots, we'd all be on that page."

"Speaking of that," said Clarise, "let's have a look at your finger."

Everyone moved closer to where Brian was sitting as he unwrapped the gauze. Where there should have been a fresh wound, there was only a faint, whitish line.

"Man, *that* is mind-blowing," Ward gasped.

"It's like magic," Madison said, shaking her head.

"No magic, just technology," Malcolm corrected her, grinning with satisfaction. "Another five minutes, and you'd never know he'd been cut."

"I want you in the lab right after breakfast tomorrow," Clarise effused. "I want to scope some blood, if that's all right."

"Sure."

"Have you two ever wondered if your children might have these nanobots?" Fern asked. "Some blood-borne infections can get passed on. There have been cases where HIV was passed to the child, but not the mother, when the women were unknowingly artificially inseminated from an HIV-positive donor. Those nanobots are smaller than the HIV virus."

"There's really no chance of that," Brian answered.

"How do you know?"

Brian looked at Melissa. She nodded. He took a deep breath. "It's time you all know that we're not actually married. In fact, Melissa doesn't know *how* she's pregnant. The babies aren't mine."

"You mean Melissa's pregnancy is just like Dee's?" Clarise gasped, shocked.

"Right," Brian replied. "We pretended to be married for the sake of our situation at the college. Even Father Fitzgerald doesn't know we aren't really married."

"We planned to give the babies up for adoption," Melissa explained. "Every test I've had says the twins are normal. I wouldn't abort them unless there was some sign they aren't normal."

"You mean if they aren't human," Dee jumped in. "Now you all know why I want mine terminated—you know where we've been and what we've seen. And for the record, I haven't changed my mind."

"Abortion isn't something I want to go through," Melissa added. "I've had one before, after I was raped in college."

"I'm stunned—again," Neff said, shaking his head. "We never suspected you two weren't a real couple."

"We *are* a real couple," Melissa corrected him. "We're just not married—yet."

"Sounds like you two had a bit of a breakthrough," Dee said, her expression softening.

"We did," Melissa replied. "And you were right. What you said was spot on."

Dee smiled and nodded appreciatively.

"We want to get married for real," Brian explained, "but we think it best to wait until after Melissa has the babies. Think of us as engaged. Malcolm—"

"Absolutely," Malcolm answered, flashing a wide grin, anticipating the question. "It would be a thrill."

"Why not keep the babies?" Fern asked. "Even though you were impregnated without your knowledge, you could still give them a good home."

"They're not mine, or ours."

"Neither are adopted babies."

"This isn't the same."

"Dear," Fern said gently, "I know the decision is a very personal one, but I'm pressing you a bit for a reason. I want to see if you are completely convinced the babies are normal. I can see that you're not—and that's quite understandable."

Melissa sighed and glanced at Brian. "I guess I'm not," she admitted. "I just don't know how I could be."

43

Great perils have this beauty, that they bring to light the fraternity of strangers.

—*Victor Hugo*

"Good morning," Fern said cheerfully as Brian and Melissa sat down at the table in the Pit. "Most everyone has already had breakfast. What can I make for you?"

"Thank you, but just show us where everything is. You don't have to wait on us," Brian said.

"That's no problem," she replied. "My age makes me everyone's mom or grandma, and I like it that way." Fern filled a cup of coffee at an adjacent setting. "This is for Graham. Doug was just here but went to get Graham," she added, her mood shifting.

"Is something wrong?" Melissa asked, picking up on the change.

"I don't know for sure. Doug was looking at his phone and said he had something Graham needed to see right away. To be honest, that's usually not good news."

"I guess we'll find out shortly."

"That we will," Fern replied. "Now, what can I get you?"

Brian and Melissa obliged Fern's hospitality and were joined moments later by Ward, who did the same.

"Clarise has been up for a couple hours already," Ward said, taking a sip of his coffee. "Not to sound too ghoulish," he said, looking in Brian's direction, "but she's prepping the lab for your visit."

"'Prepping'?"

Ward laughed. "Oh yeah. When Clarise gets fixated on a problem or something she's discovered, she gets a little obsessive."

"Reminds me of somebody," Melissa said, grinning.

"I don't obsess," Brian objected with a chuckle. "I just like to see things through when I'm on to something."

"Right."

"Clarise is also wrapped up in that old printout you gave her with all the letters. She'll be useless the rest of today, for sure," Ward added. "That means we'll have to adapt our normal routine."

"For Christmas Eve?" Melissa asked, taking a plate from Fern, who had returned to the table with some toasted bagels.

"Yeah. We usually drive into civilization to go out for dinner and see Christmas lights. Clarise already told me she doesn't want the interruption. But she had a suggestion for the two of you. I tried to talk her out of it. I'm hoping you'll hate it."

"What's that?" Melissa asked, her curiosity roused.

"Shopping. She wants me to take the four of you into the city and buy you anything you need."

"That sounds wonderful," Melissa agreed quickly. "What's the problem with that? Your gender?"

"She's good." Ward smiled and looked at Brian.

"What time do we leave? There's no turning back now. Trust me," Brian said.

Melissa sighed, feigning irritation. "We can do it some other time if you two don't have the stamina."

"Told you," Brian said, stirring his tea. "Game over. This battle of wits just ended."

"Actually, it makes good sense to go now," Ward said. "Lots of sales. Both of you should take inventory after breakfast and make a list of what you need—and not just clothing. *Anything*. I'll make sure Malcolm and Deidre do the same."

"Thank you." Melissa beamed.

"If we have time, we can still drive around and see Christmas lights."

"Are we going to see the rest of Miqlat first?" Brian asked.

"We'll make an effort," Ward answered. "It's a few hours into town, so we'll plan to leave right after lunch. That gives us an hour to tour this morning, plus time for you all to check on what you need. We'll start as soon as Malcolm and Deidre have had breakfast. The first stop will be the lab, or I'll be sleeping upstairs for a while. There's a lot—" He suddenly stopped, his attention caught by something in the background.

Brian and Melissa turned to see Neff and Malone approaching.

"What's up?" Ward asked as the two men sat down at the table. Their expression told everyone that it was serious, whatever it was.

"I think we can safely conclude that this Colonel Ferguson has discovered your former whereabouts," Neff explained, sighing as he looked at Brian and Melissa.

"How in the world could he know that already?" Brian asked, startled. "It's barely been a couple days!"

"Like I said when we left Fargo," Malone answered, "things just turn up." He slid his phone toward Melissa. "This came up in my newsreader this morning. I added the RSS feeds to the major North Dakota papers before we even left."

Melissa picked up the phone, its screen open to a news story about the suicide at the coffee shop.

"It's down the page a bit."

Melissa continued reading and scrolled down to reveal a grainy photo. Despite the poor quality, she could make out Becky's face, gun pointed at her head—and her own face in the lower corner of the image. "I can't believe it," she said in exasperation.

"Believe it," Malone said. "Somebody must have turned in the photo to police shortly after it happened. The article doesn't mention you—your North Dakota persona, of course—but if your Colonel was behind the girl's death, it's a good bet he's seen this photo. And I bet he would do something to get access to the investigation."

"Is there any indication the police have matched the face to a name?" Brian asked.

"Not from that article," Neff replied. "We've done some searching for other stories, and so far no hint of that has surfaced."

"Without that, the Colonel might not be able to locate Melissa even if he did recognize her," Brian reasoned.

"That's true," Neff admitted, "but just because there's no report that the police have been unable to locate the woman in the picture doesn't mean they don't have a name and an identity."

"Someone from the college would surely see the picture and say something," Malone added. "I suspect the police have a name and aren't saying anything to reporters yet."

"Well," Brian said, trying to make the best of the news, "we're here, so all this means is that we'll never be able to go back. That's no surprise."

"You're safe," Neff said, "but someone we all know isn't."

"Who is it?" Ward prodded anxiously.

"I got an email this morning from the college," he said grimly. "Father Fitzgerald is missing."

"*Missing*?" Melissa asked, panic in her voice.

"The official email went out to all board members. It says only that Father Fitzgerald had been taken from his home, and his whereabouts are unknown. The police have been contacted. We are to wait for further information."

"Are they sure he was taken? How do they know?"

"You got some 'unofficial' news as well, I take it," Brian guessed.

"I did.... Gloria emailed me. She said she came in early this morning to pick up some Christmas presents she'd stashed at her office. Aloysius had told her he'd be in, and she planned to give him his present when he arrived. He never made it. She was concerned since he's the extremely punctual type, and he always tells her if there's a change of plans. She called the house and got no answer, so she called police and asked them to drive out and check if he was home. I'm not sure what they found, but they called her back and asked a bunch of questions—including whether she knew anyone who would ever harm him."

"Oh, God," Melissa gasped, closing her eyes. "It has to be Ferguson."

"We don't know anything for sure now, of course," Neff said, "but we will. Ward, I hate to say it . . ."

"No problem. Should I leave now?"

"No, we'll give the police time to learn what they can. It'll take a couple days, especially with Christmas. Malone and I will go back to North Dakota with you, but you'll have to be the one who deals with the police."

"How are you going to get the police to tell you anything?" Brian asked.

"I'm licensed as a private investigator," Ward answered. "So are Neff and Malone, but we can't take the chance that someone will ID them from the scene."

"Malone might get away with that role, but I wouldn't," Neff added. "Aside from being on site in Fargo, enough people on campus know me as a board member. I can't get caught prying into police business."

"For sure," Ward continued. "I'll learn what I can."

"We need to pray that Father Fitzgerald doesn't end up like Father Benedict," Brian said somberly. "The Colonel is ruthless. If only Andrew hadn't gone back to Area 51 after we got off the base."

"He did what he thought was best," Neff said. "And trust me, I'm scared for Aloysius, especially after reading the autopsy report on Father Benedict."

"I'd forgotten about that," Brian remembered. "How did police identify his remains?"

"Well, this is probably as good a time as any to tell you . . . they ID'd him by dental remains and fingerprints on his shoes. The body had been exposed in the desert for a long time—at least a month, though based on your story it was probably longer."

"Could they tell how he died?"

"Not specifically, but the report speculated it was very violent. Most of the major bones had fractures—two broken neck vertebrae. . . . There were far too many fractures to be accounted for by the act of dumping the body, even if it had been from a helicopter. There's little doubt he'd been severely beaten. God help Aloysius."

44

If everyone is thinking alike, then somebody isn't thinking.

—*General George S. Patton, Jr.*

"Here you go," Clarise said, handing Melissa a folded sheet of paper, visibly tattered and worn at the edges. "I hope you've had more success than I have, whatever you're working on," she added, glancing curiously at the table.

"Not really," Melissa answered.

"I've spent the better part of three days trying to analyze it and can't get beyond the obvious. I'm ashamed to say I couldn't even stop thinking about it over Christmas."

"To answer your question, mom, we're getting nowhere," Madison said abruptly, hunched over the photocopies of the circle fragments from Becky that Brian and Melissa had spread out on the dinner table in the Pit. She blew a strand of hair from where it had fallen on her nose and sat up straight.

"I know how you feel," Clarise said, unable to hide her disappointment. "At this point, I can't tell you any more than you already knew. The letters on the paper are certainly part of a DNA sequence, but I have no idea why parts of it are circled. Are you sure you can't remember any other details?"

"There aren't any to remember," Melissa said grimly. "Neil was pointing a gun at us when he handed it to Brian back at Area 51. It was bizarre—he was sputtering about how millions of people would die if he didn't kill me. He didn't get the chance to say anything else before the Colonel's men shot him."

"He wasn't interested in elaborating," Brian said matter-of-factly. "He was ready to kill us both." He shook his head. "Sorry, Clarise. We haven't got anything that would help. Are you sure you don't want to keep the page?"

"No need. I scanned it and ran it through OCR software to keep a digital copy. Summit's been checking the OCR results since this morning to make sure we have an exact version. She won't quit until she's done, which should be soon. Nili's keeping her company in the lab."

"Pardon me for asking," said Malcolm, "but is Summit reliable for something like that?"

"More than anyone else here," Clarise answered. "I wouldn't say we could add obsessive compulsive to her profile, but Summit has a fixation with numbers. She won't let a digit go unchecked."

"Interesting."

"That's one way to describe it," Madison said absently, shuffling the papers on the tabletop again.

"How's Deidre?" Clarise asked Malcolm.

"She decided to lie down. She was wasted—hasn't been sleeping well. Too much movement."

"Good. She needs all the rest she can get."

"How's the puzzle coming?" Fern asked, approaching the table.

"It *isn't,*" Madison blurted out in frustration.

"What's this?" Fern asked, holding up a white napkin sitting in front of Malcolm that had a line of hand-written numbers and letters.

"That's what Becky chanted before she killed herself," Malcolm answered. "I wrote everything down. Once she started repeating herself, I assumed it was a message. I figured we should get to work on it, so I brought it out."

"Something else to torment us," Madison groused, looking at the small square.

"Madison hates it when she can't find patterns in data," Clarise whispered through a proud smile.

"I heard that."

"113619, HGWESTON, 80503," Fern recited. "What does all that mean?"

"Who knows?" Malcolm shrugged. "I put commas in between to mark where Becky paused. That might indicate starting and stopping points, but we can't be sure. Basically, Madison's right. We've got nothing."

"There's got to be some way to make sense of this stuff," Madison moaned again. "There *must* be some point."

"I don't doubt that," Brian replied. "She was programmed by the Colonel, and he never does anything without a reason. He wanted to send a message."

"Don't get frustrated, dear," Fern said, rubbing her hand over Madison's shoulder.

"Too late," Madison said irritably. "Anyone else want a snack? Popcorn always clears my head."

"Ward sends his greetings, by the way," Clarise informed her daughter as she began to rise from the table. "Got an email from him about an hour ago."

"Does he have anything to report?" Brian asked. "I know he's only been there a day."

"Well, he's been to see the police. He said they're completely stumped."

"Did they share any clues?" Madison inquired, lingering.

"They say there aren't any—except for the material at the crime scene, and they weren't sharing photos. They're more than willing to talk to him, though. Ward says they're probably hoping that anyone who is too inquisitive will accidentally reveal something only the criminal would know. If that's the state of the investigation, they're pretty much at a standstill."

"Strike three," Brian grimaced. "We haven't learned anything new on the Antarctic base blueprints, the DNA printout, or what happened to Father Fitzgerald."

"Maybe we'll know more by tomorrow," Fern reassured them. "Hopefully Graham will learn something at the emergency board meeting. And Madison, if you're going to make something, you should ask Summit if she wants anything." She motioned with her eyes to one of the entryways off the outer circle of Pit.

Madison turned and saw Summit and Nili emerging. Summit headed for a refrigerator, while Nili joined them at the table.

"Summit's finished checking and correcting the OCR," she said, taking a seat. "Has anyone seen Kamran this morning?"

"He told us he'd be in his room working on something for Dr. Scott," replied Clarise, looking in his direction. Brian shrugged, having no idea of the project. "Plus, he's on call."

"What does that mean?" Melissa asked.

"It's Sabi. Whenever he sleeps, he has devices attached to him to monitor his vitals. They send signals wirelessly to a mobile monitoring unit. It's Kamran's turn to keep it with him. Sabi had trouble sleeping last night. I was up with him a couple times."

"Nili," Brian turned to her, "I've been wanting to ask you about what you meant earlier—about how my work helped your father. Is this a good time?"

"Of course," she replied, smiling warmly. "My father was a cantor in our local synagogue. He was very upset when I embraced Yeshua and Christianity. At first we argued a lot, but eventually we agreed this should not drive us apart. That meant a lot. I loved my father."

"He passed away?"

"He had cancer. I tried many times to bring him to faith in Yeshua, but for so long he could not accept the gospel story. He said he felt like believing Jesus was the God of Israel in a body was blasphemy, that it violated the *Shema*. 'Ha-Shem our God is one,' he would say, 'and so Jesus cannot be God.'"

"That's a common obstacle for Jews."

"Yes. I did not know what to say—until I found your work about the two powers in heaven, and how the Angel of God was a man with ha-Shem within him, right there in the Torah . As soon as I read it, I knew my father would understand."

"And he did."

"Yes." She smiled gratefully. "He believed because he could see the truth in the Torah. He understood how a Jew could worship Yeshua and not be worshiping another god. After that, his heart was open. He died believing. You were God's instrument."

"That's wonderful," Brian said softly, unsure of what else to say.

"What is wrong?" Nili asked.

"Nothing's wrong. It's just . . . gratifying . . . to know that all that study amounted to something besides a degree. It's been easy to think that it didn't mean anything, especially because of the way things have turned out."

"You mean that you have no post at a university?"

"Yeah. But when I hear it expressed that way, the idea sounds even less important."

"You must not be ashamed. Your path has been difficult and unusual—like the rest of ours. But we are here together. If we serve Yeshua as He wishes, we may have to wait for recognition, but it will come."

Brian looked at her appreciatively. "Thanks."

"Even you can't argue with that," Melissa said affectionately, stroking his arm.

Summit appeared at the table, a soda bottle filled with a yellow liquid in her hand. Squish again seemed to appear from nowhere to trot lightly behind her.

"Curry Ramune *again*?" Madison recoiled, turning up her nose. "That must be what bile tastes like. How can you stand that stuff?"

Summit eyed her dismissively and took a swig. "It's good," she said and put the bottle down on the table. "You can't have any."

"Don't put it there!" Madison scolded. "That napkin has important numbers on it. The sweat from the bottle will wash them out!"

Her hand still on the bottle, Summit looked down at the small white square. She made no effort to pick it up.

"Come on, Summit! Don't be stubborn—"

"Wait!" said Clarise in an urgent but even voice. *"She's processing."*

Brian, Melissa, and Malcolm watched in fascination. Summit stood silently, staring at the bottom of her bottle where it rested, occasionally blinking, but otherwise not moving. The pink strands of her hair hung motionlessly around her shoulders as her gaze remained riveted on the napkin. Brian leaned in and looked closely. The position of the bottle had left only the numbers 113619 visible.

Fear suddenly contorted the young girl's face. *"No—Nazis!"* she wailed, backing away from the table.

Nili rose quickly and put her arm around her. "It's okay, Summit; you're safe here." Nili looked at the others, bewildered.

"He's a *Nazi,*" Summit said, her voice more controlled, but visibly shaken.

"What do you mean?"

"I won't look at it again!"

"You don't have to," Fern said, coming alongside the stricken girl. "Let's go to the kitchen and get something to eat, sweetheart."

No one said a word until Fern had walked Summit out of earshot. "What was *that*?" Melissa gasped. "Is she okay?"

"I'm checking on it," replied Madison, already at work on her laptop.

"Summit will be fine," Nili answered. "Growing up in Israel . . . The Nazis are still part of life, among other enemies."

"I need to explain," Clarise said. "I told you earlier that Summit has a gift. You just saw it."

"What exactly did we see?" Brian asked.

"Summit has a photographic memory, what some call an eidetic memory. Some people with autism have this ability. In her case, she has phenomenal recall, especially of numbers, but it can include visual memories as well. She has the call number and shelf location of every book in our library memorized—all 20,000 of them. You can ask her if we have a book, and if we do, she'll give you that information."

"That's incredible," Melissa gasped.

"It is, but it's unpredictable. While numbers are nearly instantaneous, other information recall sometimes takes a few minutes—her mind has to be diverted before the information pops into her head. Other times she sees something that just triggers recall on the spot."

"Like right now?"

Clarise nodded.

"A Nazi number?" Brian asked incredulously. "What does that mean?"

"Every Nazi Party member had an ID number," Melissa mused. "SS members also had personnel numbers."

"Nice call," Madison exclaimed, waving her phone. "That's it—it's an SS personnel file number. Summit must have read it somewhere. Does the name Hans Kammler mean anything to you?"

"Hans Kammler?" Melissa repeated incredulously.

"Yep. You two know anything about him?"

"Yeah," Brian replied, "at least what there is to know. Kammler was in charge of advanced weapons projects during World War II and the concentration camps that provided slave labor for them. He's rumored to have been the last person in charge of Nazi wingless aircraft experiments."

"Wingless aircraft?"

"Saucers—UFOs."

Madison's rosy complexion began to dissipate. Brian saw fear in her eyes. She went back to her phone.

"Can we really be sure about this?" Malcolm asked Clarise. "Is Summit ever wrong?"

Clarise shook her head. "I know it sounds crazy, but we've all seen her pull incredible things out of thin air before. She's never been wrong. Part of the sequence implanted in Becky's mind has to be Kammler's SS number. It can't be an accident."

Malcolm slid the receipt out from under the bottle, patting it dry. "God only knows what that means—and exactly what other breadcrumbs the Colonel wants us to find."

45

Secrecy is the beginning of tyranny.

—*Robert Heinlein*

"I'm sorry to call you all out here," the detective began, surveying the faces of the men and women seated around the oblong, cherry table, "but the truth is, we've hit a wall in our investigation. We're no closer to finding Dr. Fitzgerald today than we were a week ago."

"You have no leads at all?" a slender, white-haired man asked, stern faced and leaning forward in his chair.

"We have one piece of evidence to go on, which I'll be showing you today. We haven't divulged this to the public—and it's critical that you keep what you've seen and heard here confidential. There were no witnesses to the crime, no fingerprints, and no forensic evidence left behind—at least that didn't belong to the victim."

"Do you know for sure Father Fitzgerald is alive?" a middle-aged woman in a business suit asked, her anxiety evident in her tone and expression.

"Honestly, ma'am, we don't have anything tangible in that regard, though we believe that's the case. The person who did this left a message—a cryptic, violent one—so we believe Father Fitzgerald is being held as leverage for receiving some response to that message. We've made no attempt at that since we don't understand what the message might mean. That's really the reason why we've asked the board to assemble on such short notice. We're hoping one of you will provide some assistance."

"There isn't a person in this room who wouldn't do everything possible to help, detective."

"Thank you, sir. You're Graham Neff, correct?"

"Yes."

"Don't look surprised. I recognize you from the pictures out in the hallway. Father Fitzgerald's secretary told us that you've spent some time on campus recently and talked quite a bit with the president. I'd like to talk with you about those conversations and whether you saw anyone with the president that you didn't recognize."

"Of course."

"Good. Now I'll show you what little we have. I'm going to project one of the crime-scene photos on the screen," he explained, grabbing a remote and pointing it at a projector mounted on the ceiling. The projector whirred softly, and a bright white square appeared on the screen. "If any of you are squeamish, I apologize ahead of time. This will be disturbing, but we need to know if any of you can make sense of it." He pressed the remote.

It took a few moments for the onlookers to understand the image. The first to comprehend what they were being shown gasped.

"*Good God!*" Neff heard one of his colleagues exclaim. Some turned away, covering their eyes as though the gesture could erase the sight from memory. Neff stared at the picture, trying to control his own rage and revulsion once he understood what he was looking at.

The picture was a close-up of Father Fitzgerald's desktop. There were five books stacked atop the desk, neatly aligned so that the titles showed right-side up. The priest's desk blotter was covered with blood. A blood-stained scissors lay at the periphery. At the bottom of the stack, positioned precisely in relationship to each other, were two severed ears.

"It's the books we're wondering about," the detective droned on, matter-of-factly, accustomed to such images. "It's obvious the perpetrator intended them to be read, perhaps in order, but we're not sure about that last part."

"What are they?" a pudgy but dapper bald man seated at the far end of the table asked. "I can't make all of them out."

"Here's a list." The detective turned off the projector and began distributing sheets of paper around the room. "You may show these to other people," he noted, "but please keep the violent circumstances to yourself."

Neff took the page from a woman seated next to him whose face had turned pale. He perused the titles from top to bottom, consciously controlling his facial expression and body language. He knew their meaning in an instant:

Carl Sagan, *Contact*

E. Theodore Mullen, *The Divine Council in Canaanite and Early*

Hebrew Literature

Melissa Kelley, *Esoteric Nazism and Apocalyptic Christian Cults*

Deidre Harper, *Mass Hysteria: Psychogenic Illness and Social Delusions*

Malcolm Bradley, *Environmental Biology and the Christian Humanist*

"It seems obvious that the Sagan title is a request for contact," the detective said, surveying his audience closely. "But we have no idea as to whom the message is directed or what the other titles mean in that context."

"They're so . . . different," a man across the table from Neff observed with chagrin. "They don't seem to be related at all. They seem completely random."

"Anyone have any guesses? Mr. Neff?"

Neff looked up from the list and shrugged helplessly. "I haven't the slightest idea."

46

Fishermen know that the sea is dangerous and the storm terrible,
but they have never found these dangers sufficient reason for remaining ashore.

—Vincent Van Gogh

"That was Nili," Neff said, slipping his phone into his pocket. "They're just about set up. She said they'll call back tonight for the message. I'm not sure what making contact with the Colonel will mean for the four of you, but he won't be able to trace us."

"You're sure about that?" Dee asked tensely. She was sitting at a desk in one of Miqlat's training rooms, her hands clasped around a cup of coffee to absorb the warmth and distract her mind. She looked apprehensively at the boxes, circles, and chicken-scratch abbreviations scrawled on the room's whiteboard.

"I'm certain," he answered. "It'll work beautifully. Madison knows what she's doing, and Nili can help her procure everything she needs. I called for all of you just now to explain the plan."

"I hope you're right; she'd better know what she's doing," Melissa replied uneasily.

"Madison's created untraceable phone networks before," Neff explained. "It's not that complicated. You buy two anonymous prepaid phones from two different carriers. The phones come with phone numbers, so there's no personal name attached that anyone could use for ID. You just need to use a public computer to change the IP addresses, then set up call forwarding for one phone to call the other, make sure caller ID is blocked on both, and then set the second phone to call forward to the number you really want to call after it receives the call from the first phone."

"Well, that's clear." Dee smirked.

"Why did you send Nili, Madison, and Malone to Israel for this?" Brian asked.

"And Clarise told us this morning that Ward left in the middle of the night for North Dakota," Malcolm added. "I assume that's also part of the plan?"

"It is," Neff answered. "I'll try to explain. Ward will be landing in the next hour or so. When we tell him we're set, he's going to call Minot Air Force base to leave our message for the Colonel. The message will refer to the five books left on the desk, so the Colonel will know we've received his message and are following his wishes. I presume that, in response, he'll follow the directions we give him."

"But what if someone else takes the call for him? Won't that person then know that the Colonel is involved in a crime?" Melissa asked. "I'd think that would piss him off, which isn't what we want."

"We've thought about that. Colonel Ferguson has a personal extension at the base. Ward learned that by calling and asking a receptionist. If, by chance, anyone else hears his messages, that's his problem, but we'll try to keep the message as innocuous as possible. I don't want him to think we're trying to incriminate him. That would likely be very bad for Aloysius. I doubt, though, that the Colonel is having anyone else screen his messages."

Dee shrugged. "I just can't help thinking there's no winning with this guy."

"Well, we got you out of Area 51 and have stayed a step or two ahead of him since then."

"He's right, Dee," Malcolm chimed in.

"At any rate," Neff continued, "Ward will use Madison's phone configuration. If the Colonel actually picks up, Ward has the tools to electronically disguise his voice if he wants to. He'll be making the call in North Dakota and will destroy both phones with acid as soon as the message is delivered. He'll make the call inside his car along the highway between Fargo and the college where there are no cameras. He won't be traceable in any way."

"Don't forget who this is," Dee warned. "He's a gangster in a uniform and has access to everything imaginable for finding people. The creep runs the black-op candy store."

"You can't trace what doesn't exist," Malcolm said, trying to calm her nerves. "Once the phones are gone and long separated from the caller, he's got nothing."

"What instructions will we be giving the Colonel?" Brian asked.

"We're going to tell him to invisibly post what he wants from us on the Minot base website within a specific time window."

"Invisibly?"

"We're telling him to put his instructions in text of the same color as the white portions of the front-page background."

"But won't their web people know the Colonel is involved in a crime?"

"Again, how he keeps that a secret is his problem. He'll be motivated to make it happen once he knows we've gotten his message. Anyone viewing the site during the time the message remains posted would never see the words. Madison will take a snapshot of the page's code and get the text that's posted. That's why we sent her and Nili to Israel. Once they access the Minot base homepage, their visit could be traced. We assume the Colonel will try that."

"But why Israel?"

"So they can set up their own server network and can connect to the Internet at a completely secure access point, one that Nili's intelligence contacts in Israel will provide. Madison will have everything set up with encryption and a VPN to hide where the visit is coming from. She's an experienced hacker and knows the techniques used to trace. She won't overlook anything. A secure access point, encryption, VPN, and control of the servers will prevent a trace."

"I don't know . . ."

"We could do everything I described here or somewhere else, but we don't have the time it would take to make sure all the possible connection points for accessing the Web are totally secure. If we use Nili's Israeli resources, everything's in place except for buying some new hardware that we'll destroy afterward."

"It's been almost four days since you got back from your board meeting and they took off with Malone for Israel," Dee replied. "That doesn't seem like saving time."

"It would have taken weeks some other way," Neff responded. "It's the best we could do. I'm worried about Aloysius, but I'm certain the Colonel's goal isn't to kill him—it's to find you. Once we know exactly what he wants, we'll know how to approach things."

"What if he wants a trade?" Melissa asked.

"There won't be any."

The four of them looked at Neff's face and saw a mixture of calm and hard resolution.

"He's your friend," Brian spoke up.

"He is—but so are all of you. We don't trade lives. And to be honest, Aloysius would be incensed if I made any such deal. Knowing the efforts Andrew undertook to get you out and hide you, he'd never want that to fail. He'd die first."

"I believe it," Malcolm said. "That's exactly what Andrew would have done."

"And in all likelihood, did," Brian added soberly.

"One more thing," Neff said. "We have to assume that the Colonel knows that the board meeting took place."

"But if he draws that conclusion, doesn't that make you—and us—vulnerable?" asked Melissa.

"Not really," Neff replied. "No element of the contact attempt is taking place anywhere near here, and the hardware will be liquidated. Even if the Colonel visited every board member for an interview, there's nothing to tie anyone—particularly us—to the contact effort. He might deduce someone in the room knows your whereabouts, but that suspicion doesn't get him anything specific if the contact is untraceable. Besides, he's using Aloysius to draw you out. Whether the point of leverage is connected to the college or not is incidental."

"That's been bugging me, actually," Malcolm said. "It's easy for us to see that the book titles finger each of us, but the picture that surfaced from the coffee shop only had Melissa in it. We assume that someone at some point identified Melissa, and that was how the Colonel would have been led to the college. The Colonel would assume Brian was with her, but how would he know Dee and I were with them?"

"I can answer that," Neff replied. "After the meeting, I had a conversation with Gloria."

"Father Fitzgerald's secretary?" Malcolm asked.

"Right. She happened to tell me that a uniformed Air Force officer had visited her office the day before Aloysius disappeared. He actually spoke to several people who work in the administration building, asking about Brian and Melissa. Gloria told me she mentioned seeing the two of you with your friends—an African American couple. That was all he needed to hear."

"Makes sense." Malcolm sighed. "She'd have no reason to think she was talking to a psychopath. I'm sure the Colonel was tickled to pick up the trail of all four of us."

"Tickled?" Dee scoffed. "More like a shark smelling blood in the water."

Neff sat down next to Dee. "Deidre, you can be sure I understand the kind of person we're dealing with. I've dealt with enough warlords and mercenaries with no regard for human life to know that this guy is cut from the same cloth—especially after seeing what he did to Aloysius. We don't take any uncalculated risks."

"I'd prefer no risks at all, Mr. Neff, but I know we have to try to get your friend away from him. . . . I know it all too well."

47

Without courage all virtues lose their meaning.

—Sir Winston Churchill

"I'll get it," Brian said, hearing the knock on the door. He set his laptop on the floor next to the recliner. Melissa anxiously looked at him over her glasses and put down her book. He opened the door to their pod. Neff stood on the other side, a foreboding look on his face.

"Do we have something?" Brian asked with urgency.

"We do. I've asked everyone to meet in the Pit. This will involve all of us. As soon as you can, please." He glanced at Melissa.

Without a word, Melissa rose from couch and put on her shoes. The three of them walked the short distance to the foyer and The Pit in silence. Brian and Melissa saw that most everyone had already arrived. They took a seat next to Malcolm and Dee. Neff stood and waited until everyone was accounted for.

"I just received a message from Madison. She, Nili, and Malone are already in the air, en route to the East Coast of the United States. Ward should be home tonight."

"The East Coast?" Fern asked. "Why there?"

"Because of this," he said, holding up a piece of paper. "The good news is that everything went as planned for getting a message from Colonel Ferguson."

"What does he want?" Malcolm asked.

"That's the bad news," Neff answered. "But of course we couldn't expect anything comfortable. I'll read it to all of you. It's simple and direct."

> *Congratulations. To acquire the package, meet me at the coordinates below precisely forty-eight hours from now. The location is a restaurant. Dr. Scott and I will have dinner. After I see that Dr. Bradley, Dr. Harper, and Dr. Kelley have also made the trip, I will release the package at coordinates provided to Dr. Scott. Failure to follow these directions will be*

most regrettable. Do not disappoint me.

41°22 35.14 N, 71°30 45.13 W

Neff folded the paper and put it in his pocket. The four named in the message sat in silence. There was no need for words.

"Do you know this location?" Sabi asked softly.

"It's a restaurant on the coast in Narragansett, Rhode Island," Neff replied.

Sabi nodded quietly. Clarise whispered something in his ear. He shook his head.

"Does Nili have any thoughts?" Clarise asked.

"She does. She's already sent me a sketch of how to approach the location with exit strategies. She likes the layout of the area. It offers several tactical advantages."

"I don't like the sound of it even now," Fern said anxiously.

Neff continued. "Forty-eight hours from the time of reception would put us around dinner time, no surprise there. Given the venue, there should be a lot of people on the scene, so that bodes well."

"Like hell it does," Dee exclaimed with worry. "This guy isn't going to give a rat's ass for anyone who comes between him and what he wants."

"I don't doubt that, but the demand is pretty straightforward."

"Don't be naïve."

"I'm not. I'm sure there's more to it. But the message is interesting for what it *doesn't* say, at least in my experience."

"What do you mean?" asked Brian.

"He only wants to meet with you, for one. Second, he doesn't demand that you come alone. Granted, he wants some sort of visual proof the others made the trip, but he could have been far more restrictive. Be that as it may, I can tell you all right now that, other than Brian, none of you are going near this guy. We'll see to it. We'll provide the visual verification he demanded at a distance, since he didn't give us specifics."

Brian remained silent.

"He could come with his own private army," Melissa said ruefully.

"He *could*, but I doubt he will."

"Why?"

"Madison said there haven't been any attempts to trace the reception. That gives me some insight into this guy already. He knows he's in control of the situation and is pretty arrogant about it. He doesn't need to trace us. We have to come to him."

"That's entirely familiar," Dee said under her breath.

"I could be wrong," Neff continued, "and we'll plan as though I am, but this guy seems so cocksure of himself that I'm betting he'll show up with only a driver, maybe even alone. He's sure he will get what he wants. I'm sure he knows he could have asked us to do practically anything, and we'd do it. But all he asks for is face time with Brian. It's totally ego-driven."

"He's absolutely a narcissist," Dee replied. "But he's also a highly intelligent manipulator. He's capable of anything. Even if he's alone, he could take hostages and demand an exchange for us. Or he could poison Brian. He could—"

"Let's think about who he is a bit more," Neff interrupted. "I'll give the devil his due, but he does have something to lose here with that kind of behavior."

"Like what?" asked Melissa. "This guy is tripped out on his own power."

"That's my point."

Melissa eyed him curiously.

"The Colonel obviously loves holding that position," Neff explained, "and whatever he's up to mandates that he holds the position he does. He's not going to do anything *publicly* that could get him arrested or court-martialed. If he makes sure to keep what he's doing isolated to the four of you and his own cronies, he's immune to any trouble."

"How so?"

"Remember, there's no evidence that actually ties him to Father Fitzgerald's abduction except our interpretation of the books on the desk. The same goes for what he did to Becky. He knows we aren't going to go public with anything since, if he got hauled in by the police, he'd make you sound like conspiracy nuts in five minutes. Are you really going to testify that the guy who abducted Aloysius runs Area 51, kidnapped you to work on a secret project about alien disclosure, artificially inseminated you and Dee, and now wants to track you down because he's pissed that you got off the base after threatening to destroy his UFO fleet with a nuclear bomb in a briefcase?"

"Okay." Brian sighed. "We see your point."

"He'll do all he can to terrify you and get what he wants—and he doesn't need to spray a restaurant with bullets to do either. It's an ego trip."

"That doesn't mean he won't try something," Malcolm objected. "I don't doubt for a minute this is bigger than getting reacquainted with Brian. He wants something else."

"Probably. If any of you have an idea, I'd love to hear it. It may help our planning. The only thing I can say now," he said, looking at Brian, "is that if he does try anything, we'll have a few surprises for him. Unless he comes with a small army, we'll be prepared—and so will you."

48

Bravery is the capacity to perform properly,
even when scared half to death.

—*General Omar Bradley*

Neff squinted as he scanned the front of the restaurant from the driver's seat of a rented black SUV while Brian, seated next to him, peered through a set of binoculars. Nili and Melissa sat quietly behind them, watching as best they could through vehicle's windshield. They were parked in the second row of the parking lot facing the small seaside restaurant where the Colonel had dictated their contact would occur.

"Anything?" Neff asked, without glancing at Brian.

"Nope."

Neff tilted his two-way radio toward his mouth. "Still no sign of him, Malcolm?"

"That's a negative," Malcolm's voice came back through the speaker after a few seconds of delay.

Neff glanced to his left at a second SUV, this one silver, idling at the opposite end of the parking lot. Malcolm, Dee, Madison, and Clarise occupied the vehicle.

"Everything okay on the island, Ward?" Neff asked, making the rounds. Nili's tactical plan called for helicopter and water escape options.

"Quiet—boring as all get out," Ward replied from the cockpit of the transport helicopter they'd chartered.

"Let's hope that doesn't change," Neff replied. "Malone, you seasick yet?"

"A little—doing better than Kamran, though."

Neff smiled, remembering the last time his friend had drawn the short straw of staying on the water. He hoped the high-speed passenger boat was overkill, but agreed with Nili that all options should be available.

"Anybody know why they call this place George's of Galilee?" Malcolm asked, trying to make small talk.

"Beats me," Neff replied. He shook his head when he overheard Dee scold Malcolm for asking the question.

"It's still early," Nili observed, looking at her watch. She looked over at Melissa, who had a mixture of terror and concentration etched her face. "Do not be frightened," Nili said calmly. "He will *not* be taken. We are prepared to use force and will not hesitate."

Melissa nodded, unable to engage her.

"You're not going to believe this," Malcolm's voice broke the air, this time conveying both surprise and urgency. "But I see him. *Inside* . . . main floor, third window from the end . . . civilian clothes . . . wearing a brown leather bomber jacket."

"Are you sure?" Neff asked, startled. "We haven't looked away for even a second."

"Ditto," Malcolm responded. "There is a bar in there. Maybe we just couldn't see him before."

Brian trained his field glasses on the door. A cold chill shivered through him. "That's him. He's talking to a waitress."

"I don't know how we could have missed him," Neff said thoughtfully. "But at least we have visual now."

"That's how it is with the Colonel," Brian replied, his voice betraying both apprehension and irritation. "Just when you think you're ready to deal with him, he puts you on the defensive."

"Do you have everything?" Nili asked, all business, unperturbed by the epiphany.

Neff held the button down on his two-way so the other car could hear the conversation. "Yes."

"Remember your training scenarios," Nili said. "Be decisive. We're here and ready."

"I will. Be ready when I signal."

"We will."

Brian zipped up his coat and opened the door. The cold breath of a clear Rhode Island winter night blew into the car. "Pray for me. And Melissa?"

She looked up.

"I love you."

49

If we understand the mechanism and motives of the group mind,
it is now possible to control and regiment the masses
according to our will without them knowing it.

—*Edward Bernays*

Brian stood at the door of the restaurant. The erratic drumbeat inside his chest made him pause for a moment to catch his breath. He exhaled deeply to calm himself before reaching for the door.

Despite the freezing temperature, his fingers slid on the handle from the sweat that had moistened his palms. He tightened his grip and swung the door open, momentarily stepping aside for a couple on their way out. The friendly chatter of dozens of voices merged into an indecipherable hum in his ears. His glasses began to fog. He took them off and unzipped his coat so he could clean them on the corner of his shirt. The savory aromas emanating from the kitchen gradually cleared his head.

"Are you Professor Scott?" a woman's voice asked.

Brian put his glasses back on and turned toward the voice. A dark-haired, shapely young waitress in jeans and a powder-blue George's polo shirt came into view.

"I am."

"Your friend gave me a description and told me to watch for you," she explained, smiling politely. "Follow me."

Brian nodded and did as he was told. Turning a corner, he caught sight of the Colonel. The leather bomber Malcolm had noted had been laid to the side of the booth. The Colonel wore a precisely-pressed white dress shirt, buttoned to the wrists.

The crew-cut officer looked up at Brian as if on cue. Brian slowed his pace but didn't stop. The surreal vision of the Colonel gesturing him to the table made his stomach flutter.

The two of them locked eyes as Brian cautiously slid into the booth. The Colonel waited until the waitress departed to speak.

"Well, Dr. Scott," he said, clasping his hands, elbows on the table, his voice dripping with satisfaction, "we meet again. I've *so* missed your company."

"I can't say the same."

"A pity."

"Where's Father Fitzgerald?"

"Now, now," the Colonel patronized, "patience. We have a lot to talk about tonight."

"Do we?"

"Oh, yes—*my yes.*" His blue eyes penetrated Brian like two cold steel stilettos. "Tonight's conversation will be one you won't soon forget—and lest you misunderstand, I don't mean that in a personally threatening way."

"Of course not. It's not like you're dangerous."

The Colonel smirked. "When I want to threaten you, I will—but that's for some other time. Tonight we're going to talk about some things dear to your heart."

"I'm not discussing anyone except Father Fitzgerald."

"Oh, I'm not talking about your friends—especially Dr. Kelley. Is she well, I hope?"

"Splendid," Brian replied, trying to move things along.

"I'm quite sure she's all that and more. At any rate, I want to talk about your work. You and I are going to talk theology tonight . . . and mythology—how they're the same thing, but yet different. I think you'll find it fascinating."

A conceited grin pursed the Colonel's lips as he read the surprise in the younger man's expression. He didn't wait for a response.

"I'm going to do something for you tonight that I didn't do for Andrew."

"Before you killed him?"

"Of course. He couldn't very well hear me after he was dead," he replied indifferently.

"Bastard."

"You would be wise to hold your temper, doctor. Do you want what you came for tonight, or not?"

Brian held his tongue. He nodded.

"A wise decision. Tonight your job is to listen—very closely. But I won't be too hard on you. You've justified my faith in you already this evening."

Brian remained silent, waiting for an explanation.

"You've shown again that you have some pluck to you. I like that, but only because I hate to be bored. You also know when to shut your mouth—another good quality. But those aren't specifically the reasons I've chosen you."

"*Chosen* me?" Brian asked with a slightly incredulous tone.

"Yes. But before I explain . . ." He stopped and glanced over Brian's shoulder at the approaching waitress.

"Here you are," she said pleasantly, placing platters in front of each of them, along with a tall glass filled to the brim with beer for the Colonel. "Would you like anything besides water?" she asked Brian.

"No, that's fine."

"If there's anything else I can get you, let me know."

"Thank you," the Colonel replied.

The waitress smiled at him eagerly, giving every impression she liked what she saw. The Colonel watched her leave and then turned to Brian.

"I took the liberty of ordering for both of us," he said with a plastic smile. "The fish here at the Galilee is excellent."

Brian looked down disinterestedly at the fillets.

"In case you're wondering," the Colonel said, starting into his meal, "it's not poisoned. I'm not going to kill you—at least not any time soon, I hope."

"Can we get down to business?"

"I just want to assure you that you're in no danger tonight," the Colonel continued, ignoring Brian's urgency. "I want you alive and well. I'll explain why a bit later. Like I said, I'm going to do something for you that I didn't even do for Andrew. I don't have time to wait for you to grow up and learn things on your own. Even I have schedules."

"Must be awful."

The Colonel chuckled slightly. "I'm going to enjoy this relationship," he said to himself as he took a bite.

"So what is it you're going to do for me?" Brian asked. He watched the Colonel chew at what seemed to be an overly deliberate pace, all the while keeping eye contact with Brian.

The Colonel swallowed slowly. "I'm going to tell you what we're up to . . . what this past summer was all about . . . what the future portends, that sort of thing."

"I find that hard to believe. Keeping secrets is the air you breathe."

"But you're *hoping* it's true," he replied in a calculating tone. "I can read it on your face. You're the type who wants to *know*."

Brian didn't answer.

"Truth be told, I'm not going to spell *everything* out for you, but I am going to tell you what you need to know to figure things out. But let's get the preliminaries out of the way first, shall we?"

"Where do we find Father Fitzgerald?"

"A few miles from here. Before I give you the location, I want confirmation that my other-long lost acquaintances made the trip with you. Did they?"

"What do you think? It's not like we had a choice."

"Quite right. And so . . ." He waved his fork in the air impatiently.

Brian looked at him contemptuously, took off the baseball cap he was wearing, and set it on the table. "Keep your eye on the street that runs past the window. You'll see them in a minute."

"What a clever signal," the Colonel mocked. "How imaginative." He took another bite.

Barely a minute passed before they saw the flash of headlights bounce off the window glass. The Colonel put down his fork. A silver SUV rolled into view, the rear window descended slowly. Brian watched his adversary's brow tighten as Malcolm and Dee's faces came into view. Dee's terror was transparent. Malcolm's face was grim, but calm. The car kept moving, followed by its black counterpart. Only Melissa's face was visible, but she refused to look at the Colonel, fixing her gaze on Brian instead. He nodded slightly and then she was gone, into the blackness down the end of the road.

"You saw them, and they won't be back," Brian said.

"Won't you need a ride home?" he asked smugly.

"We've followed your directions. Now where's Father Fitzgerald?"

"Who are your new friends? Imagine my surprise when I discovered all of you had somehow found each other."

"They're . . . acquaintances of Andrew."

"Ah, Benedict, resourceful even in death—a worthy adversary."

"Where are *your* friends?" Brian asked.

"Friends? I'm alone."

"I'll bet."

"Think what you will, but it's true. We have our own agenda, professor, as you'll learn this evening. We interact with others in the positions we hold, but we tend to work alone when it comes to our own special interests. At any rate . . ."

The Colonel reached into his jacket. Brian presumed there was no danger in the gesture, but he stiffened. He breathed a silent, undetectable sigh of relief as the Colonel pulled out his wallet and extracted a piece of paper. He unfolded it and slid it to Brian.

"I presume you have a phone?" the Colonel asked.

"Yes."

"Text these coordinates to your friends. It won't take them long to get to the location from here. I'll radio the priest's release when they should be on site."

The Colonel picked up his fork and resumed eating as though nothing unusual was happening. Brian pulled out his phone but held it under the table. He finished the task quickly.

"Very good," the Colonel observed, taking a sip of his beer. "Someone has trained you well, keeping your phone out of my line of sight so that I don't know the make, model, or number."

Brian waited, offering no reply.

"Really, have something to eat. It's on me, of course," the Colonel beckoned. "And take off your coat, you look uncomfortable. You want to look natural, don't you?"

Brian hesitated before taking off his coat and putting it next to him in the booth. He watched the Colonel eat, every movement filling him with disgust as he contemplated the man across from him. He was in no hurry.

"How did you become what you are?" Brian asked abruptly.

"Pardon?" he asked, looking up.

"What happened to you that you've become someone who can just torment and kill? You were someone's kid, for crying out loud. How did you get to this point?"

The Colonel took a long drink and carefully set his glass on the table. He glared at Brian. "I know what's running through your head, Dr. Scott. Don't you dare talk to me about life and death, or of second chances. You have no idea to whom you speak. There is no redemption for me or those who walk my path."

Brian felt another chill as the Colonel glowered at him. He could feel a searing malice held in check by a powerful, deliberate force of will. The Colonel finished his beer before continuing.

"Tell me, Dr. Scott, do you believe that UFOs have something to do with Armageddon?"

Brian eyed him carefully, startled by the odd direction the Colonel had taken the conversation. He was uncertain whether it was wise to divulge any thought to his enemy, but he suspected that, if he refused to play along, it would send the Colonel into a rage.

"Not really," he answered. "I think the UFO myth might have some role to play in terms of a global deception for some reason, but I don't know what that might be."

"I see." The Colonel paused briefly. "Some Christians think the antichrist will be an alien or an alien hybrid. What are *your* thoughts?"

Brian sighed, making no attempt to disguise his aggravation. "Andrew tried to nudge me in that direction, but I can't see anything in the text that justifies any extraterrestrial element. The antichrist isn't described as anything other than a man."

"Ah, yes—with you it's always about the *text*," the Colonel replied blankly. "Those were carefully worded responses," he continued, "and 'myth' is an apt word considering the context of this evening. You deftly distinguished the extraterrestrial idea from the antichrist. To an uninitiated listener, it would also seem you've divorced the antichrist from the supernatural, but you haven't. I happen to know you *do* allow for the possibility of the antichrist figure being in some way supernatural in origin."

He continued, "And of course, in today's world, where many would understand 'extraterrestrial' and 'supernatural' to be synonyms, a supernatural antichrist could be marketed to the theologically illiterate public—which includes most of the Church—as having an extraterrestrial connection. But the word 'description' allows you to hesitate, since no 'description' of that is found in the New Testament. Isn't that right?"

Brian didn't reply. The unexpected parsing of his answer gave him an uneasy feeling about where the discussion was headed.

"Let's be more precise—or perhaps *honest*. Tell me what you *really* think. It would take the fun out of this evening if I had to tell you myself what you think."

"Give me a break," Brian scoffed, irritated. "How would you know what I think about theology or the biblical text, or anything like that? You only know what we discussed this past summer."

"That's incorrect," the Colonel replied, a look of amusement on his face. "I know all about you, doctor. I've read every email you ever sent to Dr. Bandstra, all the way back to your undergraduate days at Johns Hopkins. The computers at his offices and home were all an open book to me—legally or illegally."

"I first came across your name by reading through his correspondence," he explained. "The two of you could have filled several volumes. You shared your thoughts on dozens of subjects. You sent him notes, outlines, papers, articles—I've read them all and followed your interactions. Once you became a person of interest to him last summer, I had your own computer hacked remotely before we ever took you. I've literally consumed every word you've cared to put to keystrokes. What I learned convinced me to encourage the Group to approve Dr. Bandstra's request to add you to the team."

"So tell me what I think," Brian said, irritation turning to anger.

"Promise not to lie when I'm right?" the Colonel goaded, not waiting for a response. "You've thought clearly about a good many things that factor into what we'll talk about tonight. For instance, it's true that the New Testament never describes this antichrist as anything more than a man—hence your circumspect response. But you also know there are some obscure connections between ancient non-biblical Jewish texts and the New Testament writings that suggest otherwise—texts that, in fact, might connect the antichrist figure to the Nephilim, which your Bible tells you were more than merely human. And yet you aren't sure how much weight to give those texts. That hesitation was behind your resistance to Andrew's urgings."

"Not good enough," Brian scoffed, trying to not to convey the feeling of dismay surfacing in him upon discovering that his thoughts had been digitally pilfered.

"All right, then. You know that the Nephilim giants are described as 'lawless ones' at the end of the seventh chapter of the Book of the Watchers. The word in the Greek version there is the same one used to describe the antichrist figure in Second Thessalonians 2:8. That's interesting because of the phrase in Matthew about Jesus returning at the Day of the Lord 'as in the days of Noah.' . . . How am I doing?"

"Okay, you've made your point. What of it?"

"These are the sorts of things that make you so interesting—and useful. You see things others don't because with you it's always about your precious ancient texts—not creeds or traditions. It's so quaint . . . almost endearing."

"You still haven't made your point," Brian replied gruffly.

"That's because I'm not ready to give you one yet. We'll get there, I can assure you, but I have some other questions first. As we proceed, it's imperative that you realize that the fundamental key to understanding our plan is that we don't care about truth—we care only about what is *believed*."

"Fine."

"Let's start with your encounter with Adam. Didn't he convince you of the possibility that aliens from the far reaches of space might factor into end times?"

"No. I don't think he was an intelligent alien."

"Was he a *stupid* one?"

"He wasn't one at all."

"So sure, are you?"

"Actually, yes."

"Tell me why."

"He didn't heal me. We figured that out at the base. I have nanobots swimming in my blood that one of your people put there."

"You should appreciate the gift."

"Whatever. If he didn't heal me, the whole thing was a premeditated deception designed to make us believe he was extraterrestrial. If he was really an alien, you wouldn't have needed to deceive us."

"But he communicated with you, and with others."

"*Something* was inside our heads, but I don't think it was Adam. It makes no sense that something who could do that couldn't also heal me. So why the ruse?"

"Maybe he's alien but not a healer. Maybe we thought a healing would take you off the fence of unbelief."

"Major Sheppard told us that you could create the Adam we experienced."

"Are you sure he wasn't lying?"

"He was ready to lose his life to have that conversation. I believe him. It may shock you, but some people can feel guilty enough about the crap they've done to try to make amends."

"How sentimental. What else did Sheppard tell you?"

Brian thought for a moment, not only for memory's sake but also to weigh his response. "He told us that he saw another creature at the base, one that was very tall. . . . He said he saw it kill Kevin Garvey but wasn't sure exactly how. Sheppard was the one who'd given him directions for access and was hiding in the Auroral room. I don't know what he saw, but if it was a real extraterrestrial and you wanted us to believe in them, you could have made that meeting happen. You didn't."

"Well, there you have it," the Colonel answered coolly.

"There I have what?"

"He lied. I killed Garvey. I killed him just before I went to our meeting and invented the heart-attack explanation."

Brian balked at the brazen admission. He tried to retrace the events of Kevin's death through his mind—the layout of the base facilities, the timing of the Colonel's presence at their meeting—but the details were blurry.

"I can certainly believe you'd do it," he finally responded, "but regardless of what really happened to Kevin, I still believe Sheppard's explanation of what was going on, at least as far as he knew."

"Why?"

"The phony bodies Melissa and I found in our beds. Sheppard said you could do that with nanotechnology. It's a workable explanation. The bodies would have nothing to do with anything alien. It was another misdirection."

"More like a *demonstration*," the Colonel corrected him. "Sheppard was wrong about that, too—at least about how we did it. We don't need nanotechnology for that, though it could add some nice effects. You must realize that Sheppard was muscle, a paid assassin, not a scientist. All we need to create bodies like you saw is a DNA sample and a 3-D printer. We had those devices long before the public knew about them. Should I describe the process?"

"Sure."

"I thought you'd be interested," he said with a knowing expression. "We had your DNA as soon as you got to the base, of course. Any number of items were useful for that—blood taken from you while you were sleeping, a single hair collected during housekeeping, and so on. Once we reconstructed a DNA sequence, we compared it to millions of other sequences that are part of the human genome database. Based on that comparison, we learned about your ancestry and a range of genetic markers, some of which relate to things like body type, facial features, and hair color. We add other known elements, like your age, weight, and height. Those data get put into a computer, which in turn tells our 3-D printer what to produce. The printer utilizes a chemical mixture that's similar in composition to artificial skin that is produced around the world today in hospitals and burn centers. The goal, of course, is a familiar look and feel. With me so far?"

Brian nodded.

"So what's the obvious gap at this point?"

"Adam," Brian replied without hesitation. "You had no DNA sample to make him. Consequently, he was something else, or he was made through a different process."

"Excellent," the Colonel said. "You are indeed paying attention. So hear this *clearly*." The Colonel leaned in toward Brian, his eyes wide with enthusiasm. "There are no extraterrestrials, Dr. Scott," he said in a low voice, "*except* the ones we make. And if there are no real aliens, there are no real alien hybrids, unless we make those as well. All that is another way of saying your intuition about Adam was correct, even though you lacked knowledge of the method." He sat back.

"So what's the process?" Brian asked, deciding to press for as much information as he could while the Colonel was predisposed.

"Have you ever heard of synthetic biology?"

"Yes, but I doubt that I could define it accurately."

"Then let's begin with some things with which you're vaguely familiar. You know about nanotechnology, of course. That's essentially about creating working machines at the nanoscale from existing material, such as DNA, and then assigning certain tasks to those machines. Genetics and genetic engineering are, of course, about DNA. Scientists safely inside the secrecy of the military industrial complex that you were exposed to this summer have been working in both those fields for some time now."

"How is synthetic biology different?"

"In terms of public science—the kind that operates under the auspices of law and public scrutiny and the wider scientific guild—synthetic biology is still largely the stuff of science fiction. At Dreamland we're playing in our own sandbox, as you well know. To put it simply, synthetic biology is *artificial*. It's the ability to construct or redesign biological organisms from the elemental level on up. In other words, today we have the capability not only to read and use DNA—we can *write* it. Do you understand the implications?"

Brian looked down at his untouched meal, trying to process what he was being told. It didn't take much imagination, especially in the context of his present company. "Whoever can do that can create life—new life forms that have never existed," he said. "It's well beyond splicing DNA and altering a life form's genetic code. A capability like that means you're as God—or *gods*, if you prefer."

"I do." A sinister chuckle escaped from the Colonel's curled lip. "You're correct. We can create life forms as we see fit. Biologically speaking, this also explains Adam's consciousness, though not necessarily his communicative powers. Many higher animals have consciousness 'according to their kind,' to borrow a biblical phrase. Dogs, cats, elephants—those sorts of animals with higher brain function—have dog, cat, and elephant consciousness, if you will. They can remember, respond to non-verbal cues, be trained to behave contrary to natural instinct. All of that is produced by their biology."

"So Adam was essentially a skinny, gray, upright puppy?"

The Colonel smiled darkly. "You have such a knack for distilling complicated things in memorable ways. That's far more droll than calling him a biobot. Yes, that's a workable understanding."

"So what about the communication?"

"That came from another source—but that's a peripheral matter for now. I want to venture down the road of synthetic biology a bit more with you. Now that you understand the biological power we wield, I'm sure you can imagine the application. What might we do *as gods* with synthetic biology?"

"From what I've heard," Brian began, choosing his words thoughtfully, "a catalyst for moving the world to believe that extraterrestrial life is real is completely within your grasp. You don't need an actual panspermia discovery. You don't need NASA to go public with some organism found on a Mars rock. You can just make the biological proof yourself, at will—DNA that has never been known on earth and whose composition can't occur naturally on earth in any evolutionary circumstance. You'd only need to concoct a scenario for public consumption as to how the life form was 'discovered.' And that would depend only on its nature—is it microscopic, or a large, intelligent being? And since so few know what was done to fabricate the proof, the world's scientists would be in the dark. They'd have no ammunition for denial."

"Precisely—and well said," the Colonel replied with an arrogant tone of approval.

"It begs a question, though," Brian added. "If you're capable of all this, why scoop us all up this past summer and feed us a bogus environmental scenario, followed by a contrived ET disclosure plan? You don't need any of that if you can write your own extraterrestrial DNA."

"There are many ways to answer that," the Colonel replied.

Brian could tell from his tone that he was being forthright, but had no idea why.

"For one, last summer the Group never actually got down to mapping out how their ET disclosure plan would work. Synthetic biology would eventually have become part of the conversation. For another, our plans are not the Group's plans. Don't presume that the Group's strategy reflects our agenda."

Brian sat up straight in the booth, his surprise evident. "So . . . you were part of the Group but were working against them?"

"I wouldn't say *against*. The Group proved useful at times. *Indifferent* probably captures our attitude more accurately. You must realize that even in the world of black-op projects, there are competing agendas."

"You keep saying 'we' and 'our.' Who is 'we'?"

The Colonel sat back again, cocking his head to one side. Brian could tell he was thinking about how to answer.

"Me and my . . . associates."

"Oh, that's clear."

"Trust me, doctor, it will become *frighteningly* clear. But you'll have to work for the more transparent answer. Waiting for people like you and Benedict to experience the terror of such discoveries is what keeps me entertained."

50

No enterprise is more likely to succeed than one concealed from the enemy until it is ripe for execution.

—*Niccolò Machiavelli*

The Colonel pushed his empty plate to the side before continuing. "Understanding the power of synthetic biology is fundamental to discerning what lies on the horizon. It not only allows us to create life, but also to create and mold *thought*. And thought, or *belief*, is the primary mover."

"You're talking about giving life to myths—like new Nephilim?"

The Colonel smirked. "That was part of the Group's thinking. We're not so naïve. Once they saw your credentials, it wasn't hard to convince them to get you involved. They viewed you—as do I—as useful. Our reasons for that assessment, though, are miles apart."

"The Group would have known I wasn't buying the idea."

"They could see you were hesitant. That was partly why they decided to allow me to introduce all of you to Adam."

"But a scrawny, gray alien? Even if I believed he was real, the relationship to Nephilim wasn't at all coherent."

"Agreed. Frankly, the Group was too influenced by simplistic end-times thinking. They presumed you'd buy what other Christians interested in these subjects were selling. Have you ever heard of the Collins Elite?"

Brian rolled his eyes.

"I see from your reaction that you have. I share your low estimation, but you should know that they're real."

"Seriously? There's a secret, informal faction of Christians inside the intelligence community that talks about creating an American Christian theocracy to protect us from demons riding around in UFOs?"

"As absurd as it sounds, the answer is yes," the Colonel said with no hint he was kidding. "Many of its members are DIA and Air Force intelligence."

"They're theologically under-informed, if they're real."

"Again, I agree, but you have to admit their flawed thinking would resonate with many of your fellow travelers—how we need to conform society to God's laws so that God would be predisposed to bless this wonderful country and save it from invading demonic hordes. I know that pains you, but many would think it reasonable. This sort of theocratic thinking is plied by the power-hungry right-wing in American politics. Some of the Collins Elite have also found a home within The Family."

"The Family? What's that?"

"Not what, but who," the Colonel corrected him. "The Family is a vast network of evangelical Christians who have very serious political ambitions. It was established in 1935 to oppose FDR and his New Deal. They've been the force behind every Washington Prayer Breakfast since 1953. They have deep connections with members of Congress, the Supreme Court, and of course Washington's military and intelligence agencies. Their agenda is simple: They want a Christian state—a benevolent theocracy, as they'd cast it. But let's not get distracted by what's behind the American political charade."

Brian sighed and shrugged.

"You should know that the Collins Elite has something of a history with the Group."

"How so?"

"The Group introduced one of their own into the Elite to learn what they were thinking. They liked the Elite's notion that UFOs are demons or piloted by demons from another dimension—opened by occultists like Aleister Crowley and Jack Parsons, the founder of JPL. Recall that the Collins Elite was formed in response to the activities of those occultists, and the UFO angle eventually became a significant focus. The specific demonic connection to UFOs became grist for the Group's mill. Frankly, it went to their heads and became the linchpin for their own over-reaching fantasy of a global police state. Once a strategy for that began to take shape, they leaked elements of it to the outside in an effort to conduct what one might call a *disinformation thought experiment*. I'm sure you've heard of Project Blue Beam."

Brian nodded. "So the Group poisoned the mind of that guy from Quebec who published the Blue Beam book? I can't remember his name, but he died young—more of your work?"

"His name was Serge Monast, and no, in this instance neither I nor anyone in the Group can take credit for his death. Monast was a Christian fundamentalist and an easy target, given his distrust of the Canadian government and his desire to see Quebec secede. Think we could find anyone like that in the Tea Party today?" he taunted.

Brian said nothing, knowing the answer was obvious.

"Like I said, Blue Beam was a thought experiment. The Group combined elements of the theology of the Collins Elite with science-fiction scenarios—from Gene Roddenberry of Star Trek fame, to be precise—in order to incrementally plant the idea that NASA and the UN were conspiring to install a global New Age religion and the New World Order with the antichrist as its leader. Lots of gullible Christians bought it, and still do."

"So that's something you *aren't* on board with?"

"It's far too impractical. Think about what Blue Beam included: artificially created earthquakes, an aerial display of spaceships projected onto the sky in three-dimensional holograms, electronic telepathy imposed on the masses, a faked rapture, and then a staged alien invasion—for what? To convince earth's religions that their God was on the scene or to start a nuclear war so that that the UN could intervene and subsequently be put in place as earth's protector? It makes no sense at all."

"Can't you do those things? What about HAARP?"

"We can do all of them, but only in isolated contexts, which means the entire scenario is terribly vulnerable. There are so many things that can go wrong or that cannot be controlled. While HAARP can be used to transform the sky into a screen, it can't transform the sky all over the globe, only a handful of square miles. What's more, a single radar scan from a single airport from anywhere in the region would fail to detect a solid object. The whole idea of faking a UFO armada is fraught with difficulties. But it doesn't seem that the Christian conspiracists hawking the idea have a firm grasp on any of the weaknesses."

"Can't you use your own UFOs?"

"We don't have enough. The world is a very big place, professor. And think of what else Blue Beam would require. How could earthquakes all over the world be caused? HAARP and other technologies can cause weather and geological phenomena here and there, but not on a global scale. After all, prophecies of the end times pertain to the whole world, not just the places most densely populated by evangelical Christians who buy into the kind of literal tribulation we're talking about," he added with contempt. "And it's absolutely sophomoric to think the world's religions would believe their God drives a spaceship. I don't have to convince you of that."

"No, you don't," Brian replied, "In today's world, people would flood the Internet and all their social connections with what they were hearing from a phony saucer God. As soon as followers of the world's religions started posting messages that contradicted other religions about what the space God was saying, the whole notion of uniting the world's religions would fall apart. Couldn't the Group see these problems?"

"Certain members of the Group did see the weaknesses of the idea. The Group began to think about how the idea of alien disclosure could be used in *other* ways—ways that would allow them to peacefully gain control. A kinder, gentler worldview coup would still allow them to gain control. It seemed more reasonable and more workable."

"I'm guessing we were part of that new angle—especially me and Melissa—to probe us for how disclosure might work with respect to the religious world."

"That you were. An alien disclosure could steer the masses toward the political Utopia the Group would craft and control. For example, disclosure might come with the promise of technological solutions to problems of energy, climate, or disease. The Group could use synthetic biology and nanotechnology to create an alien organism that, say, cured cancer or produced an alternative fuel. Mere *acknowledgement* by the nation's highest officials that a 'genuine' extraterrestrial discovery led to this incredible blessing would fire the imaginations of millions, convincing them that intelligent ET life must be out there and that it offers the prospect for solving all earth's problems and the next phase of human evolution."

"You've already acknowledged you're going to use synthetic biology to move people toward the belief that ET life is real," Brian interjected. "Sounds to me like your thinking isn't entirely different than the Group's."

"It doesn't differ entirely, but significantly. We aren't interested in starting a global religion, as if there could ever be such a thing. Whether religious or irreligious, people will react to disclosure in many ways. All we care about is that people *believe* the reality we've created is real. And the belief in ET is part of our own strategy. We'll bring humanity's childhood to an end for other purposes."

He went on. "The Group planned to cast itself as the receiver of alien blessings and just make up a narrative about ET's eventual arrival—conditioned, of course, on whether humanity formed the sort of society that the Group wanted. Again, it was all about what people could be made to *believe*, nothing more. We'll be using a similar strategy toward a different end."

"So what part of the Group's thinking included new Nephilim?"

"The Group was divided on what happens *after* the ET myth went viral. Several members had a deep hatred of Christians and Jews. They thought something needed to be done to make villains of those two groups once people believed the lie. That's where the Nephilim issue comes into play."

"You say they *thought*?"

The Colonel gazed at him thoughtfully. Brian could tell instantly that the innocuous question had somehow given the Colonel pause.

"Yes, past tense. The Group has been . . . disbanded."

"There's no more Group?"

"Not for the time being. No doubt it will reconstitute itself at some point." He paused briefly. "But back to your Nephilim question. Leaking the idea that the extraterrestrial reality was somehow connected to Genesis 6 would certainly—pardon the pun—*demonize* any ET disclosure in the minds of those who consider the Bible authoritative, no matter how wonderful an eventual ET visitation could be marketed. That would, in turn, place those Bible-believers in opposition to humanity's progress—an opposition that simply could not be tolerated with humanity so close to realizing solutions to all its problems. The malcontents would simply have to be eliminated."

"But you also *don't* favor that?"

"Our use of Nephilim mythology has a different goal. We can capitalize on the Group's successes in that area."

"How do you plan to link the mythical alien benefactors to the Nephilim?" Brian already suspected the answer but wanted to draw the Colonel out.

"That's already been done. The Group used the alien-abduction mythology, which of course has nothing to do with aliens."

"So you're admitting the whole abduction mythology is your invention."

"It's simple psychological warfare, along with mind-control techniques. We feed abductee testimony about alien-human hybrids to people through screen memories we put there. It's about implanting the idea that humanity is on the verge of becoming more than human—a very productive meme. People eventually share those memories, which then find their way into popular culture . . ."

". . . where the media picks up the meme and makes it global," Brian completed the thought.

"Precisely. The result is that thousands of people who aren't really abducted parrot the experience as part of a natural, brain-driven experience we have nothing to do with. These mind-control techniques were pioneered by German psychologists and psychiatrists who came to the United States under Operation PAPERCLIP. The Nazi rocket scientists brought here under that program were, of course, more famous, but the psychological warriors were just as effective. You saw an example of it with Ms. Leyden."

"You make abusing people sound like applying for a grant. You programmed Becky and just threw her life away because you could."

"My use of Ms. Leyden was a little more strategic than that, Dr. Scott. I had to flush you out of hiding. Perhaps if that had been easier, she'd still be alive. Perhaps if her boyfriend hadn't stolen government property—"

"Cut the crap, Colonel. You killed her."

"If such a childlike approach helps you parse recent events, so be it. Ms. Leyden had important information. She never admitted to showing you and Dr. Kelley the fragments of the Nazi plans for the Antarctic base, but I'm sure she did. We need to control all such information. It will serve a purpose now that we know of its existence."

"How could it possibly matter?" Brian demanded angrily. "Why couldn't you just leave her out of this?"

"It's easy to arrange a marriage between Nazi eugenics and the occult mythology of the SS about how the master race came from space gods, professor. Ever heard of Miguel Serrano?"

"No."

"I'm certain Dr. Kelley has. She could spell it out for you with little effort. Serrano was a Chilean diplomat and intellectual leader in global neo-Nazism. He believed in the celestial origin of the Aryan race. In his view, they came from a race of gods called the Hyperboreans who dwell at a remote place in the galaxy that is illuminated by the Black Sun, which is far beyond our own golden sun and invisible from earth. He thought Aryans came here and took embodied form—an original race of divine men. Serrano wrote much about these origins and the noble struggle of the Aryan against the Demiurge, whom Jews call Yahweh, an evil deity who controls this planet."

"That's just Gnosticism."

"Serrano adapted Gnosticism to his own tastes and made it serve his mythology of the Aryans, or as he called them, *divyas*, a Sanskrit term. These are the intellectual seeds of the Aryan war against the Jew. But do you see how easily these threads can be married to ancient astronaut beliefs in a distant planet inhabited by alien gods? It's a trivial task to associate this with Nibiru, the mythical Planet X that's so popular these days."

"I do," Brian replied.

"There's so much more. Serrano was quite eclectic in his thinking. He proposed that the *divyas*, or Aryans, arrived here from Venus through a cosmic portal that allowed them to get to this solar system. In an attempt to destroy them, the Demiurge created bestial creatures, soulless, ape-like *golems* in the Jewish vocabulary. Descendants of the high gods from which the Aryan race came tried to put a stop to all this, but when they came to earth, some of them betrayed the cause by interbreeding with the female creatures—and so the sons of the gods mingled their seed with the daughters of the beast-men. I believe you know the story."

Brian sat quietly, absorbing the implications.

"The result of all this, as you can surmise, was the rise of the impure races of less divine quality than the Aryan. This in turn caused chaos in the cosmic order—a frightful turn of events, that was. The earth was hit by comets that caused a global flood. The remaining Hyperboreans vanished into refuges at the South Pole and in underground cities like Agartha and Shamballah. Of course, when the comets hit, that caused a pole shift, and so the Hyperborean refuge wound up in the far north—which is what the term *hyperborean* means. I presume you remember your Greek."

"Go on," Brian growled.

"Do you remember any Greek mythology associated with Hyperborea?"

"Yeah. It's the place the god Apollo went every nineteen years to rejuvenate his body and mind."

"Quite. Hmm, *Apollo* . . . Where have I heard the term before?" The Colonel's face twisted into one of menacing glee. "You have to hand it to the Nazis working in the space program. They had a wonderfully dry sense of humor—or an idea to telegraph."

Brian remained silent.

"So you see, Nazi mythology is therefore quite useful for demonizing an ET disclosure or promised visitation. We have every reason to be interested in what Ms. Leyden's boyfriend discovered. We must control the narrative."

The Colonel paused, watching Brian's passive expression turn to one of undisguised hostility. He smiled again.

"Love your enemy," he taunted with a whisper. "What would Jesus do if He were here?"

"I'd like to think He'd send you straight to hell."

The Colonel chuckled lightly through pursed lips. "You can enjoy that thought later. I need you to set aside your hatred for me and think clearly for the remainder of our evening. I've now given you the first two phases of our plan. Do you see them?"

"You're going to use synthetic biology in some way to convince people that ET life is real."

"Yes, that's step one. The discovery of even one utterly unique microbe foreign to earth will propel the idea that life must have evolved to intelligence elsewhere. Synthetic biology not only allows us to produce entirely new DNA, it allows us to steer the narrative altogether. Convincing people that they aren't alone in the universe and that their cosmic neighbors are the key to human survival and evolution will be easy. I won't tell you precisely how we'll do it, though—that would ruin the suspense. Perhaps we'll simply borrow the Group's approach: fabricate ET life with very evident benefits to humankind and then simply tell the world it was a peace offering, a message that an alien race wants open contact with humanity someday, if only we'll change our behavior. People will believe it and wait with eager anticipation. Our lab work will be done. It's all about creating the belief."

"And by isolating the myth to yourselves, you localize it—you won't need to create contact on a global scale like Blue Beam required. You could use a couple UFOs as props to make a visitation event real, whether people see an alien or not."

"Correct. It's a much more economic and manageable plan."

"I take it step two is about the Nephilim mythology," Brian went on. "I'm still not sure how you'll use that."

"We're going to use that to demonize the alien race we've introduced to the world. You understand why now—at least partially."

"You want to marginalize the Bible-believer."

"Our goal is to winnow them from the masses. We have no need for most people to awaken from the benevolent alien slumber we've put them in. We only need to filter the serious Jew and Christian—not for physical harm, mind you. Many gullible Christian ufologists have already spread the gospel of Serrano for us. They've served our purposes as psychological—and mythological—evangelists. We're so grateful," he added in a patronizing tone, then stopped, enjoying the perplexity in Brian's eyes.

"For the believer," the Colonel said evenly, "the destruction of the body is no threat, only the destruction of the soul. The convergence of all these ideas is necessary to herd our targets toward the conclusion we want them to embrace in our final phase."

Brian moved to respond, but stopped, unsure.

"How well do you *really* know the Scriptures, Dr. Scott?" the Colonel asked, leaning forward again, a wicked gleam in his eyes. "The heavens and the Scriptures declare—as it is written—*the glory of the Lord shall be revealed, and all flesh shall see it together.*"

"Isaiah 40," Brian said in recognition, "which leads me to note that while your technology makes you and your co-conspirators as gods, it doesn't make you Lord. I think you've left that detail out of your plans."

"Appealing to Jesus . . . How predictable. We haven't overlooked Him at all. He'll be on *our* side."

"Sure He will," Brian laughed, nervously.

"I suggest you think more carefully about Isaiah 40. Why might I be referencing it the way I am? Why would I be answering you in this fashion? What does 'together' mean in the verse? And what does the rest of verse 5 say? *For the Lord has decreed it.* Certainly the faithful won't want to resist the Lord."

Brian shook his head. "You're unhinged. You can't expect me to take that seriously."

"But you *will* take it seriously. I despise what you stand for, Dr. Scott, but you are no fool. I don't suffer fools. I eliminate them."

Brian became silent. He watched the Colonel as he motioned to a passing waitress for another beer, trying to judge the intent of the remark. The Colonel returned his attention to Brian.

"Every clue I'm giving you has a role to play in the larger picture. We will use the expectations and predispositions of what the masses believe, especially Christians, to propel our agenda. They're blinded by their provincial views of end times and demons. They'll just make their own audiences more vulnerable to what we'll present to them."

The Colonel paused again. Brian could see he was pleased with himself.

"With respect to clues," the Colonel went on, leaning forward, "have you deciphered Ms. Leyden's message yet?"

"We know part of it was Hans Kammler's SS number."

"Very good. I'm sure the rest will come into focus eventually—you're all so clever."

"Kammler no doubt points to both UFOs and Nazis. I don't suppose you have anything to add."

"Of course. As I hinted a moment ago, the UFO mythology is a component of one aspect of our agenda, as are the Nazis. Kammler's work is a useful component of the overall narrative."

"That's not news to me," Brian replied.

"Since Dr. Kelley will no longer be gainfully employed, she has the time to look into some items of interest . . . something called the Huemul Project and San Carlos de Bariloche. And you must make sure she isn't distracted by the official commentary."

"What's your role in all this?" Brian asked.

"As I said earlier, our agenda is our own. Exploiting the connections between Nazis, occult Aryan myths, and aliens—or should I say, 'cosmic intelligences'—is how we've decided to play this game. As scholars, you and Dr. Kelley know those connections are secure and deep. Soon we'll be readying the masses incrementally to embrace the impending points of our narrative. The two of you are going to be very busy in the future tracking the mind shift. . . . And perhaps it's already begun."

Brian stared blankly at the Colonel, his lips pressed together in thought. The question of *why* kept exploding in his mind. The Colonel's strategy was clear, but the endgame made no sense. The Colonel paused and looked at his watch.

"Your friends should be approaching the checkpoint," he informed him, and then removed a small radio with a blunt antenna from his belt. Brian waited expectantly.

"Ferguson here," the Colonel said into the radio. "Our guests should be on site. You have visual? Good. It will be either a black or silver SUV. Confirm and tell me which one. . . . Excellent. . . . Proceed as instructed and unload the priest." He glanced at Brian, who could see the façade of cordial contempt was gone, replaced by icy disdain. "Then you may leave. I'll contact you later for pickup."

51

Violence is not a catalyst, but a diversion.

—Joseph Conrad

"This is it," Madison said. The GPS device in her hand bathed her face with a soft glow in the dark of the SUV.

"Other than a beach, where are we?" Malcolm asked as he brought the vehicle to a halt and turned off the headlights, letting it idle.

"A place called East Beach," she replied and turned the screen toward him. "You can see it's just a long strip of beach, about three miles."

"A barrier beach," he mused. "So we've got the ocean on our right—Block Island Sound—and inlet on the left."

"I'm not sure, but the way we entered looks like the only exit."

"Narrow road, grit and sand—doesn't exactly lend itself to speed and maneuverability."

"I don't like it," they said simultaneously.

"At least when the Colonel's people show up, they'll have to come in the same way," Malcolm offered, looking for some point of advantage.

"Unless they're already here and we don't see them," muttered Dee from the back seat.

"I'm gonna turn the car. We can at least be pointed in the right direction," Malcolm said, deflecting the thought.

"Are you getting this, Ward?" Clarise asked into her radio as Malcolm restarted the car.

"Yep. Got your location on my GPS now. It's actually directly across from where I am on Block Island—looks like ten miles across the water of the Sound. I can be there pretty quickly if needed."

"We'll stay on line."

After the car was repositioned, they all sat quietly, looking out of the windows on both sides.

"I think I saw a light," Madison said unexpectedly, pointing. She put a pair of night-vision goggles to her eyes. "Out there, on the beach.

There were a couple quick flashes. . . . I don't think it's a beacon, since it stopped."

They waited about a minute before they all saw what had drawn her attention.

"That's it again. Maybe it's nothing."

"Only one way to find out." Malcolm pulled out his handgun and undid the safety.

"Stay here with Dr. Harper," Clarise told Madison. "Take the wheel and keep it running. And keep an eye on us."

Madison nodded.

Clarise and Malcolm got out of the vehicle. Clarise took the small backpack that Madison was passing her through the window, which was loaded with medical supplies in case Father Fitzgerald needed immediate attention. The two of them circled around the back of the vehicle and opened the rear door. Clarise unzipped a large duffle bag and retrieved two TARs. She handed one to Malcolm, who slung the assault weapon over his shoulder. Clarise did the same. Malcolm reached under the seat and produced two flashlights, handing one to her.

They closed the door and cautiously headed off the road in the direction of the light they had seen. The sandy ground was lightly covered with a thin layer of snow. Here and there they could see frozen strands of seaweed underfoot and protruding tufts of stiff beach grass as the light from their flashlights danced across the surface. There was nothing in sight that would offer protective cover.

The two of them shut off their flashlights and crouched down on the cold sand as they reached the beach line. Though their eyes had adjusted to the darkness, there was little they could see with clarity at a distance. There were no lights on the beach, and clouds masked what little light the moon offered. As far as they could tell, they were alone. Clarise looked back at the car, which was discernible only by its faint shape on the otherwise light gray line that they knew was the road.

"Now what?" Malcolm asked. "There's nothing out here."

"But we saw a light," Clarise answered apprehensively. "Where did it come from?"

"Maybe the water—maybe it was a beacon after all."

They looked out over the deep, inky blackness of the water. A small but clear white light suddenly pierced the darkness on the surface of the water. It didn't flash.

"Is that a buoy?" Clarise asked.

"No idea. How close are those things supposed to be to shore? I can't really judge the distance, but that's got to be at least a couple hundred yards out."

"Maybe they're delivering him by boat."

The two of them watched the light for a couple of minutes. It didn't appear to be getting any closer. Malcolm scanned the beach on either side of them.

"Whatever the light is, it's stationary," he finally said, looking at Clarise as he voiced his thoughts. "I don't think that's them. Let's go back to the car."

"Hold on." Clarise beckoned. "It's gone." She pointed to the now opaque darkness. Suddenly the solitary light reappeared.

"Sorry," she said, disappointed. "I guess I just lost it in a wave."

"Do you hear that?"

Clarise listened. "It sounds like the water's getting rougher. I don't feel any wind, though. The light looks a little higher. . . . Is it coming closer? I'd say we have a boat approaching, but it's odd that it doesn't look any closer."

Malcolm didn't reply. He stared straight ahead, intellectually trying to deny the realization forming in his brain. He wasn't succeeding.

"Sherlock Holmes," he whispered nervously. The faint wisps of his breath vanished quickly in the frigid air.

"What?"

"When you eliminate all other *possibilities,* what remains—no matter how improbable—is the answer. *Get ready, Clarise.*"

Malcolm pulled his TAR from his shoulder and steadied himself on one knee. Clarise didn't ask why, but followed his lead. The two of them watched expectantly as the small white light kept slowly rising in the distance. The sound of water churning steadily gained volume. Off in the black expanse they could see tiny flecks of white spray extending in a long line parallel to the shore.

"What the—?" Clarise mumbled.

Suddenly a massive black object broke free of the surf and rose into the dark sky, the water spilling off its curved edges into the waves creating a thunderous splash.

"Holy God," Clarise gasped as the round, black sphere rose and then halted its ascent, hanging mid-air above the water. It began to drift toward the shore in their direction.

Malcolm gazed at the craft, wonder and dread coursing through him in unison. The saucer was at least a football field in diameter, monstrous in comparison to the one he'd been in the previous summer.

He stood up.

"Clarise?"

There was no reply.

Malcolm turned his head. Clarise was sitting, her mouth slightly agape, hands in her lap, staring in transfixed awe. Her rifle was lying next to her in the snow.

Now that the saucer was out of the water, there was little sound, save for a dull hum. The saucer had reached shore and was almost directly overhead at a distance of a couple hundred feet. It stopped.

"Clarise!"

The woman jerked her head toward the voice, snapping back to the reason they were there. She grabbed the TAR and stood up.

"I don't know what's going down, but be ready for anything."

"Sorry, I've just never seen—"

"Trust me, I get it."

A series of bright lights unexpectedly flashed on the underside of the craft and began alternating in a pattern that created the illusion of rotation. A smaller light at the very center of the saucer appeared and began to expand in diameter. Malcolm and Clarise squinted at the center light. To their surprise, they saw human forms.

"Landing party?" Clarise asked without looking in Malcolm's direction.

"I've got a bad feeling about this," Malcolm said, shaking his head. "Lord, not this way. Not—"

His prayer was cut short by a terrified scream. They watched in horror as one of the forms disappeared from the light into the darkness. They caught one more fleeting glimpse of the doomed man as the beams of light from under the craft hit the flailing body hurtling downward. They lost visual, and seconds later the body slammed the cold, wet sand just yards from where they stood with a sickening smack, loud enough to make them both jump.

Clarise bolted toward the crumpled form, with Malcolm close behind. Father Fitzgerald's face was buried in the sand, his head twisted unnaturally, blood seeping from the holes on the side of his head where his ears had been. His shoulder was smashed so severely that the collar bone had broken through his shirt and was now thrust deeply into his neck. The contorted position of the legs told Clarise the priest's pelvis had been shattered as well. In despair, she cleared the neck wound as best she could and tore furiously into her backpack. She produced a wad of gauze and pressed it tightly to the puncture, trying to stop the flow of blood. She checked for a pulse, then looked at Malcolm and turned away.

Malcolm looked skyward and watched the inner circle of light close into blackness. The pattern of lights on the outer rim continued rhythmically. He gritted his teeth and raised the TAR.

"Don't!" Clarise yelled, having caught the motion from the corner of her eye. She lunged at the wiry black man and pulled the weapon down as he fired. The bullets ripped harmlessly into the sand.

"Don't," she said breathlessly. "They could kill us all—and you know it won't do any good."

Malcolm looked at her, his face filled with enraged desperation. She held on to his arm, waiting for him to return to reason. "We have to tell Brian—*now*," she urged. "The Colonel may have something else planned."

Clarise released Malcolm's arm and took the radio from her belt. She pressed the button to communicate. The device was unresponsive.

"It's dead! But the batteries are brand new. What—?"

"It's the saucer," Malcolm said, looking upward. The low hum and rotation pattern were the same as before. "They're sticking around just to jam our communications. We have to get away from here." He looked down helplessly at Father Fitzgerald's body. "I don't want to leave him."

"We can drag him to the car. Madison can help if we need her to." She looked back at the car.

Malcolm put his rifle on his shoulder and moved toward the dead priest's feet. He felt Clarise grab his arm once more and looked up at the car as she pointed. The inside light was on, but no one was visible.

They sprinted toward the SUV as fast as they could. Clarise began calling for Madison, frantic for her daughter. When she was within ten yards, she screamed even louder—not seeking a response this time, but because she now saw why the door was ajar: Madison's foot was dangling out of the driver's door, preventing it from closing.

Clarise got to the door and pulled it open. Madison was slumped across the tray that separated the two front seats, her head resting awkwardly on the passenger seat. Her strawberry blonde hair was draped over her face, revealing a small dart in her neck. Clarise quickly felt for a pulse. Malcolm pulled open the driver's side back door. The car was empty.

"She's alive!" Clarise exclaimed through tears of panic. "But she's out cold."

Malcolm ran around the outside of the car, looking for signs of Dee in the ambient light. The low hum abruptly ceased, and the two of them looked up. The black saucer was drifting low over the water, heading out to sea. Without any warning, it shot up and out of sight at a tremendous speed, and then it was gone.

Malcolm suddenly remembered that he'd tucked his flashlight into the back of his trousers. He pulled it out and turned it on. It worked. He frantically scanned the ground and found two sets of boot prints leading to and away from the vehicle. He jogged after them, calling for Dee, flashing his light down toward the recess on his left filled with water.

Farther down the road, the light revealed a small mound. He recognized Dee's coat and ran toward it. He picked it up and felt moisture. He dropped it and shined the flashlight on his hand. His fingers were streaked with blood.

52

There is no neutral ground in the universe. Every square inch, every split second, is claimed by God and counter-claimed by Satan.

—*C. S. Lewis*

"So why are you telling me all this?"

Now that Father Fitzgerald's rescue was underway, Brian wanted to bring the meeting to an end as quickly as possible, but the urge to discover the Colonel's motivation for the conversation was irresistible.

The profanely haughty expression appeared once again on the Colonel's face. Brian could tell he was more than eager to provide an answer.

"It's simple, actually." The Colonel looked again at his watch. "I'm telling you all this because I want you to suffer," he answered coldly. "I want you alive and well so that you feel the full brunt of defeat—not only that of Andrew's hopes, or those of his associates, but that of the people of your God."

"You're delusional."

"Really?"

"Yeah, *really*. The whole history of the Church shows that believers will resist evil unto death—and persecution and martyrdom has been the seed of the Church all over the world. You'll never kill it off."

"Exactly. Real believers won't be forced by death to deny the faith. Spiritual suicide is more what we have in mind."

Brian tried to be coy, but once again couldn't disguise his confusion.

"You can't yet understand the coherence of all that I've told you this evening. That will require some discovery on your part."

Brian gave a slight shrug, trying to look calm. "You said Jesus would be on your side. Are you going to try to convince everyone that Jesus was really an alien and then turn people against Him? Maybe the alien Jesus raptures everyone but the real Christians, destroying their faith?"

"Please, professor. We aren't planning something so intellectually childish as a fake rapture. But we'll certainly make use of such shallow end-times thinking. There's a much better way to strangle the life out of the Church than some nineteenth-century contrivance like a rapture. Many Christians don't even believe in one—but they *all* believe that Jesus promised to return."

"Seems like a waste of time," Brian replied, hoping to get more detail.

"Our agenda will produce the right villain to move the target audience to the right savior."

Brian sat silently again, choosing to let the Colonel follow his train of thought uninterrupted.

"You're too quiet, professor. I know it isn't because you're not following. Perhaps a question will get you to open up a little." The Colonel smiled as he held his hands in front of his face, tapping his fingertips together. "Tell me, Dr. Scott, do you believe that those who express faith in Jesus are eternally secure?"

Brian didn't move. In any other context, he'd have enjoyed the academic discussion, but he could sense this wasn't about scholarly jousting.

"Your continued silence tells me that you understood immediately that I worded the question very deliberately. *Expressing* faith and *possessing* faith are two different things, especially for someone like you who pours over the text so diligently—a quaint obsession that will indeed bring you to suffer in the wake of this conversation."

Brian held back, unsure how the Colonel had managed to weaponize this point of theology.

"The idea of eternal security is a good example of something millions of Christians consider obvious, but that you don't—because you see something hidden in plain sight. Untold masses of Christian believers feel secure in their path to heaven for one of two reasons. Some find assurance because they think they're chosen by God—*elect* is the word they'd used. But they never stop to consider that their Old Testament has every Israelite elect—but that didn't keep huge numbers of them, maybe *most* of them, from worshiping other gods and perishing in Nebuchadnezzar's conquest and the exile in Babylon. How tragic—how *confusing*. How can you have the *elect* going astray after other gods if election means salvation? Do those who *don't* choose to worship Yahweh find a home in the presence of Yahweh?"

"Of course not," Brian replied, now discerning what was coming.

"But if they're not in heaven, then what did being elect mean? You know the answer to this because you see it clearly in the text—election and salvation are *not* synonyms. That means people who at one time expressed loyalty to the God of Israel—and by extension, to His Christ—*could* turn to unbelief and forfeit salvation of their own free will. I do hope you noticed I used the word *express* there as well."

"I did."

"Good. And let's not forget that all humans—God's imagers, as you taught us all this past summer—*must* have true freedom of will. If they didn't, they couldn't image God—they could not be like God without sharing that attribute. That brings us to the second reason so many presume their heavenly destiny is sure: because their faith is in the gospel story of the New Testament."

"That's obvious," Brian objected. "That's *biblical* theology."

"Of course it is. . . . It's also the perfect tool to eviscerate the Church."

"What's that supposed to mean?"

A cocky grin creased the Colonel's mouth. "What if millions *believed* they had put their faith in the right thing—or person—but they were deceived? What if the Jesus they thought was the object of their faith was—but also wasn't—Jesus? I'll ask it this way: If one *believes* a lie, isn't that belief still unbelief? Oh, dear. What would the writer of the book of Hebrews say?" He paused, as if waiting for an answer. "You do recall that he was worried about this sort of thing. Would your loving God have *believing unbelievers* as His children? He didn't do that with the Jews, *did He*?"

"Are you done?"

"*No,*" the Colonel growled, his demeanor suddenly shifting. He hadn't raised his voice, but his tone was commanding.

Before he could respond, Brian saw the Colonel's attention was once more diverted. He turned and looked over his shoulder. The waitress was approaching.

"Is there something wrong with your fish?" she asked sincerely, looking at Brian.

"No," he said apologetically, then glanced at the Colonel. "I just didn't have an appetite this evening. You can take it away."

"Would you like dessert?" she asked the Colonel with a smile.

"No, thank you, dear," he said with feigned charm. "You can bring me the check."

Brian waited for the waitress to leave and then went on the attack. "It wouldn't be hard to expose a false Christ. The New Testament clearly warns that false Christs will show up. It's too clear about the nature and character of Jesus. Even miraculous acts won't be enough, since anyone with an ounce of biblical knowledge will know other divine beings have real power. Nothing short of Jesus Himself is going to draw the attention of real believers."

"Right again," the Colonel answered confidently, eyebrows raised. He went on with deliberation, choosing his words carefully. "What if there was no ambiguity that the resurrected Jesus had returned, precisely as promised, to do exactly what He's supposed to do—crush the antichrist and his minions and usher in the earthly kingdom of God, the renewed Eden? What if there was a way to confirm the reality of His resurrected flesh, validating that most crucial element in the New Testament story? *Would there be any reason to doubt*? Would there be any reason *not* to believe when that Jesus rescues Jerusalem from assured devastation and conquers an unconquerable enemy?"

Brian hesitated, knowing he was being led to a predetermined conclusion. Rather than protest, he decided to go along. "I suppose not."

"And so the end will come," the Colonel replied. "There are other ways to destroy the faith of those who say they believe. This is just the most interesting to us. And you'll have a front-row seat for it. You're here for my entertainment, Dr. Scott. When you see the myth emerging, I want you to *know* it's all a trap, that it's all a horrible mistake."

The Colonel smiled menacingly. "We'll give every dimwitted Bible believer what they've longed for—proof that their Scriptures are absolutely genuine—while we steal their place at Yahweh's table. We won't have to threaten them with death—they'll voluntarily forfeit their faith without ever knowing they're doing it. Jesus *has* to save the day, and the faithful *must* rally to His cause or be cast into outer darkness. Isn't that what He said?"

"You're talking in circles," Brian challenged him, trying not to erupt. "You're so enamored with your position and whatever little cabal you lead that you're drifting toward insanity. Your ego is what will destroy you, not to mention God's own plan."

"No doubt it feels that way now," the Colonel answered bitterly. "But in a short time, all of this will be disturbingly clear."

"You'll fail," Brian replied with an unexpected calm. "You act as though you're God. *You aren't*. You'll learn who is, one way or the other."

"Oh, we know who God is, professor," the Colonel said though gritted teeth, his eyes narrowing. "It isn't that my associates and I don't believe the God of the Bible exists. We do. *It's that we hate Him*. We may never be able to defeat Him totally, but we can rob Him of His children. Didn't Jesus wonder whether He would find faith on the earth when He comes again—right after saying that many who call Him Lord and who do great things in His name are told to depart into darkness?"

"*You're going to fail,*" Brian repeated.

"Have you mentally put yourself in our scenario yet, Dr. Scott? It's an exquisite place. Unless your God mercifully takes your life early, you'll be here when all this transpires. You'll have the unenviable task of telling people that what they see happening in real time isn't true—that it's the work of some insane Air Force colonel. And when Jesus shows up and ends the threat on cue, you'll get to tell everyone that was the point—that they shouldn't believe the salvation they just witnessed, which is in precise fulfillment of the Bible you say you're trying to defend."

He went on, "I wonder, what will the masses believe—an epic conflict played out right before their eyes and a Jesus who arrives according to script with phenomenal power to save the day . . . or your pathetic, isolated voice telling everyone it's a theological scam? I think we both know the answer. You can always say nothing, of course. And so the end result is that Yahweh's children are damned if you do, and damned if you don't."

"You're a bit too convinced of your own omniscience, Colonel," Brian cut in. "God will find a way to undermine your fantasy."

"If you really believe that, why don't I see confidence on your face?"

"How I feel," Brian said evenly, "has nothing to do with what's true and what isn't—or where sovereignty resides."

The Colonel's eyes darted away from Brian's.

"Here you are," the waitress said melodically, handing the Colonel a small folder with the bill. "Have a good evening."

"I already have," the Colonel said through a smile, glancing at Brian as the waitress turned and left.

"Bravo, Dr. Scott," said the Colonel as he retrieved his wallet. "I'm so glad we could have this chat."

Brian watched his adversary carefully flipping through a wad of cash, calculating the expense and tip like any other customer. He tried to control his thoughts, to avoid the distraction of what he'd just heard in order to focus on what to expect as the meeting ended. The Colonel flipped the pad closed and waved it at the waitress, who was now attending to an adjacent table. She took it with another smile and left again.

The Colonel turned to Brian. "I've enjoyed this evening so much that I have one more revelation for you about me and my associates. Then you're free to go. No one will be following you. But first, I need to use the restroom—the beer just goes right through an old man like me. I'll only be a moment."

The Colonel stood and put on his jacket, and then went toward the restroom, which was clearly visible from where they sat. Brian slid his coat on and then his hat, which was the signal to Neff and the others in the car that he was preparing to leave. He waited, resisting the urge to just run out. He was afraid that an early exit would draw some sort of retaliation, for him or the others.

"Sir, I think there's some mistake."

Brian turned and saw their waitress. Her complexion was slightly flushed, but she was still just as pleasant as before.

"What is it?"

"Is your friend still here?"

"He's in the restroom."

"I think he gave me the wrong bills."

"I saw him count everything out. Trust me, he's not the type to overlook any details."

"Well," she looked at him, a little flustered, "it's just that he left me the biggest tip I've ever had—$153! I can't believe it. I'll come back in a minute to make sure."

Brian nodded as she left. His thoughts were interrupted by the ring of his phone. He retrieved it from his pocket and answered.

"Neff? I'll be a minute yet."

"Brian—you have to get out of there now!" shouted the voice on the other end.

"Why?"

"We just heard from Clarise. We've been played. I have terrible news."

Brian listened in dumbstruck dismay as Neff relayed Clarise's description of the events on the beach, his eyes riveted on the door of the restroom.

"Get out now. Don't confront him. He could have soldiers stationed somewhere in plainclothes. Just get out now—we're right outside."

Brian hung up. He rose quickly and headed straight to the restroom, fury welling up inside him. He pushed the door open and froze as it closed behind him. In panicked disbelief, he thrust open the two stall doors. The undersized, windowless restroom was empty.

53

All the world is full of suffering. It is also full of overcoming.

—Helen Keller

"Dr. Scott." Nili bent over Brian's seated form. He was resting his head between his folded arms on the hard wooden table, which was covered with stacked books and scattered articles. She gently shook him on the shoulder. "Brian."

Brian slowly stirred, first opening his eyes and then lazily lifting his head. For a moment he was confused. Why was he sleeping in a library? His mind soon started to clear, the events of recent days rebooting into his consciousness—the race to the beach in the car, the horrible, mangled form of Father Fitzgerald, the abduction of Dee. He could still see the flashing lights on the helicopter as Ward descended onto the beach.

Conflict about what to do with Father Fitzgerald's body had surfaced almost immediately. Clarise had insisted on keeping it, believing there was something important to learn. Others had wanted to leave everything untouched and call the police anonymously to direct their identification of the John Doe.

The debate hadn't lasted long, as Malone had picked up a 911 call on the police monitor he'd brought with him on the boat. Someone had seen the chopper land on the beach and had alerted the authorities. Ward and Clarise had decided to take the body to Minnesota, to their friend Cal. His pathology office—the one where Brian and Melissa had first met Clarise—would have everything necessary to store the body, examine it, and preserve anything Clarise might consider useful. Cal could be trusted to make up a scenario in case anyone discovered the new resident in his morgue and asked questions.

"What time is it?" Brian asked.

"Seven o'clock a.m.," Nili answered. "I was on my way to swim in the lap pool when I saw the light from the library. You've been here all night?"

Brian nodded through a yawn. "Yeah . . . research. Summit was here till midnight finding things for me. She's amazing."

Nili smiled, then turned serious. "Fern is making breakfast. She's already served Malcolm."

"Malcolm? Really?"

His friend had been inconsolable on the trip back. Once at Miqlat, Malcolm had gone to his room and isolated himself, refusing to speak to anyone. It had been three full days since anyone had seen him. Brian knew he was paralyzed with guilt for what had happened.

"Yes," Nili confirmed. "We didn't speak, but he told Fern he had agreed to meet with Sabi in the chapel. They're there now. When he's ready, he should listen to the recording."

"I'll say something to him," Brian assured her.

The recording was the one small victory they'd managed in the whole affair with the Colonel. Brian had worn a voice-activated recorder during the episode, and it had worked like a charm. With the exception of Malcolm and Summit, everyone had listened to it repeatedly and begun pouring themselves into deciphering the Colonel's comments, searching for any clue about what he might be intending to do with Dee. It was now apparent that the entire episode had been engineered for the purpose of reclaiming her. But why?

The door to the library opened. It was Madison, still in pajamas and slippers, her tussled hair tied back in a careless knot. Her usually cheerful face was drawn. The young woman had been traumatized as well, silently competing with Malcolm for who should take the blame for what had happened to Dee.

"Did you hear?" she asked, barely above a whisper.

"About?" Nili asked, hoping there was nothing new to worry about.

"Malcolm's out."

"Yes. I was just telling Brian."

"What's he going to say to me?" Her face knotted up, and she started to cry.

Brian got up and walked over to her, putting his arms around her. "He won't blame you—I guarantee it."

"I keep running everything through my mind, trying to figure out what I could have done differently," she sobbed.

"There's nothing you could have done," Nili said soothingly. She'd already offered Madison this reassurance repeatedly since their return. She reached out for Madison, and Brian released her.

After a few moments, Madison was calm enough to speak. Nili pulled out a chair from the table so she could sit. "I got out of the car to look at the saucer," she sniffed. "It was so fantastic, I wanted to see it. I was out less than a minute when I felt the sting of the dart. I reached for my neck, and knew what it was. I tried to get back in and lock up, and that's the last thing I remember until I woke up in the car next to mom on the way back to the plane. *Why did I get out of the car*?"

"Because they planned it that way," Brian replied. "They were counting on the spectacle to be a distraction."

"If you hadn't gotten out, they probably would have killed you," Nili said with confidence. "If they couldn't draw someone out of the car quickly, they may have opened fire to get at Dee with speed. You're blessed to be alive."

"I don't feel blessed. And what about poor Dr. Harper? I can't stop thinking of what they might do to her."

"We must trust God," Nili said sympathetically, then fell silent. She looked at Brian from behind the seated girl. Her eyes betrayed his own thoughts. It was hard to muster any hope. But there was nothing else to do.

"Nili's right," Brian said faintly. You aren't to blame for the evil others decide to do. Malcolm knows that—we *all* know that."

She nodded weakly.

"Did you eat yet?" Nili asked her, touching her shoulder.

"Just a little coffee."

"Let's go; you'll feel better."

"I'm gonna see if Melissa's up yet," Brian said, "and then we'll go talk to Malcolm."

54

The cost of quitting will be a life of peaceful stagnation.
We sons of eternity just cannot afford such a thing.

—*W. A. Tozer*

Brian and Melissa walked silently, hand-in-hand, down the dimly lit corridor, their hearts heavy not only because of their fears for Dee, but because of the lingering uncertainty over Malcolm. Their friend's reaction to the tragedy in Rhode Island had been expected, but unnerving.

They'd come to rely on Malcolm's optimism and stability. Even though he'd played a game of misdirection back at Area 51, they'd known he was dependable. His ability to cut through tension, and his flair for saying the right thing at the right time, had helped them both through difficult turns. They wanted to return the favor now but felt completely inadequate.

As they approached the chapel, they could hear instrumental music emanating from the room. Brian stopped to listen before opening the door. The tune was familiar.

"What's wrong?" Melissa asked, looking up at him.

"Nothing, just listening," he answered. "It's my favorite hymn, "Be Thou My Vision." I'm just struck by how long it's been since I heard it."

"That was one of my favorites as a girl, too," Melissa replied distantly.

They listened for a few more moments before going in. The chapel was one of the smaller spaces at Miqlat in terms of square footage. It was deliberately plain, yet charged with symbolism. The room was circular with a high ceiling. A solitary, upright padded bench formed a perfect circle within the room, broken only in one place for entry into the center and out to the walking space behind it.

At the center of the room was a tall, unfinished, rough-cut wooden cross nearly fifteen feet in height. There was literally no place you could go without being confronted by it, without your attention being arrested by its presence. No one had a better seat than anyone else in the chapel—everyone had equal access to the cross. There was no choir, no pulpit, no band, no screens. There was only the towering fixture dominating the room, at once a compelling memorial to the horrible event that gave it meaning and a comforting refuge to all who believed its message. It was spectacularly simple, communicating all that needed to be said without the utterance of a single word. Brian loved it. Every time he entered the room, things came into focus.

Malcolm was seated at the edge of the break in the circular bench, where Sabi had guided his wheelchair through to the center, adjacent to the cross. Their heads were bowed in silence, each of them listening to the music with closed eyes. Brian could see the end of Sabi's prayer rope dangling from the side of his wheelchair under the armrest. It was a familiar sight by now; he'd rarely seen Sabi without it on his lap. He'd explained that the object was his constant, visible reminder to pray without ceasing, orienting his mind as his fingers, awkwardly but doggedly, fumbled for each knot.

They took a seat as quietly as possible. Melissa leaned into Brian, resting her head on his shoulder. He put his arm around her. They waited, gazing at the cross in silence, their thoughts absorbed by the circumstances they'd experienced that had led up to this moment—events terrible and tragic, inspiring and uplifting. It was impossible to deny the unseen hand behind it all, but their hearts ached for Malcolm.

Brian closed his eyes and tried to pray. He understood this sort of emptiness all too well, but words failed him. The hymn drifted to an end, replaced by new lyrics carried along by an understated piano tune that filled the void in both his mind and his heart:

Tears are falling, hearts are breaking
How we need to hear from God
You've been promised, we've been waiting

Welcome Holy Child
Welcome Holy Child

Bring Your peace into our violence
Bid our hungry souls be filled
Word now breaking Heaven's silence

Welcome to our world
Welcome to our world

So wrap our injured flesh around You
Breathe our air and walk our sod
Rob our sin and make us holy

Perfect Son of God

Perfect Son of God
Welcome to our world

"That's who we need."

Upon hearing the familiar voice, Brian opened his moistened eyes and turned toward Malcolm, whose eyes were closed, a faint smile on his face.

"He is why we endure," Sabi added softly. "And one day, as the Scriptures say, Jesus will present us to God's council . . . the great cloud of witnesses . . . as His brothers, sisters, and friends."

Malcolm opened his eyes. He leaned forward and touched Sabi's shoulder, whispering to him. Then he turned and looked at Brian and Melissa.

"Sorry for the past few days," Malcolm apologized, coming toward them. "It's been really rough . . . for a lot of reasons."

"No need," Melissa answered, dabbing her eyes. "We missed you. We need you with us."

"I don't plan on going anywhere. That's been part of the struggle, or maybe the resolution to a struggle. What happened with Dee . . . it has forced me to come to grips with some other things. It just brought everything to a head."

Sabi remained silent, his head bent in concentration. Brian could see him once again fingering his rope. "What is it?" Brian asked.

Malcolm sighed. "Everything, really. Since I learned Andrew was dead, I've felt lost. He was the reason I entered the priesthood. That's no doubt misguided, but he reoriented my whole life—and that's part of the problem."

"What do you mean?"

Malcolm pursed his lips, mulling over an answer. "Andrew was consumed with his mission to expose the evil inside the Church. You both know he spent part of his career in the Vatican. He'd heard stories from curia members he trusted that satanic rituals had been performed in the Vatican by some rogue priests as sort of a surrender of the Church to darkness. He believed it and wanted to identify the people responsible for the sacrilege and have them removed. Over, the years he'd recruit people inside the Church hierarchy and on the outside to gather information. The obsession exposed him to some really strange stuff. He was never one to just stay out of things, either. He'd get involved and make serious enemies.

"We met while I was in graduate school, and I decided I wanted to be part of it. It gave me a mission that went beyond my love for science. I'm not saying I didn't see eternal value in that, but what Andrew was doing felt more immediate—more in the trenches. Honestly, it was seductive, but in the right sort of way. I wanted God to use me."

"You don't want that now?" Melissa asked.

"I've been wrestling with how I can still be useful . . . how I can stay on the front lines. I've been struggling to see how I can be without Andrew. I don't know anyone on the inside. I don't know who is on Andrew's side and who isn't. I have no contacts. I was basically his understudy. I just don't know who I can trust to keep going in that direction now."

"What about just being a priest?"

"It's not that easy. There's so much corruption and complacency. Without Andrew to help me navigate, I can't help thinking I'd spend too much valuable time trying to work around the authority above me. And I don't believe I have the pastoral heart I need to stay put in a parish."

"That's understandable," Melissa observed, "but as a Jesuit, you could still have the life of a scholar."

"That's true—and it brings up another part of the problem. I actually haven't taken my final vows yet. I'm at the stage called Tertianship. This latest episode is making me seriously consider asking to be released from the order and my earlier vows—or just walking away without even asking. I'm thinking in ways someone in my position shouldn't, and in my mind, that disqualifies me."

"Wow," said Brian. "I had no idea you were struggling like this, Malcolm."

"I'm good at hiding that sort of thing. There's more to it, too."

"Like what?"

"I don't want to forgive the Colonel," Malcolm admitted frankly. "I want him punished. In fact, if I'm honest, I want him to die. I can't see him sparing Dee once he's done with her. He needs to pay. I know it's not right—a priest has to be able to do things that he'd tell others to do. I'm just not there. Forgiveness is a great concept until you have someone to forgive, especially someone this wicked."

"Rage against evil is no sin," Sabi's calm voice interrupted. "but we must let Jesus fight such battles for us. I have known such anger as well. Where I was kept before the Lord delivered me . . . it was a terrible place. The people there did horrible things to me. I was powerless to defend myself. But you must release this to God in prayer. The only place to find a spiritual victory is on the other side of a spiritual battle."

"He's right, Malcolm," said Brian. "That's what imprecatory prayers teach us. God will curse those who curse us. As believers, we've inherited that covenant promise. We can't take matters into our own hands.

But I'll admit, I'm guilty there, too. After I got Neff's call, I wanted to just pound the guy right there in the restaurant." He paused. "And since we're being honest here, I'm with you. I want him to get what he deserves. He's taken so many lives. . . . But Sabi is right. Frankly, we both need to pray we don't get the opportunity."

"I hear that."

"Malcolm," Melissa broke in.

"Yes?"

"Look at me. Do you remember who I was—and why?"

Malcolm started to reply, but stopped. He looked at Melissa's face, which was full of sincerity and concern. The episodes of the past summer she was referring to hadn't faded from his memory.

"Let it go, Malcolm. Things *will* come full circle."

"Such battles are what forge true disciples," Sabi encouraged him. "You can train a chimp to carry a Bible. Such outward things do not demonstrate a heart humble enough to be obedient unto death. We put down the sword that would punish our enemies, because the resurrection and the judgment will demonstrate before every spectator—from worlds seen and unseen—who won and who lost. We can wait for resolution."

Malcolm nodded gratefully. "Amen. I'll need all of you to keep me accountable, though."

Sabi smiled. "All of us here—we are our brother's keeper."

"Right," he nodded, and returned the gesture.

"As for service to God," Sabi said, "my prayer is selfish. I pray that you will find your calling here. The task is great—even greater now after what we have learned. We must work to complete the mission set before us while it is yet day. We must believe that we will see our sister again, in this life or the next."

"That's actually been on my mind a lot," Brian confessed.

"Do not fear," Sabi replied. "Many who we find estranged from Jesus are not in that condition because they do not know the truth. Many are in pain, seized by anger and loss."

"How do you know that's the case with Dee?" asked Brian.

"Fern and I spoke with her several times. Your friend knows the gospel. She grew up with it. But she has suffered many things, sometimes because of the words and deeds of those who would take the name of Christ. At other times . . . there were abuses that seem connected to the evil that knows your names," he said ominously, yet without fear.

"What did you say to her?"

"We shared our stories. Her pain was no barrier to us, for we have known terrible things. That is where evil is blind. It cannot see that those who suffer speak the same language. God had one son on earth without sin, but no son without suffering. When this penetrates the heart, it becomes hard to continue to rage against the one who loved you enough to suffer in your place.

"That was our message. I believe Jesus will have the final word in her heart, regardless of what the rest of her life here holds. The Spirit will attend to her though we cannot."

55

There is strong shadow where there is much light.

—Johann Wolfgang von Goethe

"I want you all to hear me out," Clarise began, surveying the troubled expressions in front of her. "It might sound a little crazy, but I'm absolutely certain this whole episode—the whole reason Father Fitzgerald was kidnapped—was about Dee from the beginning."

Brian looked at Melissa and Malcolm's unsettled faces. "What are you saying?" he asked. "How do you know that?"

"The more I think about what I know now, any other conclusion doesn't seem possible. Where's Fern—and Nili and Sabi?"

"They took Summit to her room to play a board game after lunch," Ward explained. "We didn't want her to feel excluded again. I told them she wouldn't do well with this stuff—no need to fill her head with the details."

Clarise nodded. She opened a manila folder she'd brought to the gathering. "Let me just lay out the facts." She began distributing papers. "I've got two sets of DNA test results here."

"Two sets?" asked Neff, holding a page, lines forming on his brow.

"Yes. Dee and her baby."

"How did you manage that?" asked Malone.

"It was actually pretty straightforward. There was no problem matching the blood on Dee's coat to blood I'd drawn earlier in Maine. Once we got Malcolm and Dee stateside, given her condition, I gave her a complete physical. It didn't take long to learn she was anxious about her pregnancy, though I didn't know why at the time, so I suggested we conduct some tests. Malcolm convinced her to let me. One of them involved a draw of amniotic fluid, which you can get the baby's DNA from. I kept some and brought it here."

"If this was all about her like you think, I can't believe they'd harm her," Melissa said, removing her glasses. "What do you think happened?"

"I don't know, but I agree. I can't see them harming her deliberately. It's not unusual for a pregnant woman to be jolted into serious labor if she's severely stressed or injured."

"Was she far enough along for that?" Malcolm asked

"Dee was close to thirty-two weeks—a week or so ahead of Melissa. If she delivered, the baby would have survived, unless whatever caused Dee to hemorrhage involved an injury to the fetus. I think we can assume the Colonel's people had the medical capability to take care of her and the baby on board the craft. After all, that's what they came for."

"So you said," Brian replied. "But why? I take it that the DNA results are driving the conclusion?"

Clarise took a breath to steady herself. "The first set is Dee's. The page after that . . . I don't know what this means. I had a hunch on the way back here." She paused again and looked at Melissa, then Brian.

"What is it?" Brian pressed.

"That computer printout you took from Area 51 . . ."

"Yes?" Melissa sat up and looked expectantly into Clarise's eyes.

"Well, that wasn't part of your DNA profile. . . . It was part of Dee's."

"*What*?" Brian gasped.

"The printout was a section of Dee's genetic profile, not Melissa's. The second page of what I just handed you is from that printout. I marked the place on the profile I just took from Dee's DNA so you can do a visual comparison of the sequence if you want to. It's a perfect match."

"How in the world can that be?" Brian asked. He turned to Melissa, who was speechless, caught totally off guard.

"I don't know," Clarise answered. "I've been running your story through my mind. I can only guess that when your friend Neil saw that printout and took it, he thought he was looking at something associated with Melissa. He must have made a mistake, at least about who it belonged to. He didn't know what he was really looking at. But I do. It belongs to Dee."

"I don't know what to say—to even think," Melissa stammered. She stopped and looked at Clarise. "What about the marks on the paper?"

"I can't be *completely* sure about them, but I can say I have some reasonable guesses. I looked through a dozen journal articles this morning after I confirmed the match with the printout. If I had to guess, I'd say that Dee was being genetically inspected to make sure she could carry a child to term. At least two of the locations on the printout are consistent with some things that geneticists have studied to explain spontaneous abortion after implantation of the conceptus on the uterine wall. I think they wanted to make sure she was a good candidate for implantation. There's nothing else I can see with the marked locations on the printout that would be amiss."

Clarise paused to let the news sink in. She wanted to give them a minute. She'd been wondering how to approach what she had to say next, and she still didn't know, but the time had come. Malone could tell from her expression that she was a little on edge. He nodded to her as if to say, "Whatever it is, it'll be okay."

"What about the baby's DNA?" Neff's voice broke into her thoughts. "Is there something unusual about it?"

"Well, yes and no," she answered. "Or maybe I should say yes and *maybe.*"

"Just tell us," Malone pressed gently.

"As far as the DNA itself, there's nothing unusual. Dee was pregnant with a normal baby boy . . . but it had no genetic relationship to her. The child is Caucasian by race. She was obviously a surrogate."

"That's not unexpected," Brian replied. "We all knew she and Melissa had been implanted." He paused. "Is there something else?"

"I'm not sure . . ."

"You've got to be sure!" Melissa blurted out. Brian took her hand. She sank back into the couch and covered her mouth with her hand.

"I'm so sorry." Clarise got out of her seat and crouched in front of Melissa, touching her knee. "I don't mean there's anything wrong the baby. I know this brings back the fear all over again, but I have no reason to think there's anything unusual about any of the babies—really. I'd tell you if I did."

"I apologize," Melissa said, catching her breath. "I—"

"There's no need. What I'm not sure of is that, for some reason, I can't shake the notion that I've seen this DNA somewhere else."

"How could you remember a DNA profile?" Malcolm asked. "A sequence is phenomenally long."

"It's not the sequence that's familiar—it's certain features that derive from the description. The thought may be completely wrong, but it keeps nagging at me."

Melissa touched Clarise's hand. "Really, I'm sorry for overreacting. You've helped us so much already."

"Forget it," Clarise said. "Maybe we should switch gears a bit. That article you asked me to read—I'm through that, too."

Melissa's expression became more focused. "And?"

"It's legit. The research and the conclusions are solid. Whatever you're angling for that rests on the work described in that article should be secure."

"Thanks." Melissa paused. "I don't know whether to be enthused or troubled."

"Ward also got the autopsy reports you asked for."

"Autopsy reports?" Brian gawked at her. "What did you—?"

An abrupt, unexpected commotion coming from one of the corridors that opened into Miqlat's central foyer caused all their heads to turn in that direction. A rapid crescendo of footsteps, accompanied by indiscernible shouts, reverberated louder and louder. Without warning, Kamran shot through the opening, one arm holding his laptop, the other grabbing a rail to divert his momentum toward the bewildered cluster of onlookers. He put the laptop down on an end table and began grunting and gesticulating wildly, trying to communicate.

"Slow down!" Madison shouted, trying in vain to read his signs. "Just calm down and tell me!"

Kamran's signals slowed a bit, but his urgency didn't diminish.

"He says he's found something ... terrible ... and exciting—but more terrible than exciting," Madison sputtered, trying to translate. "*Slower!*" she demanded.

Kamran bent over to both catch his breath and gather his composure, hands on his thighs. After a few seconds he stood up and, wearing a determined expression, resumed signing to Madison. They all watched the look on her face change from concentration to curiosity, and then to uneasiness. Kamran nodded insistently, pointing to Brian. Madison turned to him.

"Kamran says he understands something the Colonel is planning. It has to do with something his priest friend told him."

"Father Mantello?"

Kamran clapped and waved a finger at Brian.

"He wants to show you," Madison explained.

"How does he know ... whatever it is he knows?"

"Isaiah 40. He says he knows why the Colonel quoted Isaiah 40—and it scares him."

56

"To whom then will you compare me, that I should be like him?" says the Holy One. "Lift up your eyes on high and see: who created these? He who brings out their host by number, calling them all by name, by the greatness of his might, and because he is strong in power not one is missing."

—*Isaiah 40:25–26*

"What do you think he's come up with?" Brian asked Malcolm.

"Well, Andrew and I discussed Father Mantello's ideas a couple of times," Malcolm answered as he, Brian, and Melissa watched Ward and Madison setting up the equipment for Kamran's presentation. "My guess is that it's going to be something about signs in the sky. But with this kid, I'm expecting the unexpected."

"Why?" Melissa asked.

"He's way outside the box. He's brilliant, but half the time you're not sure what he's talking about. I don't have any background in astronomy to speak of. Madison and Nili told me he spends almost every free minute fiddling with his astronomy software. If he comes out here, it's basically for food. When I talked to him it was like listening in on a conversation between Origen and Isaac Newton. I'm amazed sign language even works for what's in his head."

"Seriously?"

"Oh, yeah."

"Okay, folks, looks like we're ready to roll," Madison announced as she walked up to the front and handed Kamran an open laptop. She paused as Nili, Summit, and Fern found seats in the Pit, accounting for everyone. She motioned to Kamran and pointed to a lead on the floor, which the young man promptly picked up and plugged into the laptop.

"I've helped Kamran get his material together so that we can go as quickly as possible without needing to sign or text back-and-forth. I put all his material into a text-to-voice program and saved the results in an audio file that I mapped to his slides. The result is that you'll be able to hear what you are seeing as though he is narrating it. If you have questions, feel free to ask them as he goes. He'll type responses onto his laptop, and you'll all hear the audio results through the speakers. Got it?"

Madison saw some nods and then sat down on a stool adjacent to Kamran. Kamran began typing on his laptop. A computerized voice began the lecture, its artificial, awkwardly-punctuated rhythm articulating Kamran's thoughts: "In order to understand what I see in the Colonel's words to Dr. Scott, we must begin with the birth of Jesus. We all know that Jesus was not born on December 25. That is just the day that Christians historically celebrate his birth. We will see tonight that we can know the real date. Once we have that date, you will begin to see what I see. First we'll talk about Revelation 12 and how it helps us understand what the magi saw when Jesus was born. Let's look at that passage as we begin the slides."

Kamran hit his remote.

> *And a great sign appeared in heaven: a woman clothed with the sun, with the moon under her feet, and on her head a crown of twelve stars. She was pregnant and was crying out in birth pains and the agony of giving birth. And another sign appeared in heaven: behold, a great red dragon, with seven heads and ten horns, and on his heads seven diadems.*
>
> *His tail swept down a third of the stars of heaven and cast them to the earth. And the dragon stood before the woman who was about to give birth, so that when she bore her child he might devour it. She gave birth to a male child, one who is to rule all the nations with a rod of iron, but her child was caught up to God and to his throne, and the woman fled into the wilderness, where she has a place prepared by God, in which she is to be nourished for 1,260 days.*

"The signs that appear in the heavens are astronomical: sun, moon, and stars," the mechanical voice communicating Kamran's words explained. "It is also clear that this passage is not describing an angelic rebellion before or at creation. The 'third of the stars' are not called angels, but even if they are angels, as many think, they are swept down after the birth of the child, which is clearly Jesus."

Kamran paused the presentation and typed a short message into his laptop. "Do you agree, Dr. Scott?"

"Look out," Malcolm whispered.

"I do," Brian replied. "Verse 5 quotes Psalm 2, a messianic psalm.

The 'rod of iron' reference comes from Psalm 2:9. The child is certainly Jesus the Messiah, and so this casting down of a third of the stars has nothing to do with primeval creation, though a lot of Christians think that. There's nothing in the Bible about a third of the angels falling before creation. It's a myth."

Kamran nodded appreciatively and began typing once more. "Please stop me if you hear anything you disagree with. If you don't, I will assume you are in agreement. I will also ask questions now and then for you to answer. We must all know your thoughts."

"Sounds fine," Brian answered.

Kamran pressed the remote to continue. "Several points of the description need our attention. The woman in the vision is described as 'clothed' with the sun. She has twelve stars around her head. The woman gives birth to a child, who is the messianic Jesus. After giving birth to the Messiah, the woman is persecuted and has to flee into the desert."

Kamran paused to type. "Dr. Scott, who do scholars—including you—think the woman in the vision is?"

"Just about everyone would say the woman is Israel," Brian answered, "because the Old Testament describes Israel as the virgin daughter of Zion who produces the messiah in fulfillment of prophecy. We, of course, think of Mary, but Mary was not persecuted and never ran into the desert for safety—her life in the New Testament has no parallel to the description here. Israel was scattered after Jesus was here—mainly in the Diaspora after the resurrection and the destruction of the temple. The 'Virgin daughter Israel' is obviously the best fit for both parts of the description."

"Thank you," Kamran responded. "Let's talk about the twelve stars."

He resumed his presentation: "The twelve stars around the head of the woman are easily traced to Old Testament and other Jewish religious writings. In Joseph's dream in Genesis 37, the sun, the moon, and eleven stars represent Jacob, his wife, and the eleven tribes of Israel. Joseph, the twelfth tribe, would be the twelfth star in the vision of Revelation 12.

"Jewish writers like Josephus and Philo thought the stars were also a description of the garments of the Israelite high priest, since he represented the twelve tribes before Yahweh in the temple. Those writers believed the twelve stars of the tribes of Israel corresponded to the twelve signs of the zodiac. This is known from several zodiac mosaics found in ancient Jewish synagogues."

Kamran cut in to type more, "The point I am making is that the vision of Revelation 12 has a long history of being understood by Jews in terms of both the Old Testament and astronomy. Now for the dragon."

The pre-recorded mechanized voice continued: "The dragon is a well-known Old Testament symbol. Many scholars have identified the dragon as the chaos sea-monster symbol of Israelite religion. Revelation 12, 13, and 15 describe this dragon as coming from the sea. This links the dragon to the fourth beast of Daniel 7, who also came from the sea. The four beasts of Daniel 7 were four kingdoms, aligned to the great image made of four different metals in the vision of Daniel 2."

"Dr. Scott," Kamran typed, "what was the identity of the fourth kingdom?"

"Most scholars take it as Rome, though there are some exceptions. Rome makes the most sense to me. The key is Daniel 2. In that passage, the kingdom of God appears in the fourth kingdom, the stone made without human hands in Nebuchadnezzar's dream. The New Testament is crystal clear that the kingdom of God began during the first coming of Jesus, which was during the rule of Rome, so it's sensible to have Rome as the fourth kingdom."

"I agree," Kamran typed. "These comments are good enough for understanding the astronomy, as we will see. I want to focus on the birth and not the interpretation of events after the birth."

He resumed the presentation: "Once more, it is important to note that the images of Revelation 12 are easily known from the Old Testament. Less obvious is how people who were not Jewish, but who lived at the same time and needed the same message from God, would have receive the message. The Apostle John was a Jew, but he also lived in a Greek and Roman culture."

Kamran paused to type, "Still in agreement, Dr. Scott? If so, we can move on."

Brian nodded.

"Paul tells us in Romans 10:18 that all people could have known about the arrival of the Savior because the voice of the stars went out to all the earth. Paul is quoting Psalm 19:4, which describes the heavens as communicating the glory of God. The voice of the stars, according to Paul, means that all nations heard the news of the coming king."

Brian's mind suddenly drifted back to his confrontation with the Colonel, to Isaiah 40:5, *The glory of the Lord shall be revealed . . .*

"Some Hebrew manuscripts of Psalm 19:4 say that the 'line' of the stars declares their message, not their 'voice,'" Kamran's recording continued. "The line of the stars describes the ecliptic—the path of the zodiac constellations. The wording is different, but the idea is the same no matter the manuscript difference."

Kamran hit the keyboard again. "We are now ready to read the vision of the night sky. Please watch the video on the screen as I narrate what you see. My comments will reflect the point of view from Israel, since the Apostle John is giving us the description. The magi in Babylon would have seen the same events and more as they journeyed to Israel, but the exact timing of the birth of Jesus requires viewing the sky from the ground in Israel, the place of the birth.

"The key figure is the woman. Revelation 12:1 gives us clear details: the woman is 'clothed' with the sun, there are twelve stars around her head, and the moon is at her feet. The 'birth' of the Messiah is associated with this heavenly scene. The word John uses to describe this vision is 'sign'—*semeion* in Greek. Scholars say this is the same word used many places by Greek writers to describe constellations.

"Since the sun and moon have positions relative to the woman, the language is astronomical. The ecliptic line, the sun, and the moon are in color in the image you see. In the night sky the woman would be a constellation located within the normal path of the ecliptic line. This line will speak to us now—as Psalm 19 said.

"The only zodiac sign of a woman that exists along the ecliptic is Virgo—the Virgin. Modern astronomers list twelve stars around what is considered the head of the woman of this constellation.

"In the period of Jesus' birth, the sun on its annual course through the heavens entered into the constellation of the woman on about August 13, and exited from her feet on about October 2. But the Apostle John saw the scene when the sun was 'clothing' the woman. This indicates that the sun in the vision was located in the woman's body.

"There is a twenty-day period in the year when the sun is inside Virgo. But that occurs every year. We need to know a specific year. That year is determined by the other elements in the vision as well as astronomical events that explain the movement of the star in Matthew and that align with Luke's chronology for the priestly service of Zechariah, John the Baptist's father and Jesus' cousin. Recall that both the pregnancies of Mary and Elizabeth, John the Baptist's mother, were divinely announced.

"The year that accounts for all the elements is 3 BC. I will show you all the signs that need to be accounted for as we proceed so you will all see that 3 BC is the precise year. For now, we will focus on the sun clothing the Virgin in 3 BC.

"In 3 BC, the sun would have clothed the Virgin from about August 27 through September 15. Jesus would have to be born within that period. This timeframe correlates precisely with the chronology of Luke concerning the timing of the birth of John the Baptist and his father Zechariah's scheduled time of service at the temple, where the angel met him to announce John's birth.

"From the religious perspective of the magi, just these signs would have denoted a divine birth. We know the magi were familiar with the virgin-birth prophecy of Isaiah 7:14 since they journeyed to Judah and asked for the whereabouts of the king of the Jews. They knew the Scriptures since the prophet Daniel, a magi himself, had brought the Scriptures with him to Babylon.

"We must now account for the moon at the Virgin's feet. The position of the moon pinpoints the birth to one day within the twenty days the Virgin is clothed with the sun and really to within ninety minutes on that day. According to John's description, the moon must be under the woman's feet at the same time the sun is clothing the woman.

"In the year 3 BC, these two events occurred from 6:15 p.m. until around 7:45 p.m. on September 11. This is the only day and time window in the whole year that the astronomical phenomenon described in Revelation 12 could take place. This means that Jesus was born just after sunset on September 11, 3 BC."

"That's awesome," Malcolm marveled.

"I'd say it's creepy," Melissa added. "September 11? Are you kidding?"

"I'm with Melissa," Clarise spoke up. "It's a really weird coincidence—and we don't like that word here. Do you think this gives our modern September 11 some sort of added meaning, Kamran?"

Kamran took to the keyboard quickly. "I can think of messages that the unseen world of evil ones could communicate by the date and the symbol of the two towers in New York, but I am cautious. I don't want to let my imagination go too far. I think it must mean something, but I'm not sure what. But for our discussion, September 11 is not the important date formula—the Jewish dating will be our focus. This focus will become more important as we proceed with the things we can know. They are much more strange."

"*More* strange?" Ward asked. "It feels like we just shot the bull's-eye out of strange."

Kamran shook his head. He wasn't smiling.

"What else is there?" Neff asked, intrigued by Kamran's assertion.

"Much more."

He resumed the presentation: "You can see the Virgin and the elements of Revelation 12. There are more signs for the birth date that would have been very important to the magi. Notice in this slide that above the head of the Virgin there are two celestial objects: Jupiter and Regulus. You only see one object, but there are two names. That is because Jupiter and Regulus are aligned.

"Jupiter and Regulus are called the 'king planet' and the 'king star' in ancient Graeco-Roman astrology. This is because Jupiter is the largest planet. Regulus is very bright, so it is prominent. For that reason and the constellation of which it is a part, it was considered the star of kings."

"What constellation is Regulus part of?" Sabi asked, moving his wheelchair a bit closer to the screen.

"*Leo.*" The answer appeared on the screen, as Kamran had anticipated Sabi's question. "Leo is the lion, and the Messiah is—"

"The lion of Judah," Nili finished the sentence, wide-eyed at the correlation.

"Yes. Revelation 5:5 calls the lamb that was slain the 'lion of Judah' and the 'root of David.' The night sky on September 11, 3 BC would have looked like this, with Leo present."

The image popped up on the screen.

Kamran continued, typing as quickly as he could. "For the magi, the conjunction of Jupiter and Regulus in the same sky as the Virgin clothed mid-body with the sun would have announced a royal birth—a divine royal birth, since they were thinking in terms of the Jewish Scriptures. Other wise men who perhaps had no knowledge of the Jewish prophecy would nevertheless have expected the same thing, given their belief in astrology—that the stars gave messages from the gods about what they were doing and going to do on earth. And all these celestial events occur together only on this date in this year."

"Good grief," Malone said, shaking his head. "This is mind blowing. I'll never accuse you again of just playing Halo on your time off."

The quip produced laughter all around the room, but Kamran offered no expression. He began to type feverishly again. "No—this is not the strangeness I spoke of. There is more."

"What about some of the obvious problems with a 3 BC date?" Brian interrupted. "Things like the date of Herod's death. The New Testament has Jesus born before Herod died—and that was in 4 BC."

Kamran shook his head and waved Brian off and then started in on the keyboard again. "That date is based on a solar eclipse that Josephus says occurred shortly before Herod died. There was more than one eclipse between 5 BC and 1 BC. The details of Herod's death can be aligned to the 1 BC eclipse."

"Really?" Brian asked. "Josephus has other chronological indicators besides an eclipse. Scholars have spent a lot of time correlating his work with Roman records."

"Have they considered that Josephus and the biblical writers might be using different calendars at different times—one political, the other religious?" Kamran asked.

"Well . . ."

"Herod's death by the political calendar is 4 BC. By the Jewish religious calendar, it's early 1 BC. A Jew could be looking at a date for Herod in one calendar and talk about it in relation to the other. Scholars who study ancient Herodian coins have shown that to be true. Therefore, the 4 BC date and the 1 BC date are not actually contradictory."

Brian glanced at Malcolm, who had a look on his face that said, "I told you so." To Kamran he replied, "I'll have to check on that."

Kamran nodded and held up a flash drive to draw Brian's attention.

"It's all on the flash?"

Kamran nodded again and tossed it lightly to Brian.

"I suppose," Brian continued as he slid the object into his shirt pocket, "that I'll find an answer to the problem of how the 3 BC date can work with the governorship and census of Quintillus Varus as well?"

Another nod.

"Alright then."

"Looks like you found a graduate student," Melissa leaned in and whispered to him.

"Or maybe Kamran found one," he replied under his breath.

Kamran pointed to the screen and resumed the presentation. "One month before September 11, on August 12, 3 BC, Jupiter was in conjunction with a different object than Regulus—Venus, the 'morning star.' In Gentile astrology, Venus was Ishtar, the Mother, the goddess of fertility. Jupiter was the great Father. Therefore, a Jupiter-Venus conjunction would have signified to the Gentile that a divine royal birth was at hand."

"Isn't Jesus called the 'morning star' in the Bible somewhere?" Fern asked, leaning forward, visibly captivated by what she was seeing.

Kamran nodded and pointed to the screen, continuing the presentation. "The New Testament refers three times to Jesus as the 'morning star.' It was the brightest morning star; it 'ruled' the others, so to speak. That makes perfect sense given the astronomical signs. Second Peter 1:19 and Revelation 22:16 are the two clearest uses pointing to Jesus. The third is in Revelation 2:28, where Jesus tells the Apostle John that all those who overcome will be set over the nations—believers will displace the ruling, fallen sons of God who now have dominion.

"And then Jesus describes us, His children, as ruling with a rod of iron—which is what Psalm 2 says about Him! And after all that, Jesus promises to give the believer the morning star. This means that we will rule as the Messiah rules—we'll rule and reign with Him. We are morning stars as He is the morning star. See Dr. Scott's dissertation if you want to know more."

Brian smiled to himself. "You make the theology sound so much cooler than I could."

Kamran beamed at the compliment before continuing. "Venus was therefore a special 'bearer of light' before the major conjunction of Regulus and Jupiter, the signs that the king was born. God, of course, is called the 'Father of Lights' in James 1:17. Jesus is the 'radiance' of the Father in Hebrews 1:2."

"And the light of the world!" Madison added enthusiastically.

Kamran clapped his approval, enjoying her response. He pointed again up to the screen and resumed the recording. "All of this was foreshadowed in Isaiah 60:3, which prophesies the future return of the Glory—the presence of God—to Israel. The prophecy is filled with astronomical language: rising, brightness, a light."

The words of that passage appeared on the screen:

Arise, shine, for your light has come,
and the glory of the LORD has risen upon you.
For behold, darkness shall cover the earth,
and thick darkness the peoples;
but the LORD will arise upon you,
and his glory will be seen upon you.
And nations shall come to your light,
and kings to the brightness of your rising.

Isaiah 40 again beckoned to Brian's consciousness. *The glory of the Lord shall be revealed* . . . He closed his eyes in thought. *But the glory was revealed earlier. Luke quoted the passage.*

Kamran paused the presentation. His expression turned somber. "I won't take time to show you how the Jupiter-Regulus conjunction explains the apparent movement of the star of Bethlehem. All astronomers know about that—how Jupiter's retrograde motion solves that part of the birth story. I want to move to the very startling material I learned from Father Mantello, my friend, the evening he died."

Kamran sighed and closed his eyes, collecting himself and his thoughts. He blinked and began typing. "I believe these signs in the sky are what Paul was talking about in Romans 10:18, where he insisted that all people had received the good news about the coming of the Messiah. Dr. Scott?"

Brian focused his attention on the young man. "Yes?"

"Look at Isaiah 40:5. I have the verse on the screen."

Brian looked up at the familiar words:

And the glory of the LORD shall be revealed,
and all flesh shall see it together,
for the mouth of the LORD has spoken.

Kamran continued. "Isaiah spoke of the birth of Jesus. We know this is true because this passage is quoted in Luke 3. Here is what Luke says about the message of John the Baptist." He gestured to the screen.

As it is written in the book of the words of Isaiah the prophet,

"The voice of one crying in the wilderness:

> *'Prepare the way of the Lord,*
> *make his paths straight.*
> *Every valley shall be filled,*
> *and every mountain and hill shall be made low,*
> *and the crooked shall become straight,*
> *and the rough places shall become level ways,*
> *and all flesh shall see the salvation of God.' "*

Kamran typed out his next question: "How did all flesh see the coming of the king—the salvation of God—together? The Colonel asked you what 'together' meant. Do you see now?"

Brian sat in stunned silence as the answer broke through, invading his thoughts. "The heavens," he said, looking at Kamran. "The other passage that has the heavens revealing the glory of God is Psalm 19—the one Paul was quoting in Romans 10:18. The heavens declare the glory of God . . . and the glory that was revealed was Jesus. All people saw together because all people can see the sky."

"Exactly. But do you see how Isaiah 60 fits all this? We saw that part of Isaiah a few minutes ago." Kamran began clicking back through his presentation. "It is the reason for my worry. Consider the slide."

> *But the* Lord *will arise upon you, and his glory will be seen upon you. And nations shall come to your light, and kings to the brightness of your rising.*

"It's projected into the future," Brian spoke his thoughts loud enough for the others to hear. "It's about the kingdom come to earth in the future, when all nations will be drawn to God, so it's not about the first coming of Jesus. The language of light . . . and brightness rising . . . the glory will be seen *again.*"

He turned to Kamran. "The Colonel is going to use the heavens, isn't he? He's going to use some astronomical event as part of his plan—all that stuff about a real but false Jesus showing up. That's your point."

Kamran nodded.

"Kamran?" It was Malcolm. The young man nodded in his direction. "You can see ahead in time—astronomical time. Are these signs of Jesus' arrival the first time around? Will they ever all repeat? Do you think that's what the Colonel is going to use to dupe people?"

"Yes . . . and yes."

Brian heard a few gasps.

"But there's no clear indication in the New Testament that the second coming will have the same set of signs," Brian pressed.

"Brian," Melissa replied, shaking her head, "what would the Colonel say to that?"

Brian closed his eyes tightly, realizing his mistake. "He'd say it doesn't matter. He'd say the only thing that matters is what people will expect . . . and believe."

"But what's the connection to Genesis 6?" Neff spoke up. "We've all listened to the recording by now. He kept going back to using that passage for his homemade myth. Unless all these signs in the sky dovetail with that somehow, I can't see him being interested in this."

"But he's the one who quoted Isaiah 40," Melissa protested. "He wouldn't have done that if he didn't see a connection."

"True, but what is it?"

"Dr. Scott," the mechanical voice cut into the discussion. Brian looked at Kamran. "Do you know what day in the Jewish calendar corresponded to September 11, 3 BC?"

Brian shrugged and looked around the room. "I haven't the slightest idea. But after all this, I'm sure it will mean something."

"Yes, it means something . . . perhaps everything."

Brian gazed at the young man's earnest face. Brian could see that what he knew frightened him. "Go ahead."

"The date was the birthday of the world . . . a date that Jewish tradition considered the birthday of Noah."

Brian lowered his head, his mind racing through line after line of ancient Hebrew and Aramaic texts he'd translated and studied over the years. The full force of the mute prodigy's words crashed into his mind. "Are you serious? Tishri 1?"

Kamran nodded.

57

There are things known and there are things unknown,
and in between are the doors of perception.

—*Aldous Huxley*

"I do not understand," Nili broke in, a look of confusion on her face. "Tishri 1—it is Rosh Hashanah. But what does this have to do with the flood and these other things?"

"You'd better explain to everyone first that there's more than one Jewish new year date," Brian said to Kamran, still trying to process the implications of Kamran's revelation.

"Yes, there are four new year beginnings in Israel," Nili noted.

"Four?" Fern asked. "I'm confused already."

"There are four. America has this, too."

"You mean like when a fiscal year begins and ends, or a school year begins and ends, versus the solar year—they can all have different beginning and ending points," Neff observed.

"Correct. In Israel there are four, but two are especially important. The first month of the calendar that follows astronomy—specifically the months or new moons—is Nisan. So the first day of Nisan is the beginning of the new set of month cycles for the Hebrew calendar year. In the Bible, God set Nisan as the first month for Israel because it is the month that our people were set free from Egypt by the hand of Moses."

"Nili is referring to the first two verses of Exodus 12," Brian explained. "Nisan was the month of Passover, which was first instituted in connection with the last plague, the death of the firstborn, and the subsequent exodus from Egypt."

"But Nisan 1 is not Rosh Hashanah—which in English means 'the first day of the year,' " Nili continued. "Rosh Hashanah is Tishri 1."

Brian could see there was still confusion on most of their faces. "Before Moses instituted Nisan as the first month for the new community of Israel that came out of Egypt, the Hebrew people already had a calendar—an agricultural one, like most ancient societies. Since that calendar pre-dated the Mosaic calendar, the rabbis regarded it as the *original* calendar of the world, going back to Genesis."

"Yes, Tishri was the first month of that original calendar," Nili picked up on the thought. "But in the more recent Mosaic calendar, Tishri became the seventh month of the year since Nisan was made the first month after the exodus. God did not change the order of the months; He changed the starting point of the year, making Nisan the beginning. It commemorated Israel's new beginning."

"So Rosh Hashanah is sort of the *original* new year's date on the older calendar?" Clarise asked.

"Yes," Nili replied. "But to understand what Kamran is saying, you must know that the rabbis teach that Tishri 1 was also the day that marked the time when God finished creating the Garden of Eden by creating Adam and Eve. It was the first day of humanity in the world."

"Why would they think that?" Ward asked.

"Because of the garden of Eden."

"I don't get it."

"I will try to explain," Nili replied. "Nisan—the first month of the *astronomical* calendar—corresponds to the early springtime in Israel. That's April in the calendar used in America. Move seven months ahead to Tishri, the seventh month in that calendar, and you are then in the fall season—September in the American calendar. The fall season is the time of the fall food harvest in Israel. The book of Genesis says the Garden of Eden was created full of vegetation, including plants for food. And so the rabbis believed that since Eden was created full of plants for food, it must have been created at the fall harvest."

"And therefore," Fern jumped back in, "the first fall month is Tishri, and the first day of Tishri is Tishri 1—and that day, by the rabbis' logic, was the first day of the finished world."

"Yes, that's it," Nili replied.

"The link between the Genesis creation account and Tishri is what's significant for understanding what Kamran told us," Brian added, looking at him. "If Kamran has a Bible on his laptop, that would be helpful for explaining that—we can start in Genesis 7."

Kamran quickly brought up the book of Genesis on the screen. Brian took the cue.

"The first thing to notice is that Genesis 7:6 says that Noah was 600 years old when the flood came upon the earth. Five verses later we find out that 'in the 600th year of Noah's life, in the second month, on the seventeenth day of the month, on that day all the fountains of the great deep burst forth, and the windows of the heavens were opened.' Notice the verse refers to the second month—the month after Tishri in Jewish tradition. The rabbis reasoned from this wording that Noah was *already* 600 by the second month—meaning he had turned 600 in the previous month, the first month, the month of Tishri."

"Clever logic," said Malone, stroking the handlebars of his mustache.

"According to Genesis, the flood lasted a little over a year. The ending of the flood is important to this whole Tishri issue," Brian continued. "In Genesis 8:13–14 we get some more detail about Noah's age."

Brian began reading: "'In the six hundred and first year, in the first month'—that would be Tishri—'the first day of the month'—that would be Tishri 1—'the waters were dried from off the earth. And Noah removed the covering of the ark and looked, and behold, the face of the ground was dry.' "

He explained, "The reference to the 601st year in the verse would be Noah's age, since earlier it said he was 600 when the flood started. Everyone follow?"

"Then the math would suggest," Ward reasoned, "that Noah had turned 601 sometime before the second month of year that saw the flood end."

"Right—and that would have been in Tishri. Early Jewish tradition took all this to mean that Noah's birthday was Tishri 1."

"So . . . a Jewish reader who took Revelation 12 as describing the birth of Jesus and who did the math would have Jesus and Noah sharing birthdays?" Neff reasoned.

"Yes, but that's just the tip of the iceberg," Brian said. "Tishri 1 was also the date that marked the beginning of a reign of a king of Judah—those kings in the line of David. Remember from Old Testament history that after Solomon died, the Israelite kingdom split into two smaller kingdoms—one in the north that went by the name Israel, and one in the south that called itself Judah. Kingship years in Judah were marked from Tishri to Tishri. The coronation for each new king was held on Tishri 1."

"So the birth of Jesus, as Kamran has plotted it out, was on the same day the king of Judah, the lion of Judah, the king from the line of David, began his rule," Nili summarized.

"That's remarkable," Melissa replied. "The timing is perfect, and the symbolism is unmistakable."

"The connection with Noah's birthday naturally ties the symbolism to the great flood," Brian added. "In the biblical passages we saw, Noah's birthday would have been a sign—a portent—of the impending flood. And the next month—the second month of the calendar, when the flood actually began according to Genesis 7:6—would have been the time of the harvest. That's part of what the Colonel must be angling for since it would connect the idea of aliens to Genesis 6 and the flood."

Ward held up his hands. "Whoa—you just lost me, big time."

"Remember that Israel's original calendar was agricultural," Brian explained. "The night sky had a lot to do with how the ancients marked the seasons—and Genesis 1 tells us as much, that the objects in the sky were for times and seasons. Harvest time in Israel was marked astronomically by the rising of the stars of the Pleiades. That would mean that the rising of the Pleiades marked the coming of the flood. Anyone acquainted with UFO contactee stories knows the Pleiades are important in so-called alien messages."

"That's for sure," Malone added, shaking his head. "You don't have to read very long before you run into stories from alien contactees that have the aliens saying they're Pleiadians. It seems to be a common theme."

"It is," said Brian, looking in Kamran's direction, "and I'm sure Kamran is tracking on that—it's got to be part of the strangeness he alluded to earlier."

Kamran nodded in agreement.

Brian continued. "In the Hebrew Bible, the word for Pleiades is *kima*. It occurs three times, always in association with another word, *kesil*, which is the word for Orion."

"And in Greek mythology," Melissa quickly connected the dots, "Orion is frequently associated with giants—since the constellation Orion was conceived of as a giant man, a hunter."

"Yep. And in one Targum—or Aramaic translation—of the book of Job found with the Dead Sea Scrolls, Orion is found in parallel to the word *naphila*—"

"The Aramaic word behind *Nephilim*," Malcolm said grimly. "I remember Andrew talking about that scroll. Man, who would've thought the birth of Jesus could be connected to Genesis 6?"

"The Colonel," Melissa said, frowning.

"You know," Brian said slowly, "there's even more to it . . . in Jesus' genealogy in Matthew."

"How many layers does this have?" Madison asked. "I mean, this gets freakier by the minute."

"This is why God brought you all here," Sabi said with conviction.

The conversation was suddenly interrupted by a series of loud taps. Heads turned to Kamran, who hit his keyboard after he had everyone's attention. "What is in the genealogy?"

"Finally," Brian said, grinning, "something you don't know."

Kamran smiled and shrugged innocently.

"It's a little hard to explain briefly, but I'll give it a shot. Why don't you put Matthew 1 on the screen so everyone can follow." Kamran did so.

"To understand this," Brian began, "you have to know the basics of the Watcher story—the Genesis 6 episode according to the book of *1 Enoch*. In that story, the Watchers—*Enoch*'s title for the sons of God—left heaven, had sexual relations with human women, and then taught humanity forbidden skills and dark arts—things like astrology, use of cosmetics, learning to make instruments of war, divination, and other enchantments. The offspring of those unions in *1 Enoch* were giants, and they were very violent, killing and even eating people. Eventually the giants were destroyed by the flood and by other angelic beings sent by God. When one of the giants died, its evil spirit, now disembodied, remained on the earth to plague and torment humans."

"Sounds like demons," Malone noted.

"That's the point. *Enoch* gives us the Jewish explanation for where demons come from, something that isn't discussed in the Bible. In *1 Enoch* we get demons as a direct result of the sin of the Watchers. Clear so far?"

Heads nodded.

"Now, try to think of the Watcher story in terms of its specific negative plot elements: sexual transgression, some sort of illicit interaction with divine beings, unusual or detestable offspring that caused harm to humanity. Still clear?"

"Sure," answered Neff.

"Good. With that in mind, we can get to Jesus' genealogy. The issue with that revolves around the four women it. The presence of those four—all of them apparently Gentiles—has puzzled scholars for a long time, but I think there's some messaging going on under the surface that's pretty telling, especially after what we've seen here."

"Ruth and Bathsheba are two of them," Clarise said, reading the screen.

"Right."

"And Tamar and Rahab," Madison finished the list, looking up at the text.

"Right again. Now, believe it or not, each of those women have some element in their lives—at least how we know them from the Old Testament and Jewish tradition—that in some way telegraphs a *reversal* of the negative plot themes of the Watcher story."

"You're kidding," Clarise said in a dubious tone.

"Really. It's in there, but you can't really see them all in the English translation. Let's take them chronologically and start with Tamar. Tamar was the daughter-in-law of Judah, one of Jacob's twelve sons. She's infamous for having disguised herself as a prostitute to have sex with Judah in retaliation for him neglecting to arrange her marriage to his son, Shelah."

"Shelah was Judah's third son," Nili added. "The other two, Er and Onan, had a sexual relationship with Tamar. God killed them both."

"Right—that's all in Genesis 38. When Judah wouldn't give his third son to Tamar as a husband, she got revenge by tricking him into sleeping with her."

"What a mess." Madison shook her head.

"No doubt. The Tamar story is interesting for our sake for two reasons. Judah's own wife—who died right before he unknowingly slept with Tamar—was a Canaanite named Shua. Remember that name—you'll hear it again. Second, Tamar is also said to be a Canaanite—a Gentile—and is described in Hebrew as a *qedeshah,* a term most scholars consider a cultic prostitute. We know from the story that she really wasn't a prostitute, but the term is important—a *qedeshah* was a woman who was thought to be in sexual union with divine beings."

"There it is—the Genesis 6 connection," Nili said, fascinated by the point.

"Yep. And some rabbis taught that angels intervened in the relationship between Judah and Tamar by preventing Judah from having her executed when he discovered she was pregnant outside marriage. He spared her when he learned he was the father."

"And when Tamar had the baby, his name was Perez," Nili said, looking up at the screen. "He's in the genealogy of Jesus, who shared Noah's birthday . . . which foretold the demise of the Nephilim."

"That's the point," said Brian. "The circumstances of her story imitate a Genesis 6 element, but her story ends up counteracting the Genesis 6 incident in some way. The other three Gentile women in the line of Jesus follow suit."

"What about Rahab?" Ward asked, reading through the genealogy again.

"Rahab was the Gentile prostitute Joshua's two spies met when they went to Jericho. It's kind of odd, but the spies are referred to as *malakim* in that story—the word for angels or, in that context, messengers."

"No way."

"It's true—Joshua uses the term twice in Joshua 6. And it's because of those two instances that later interpretations of the Joshua story in rabbinic tradition considered the spies angels. Since prostitutes in general were thought to use spells to seduce men, and since these two *malakim* show up at the prostitute's house, some rabbis thought the story echoed Genesis 6. What's also noteworthy is that Matthew has Rahab as the mother of Boaz—"

"The Boaz of the Ruth story?" Fern asked, her expression betraying her disbelief.

"Yes. It's right in the genealogy in verse 5."

"I never noticed that before."

"It's there, but what's really strange is that Ruth 2:1 describes Boaz as a *gibbor*. That's one of the words used to described the Nephilim in Genesis 6:4, and one of the words the Jewish Septuagint translators rendered *gigantes*—giants—in their Greek translation of the Old Testament."

"You don't think Boaz was part Nephilim, do you?" asked Melissa.

Brian shook his head. "*Gibbor* often just means 'warrior' with no connection to unusual height. It can also just mean 'important man' like it does with Boaz. The point is that the terms show up in these stories in connection with these women, who wind up in Jesus' genealogy. Some scholars—and I agree—think these are clever literary devices the biblical writers used to telegraph spiritual significances to Jesus' birth. What we've heard from Kamran tonight about connections between Noah and Jesus goes very well with that idea."

"The third woman is Ruth," Brian continued, "who was a Moabitess, another Gentile. The rabbis thought that Ruth's marriage proposal in Ruth 3 was illicit since she uncovered Boaz's 'feet'—a euphemistic expression often used in the Old Testament for a man's genitals. They thought her behavior smacked of a prostitute's behavior, so some Jewish writers in the period before Jesus and the apostles assumed Ruth must have done other things cultic prostitutes did, like casting spells over men."

"That seems doubtful," Sabi said.

"I agree, but I'm just telling you what a literate Jew would have been thinking when looking at Jesus' genealogy. There are other connections back to Genesis 6 that are more textually based, though. Ruth married Boaz, the *gibbor,* and later Jewish writings refer to four of their children as *gibborim.* Also, Ruth was from Moab, which was the ancestral home of one of the giant clans, the Emim, according to Deuteronomy 2:10–11."

"And the reversal of the Genesis 6 transgression would be that Ruth was the grandmother of David," Nili concluded, "who was the direct ancestor of Yeshua."

Brian nodded. "It's another way of using the Old Testament plotlines that extend from Genesis 6 to communicate the idea that the story of Jesus would counteract the evil spawned in Genesis 6. There's a duel of theological ideas woven into the genealogy."

"What about the fourth woman, Bathsheba?" Neff asked. "I don't recall any of this sort of thing with her."

"Bathsheba is always described as the wife of Uriah the Hittite—a Gentile—and she's called Bathshua in 1 Chronicles 3:5."

"Literally, that means 'daughter of Shua'—that's the name from the Tamar story!" Nili connected the dots.

"Right. It's the same name. Since Shua is clearly Canaanite back in the Tamar story, many scholars think that Shua may indicate a foreign god. If so, both Uriah and Bathsheba were Gentiles. You can actually make a good case for the name Shua being a non-Israelite territory since Shua might be linguistically connected to the Shuhites, who were from either the upper Euphrates in Mesopotamia or Edom. Archaeologists still aren't clear on which one."

"What are the Genesis 6 connections?" Malone wondered.

"David is called a *gibbor,* and several members of his bodyguard are called *gibborim.* Bathsheba herself fills the role of the *gebura*—the biblical Hebrew term for the queen mother."

"And Bathsheba became the mother of Solomon," Melissa completed the description. "And he inherited the covenant promise to David and therefore produced the Messiah . . ."

". . . who brought the kingdom of God back to earth," Malcolm finished, "a mirror opposition to the evil that had overspread the earth at the time of the Nephilim."

"So what does it all mean?" Malone asked, looking at Brian.

"It means that, for a Jew who knew the flood stories of Genesis and *Enoch,* and at least some of what we just talked about, a connection between all that and the birthday of Jesus would have suggested that Jesus' arrival meant another campaign against cosmic evil was unfolding. And the New Testament would, of course, confirm that."

"How?" Neff asked, his brow wrinkled in uncertainty.

"There's actually a lot more to this spiritual reversal idea when we get past the birth of Jesus," Brian answered. "Many of the places Jesus visited correspond to giant-clan turf in Old Testament times. And what He says and does at those places is pretty significant. For instance, Peter's confession about Jesus being the Son of God takes place at an old religious site dedicated to Baal—a site that falls within Bashan, which was home to the giant Rephaim. The transfiguration happens at the foot of Mount Hermon—the place where *Enoch*'s Watchers descended to take their human women. There's a lot more, too—it's pretty stunning," he said thoughtfully.

"Until we put it in the context of why we're even talking about it," Neff reminded him.

"Yeah, for sure."

"And we've only uncovered one of the Colonel's trails."

"Actually," Melissa said, turning to Brian, then to Neff, "we have more than that—a lot more."

58

If at first, the idea is not absurd, then there is no hope for it.

—*Albert Einstein*

"Thank you," Melissa said, taking the cup of coffee Neff extended to her.

"Just let me know if you need anything else," Neff replied. "Are you sure you're okay standing?"

"I feel good now," she assured him, smiling. "I didn't have trouble sleeping last night, for a change. We'll see how it goes."

Melissa surveyed the small audience coming together in the most spacious of Miqlat's two small debriefing rooms. Kamran's presentation the previous day had energized her—a condition that had, of late, been all too infrequent.

She watched as Brian finished passing out a stapled handout, her less-than-perfect notes thrown together in too much haste for her liking. Still, she was satisfied that she'd made good progress on several fronts, and it was time to contribute rather than be waited on. The subject matter today would involve Nazi activity, so Fern had once again volunteered to keep Summit occupied somewhere else. She'd catch up with the recording of the session.

Melissa put on her reading glasses. "The arrangement of these pages is rough, but I think you'll be able to track through what I'll be explaining. Don't hesitate to ask questions."

She heard a low whistle from the front row. Ward was already inspecting a page. Something had jarred him. "These documents . . . they're for real?" he asked.

"All of them, and they're just a selection to cover the core points."

"I'm no engineer," he replied, turning another page, "but I do know something about energy . . . and aeronautics. This is pretty wild stuff."

"No argument there. And those of us in the room who've seen where the technology's gone would use words like *frightening* for it."

"*Freakin' creepy* is more like it," Madison mumbled, looking over Ward's shoulder to see what page he was on.

"It's probably easiest to start with the term that the Colonel gave Brian—his little homework assignment for me: Huemul."

"Do we know now who that is?" Malone asked.

"Huemul is a place, not a person. More precisely, it's an island off the shore of San Carlos de Bariloche, a city in Argentina. It's famous—or infamous, as most would think of it—as the post-war location of the work of Dr. Ronald Richter, an Austrian physicist."

"A Nazi?" Nili asked disdainfully.

"Richter wasn't a party member; he seems to have been more of an opportunist. Allied scientists were divided about the nature of his work at Huemul, which gets referred to as the Huemul Project. Some thought he was a genius, others a crank."

"I can see why," Neff muttered aloud as he read. He shook his head.

"Richter did legitimate scientific work before and during the war. Some of that provides the context for what you're reading. I'll cut to the chase. Richter wound up in Argentina after the war. He was recommended to President Juan Perón by a German aeronautical engineer named Kurt Tank."

"Perón—there's a Nazi lover for you," Malone grumbled.

"Tank had emigrated to Argentina and had gone to work for Perón under the cover name of Pedro Matthies. In 1948, Richter went to Argentina and presented a scientific proposal to Perón that promised the ability to develop controllable nuclear fusion—what would now be referred to as cold fusion. Perón set him up on the island of Huemul."

"Was it bogus?" Neff asked.

"Apparently that depends on who you ask," Ward mused, still reading ahead.

"And what part of Richter's work you're looking at," Melissa added. "Remember the Colonel's directive that I not get lost in what happened to Richter and the way his work gets talked about? That's a critical point. Most people who find out about Richter filter him through the Perón fiasco and never take note of some of his fundamental ideas. He gets dismissed too early."

"What was the fiasco?" Clarise asked. "What happened?"

"In 1951, Perón announced that Richter had produced nuclear fusion under laboratory conditions in a couple of bottles, the largest of which was a liter or so. Naturally, physicists around the world wanted proof. A couple teams of scientists tried to reproduce the results and failed. They eventually demonstrated that the claim was false."

Neff chuckled. "I'll bet Perón was pissed."

"Considering the project cost the equivalent of three hundred million dollars in today's terms, he was justifiably angry. Richter had to leave the country. He claimed that Perón had jumped the gun, that his work wasn't ready for announcement. He basically just fades into history at that point—unless you're following what led Richter to think he could do it in the first place."

"What was that?"

"Richter's proposal played off a discovery he'd made before the war that more famous Nazi physicists built on. While he was working in Czechoslovakia—and we'll travel there more than once today—Richter discovered that he could induce radiation by injecting deuterium into lithium plasma."

"What does *that* mean?" Madison interjected.

"I can't explain it in terms a physicist or chemist would want," Melissa confessed, "but I don't need to—you'll see why it matters in a moment. The discovery led to what's became known as the photo-chemical process, where powerful electric magnets were used to produce fluorescence in mercury."

"I remember," Malcolm recalled, "that magnetism was part of Dr. Yu's explanation of gravity modification. Does this have something to do with that—like what the Nazis were doing in their saucer development?"

"It's related, though not directly, at least in terms of the declassified documentation you can find."

"Who's Dr. Yu?" Ward asked.

"Nazi UFOs?" Nili asked, surprised.

"Dr. Yu is a scientist we met back at Area 51," Melissa explained. "And we'll hit the Nazi connection in a bit," Melissa added, turning to Nili. "Let's stick to Richter since his work is, in many respects, a good starting point."

Nili nodded.

"I can only give you a description of the photo-chemical process in layman's terms, since I'm not a physicist or a chemist. Your handout has some pages taken from the available Freedom of Information Act documentation of Richter's work. In simplest terms, mercury plasma was put inside some spinning, rotating drums. Flasks of beryllium and thorium were also put inside the drums at the center. The addition of deuterium into the mercury would cause the mercury to fluoresce, and when that happened, the mercury ions that formed would cause the beryllium to emit neutrons."

"So, this was something like a particle accelerator," Ward said. He put down the papers and leaned back in his chair.

"If you say so."

"It is. Go on."

"Well, the neutrons that were emitted were then captured by the thorium, which changed them into uranium-233."

"Hmm . . ." Ward said, closing his eyes and causing Melissa to pause. "Uranium-233 is used for nuclear energy. You're suggesting that before and during World War II, the Nazis were capable of producing fissionable uranium *without* a nuclear reactor."

"It's more than a suggestion," Melissa replied. "The Germans were the leaders in nuclear science at the time of the war. We were fortunate to get some of their scientists, like Oppenheimer and Einstein, as part of the Manhattan Project that produced our atomic bomb."

"What's important about this process for us?" Malone inquired.

"Several things," she answered. "Do you remember what the periodic table abbreviation for mercury is?"

Ward shrugged.

"Hg," Clarise answered.

"That's right. Sound familiar?"

"Not—wait a minute," Clarise caught herself. "Those are the first two letters in the letter sequence of Becky's message!"

"They are, and I think that's the point of their presence in her message."

"I presume you have reasons for that?" Neff questioned.

"Good ones. Let's follow the nuclear thread. We tend to think that the German physicists who didn't come to America didn't know how to produce an atomic bomb, or that they couldn't do it because we never found evidence of a functioning reactor. That's the accepted storyline, but it's a myth. There's good evidence that near the end of the war, prior to Hiroshima, the Nazis had the atomic bomb but lacked a delivery system for it—thank God."

"What about what the British learned?" Ward hesitated. "There was some scheme they arranged to get that information—*Farm* something."

"Farm Hall," Melissa answered.

"Yeah, that's it."

"What's Farm Hall?" Malone asked.

"Look on page 5," Melissa answered. "Farm Hall is the name of a house in Godmanchester, England. During the last six months of 1945, the British held ten German scientists in that house. Unbeknownst to those scientists, the house was bugged. The goal was to discover what the Germans knew about nuclear projects, specifically a bomb. The set-up was called Operation Echelon."

"But from what I've read," Ward objected, "the British basically learned that the Germans didn't know anything about the bomb."

"There are parts of conversations in the published transcripts that contradict that conclusion—especially if you have Richter's work in front of you, Melissa replied. "I'm assuming most or all of you know the name Werner Heisenberg?" She glanced around for confirmation. "Heisenberg was a Nobel laureate in physics. He was one of the Farm Hall ten. If you read the transcripts, there's a lot of ignorance among many of the scientists with respect to nuclear fission and bomb-building. But two days after our bomb was dropped at Hiroshima, Heisenberg gave a lecture on the bomb's design and how it worked to his colleagues at Farm Hall."

"In other words," Neff smirked, "he got real smart real fast without being part of the Manhattan Project."

She nodded. "Heisenberg knew a lot more than what he let on. The fact is, he knew about Richter's discovery and its application. The historical record confirms that he advocated Richter's method at a conference in July of 1942. Heisenberg argued for employing a heavy particle accelerator to produce bomb grade uranium-233 using thorium. There was at least one other person at Farm Hall who knew what you could do with Richter's ideas, too—one you can bet Dr. Yu would have been fond of."

"Who was that?" Malcolm asked.

"Walther Gerlach, another Nobel Prize winner. But Gerlach's specialty wasn't nuclear fission." She looked at Malcolm over her glasses. "Want to guess what his specialty was?"

"Magnetism?"

"Close—gravitation."

Malcolm sighed. "Here we go. Up, up, and away."

"Gerlach won the Nobel Prize for his work on the spin polarization of atoms. Think about that in light of Richter's process. There are passages in the Farm Hall transcripts where Gerlach complains to his colleagues about not having enough engineers for—and I quote—'his photo-chemistry project.' He insists that his work didn't neglect, to quote him again, 'isotope separation.'"

"Nice," Ward quipped.

"I don't want to get lost in the bomb physics." Melissa paused. "What we're talking about—the process—relates to two things, specifically: getting fissionable uranium for a bomb, or getting it for flight technology. The Nazis were working in both areas."

"The Colonel did allude to some of that, too," Brian reminded everyone.

"Last summer at Area 51," Melissa continued, "we saw documentation that showed saucer technology had its roots in German science—not to mention we experienced it up close and firsthand."

"Did you include any of the Majestic documents in the stack?" Brian asked.

"A couple—at the very end of the handout. The ones you suggested."

"What are those?" asked Nili.

"The Majestic documents are a set of leaked documents that ostensibly were created in the 1940s and 1950s, but only surfaced in the 1980s. They talk about how the United States recovered extraterrestrial saucers and bodies from crashes like Roswell and covered up the ET reality."

"Are they real?"

"Depends on what 'real' means. They've been tested forensically and appear in that sense to be legit, but linguistic analysis of a bunch of them shows they weren't written by the people who supposedly produced them. They have a long, shady history of how they surfaced, too. Most UFO researchers think they're either fakes or disinformation. I think they're a combination of fact and fraud, specifically to construct a narrative to move thinking in the ET direction."

"Why do you mention them now?"

"I reread a lot of them in light of Melissa's work on Richter," Brian explained. "Some of the early ones produce a conflicting narrative—conflicting ideas."

"How is that?" Neff asked.

"They combine extraterrestrial speculation with very human, terrestrial technology. For instance, they talk about saucers that can fly at 1,200 miles per hour. German Paperclip scientists and other sources make it clear that the Germans had aircraft that could go that fast, including wingless or deltoid craft. At that speed, it would take over 1,000 years to get to earth from Mars."

"That's hardly a mode of travel you'd associate with advanced aliens," Ward scoffed.

"That's the point. Other Majestic documents talk about gears and plastic and copper tubing in the recovered craft—again, hardly extraterrestrial. One document, the Air Accident Report, theorizes that the source of propulsion was a bladeless turbine. That's precisely what Viktor Schauberger, long rumored to have developed UFOs for the Nazis, was working on. But for our purposes, the significant thing I found was in a document called the White Hot Intelligence Estimate by General Nathan Twining. It specifically says that one crashed, allegedly alien saucer contained a 'neutronic power plant' that had traces of—get this—uranium-235, beryllium, and thorium."

"Good grief," Clarise said. "That's Richter's process."

"What about the bomb?" Nili pressed. "Is there any real evidence the Nazis had one?"

"There is," Melissa said, thumbing through the handout. "Look at page twelve and following. There are some reproduced military intelligence reports and other documents. Some of them come from microfilm, so the visual quality isn't great."

"Oh, my!" Nili gasped. "This Zinsser paper—"

"You're looking at the Zinsser affidavit. Hans Zinsser was a test pilot."

"This is incredible," Clarise murmured.

"And terrifying. Zinsser was debriefed in October, 1944—a full eight months before the first American atomic bomb test in New Mexico."

"He says he witnessed a mushroom cloud explosion while flying in northern Germany," Nili said, reading from the paper and shaking her head. "This sounds just like you'd see in films of atomic explosions."

"It does—and notice that he refers to the location of the explosion as a *test area*. He knew about the testing. There's another report on the next page from the same month of a similar explosion on the German island of Reugen. On that occasion, an Italian officer, Luigi Romersa, was the eyewitness."

"The Japanese had a nuclear bomb as well?" Ward had already moved on to the next series of documents.

"Hard to argue against that," said Neff as he read, tracking with Ward. "What else could you conclude from these intercepted cables from the Japanese embassy in Sweden?"

"The Japanese conducted their first atomic bomb test two days after Hiroshima," Melissa explained. "Their bomb capability is fairly well known in the mainstream historical discussion. Some historians think it was part of what prompted Hirohito to surrender."

"Why surrender when you had the bomb, too?" Madison looked up.

"I think Hirohito would have asked, 'Why continue the war?' " Malone replied, looking over at her. "He could probably see that not surrendering could mean trading nuclear bombs—if the Japanese had a way of delivering them to their enemies' territory, anyway."

"And they didn't," Melissa finished the thought.

"It's a good thing, judging by the following page," Nili said.

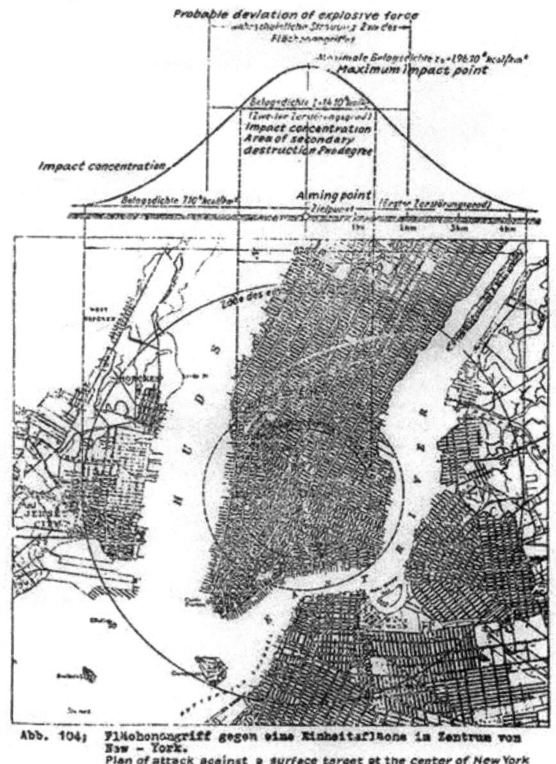

Abb. 104; Flächenangriff gegen eine Einheitsfläche im Zentrum von New - York.
Plan of attack against a surface target at the center of New York

"That's a chart that provides radiation-effect estimates of a nuclear explosion over New York City. It was prepared for Hermann Göring in 1943. A later translator added the English in the document. Bombing New York seems to have been something of an obsession for Hitler."

"He had his own Manhattan Project in mind," Brian added.

"There's really no doubt that the Nazis had nuclear know-how and were thinking of ways to weaponize it," Melissa continued. "The accepted historical narrative seems to conveniently forget that top-flight Nazi scientists like Dr. Erich Schumann and Dr. Walter Trinks filed nearly forty patent applications in Germany during the war for what we'd now call tactical nuclear weapons. Take a look at the recent *UK Daily* story I included about the Nazi nuclear waste."

"Gotta love this," Ward said, skimming the front page of the article. "An old salt mine containing 126,000 barrels of nuclear waste . . . from an era when the Nazis weren't supposed to be able to produce a single barrel."

"I'll say it again," Malcolm chimed in, "thank God they were never able to deliver anything."

"Actually," Melissa said, turning to him, "they were very close. They may have even undertaken a dry run."

"Seriously?"

"Does she look like she's kidding?" Clarise said.

"She's talking about the Junkers flight," Ward noted, again ahead of everyone. "Look at the page after the nuclear-waste article. The Junkers aircraft were long range. They would have been capable of a trip to the east coast without stopping for fuel."

"There's circumstantial evidence," Melissa began, "pointing to a German reconnaissance mission to the east coast of the US in September 1944."

"One month before the nuclear tests you told us about," Malcolm said ominously.

"Exactly. A Junkers plane apparently crashed off the coast of Maine, near a place called Owl's Head. There were reports of discovered bodies."

"How was that not news?" Neff asked. "I've read a lot of World War II stuff, and I've never heard of that."

"It was a different world back then," Melissa said, shrugging. "The military and local authorities found plane wreckage in the location with partial serial numbers and German words like '*JunkersMotorWerkes*' on it."

"Man," Malcolm shook his head and looked up from the page, "I wish I'd never heard of this guy."

"You hit Kammler?"

"Yeah," he sighed. "It's so clear. . . . Ferguson's rubbing our noses in it."

"What's this . . . thing . . . next to his picture?" Madison asked. "It looks like a huge bell."

"It's what brings all the threads together," Melissa answered, crossing her arms. "Nazi saucer research, Paperclip, Kammler, and the occult ideology of the SS. Its code name was *Die Glocke* . . . the Bell."

59

When WWII ended, the Germans had several radical types of aircraft and guided missiles under development. The majority were in the most preliminary stages, but they were the only known craft that could even approach the performance of objects reported to UFO observers.

—Captain Edward J. Ruppelt, USAF
Director of Projects GRUDGE and BLUEBOOK

"What was this . . . Bell?" Ward asked.

Melissa glanced knowingly at Brian, then looked at Ward. "Remember the photo-chemical process I described? As near as the best researchers can tell, the Bell was the container. It gets its name from its shape."

"Okay . . ."

"The story of the bell came into public view through the work of a Polish researcher named Igor Witkowski. In 1997, a Polish Intelligence officer introduced Witkowski to the Bell through original documents of a war crimes interrogation of an SS officer at the rank of Gruppenführer named Jakob Sporrenberg. He was shortly thereafter tried and executed."

"It's likely someone in that position would be trying to provide any information of real value that might keep himself alive," Ward noted.

"That's certainly possible. Witkowski began his own investigation and was subsequently contacted by a member of Polish military intelligence, who gave him access to some classified documents on the matter. The Bell was described as around nine feet in diameter and twelve to fourteen feet high. The outside was said to be made of thick ceramic material that acted as an insulator, since it absorbed incredible amounts of electricity. Inside the Bell were two rotating drums where the conversion process took place. The whole thing supposedly glowed violet-blue when it was operating."

"Well, there it is," Ward announced, leaning forward. "This Bell was, in effect, a particle accelerator. Richter's processes called for that."

"That's the supposition. It was located in Silesia, which is a region of central Europe that covers mostly Polish territory. Silesia was a major source of thorium, which was crucial to the whole process. This is where Walther Gerlach reenters the picture."

"The gravity guy?" asked Madison.

Melissa nodded. "Gerlach was head of something called Project Thor. You have the first page of a document that suggests Thor used Tesla coils or something called a Van der Graaf generator that could produce five million volts of electricity. So," Melissa added, looking at Brian and Malcolm, "we have all the elements that we learned about at Area 51 with respect to the basics of gravity modification research from Dr. Yu: huge amounts of electrical power, spinning surfaces, magnetism. The only question seems to be whether Kammler or someone else applied all that to flight. The Colonel and some of our other friends back at Dreamland filled in those gaps for us last summer."

"Essentially," Ward followed, "nuclear power and gravity modification were married—either for linear propulsion, like a rocket, or lifting."

"That's what it seems. Toward the end of your stack there are photocopies of several formerly classified documents that make a pretty strong independent case that the Germans were using this technology to power wingless craft—saucers. There's the cover page of a 1946 OSS restricted study on German experiments in electro-magnetism, a catalogue sheet from the National Archives and Records Administration that casually notes the Germans were working on a flying saucer, and, finally, a declassified document from the National Archives and Records Administration on Richter that mentions, and I quote, 'experimental approach to the unified field theory and the velocity of propagation of gravity' and 'nuclear propulsion systems under hypersonic flight conditions.' "

"If it walks like a duck, and quacks like a duck . . ."

"I hear you, Malcolm," Melissa said, looking over her glasses at him and allowing herself to smile.

"What in the world is this?" Clarise asked, holding up one of the pages. "It looks like a miniature Stonehenge or something."

"I know *exactly* what that is," Ward answered, looking at his wife, whose expression told everyone she wasn't buying it. "That's a fly trap."

Clarise started to laugh. "Shouldn't somebody close the windows?"

"He's right," Melissa confirmed with an amused grin. "Ward?"

"It gets covered with netting. Fly traps are used for testing helicopters."

"Don't tell me . . ."

"I think you already know," Melissa cut in. "There are surviving accounts of witnesses who saw saucer craft floating inside—the Nazis used it for testing. The Canadians did the same for testing the AVRO-car, their experimental saucer. There's a 1952 declassified CIA document on that in your handout."

"I asked you not to tell me," Clarise sighed.

"The 'henge' is located in a little village in Ludwikowice, Poland. Anyone want to guess what region of Poland that's in?"

"It is in Silesia, where this Bell was kept," Sabi answered. "I have been in that village."

Melissa nodded. "The Bell project went by other code names. Some of them are ironic, to say the least. One is Kronos, the Greek name for Saturn. It's probably a reference to the spinning inside the Bell. But, as Brian was quick to tell me, Kronos has another meaning."

"Kronos was a Titan," Brian explained, "the one overthrown by Zeus and thrown into Tartarus, the place where the book of Peter has the fallen sons of God imprisoned."

"That's a nice touch," snickered Malcolm.

"It gets weirder," Melissa continued. "The Bell's other code name was Der Laternenträger, no doubt because it glowed. How's your German, Malcolm?"

"Hmmm, 'the light' . . . or 'lantern' . . . something."

"'The light-bearer,' " Sabi cut in. "Or, in Latin, Lucifer."

"Great," Malone replied. "Let the record show that I'm officially creeped out now."

"Some have speculated," Melissa added, "that the Bell was eventually reproduced and fitted into a saucer-type craft to harness its lift-power capability."

"Did you see anything like that at Area 51?" Nili asked.

"No, and I'm guessing they're well beyond the design."

"There's a classic UFO crash account," Brian added, "that might be related to this, though. It's known as the Kecksburg incident. Not as famous as Roswell, but important. The object that crashed there was bell-shaped and seemed to had runes on it—which were familiar signs used by the SS. But it's still only speculation that the Bell may have been adapted for flight."

"So what happened to the Bell—and to Kammler?" Neff asked.

"Well, there are no less than five separate accounts of Kammler's death," Melissa answered, "all of them different."

"What else would we expect?" he smirked.

"No one really knows what happened to him," she continued. "All we have is conflicting witness testimony. I have a timeline in your handout, the second page from the end. It's pieced together from the debriefings of an SS general named Sporrenberg, Hauptsturmführer Rudolf Schuster, and Dr. Wilhelm Voss, the person in charge of the SS Skoda works—which was a sort of Skunk Works factory for the SS at the end of the war. Skoda was in Pilsen, a Czech province a few hours from Silesia."

"Can you summarize it for us?" asked Malone, finding the page.

"The last verifiable communication from Kammler was a cable on April 17, 1945. Kammler was turning down a request from the German high command for the use of a Junkers long-range aircraft."

"That's really close to the time of Hitler's suicide," Neff observed. "Makes you wonder why they'd want a plane for long-range evacuation."

"Albert Speer testified after the war that they wanted to fly Hitler to Japan. That, of course, didn't happen. It's unclear whether this rejection by Kammler is related. Hitler's pilot, a fellow named Hans Baur, factors into the story at this point, at least for Kammler's possible escape. In 2004 a former German soldier in his nineties testified that after the denial, on May 1, Baur ordered him to ready a six-engine Junkers to fly certain Nazi VIPs from Norway to Greenland."

"The far northern location will take on more significance when we get into the Nazi mythology," Brian inserted.

"Schuster testified that a Junkers-390 flew from Prague—that's right next to Pilsen—to somewhere near Opole, Poland. Sporrenberg also told his captors that a Junkers-390 took off from a place called Schweidnitz, which is about 100 kilometers west of Opole. He also testified that he knew of three people on that flight: mathematician Elizabeth Adler; Herman Oberth, a rocketry expert and Luftwaffe officer; and Dr. Kurt Debus, whose specialty was high voltage. The flight went to Bodo, Norway. Dr. Voss, independent of the other two witnesses, confirmed the flight from Schweidnitz to Bodo, as well as the detail about the Bell being on board. He didn't specifically mention Kammler, since Voss believed Kammler died at the end of the war, though he didn't witness his death."

"Do you think Kammler was on board?" Ward asked.

"Witnesses say that Kammler had roughly sixty scientists associated with the Bell executed before its evacuation. Witkowski and other researchers believe Kammler accompanied the Bell. It's possible, but I have to confess I'm still not sure, largely because of another issue. Wernher von Braun said after the war that Kammler talked about going underground before the Americans got to his location. He even described escaping disguised as a Jesuit priest, the way Bormann did."

"I thought Bormann died at the end of the war," Neff said. "I've read that."

"He wound up in Argentina. I've reproduced several documents from the Argentine secret police that show they knew Bormann was in their country under several aliases. They kept track of him but didn't arrest him. At least one of the documents has him with Mengele, and we know for sure he was alive and well in South America."

"It's true," Malcolm spoke up. "I've seen those documents. Andrew showed me copies once. He lived through all that, remember."

"I agree," Nili added. "I have read old Israeli intelligence reports about Bormann, Mengele, Barbie, Eichmann. . . . There was great suspicion Bormann was hiding in Argentina."

"Any word on what happened after Norway?" Ward asked.

"The Junkers went to Argentina," Melissa answered.

"That's within its range," noted Ward.

"There's really no dispute to the arrival, either," she continued. "The real question is who all made that leg of the trip. Witnesses have the plane landing at Puntas de Gualeguay. An Argentine report declassified in 1993 refers to a Bell device being unloaded. That's the only public piece of information about the Bell before Witkowski's information was published in 1998."

"Puntas de Gualeguay is a couple hundred kilometers north of Buenos Aires," said Neff. "Did the plane stay there?"

"Witkowski says he's read a classified report by a Polish diplomat who said he saw a Junkers dismantled on a German ranch. That was May, 1945."

"This is a pretty tight reconstruction," Malone mused, "but it's still hard to believe the Allies would have failed to get Kammler, in Germany or anywhere else. He was arguably the worst war criminal of the lot—all that slave labor at Peenemunde and Nordhausen."

"They may not have gotten a chance," Brian offered. "He may have had something to barter—something the Allies couldn't refuse." He turned to Melissa. "We should tell them about Operation Lusty."

"Lusty?" Madison said dubiously.

"I don't know about the name," Melissa answered lightly, "but the project was real—and very significant."

"Lusty was sort of a project that ran parallel to Paperclip," Brian explained. "It wasn't about obtaining people, though—it focused on documents and hardware."

"Project Lusty managed to find an amazingly large number of documents," Melissa began, "but the mother lode—since we don't believe in coincidences here—was tied to Skoda."

Neff shook his head and started to laugh. "Malcolm was right. You couldn't script this."

"Sometimes truth is indeed stranger than fiction," Melissa said with a shrug. "In February of 1946, the Americans got a tip—and of course, the question is from whom—about a cache of secret documents hidden near Prague. There's evidence that the documents—and perhaps the tip—were linked to the Kammlerstab, Kammler's personal staff. If it came from Kammler, then he didn't go with the Bell—unless, of course, he planted the tip earlier."

"In a nutshell," Brian summarized, "Kammler either went north to Greenland or somewhere closer to the Arctic, or he wound up in Argentina with the Bell."

"The location of the cache presented a problem," Melissa said, "since it was in territory ceded to the Soviets by agreement among the Allies. The decision to go in and get the documents led to an international incident and a subsequent American apology, but it was well worth it. "

"Holy smokes," Malone exclaimed. Melissa could see he was reading the last page of the handout.

"Stunning, isn't it?" Melissa noted. "There were 2.5 million drawings from Skoda in the cache."

"I saw that—and that's not everything."

"All in all," Melissa informed them, "Project Lusty obtained 1,200 *tons* of documents, which they transferred to the US over the course of several months. It also obtained all the records of the German Patent Office—225,000 volumes. That's a direct connection to Kammler, as he set up a system of total patent review under his command. If he was the source of the tip, he would surely have told them to go after the patent office. All patents were reviewed for military application."

"Like this picture of a triangle craft?" Ward asked.

"That's the Lippisch P-13a, created by the German pioneer in aerodynamics, Dr. Alexander Lippisch. The model 13 had passed full trials. It was completely functional and supersonic. After the war, Dr. Lippisch joined some of his friends here in the United States as part of Operation Paperclip."

"What a shock," Malone scoffed.

"I'm afraid to ask where the documents went," Clarise muttered.

"One hundred and fifty tons went to three places in the United States. Two are very familiar to anyone doing UFO research: Wright Field in Dayton, Ohio—now called Wright-Patterson—and White Sands, New Mexico. The third was Freeman Field in Indiana."

"So what do you think the Colonel wanted us to learn here?" Neff asked.

"Well, he wasn't trying to teach us that the US has UFO technology," Brian answered. "We knew that. I think the point was to show us the clarity of a connection between UFOs, which most people will presume are alien, and the Nazis. It would be easy to create the myth that the aliens he wants to demonize seeded technology to the Nazis to win the war and exterminate the Jews."

"Let me add to the nonsense," queried Malone. "The aliens were on their side to move eugenics ahead."

"All in the name of human progress and evolution," Clarise added with disgust.

"As bogus as all that is," noted Melissa, "the thoughts actually become more potent against the backdrop of where the rest of Becky's message takes us. We just couldn't see it before. Now we can. It's elegantly depraved."

"What do you mean?" Neff wondered.

"If 'Hg' is securely identified," she answered, "that leaves the letters W-E-S-T-O-N."

Clarise sat up straight with a realization. "Weston—that's the name on one of the two autopsy reports you asked for."

"It is."

"Who was the other autopsy report for?" asked Brian.

Melissa bowed her head and briefly looked away. "It's Andrew's."

60

Mortal danger is an effective antidote for fixed ideas.

—*General Erwin Rommel*

"Sir!" the MP inside came to attention and saluted smartly.

Colonel Ferguson returned the salute and strode toward the console. The enlisted man seated in front of the viewing screen never heard the door or the guard's response. He was too far away, and his headset muted one ear. His attention was trained on an array of viewing screens that, to the uninitiated, appeared to be nothing more than a random smattering of blinking dots, like you might see if you ran your finger along the edge of a wet toothbrush and sprayed a mirror. The Colonel stood behind him, searching the specks until he found the one that had present meaning. He bent slightly toward the seated operator.

"Still no movement?"

"No, sir. The object is still stationary."

"And that's been the status since the initial trail?"

"Yes, sir."

"Any activity on the other side of the border?"

"Nothing but the usual traffic, sir."

"Let's see the satellite visual."

The operator quickly complied with the necessary keystrokes. The Colonel studied the screen, though there wasn't much to look at.

"What's the refresh?"

"Thirty seconds, sir."

"Activity?"

"A trickle, sir. Mostly local law enforcement."

"NSA link?"

"Email and phone traffic. No keywords present; consistent with the movement—or rather non-movement, sir."

The Colonel stood erect and remained behind the operator in silence. He listened dispassionately to the click-clack of other operators and their occasional directives and responses. *Unexpected, but easily dealt with.*

"What's nearby? Say, within twenty miles or so."

"Not much, sir. It's mostly forest, especially to the north."

Excellent. A decision soon pushed its way into his thoughts.

"Sometimes," the Colonel said slowly, more to himself than to the operator whose attention he once again held, "you just need to reach out and touch someone when you want information."

"Yes, sir."

"Carry on."

61

Access to the Vedas is the greatest privilege this century may claim over all previous centuries.

—J. Robert Oppenheimer

"Why did you need Andrew's autopsy report?" asked Neff. "I could have given you the details."

"I needed both reports to see if there were any similarities between his death and that of Weston," Melissa replied. "It'll become clear in a moment."

He nodded.

"I started by presuming Weston was a name. It wasn't hard to run searches for it with keywords associated with the sort of things I specialize in, or that we've been talking about. I figured there had to be a relationship of some kind. Once I found some things that seemed pertinent, I presumed I had an ID. Then I widened my searches with the full name. It didn't take long to discover it in an apparently random death—in Rachel, Nevada. That was too close to Area 51 and where Andrew was found to be coincidental."

"So who is he?" Malcolm asked.

"I believe the Colonel wanted to direct our attention to Professor Claude Weston, formerly of Brown University. Dr. Weston was a professor of comparative linguistics. His specialties were in Sanskrit and the Dravidian languages, but he also seemed to have a working knowledge of Sumerian, Elamite, and Hittite. That may sound like a recipe for irrelevance, but all those fields are related to Aryan mythology."

"Boy, that's like planning to focus on every fringe ancient language there is," quipped Brian. "Makes me look employable."

Nili gave him a scolding look.

"Sorry," he apologized.

Melissa went on. "For starters, it's fair to say Weston was ethically challenged, to say the least."

"I'm positive he wasn't embezzling piles of grant money with those fields," Malcolm joked. "What'd he do, steal some antiquities?"

"Among other things," Melissa replied. "Weston had a history of being suspected of black market profiteering—paying indigenous workers to steal artifacts from museum storage or digs, assisting in forgery of artifacts, that sort of thing. He managed to get arrested for that one too many times, though he never served time. He eventually lost his position."

"He didn't lose his income, though," Ward chimed in. "After Melissa had a name, she asked me to do a little detective work on him. I got information on his bank accounts. Somebody was paying him well after his dismissal."

"Was it the Colonel?" Brian asked. "Any connection to the government?"

"No, but that doesn't mean a whole lot. It's easy to set up fronts and firewalls to avoid detection. That's part of what I do here. If it wasn't Uncle Sam, it could have been private collectors of antiquities. They pay good money for artifacts, black market or legit."

"Any next of kin we could talk to?" Clarise asked.

"He was long divorced and had no children. No immediate personal attachments."

"That sounds like a familiar profile." Brian looked at Melissa, then Malcolm. "People who'll be easily missed, and with no relatives who will challenge an excuse for an absence. That has the Colonel's stink for sure."

"How did Weston die? Was there anything suspicious?"

"He was supposedly killed in a head-on collision with a telephone pole. The collision apparently took place in the early morning hours. The area was very remote. A motorist noticed the vehicle on fire and reported the collision. The autopsy notes that the guy's face was badly smashed, as was the car's windshield. There were bits of glass in some of his facial wounds. His upper torso was also badly burned, though most of the car was not. He was positively ID'd through a passport and wallet in a briefcase in the back seat. The corpse's fingerprints matched the ID."

"Sounds pretty tidy, pardon the expression," Clarise commented. "It feels a little too easy."

Melissa looked uneasily at Brian, then Malcolm. "It's him, all right. But there's one detail that unmistakably connects him to us. It still unnerves me to be honest."

"What's that?"

"The investigators also checked dental records in the ID process. The body was missing a tooth . . . a left incisor, to be precise. It wasn't found in the car anywhere, including the windshield."

"Oh, wow," Malcolm sighed, stunned by the detail. "Do you think—"

She shook her head. "I *know*. It's the tooth Andrew found in the room at Mount Weather—the room with the Nazi Black Sun in it."

"How can you be sure, Melissa?" Brian asked.

"Andrew's file."

"Really?" Neff said, amazed, again taken by surprise.

"Ward was able to get not only the autopsy report, but other police report documentation. When I asked for the autopsy, I never imagined I'd be looking for someone else's remains, but there it was. The CSI found a tooth in Andrew's pants pocket. He wasn't missing any, so they knew it wasn't his. They had no explanation for why a dead man would have someone else's left incisor in his pants. I have one. The odds against the correlation with the tooth at Mount Weather are extraordinarily slim."

"That's just . . ."

"Providential," Sabi said quietly from the back of the room. "The One who knows all things is helping us, guiding us—even in tragedy."

Nili stood up and walked over to the coffee for a refill. "Do we know anything else about Weston that would tell us why his name was part of the code implanted in Becky?"

"A couple things," Melissa replied. "Ward can explain. Did you bring your notes?"

"Got 'em right here," he said, pulling his phone from his shirt pocket. He tapped in his password, swiped the surface a few times, and then started in. "One of the things I uncovered about Weston was a police report of an incident a little over year ago at a genetics conference, of all places. He had to spend a night in jail for disorderly conduct."

"Drunk?" Malone asked over his eyeglasses.

"Nope. Some scientist claimed Weston had assaulted him. The details are pretty tame, and charges were eventually dropped. I was curious, though, so I called the guy who had filed the charges in the first place. He remembered the incident. He said that Weston had attended a lecture of his at the conference and wanted to talk afterwards. Everything was cordial at first, but then Weston started ranting about having cuneiform tablets, and days lasting more than twenty-four hours in the Arctic, and how the two of them needed to collaborate on a paper that Weston insisted would solve the puzzle of Indo-European origins for good. The guy got freaked out. He said that when he tried to leave, Weston grabbed him and knocked him down. A witness called security, and that was that."

"Once Ward gave me the name of the scientist who had the scuffle with Weston, I put it into the scholarly databases to see what I'd find," Melissa said, picking up the thread.

"And?" Malcolm pressed, intrigued by the path the conversation had taken.

"You're going to love this, Brian," she said with transparent sarcasm. "It's the article I asked Clarise about."

"What is it?" he asked, his curiosity piqued.

Melissa opened a folder and read the first page. "'A European Population in Minoan Bronze Age Crete.' " She peered at him over her glasses, closed the folder, and handed it to him. "There are some summaries of the findings in there, too, for lay readers like us."

Brian paused for a moment, unsure of how to respond. "Crete?"

"Crete."

"And this is based on genetics?"

"Yep."

"Does it suggest a geographical origin for the population?"

"The authors suggest the Minoans likely came from somewhere in Anatolia. The genetic trail leads north from there."

"Tell me you're kidding."

"The study used mitochondrial DNA from thirty-seven well-preserved ancient Minoans," Clarise interrupted. "They were found in an undisturbed cave ossuary in east-central Crete. They were in wonderful condition. Most of them were haplogroup H."

"That doesn't mean anything to me."

"Sorry. Mitochondrial haplogroup H is the one that arose in Western Asia about 25,000 years ago. Some geneticists and geographers use the term 'southwest Asia.' But both terms refer to what's now known as the Middle East."

"And what people in my field call the ancient Near East," Brian added.

"Right, but North Africa is excluded in terms of the genetics," Clarise explained. "Paleo-genetic studies have established that haplogroup H was carried to Europe by migrations. Haplogroup H is a genetic descendant of haplogroup HV, which was also spread across that region. Haplogroup HV overlaps with haplogroup J, which isn't mitochrondrial DNA, but DNA from the Y chromosome. That's thoroughly Middle Eastern."

Melissa broke in again. "The study has the Minoans genetically similar to—and this is their term, not mine—Nordic Romans."

"You can't be serious."

Melissa looked at him with raised eyebrows. He'd learned to read that as a sign of amusement. This time was different.

"Wait a minute—Minoans!" Ward blurted out, drawing everyone's attention. He smacked his hand to his forehead. His eyes darted to Clarise, who stared at him, startled.

"What is it?" she asked.

"The police let me go through Weston's briefcase, the one in the back of the car."

"And?"

"It was just a bunch of papers, nothing that seemed important. But one was about some tablets from some place in Mesopotamia . . . it begins with an 'm' . . ."

"Mari?" Brian suggested.

"Yeah! That's it!"

Brian hung his head. He didn't seem excited about being right.

"There were papers about these tablets. They said something about Minoans and some other place called Kabri. Do you know that one?"

"No," Brian replied, now looking at him again. "I don't know the place, but it should be easy to find out." He looked around the table.

"We're not yanking your chain," said Clarise, who could see the apprehension on his face. "I don't know why this would rock your world. Why don't you let the rest of us in on it?"

"It's all about Aryan mythology," he answered, "the mythical origins of the Nazi master race idea." He turned to Melissa, a helpless expression on his face. "Where do we even begin? It's so convoluted and . . . bizarre."

"After the first round this morning," Madison said, "I think we're prepped for bizarre."

Melissa shook her head. "The only point of clarity in my mind right now is that the Colonel will milk this for everything it's worth. He knew this would get a real rise out of the two of us."

"We're going to have to start from the beginning and give them the framework. There's no good shortcut," Brian noted.

"I know." Melissa paused in thought, trying to find the right mental foothold. She looked up. "The only way to really grasp why all this is important and how it relates to the late Dr. Weston is to go back to the mid-nineteenth century, to British colonization of India. That's where the whole Aryan debate begins. That debate is really about the question of Indo-European origins—where the *singular* people that settled in India and Europe came from."

"India and Europe?" Malone questioned. "It seems the people of India and Europe couldn't be more different. I know Nazi goons like Himmler went that direction to find some people known as the Aryans, and that the swastika actually comes from ancient India, but I never understood the logic. They don't look anything alike."

"No, they don't," Melissa said, smiling knowingly, "but you're just thinking of how they look *today*. The fact is that the major language of India, at least apart from the southeastern regions, is a member of the same language family as the languages we know today spread throughout Europe. They're all in what's now called the Indo-European family. And you're right about the swastika; the name comes from a Sanskrit word, *svastika*, which means 'good to be.' It was a good-luck symbol."

"Talk about something being lost in translation," Malcolm quipped.

"Languages are grouped into families because of overlaps and similarities in their grammatical properties," Brian explained, "and where they disagree in kind with other languages. Since all the languages of European peoples belong together along with Sanskrit from India, people in the nineteenth century assumed that all the people speaking the languages in a family were of one race."

"And that's the 'master' race?" Malone asked.

"It's part of that idea. We know today you can't really equate race and language, but before the science of genetics came along, race was defined by language. It's antiquated thinking, but it was dominant until recently."

"We're getting a little ahead of ourselves already," Melissa steered the conversation. "That's easy in this subject. But let's go back to the nineteenth century."

"Agreed," echoed Brian. "This is your domain. I'll be a fly on the wall."

"I'll bet," she smiled skeptically in his direction. "Let's start with the term 'Aryan.' It's a Sanskrit word—that was the spoken language of most of ancient India. Today it's only used for liturgical purposes by Hindus. It's also a classical written language studied by scholars of Buddhism and Jainism, or linguists, like Dr. Weston. The term 'Aryan' was an ethnic self-designation in ancient India that meant 'noble' or 'honorable.' "

"Before the eighteenth century," she continued, "scholars in the European world thought the most ancient language that was linguistically related to European languages was Iranian. That all changed by the mid-eighteen hundreds, when the British began to colonize India and report what they were finding. They discovered India had its own ancient texts, written in a language that was soon discovered to be closely related to Iranian and those in Europe. The term 'Aryan' began to loosely refer to all the peoples whose languages fell into that family."

"I can't believe that Europeans would think that Indian people were ethnically related to them," Malcolm objected. "A lot of them are very dark skinned. There's no way white Europeans would have believed that."

"They didn't—and there was certainly a racist motivation undergirding that resistance."

Kamran waved to get Melissa's attention, then signed something to Madison. "He says he agrees—the upper-caste folks he occasionally met treated everyone dark like they were lesser people. It was a problem even in his father's church."

"I believe it," Melissa replied. "Bigotry became a prime motivation for what would become known as the Aryan invasion theory—the idea that light-skinned Europeans invaded India in the distant past and civilized northern India, thereby producing the 'noble' or Aryan upper caste. That provided a palatable explanation for the linguistic connection for white Europeans."

"But how could even the upper-caste Indians be the same ethnic stock as Europeans?" Neff asked.

"That was one of the great debates of the nineteenth century for several reasons. The question was inevitably tied to the issue of human origins. Remember, 1859 was the year Darwin published his *Origin of Species*. In many respects, Darwin's ideas were a direct attack on biblical ideas like monogenesis—that all humans came from one pair, Adam and Eve. The Tower of Babel story had all people after the flood as having one language—which of course had to be the language of Noah and his sons, and of Adam and Eve before him."

"There's the original one-people-one-language equation," Clarise observed.

"Everybody believed, on the basis of a literal reading of the Bible," Melissa continued, "that Noah's sons were the genesis of the other languages and peoples listed in the Table of Nations in Genesis 10. But as early as the sixteenth century, this view of human origins found trouble. Explorers began to encounter other peoples on the other side of the world—the Americas. No one knew where they came from, since the Table of Nations in Genesis 10 didn't include them. All sorts of wacky theories were invented to explain the discrepancy. And Darwin made it worse since his ideas were at the forefront of science."

"The nineteenth century really blew things apart," Brian added, "since that was the century when texts from Egypt and Mesopotamia were deciphered. All of a sudden, you had very ancient texts—older than the Bible—that had alternative histories and chronologies of civilization. When Europeans were able to read the literature of China, and of course India, you had more of the same problem. Where did the people of the world *really* come from, now that everyone knew the world was bigger than the Bible described—and what about all their languages, histories, and chronologies?"

Melissa picked up the thought. "Since India's sacred texts, the Vedas, had histories going back long before the invention of writing in Egypt and Mesopotamia, the logical impulse for scholars who cared about any defense of the Bible was harmonization—coming up with a way to align all this material with the Bible to show the Bible correctly had everyone coming from Adam and all the languages of the world emerging from one at Babel. On the other side, though, the opponents of the Bible's view of history were having a field day. Many scholars began to propose that ancient India was the true source of information on human historical origins. They couldn't wait to disassociate themselves from the Bible."

"Think about the implications," Brian said in earnest. "Europeans who found the Bible intellectually distasteful also saw a way to disassociate themselves from the people who produced the Bible—the Jews. They could dismiss the Bible and the Jews as inferior."

"Even worse," Melissa added, "in 1903 the book known as *The Protocols of the Elders of Zion* was published in Russia. This book presented a grand conspiracy of the Jews to conquer Europe and the world. By 1920 it had been translated and spread all over Europe and North America. That became another justification—for Indian or Aryan supremacy—and for what would become the virulent anti-Semitism of Hitler and the Nazis."

"It sounds as if a literal reading of the Bible drove people to reject the Jew," Nili said in a troubled tone.

"That was true in that historical context," Brian said, "but remember these aren't necessary conclusions. And that's a good thing, because the issues are a lot deeper than this. It's unfortunate, but a literal reading of the Bible at this time in history led to a lot of tragic ideas, especially when it comes to anti-Semitism."

"For a lot of people," Melissa continued, "this was a winner-take-all proposition. The debate was heated, and to read it now sounds incredibly racist, first toward the Jew and then, for those Christians who honored Jews," she looked at Malcolm, "toward the Negro race. This is why racism has historically been defended using the Bible. The stakes were much higher than blacks versus whites. India, Darwin, Adam, Noah, and the one-race-one-language teaching of the Bible were all in the mix. For a lot of people, to argue against racial hierarchy was to argue against the Bible."

"Trust me," Malcolm interrupted, "I get the racist flavor, but the fight over harmonizing all that stuff with the Bible, and producing a justification for racism, is a bit lost on me."

"Think about it this way," Melissa replied. "The issue is that those who harmonized everything to the Bible still had to posit one *original* race at the beginning—a race that must have been near-perfect, since that original race began with the first, perfect man, Adam. For sure, that's a literal over-reading of the Bible, but if you approach it in such a simplistic way, the idea of a first 'closest-to-God's-likeness' *race* goes with it. I should mention that Brian's take on the image of God undercuts all of that."

"Most Christians don't think that way today, though," Madison said confidently.

"That's true," Brian noted, "but that's largely because they've never been jolted by these issues and their implications. They're so focused on specific apologetic thinking about evolution that problems like these never get on the radar. Even people who write about Genesis are largely unaware of how linguistics, Indo-European origins, and Sanskrit affect their faith. Most know nothing about India at all."

"Except for curry and Bollywood," chuckled Malcolm. Some of the others couldn't help but laugh. Kamran guffawed loudly and rocked in this chair. The two exchanged a fist-bump. Brian smiled and shook his head.

"This is why we love you, Malcolm," said Melissa.

"The only reason?"

"Don't push it. Only you could interject some humor into all this."

"So how does this relate to migrations?" Ward asked. "You two and

Clarise were tracking on something there."

"The migration problem runs in a lot of directions—geographically and intellectually," Melissa answered. "We've already hinted at one—the Aryan-invasion idea that the great light-skinned civilizers invaded India and gave them their high culture thousands of years ago. That alleged invasion was believed to have occurred on the tail end of a long migration from the north. Naturally, native Indian people in the nineteenth century felt disrespected by the whole notion that their cultural achievements should be credited to Europeans. They turned the tables and argued that Europeans came from India—that's what became known as the 'indigenous Aryan' viewpoint."

"So that view has people from India migrating from south to north; it's a reversal," Neff clarified.

"Right—and here's another point where the Bible takes center stage again," Melissa went on. "The question of human origins in the Bible moves from Adam to Noah and, after the flood, Noah's sons. When people started thinking about tracing the human races back in time, the landing of Noah's ark became an issue, since the assumption was that the one people from which all the races came was the one that survived the flood. That led to the conclusion that the European races—remember, they were viewed as the extension of the original, perfect race—had migrated from Mount Ararat to civilize the world. This human rebirth led to the question of the precise location of Ararat, and then the precise location of the Tower of Babel. The first was most important since it was thought that the answer would reveal humanity's original homeland."

"The options for Ararat were more diverse than you'd think," said Brian. "There were serious efforts to locate Ararat in Turkey—which is the more recent name for Anatolia, the old kingdom of the Hittites. Other candidates were Iran and Armenia in the region of the Caucasus mountains."

"So that's why the reference to Anatolia caught your attention," Clarise concluded.

"It's one reason. There are others."

"It's important here to catch the implications again," Melissa said. "Europeans used all the talk about Ararat to justify the Aryan-invasion theory, since eventually you have to get the original Aryans—the original 'closest-to-perfection' race—down to India from the north. Indigenous Indians quite understandably viewed the Bible as a document that dismissed them racially."

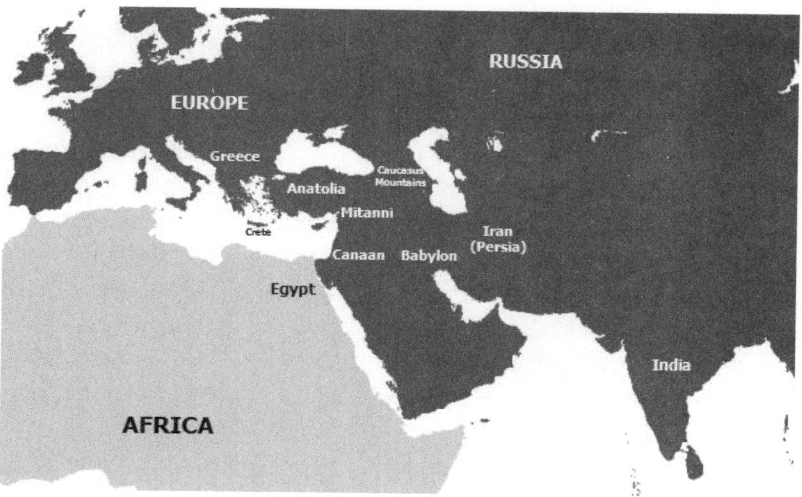

"Later in the nineteenth century," Brian added, "the Germans would tailor the idea to their own Germanic mythology to divorce it from the Jewish Old Testament. Once the British and other Europeans were satisfied that the invasion idea solved the problem of how they could be related to people in India—people they were recolonizing just like their white European Aryan ancestors had done—they lost interest in the question and careful study of Sanskrit and the Vedas. The Germans quickly took up that cause. They had their own agenda for identifying the original master race. They weren't pursuing it out of sympathy for the Indian, and they certainly didn't care about harmonizing anything with the book of the Jews. They were more interested in exploiting the links between the Vedas and Europe, especially the more remote north and the Eddas."

"What are . . . Eddas?" asked Nili.

"Edda refers to the old Norse, or Nordic, poetic and prose texts, from which we get Norse mythology—which was near and dear to the hearts of many Nazis, especially the SS. Those texts were written down in the thirteenth century in Icelandic, but the content is much earlier, dating at least to the Viking age. Himmler and his partners in crime at the Ahnenerbe basically viewed that material as sacred."

"Kamran wants to know what 'Ahnenerbe' means," Madison spoke up, once again translating for Kamran.

"On the surface, it was supposed to be a scientific institute," Melissa answered. "It was actually a pseudo-scientific research arm for gathering alleged evidence for Nordic-Aryan supremacy. It was the SS organization that did things like investigate ancient rune inscriptions in Sweden supposedly left there by the original Aryans. It also mounted expeditions into Tibet in search of original Aryan bloodlines. Nazi 'race science' was born to detect racial relationships between all the peoples in the presumed migration routes from the north down to India, with the goal of creating a mythical profile of the ancient Aryans."

"But from where I'm sitting," Malone said, stroking his mustache, "that really didn't solve some things, at least in intellectual terms. It didn't answer the question of why India isn't mentioned in the Bible, for example. And outside India, it didn't do anything about where the Chinese or Negros came from."

"On the surface, it wouldn't appear to have any impact on those questions," Melissa answered, "but the German takeover of the Aryan debate actually did provide an answer of sorts. The Germans wanted to make the Aryan question about race, not language. That separation was motivated by their wish to establish their own racial superiority over all other ethnicities—even other Europeans. Consequently, racial supremacy couldn't be about language, since German was a common member of the Indo-European language family. They had to define race a different way. They succeeded in that by defining race in terms of biology and physical anthropology."

"So any race other than the Germanic or Nordic-Aryan was inferior," Malone reasoned.

"Right."

"But don't we see race biologically now?" Malone asked.

"No," Clarise quickly answered. "Not the way the Nazis were defining biology. Today, race is about genetic lineage and differentiation. What Melissa's talking about is the stuff the Ahnenerbe did—looking at the shapes of noses and heads, skin coloration, measuring the length or stoutness of a head or skull with calipers—to create some sort of pseudo-typology by which to delineate a race. All of that is at best subjective, and at worst, contrived."

"Absolutely," Melissa agreed. She paused and slowly moved toward a chair. Neff stood up quickly and took her by the hand.

"Thank you," she said, easing herself down. "Just some back pain." She waited a moment and went on. "All of this pseudo-science gained steam at the beginning of the twentieth century. Once the argument fell under the dictatorship of science, European talk about Hindus being Aryan brethren because of a common language family became as absurd as white Americans claiming a racial kinship with Negros because they all spoke English.

"The Germans basically took the Aryan ball and then redefined the rules of the game. Their ideas dominated the intellectual discussion from about 1880 onward since they gained control of the conversation. By the time the Protocols were published and translated, race science had already gained intellectual traction. And as Brian could tell you, this was the same era that the Germans were dominating the field of the higher criticism of the Old Testament."

"That's all true," Brian noted. "Although biblical criticism served some useful purposes and had valid points, many of the leaders in the field were anti-Semitic and used their research to denigrate the authority of the Old Testament—the sacred text of the Jews."

"In terms of the Aryan question, the next steps were how to argue for a Nordic-Germanic homeland for the master race and prove a north to south migration route, Melissa went on. "Establishing a precise route would make it easier to distinguish the Aryan race from other races—like the Jews."

"How in the world could they do all that?"

"Oh, they managed," Melissa smirked. "They had a wealth of bad science and religious gobbledygook to draw on."

"Have I ever heard of any of it?" asked Neff.

Brian chuckled and glanced at Melissa, who knew what was coming. "Only if you've watched TV shows about ancient astronauts."

62

> About the Aryan Root Race and its origins, science knows as little as of the Men from other planets. . . . Even the habitableness of other planets is mostly denied. Yet such great adept astronomers were the scientists of the earliest races of the Aryan stock, that they seem to have known far more about the races of Mars and Venus than the modern anthropologist knows of those of the early stages of the earth.
>
> —*H. P. Blavatsky*

"That was so tasty," Melissa congratulated Summit as she picked up her plate. "Thank you for making it for me. I've never had a curry chicken salad before."

"You're welcome," the pink-haired girl solemnly replied, though Melissa detected the faint hint of a smile. Summit turned and walked off with the plate without another word.

"Summit likes positive attention," Fern said, making sure she wasn't heard, "at least in small doses."

"She really is amazing," Melissa said sincerely. "Clarise wasn't kidding about her knowing where everything is in the library—which is surprisingly good, at least for my research. Her memory is remarkable."

"With her it's something of a game, so she enjoys when people are doing research. She won't let on to that, though."

"I've noticed. It's hard to get an emotional read on her."

"Her emotional health is pretty good, considering the events that brought her here. Dr. Harper and I talked about her a few times, and she agreed."

Melissa bowed her head and sighed. Fern read the gesture immediately.

"Try not to worry, dear," she whispered, putting her hand on Melissa's shoulder. "I know it looks hopeless, but don't give up the thought that you'll see her again."

"That just doesn't seem possible," Melissa admitted, looking up.

"Look around," Fern said, forcing a smile. "Impossible is all around you. We must give her to the Lord."

Melissa looked around the room, trying to draw encouragement from the amazing chain of events that had brought them here.

"Do you need me to keep Summit busy somewhere else again for your next discussion?" Fern asked, changing the subject. "Since we're meeting out here in the Pit, I'm guessing she'll come and go."

"We'll still be talking about Nazi beliefs, but nothing violent."

"We'll see, then."

Melissa heard Brian call from behind her, "Almost done cleaning up." She looked over her shoulder at him, and he took a seat next to her. "How are you feeling?"

"Energized, now that I'm off my feet and have had something to eat," she answered. "Thanks again for suggesting the break, Fern. My stamina isn't predictable."

"Well, dear, you're almost eight full months; that's to be expected. *Someone* has to look after you," Fern said in a gentle but scolding tone, making eye contact with Brian.

"I admit," he held up his hands in surrender, "I deserve that. I just get absorbed in the content."

"Well, you can see your lovely bride-to-be is well along," she pressed him.

"When I look at her, I don't even see that," he said earnestly, turning to Fern. Melissa rolled her eyes, but smiled appreciatively. "I'll try to pay better attention."

"You do that," Fern added. She stood up and went to the kitchen.

"Did I say something wrong?" Brian asked as he watched her leave.

"I'll let you know later," Melissa replied, suppressing just enough of her amusement so that he couldn't be sure of her intent. "Now try to stay focused."

All evidence of a meal was soon cleared from the rugged dining table, the center of social life at Miqlat. In between bites, Kamran and Madison had set up some recording microphones and photocopied a few things Melissa had requested. Everyone was present. Not unexpectedly, Summit curled up on a couch in another section of the Pit to read to Squish, who quickly settled in her lap.

Melissa put on her reading glasses, a sign that she was ready. "I'll try to make this as brief as possible," she began. "I know you're all curious about how all this talk about an Aryan master race, Nazis, genetics, and Minoans relates to the late Dr. Weston and why the Colonel was interested in his work. It's a convoluted but important path to navigate."

"True that," Madison said, shifting in her seat.

"I hear you. Let's jump in again with racial theory," Melissa continued. "It's hard to underestimate Darwin's impact on racial theory. Once the definition of race was divorced from language shortly after the mid-nineteenth century, scholars and scientists in all sorts of fields began to speculate on human origins. Hundreds of books, academic papers, and literary works would eventually form a pool of thought from which the Nazi racial ideas we're familiar with would emerge. Much of what was produced was anti-Semitic in nature and pure nonsense when viewed against our current scientific knowledge. But for the times, it was all taken seriously."

She paused, made eye contact with Brian, and nodded. He took the cue.

"There isn't much that today's ancient astronaut and alternative history crowd says that doesn't come from nineteenth-century thinking," said Brian. "The flawed science of nineteenth-century writers is simply taken as absolute truth and repackaged for a twenty-first-century audience. The period is a goldmine for conspiracists and fringe thinkers. The rule of thumb seems to be that if an old source disagrees with science today, that source must be on to something. Melissa and I suspect the Colonel will be drawing on this material for his own mythical narrative, while simultaneously engineering circumstances and faking evidence that will prop up some of these outdated ideas."

"Human origins is a good launching point," Melissa resumed. "It didn't take long, especially with the growing prominence of evolutionary thinking, for polygenism to become not only respectable, but the dominant view of human origins."

"What's polygenism?" Fern asked.

"That's the idea that the human race had many points of origin and therefore multiple lineages. It's the opposite of monogenism, where all of humanity comes from one source—a single, original couple, like Adam and Eve."

"Polygenism is now the scientific consensus," Clarise added. "Human evolution is thought to have occurred in various places and at different times."

"That's certainly true," Melissa added, "though many Christians continue to reject it."

"But many don't," Malcolm noted. "I'm a biologist and a priest. I don't have any problem with the consensus."

"Neither do I," Clarise added. "I have my own way of parsing origins and the Bible, but I don't want to derail the discussion."

"If you don't mind, Dr. Kelley," Sabi interjected, adjusting his wheelchair so he could look more directly at Brian, "I would like to hear briefly about what Professor Scott thinks about this. I am wondering how he approaches these things."

"I was wondering that myself earlier," Clarise added. "With all the problems related to Adam and Noah and Babel, which you referred to as being read in an overly literal way, where are you at?"

Brian leaned forward. "Well, this might sound odd, but I don't struggle with it because I committed myself a long time ago to let the Bible be what it is in its original context and say what it says to its original audience. I don't look at it as something it isn't. God made it what it is, and I'm not second-guessing Him."

"You'll have to unpack that," Neff said, "at least for me."

"The Bible is a Mediterranean-centered document produced by people living between the second millennium BC and the first century AD. Those people knew nothing about any modern sciences like biology, anthropology, or linguistics. The Bible was never meant to be a science textbook for modern people—by God's design. God was the one who made the decision to prompt people living at that time, in that place, with the knowledge of that worldview, to write what He wanted preserved for posterity.

"Had God given these ancient writers advanced scientific knowledge, no one to whom the books were written would have understood it. The same thing would happen if God produced the Bible today, knowing His plan for human history would last at least two more millennia. Writers today would write using the vocabulary and knowledge they have. If God gave them advanced knowledge of the future, no one today would know what they were talking about. It would defeat the whole enterprise of communication."

Neff and the others sat quietly for a moment, processing the approach. "You know," Ward spoke up. "That makes a lot of sense, but I'll have to think about it."

"I would agree," said Nili. "You honor God's decision to do things as He wanted, at the time He decided to act, for the reasons He wanted to do them."

"That's the goal, anyway," Brian confirmed. "Whether human creation happened by a process or was immediate is of no concern. God was behind it and gets the credit. The Bible is ultimately about theological messaging—Yahweh's status against the other gods, and the outworking of His will against all opposition, human or otherwise.

To make the intent of the Bible our current squabbles or discoveries trivializes the message. And when people criticize the Bible for not being what it was never intended to be, it's like criticizing your dog for not being a cat. It makes no sense at all."

"In other words, you'd demand that a critic explain why their criticism makes any sense before even bothering to argue about it," observed Neff.

"Exactly—and it's not just a tactic. I'm being honest. I insist on the same for Christians."

"What do you mean?" Madison looked intrigued.

"Christians talk a lot about interpreting the Bible in context, but then they filter the Bible through some other context. We shouldn't filter Scripture through the early church or any church tradition, whether that's Catholicism, Orthodoxy, the Reformation, or evangelicalism. The context of the Bible is the context that produced it. Everything else is a foreign context."

"Including the nineteenth century." Clarise added.

"Absolutely. When Christians of the late nineteenth century started talking about pre-Adamic races as a way to argue against evolution, they were imposing their own life and times on the Bible. They wanted it to speak to their current concerns, but it wasn't written to address any of those concerns. Forcing the Bible into making dogmatic theological statements about issues it wasn't written to address led to distorting its contents—and some tragic theology. I'd like Christians and anyone else to interpret the Bible within its own worldview and then judge it on its own terms. I think we just need to be honest with it. I know it can scare people, but I don't think God wants me to protect Christians from their Bible."

"Well, I can see now why you had the troubles you did where you taught," Clarise observed with a smile. "No matter how much sense it makes, it would scare a lot of people if they thought the purpose of Bible study wasn't affirming their creeds or beliefs."

"I know. Been there and done that." Brian forced a smile, then looked at Sabi. "Does that help?"

"Yes," he answered thoughtfully. "This thinking is wise. Creeds have value for helping us focus on important ideas. So do the writings of faithful believers. But they cannot be placed above the Scriptures." He smiled in Melissa's direction. "Please continue."

She smiled back and picked up her thought. "Back in the nineteenth century, the idea of humans originating apart from Adam and Eve was radical, to say the least. Darwin was new, and Christians by and large wanted to resist him. But even if you hated Darwin, that didn't make the problems go away."

"So what did they do?" asked Fern.

"For those who thought monogenism was no longer possible," Melissa answered, "two forms of polygenism came into discussion among Christians: pre-Adamism and co-Adamism. Pre-Adamism was the idea that there were humans before Adam. Co-Adamism said there were other races of humanity along with Adam that were not related to Adam. Neither view caught on, which was no surprise. Pre-Adamism was actually suggested before Darwin in response to the question of where other races of humans came from. The problem became more pressing every time explorers discovered a new world with people living in it. But most Christians thought the idea of non-Adamic humans was heretical because of doctrines like original sin.

"Eventually, the focus of the fight over how to explain the non-European races became the Table of Nations in Genesis 10. The easy solution was to say the Table was incomplete. But some Christians thought even that was an assault on biblical authority, so they argued it was complete and that God must have used some process like evolution to produce the physical differences in the races."

"It's important to understand," Brian clarified, "that neither Melissa nor I would try to argue for any of these ideas. They're only to illustrate that the new discoveries of the sixteenth through the eighteenth centuries forced people to look at their Bible and human origins much differently. They were trying to solve problems in a way that let them keep their view of an inspired Bible."

"I think Brian is framing it in the best way possible. The sad result of a lot of the effort," Melissa lamented, "was a lot of racist thinking that became Bible-endorsed. For instance, to explain where Cain got his wife, some Pre-Adamite adherents taught that Cain left his own clan for a woman of inferior racial stock. The thinking was that a line of humanity that wasn't from Adam had to be inferior since Adam and his kin were the most 'God-like' race. That belief eventually led to the notion that Cain's mark was blackness—that his children were mixed or Negro. If you think about it for even a few minutes in light of the biblical story, that interpretation has no basis at all, but you'd be missing the point. Those interpretations were adopted to solve an intellectual crisis."

"The thinking gets even weirder when it comes to the writings of people who didn't feel any need to stay moored to the Bible," Brian added. "Those who rejected biblical authority were free to come up with anything. And they basically did."

"Brian's not exaggerating," Melissa agreed. "A lot of what was published in the late 1800s and early 1900s is a literary theater of the bizarre. The era birthed a lot of modern mythology, and it appears Dr. Weston bought some of it. We think the Colonel will be using some of the period's ideas to stage his ET villain, for whatever purpose he ultimately has in mind."

"Might as well start with theosophy," Brian suggested. Melissa nodded.

"What's theosophy?" Clarise asked.

"The term means 'divine wisdom.' It's a philosophical system that is part of a larger field known today as occultism or esotericism—a term that refers to alleged hidden wisdom that purports to offer its adherents enlightenment and salvation through that knowledge. When it comes right down to it, theosophy articulates an imaginary evolutionary journey of the human race, begun and assisted by advanced beings from other planets."

"Sounds like Scientology," Neff said dryly.

"It's one of the intellectual threads you'd find there. But instead of Tom Cruise or John Travolta, theosophy tends to be identified with its major nineteenth-century theorist, Madame Helena Petrovna Blavatsky."

"Russian?" asked Ward.

Melissa nodded. "Blavatsky was a Russian occultist. She was prolific, and so the system has come to be identified with her writings."

"Blavatsky's major works," Brian noted, "were *Isis Unveiled* and the *Secret Doctrine*. The latter contains her explanation of the origin and evolution of the universe. Blavatsky talks about an unseen divine being that sort of broke up and oozed out to fill the universe—sort of like describing the Big Bang as an entity. Everything in the universe from the point of its filling then evolved through seven evolutionary cycles. She claimed her knowledge came from an ancient esoteric text called the *Book of Dzyan* and otherworldly 'spiritual masters' who channeled information through her."

"After what we talked about already," Melissa kept pace, "you'll find it interesting that Blavatsky referred to these evolutionary cycles of life as 'races'—more accurately, 'root races.' She wasn't talking about skin color or other physical features, though some of what she did say would be used in later Nazi racial thinking. Blavatsky only gets to human life in the fourth root race, which for her began four or five million years ago. Her system is very complex and mixes planetary language with race terms, so it can be confusing. For example, she held that seven sub-races made up a root race; seven root races made a 'globe round'; and seven 'globe rounds' made a 'planetary round.' "

"Blavatsky's system is monistic," Brian added. "It teaches that all is one. She borrowed a lot from Gnosticism and Hinduism."

"It sounded like her first three races were aliens," Madison observed. "Is that what she was saying?"

"It's probably easier to say they weren't human," replied Melissa. "Remember, these races—the whole system, essentially—are stages of *human* evolution as well as planetary evolution. The seven root races evolve out of some undefinable divine 'stuff' that filled the universe and eventually wound up forming into life forms on earth. The first root race was the most like the divine beings not of earth—basically extraterrestrials. Those entities evolved after the universe was filled with whatever divine stuff Blavatsky believed filled the universe—essentially seeding the universe. That god-likeness was diluted as time moved on toward the appearance of humans."

"The seeding idea," Clarise mused. "Your description sounds like the way astro-biologists and astronomers talk about panspermia—that life on earth was seeded by particles from space. And that came up in Brian's conversation with the Colonel."

"Ironic, isn't it?" Brian smirked. "Theosophists would of course say they were ahead of their time by thinking that way. It's their own theologizing science, and then claiming that science legitimizes their religious views."

"But what they're talking about and what scientists today are saying differ in many ways," Melissa reminded them.

"Panspermia would have broad appeal," added Clarise. "But it wasn't clear to me whether the Colonel was going to use that idea specifically."

"Yeah," Brian agreed. "He held that card to his chest. But the bottom line is, if it's useful, he'll be on it."

"I can see him making it part of a narrative about how the aliens have always taken a benevolent interest in us," offered Malcolm. "But it won't be any use to him when it comes to demonizing his aliens."

"That's true," said Melissa. "He'd have to look elsewhere within theosophy for that. He has a couple other serious options."

"Like what?" Malone asked.

"They have to do with the other root races," Melissa answered. "Blavatsky's second and third root races were the Hyperboreans and the Lemurians."

"The Hyperboreans?" Neff perked up. "The Colonel used that term specifically."

"That he did," Brian recalled. "The term and what it stands for is a clear link to the bizarre Nazi occult theology of Miguel Serrano, which has the Nephilim as its central biblical foothold."

"In Blavatsky's system," Melissa noted, "the Hyperboreans and Lemurians refer to lost worlds or lost continents—again, don't lose sight that this is earth evolution. If any of you have studied alternative earth history or hollow earth myths, you'd have seen the terms there. Her lost races were deemed advanced races that were Pre-Adamic in the biblical sense. They were intelligent precursors to humans and were far more advanced. The divine entities channeling Blavatsky were, according to her, trying to help us evolve back to the divine wisdom from whence we came."

"That's right out of the History Channel's *Ancient Aliens* show," Fern added.

"One of your favorites," Malone teased.

"If you spent more time with me, I wouldn't be interested," she jabbed back, playfully.

"Sounds like standard new-age pop-culture mumbo-jumbo," Ward scoffed.

"That's where most people run into the ideas," Nili replied.

"For people my age, it's video games," Madison interjected. "Some of these ideas are pretty familiar."

"Like the Colonel said," Brian turned to her, "pop culture has spread the memes everywhere."

"Blavatsky's fourth root race, the one before the human race, is the most interesting and relevant for us," Melissa said, getting back on point. "Her fourth race was the Atlantean."

"Somehow I knew we'd hit Atlantis," Malone said sardonically. "What's weird ancient history without Atlantis?"

"For sure," Brian agreed. "The *Secret Doctrine* has the Atlanteans as masters of flight, physics, astronomy, and lots of other sciences. . . . And there's another thing you should know about them."

"What's that?" Neff asked.

"Blavatsky's Atlanteans were giants."

63

Spirits—or shall I say beings—came to this visible world . . . in order to fight the Demiurge on this plane, which is the real Creator of Satan: Yahweh-Jehovah, who in turn created the Jewish genetic robot in order to contaminate the planet Earth. The first terrestrial embodiment of these spirits took place in a Polar body or Hyperborean race. From there, in comes the dramatic involutionary story of the mixture of the pure race with the original earthly beings.

—*Miguel Serrano*

"Let me guess," Ward replied cynically. "The giants of Atlantis built the pyramids."

"Of course—and lots of other things," Brian replied. "Certainly humans couldn't have done that."

"Back to the History Channel," Fern laughed.

"They ought to call it the 'Fantasy Channel,'" Malone quipped, shaking his head.

"The sad thing is," Brian continued, "there are Christian researchers who say the same things today—how the Nephilim built the pyramids and other structures. It's just baptized Blavatsky. Her Atlantean giants were killed off around 850,000 years ago in a great flood. Sound familiar? Giants perishing in a flood?"

"Just a little," Malone grumbled.

"To be precise, though," Melissa interjected, "Blavatsky had the Atlanteans dying off in a series of floods and catastrophes, the last of which was the biblical flood. Since that event overlapped with historical records, Blavatsky claimed that the subsequent root race—the fifth one, which was fully human—witnessed these late events and bore witness to them in various writings recovered from antiquity."

"The Bible being one of those, I assume," Nili conjectured.

"Right," Brian answered.

"Blavatsky's view also allowed overlap," Melissa went on. "Remnants of the dying fourth root race survived a bit into the next one. That's important here, since Blavatsky taught that when Atlantis sank, a fifth continent emerged—Europe. The last vestiges of Atlantis and its giants trickled over into the next phase of the evolutionary journey—the European phase."

"Oh, brother, here we go," Malcolm said. "Europe's going to take us into Nazi mythology."

"It sure will," Melissa agreed. "The fifth root race originated in northern Asia—which, in the parlance of the day, could be anything from the Caucasus Mountains, to northern Mesopotamia, to Turkey. Blavatsky viewed her own time as the tail end of that phase. The coming sixth and seventh root races would evolve toward divinity, be androgynous and spiritual in form, and, of course, have amazing psychic powers."

"Where does Nazi ideology specifically intersect with this?" Neff asked.

"There are three writers who are mainly responsible for how Nazism absorbed and transformed these ideas," Melissa stated. "The first—the bridge from theosophy to Nordic or German racial mythology—was someone named Guido von List. Von List was a lot of things—a poet, writer, mountaineer, and businessman—but he's most important as a German mystic, an occultist who specialized in rune interpretation."

"Von List essentially married theosophy and Wotanism, the religion of the old Norse gods like Odin," explained Brian. "His brand of occultism combined Blavatsky's evolutionary cycles and races with the exaltation of the Nordic gods. He taught that since humans were part of the cosmos, and the cosmos was embedded in nature, people were obligated to live in accord with nature, in identity with their own people and race. Naturally, the race of closest descent to the Nordic gods was the Germanic one. Thus, they were superior by divine lineage. All other races were lesser by cosmic design, much like India's caste system."

"Madness," Nili fumed. "All of this nonsense radicalizing the masses to hunger and thirst for Nazi rule."

"It gets worse—very ugly," Melissa noted. She looked toward the couch. Summit hadn't moved. Fern followed her sightline instinctively.

"Von List's Nordic transformation of theosophy toward Aryan supremacy is known as Ariosophy—a philosophy of Aryanism. The second major personality in that philosophical system was an ex-monk, Jörg Lanz von Liebenfels."

"Lanz fancied himself as something of a biblical scholar," Brian broke in. "In the early 1900s he published an article entitled 'The Biblical Man-Animal' in a biblical studies journal."

"How did that ever see the light of day?" Malcolm asked.

"The editor was a follower of Guido von List."

"I guess that would explain it."

"Lanz basically argued—supposedly on the basis of ancient Near Eastern comparative literature—that those texts pointed to hominid ape-men in early historical times. He took that nugget of nonsense and used it as a filter to reinterpret the Old Testament, arguing that it contained coded references to these ape-men interbreeding with more evolved humans. It doesn't take any imagination to conclude who the subhuman ape-people turned out to be in his thinking."

"Of course," Nili sniffed with contempt, "we already know."

"Lanz came up with a philosophy within Ariosophy that he called 'theozoology' to articulate his racist views," Melissa continued. "He claimed that the Aryans originated from extraterrestrial gods, whom he called Theozoa. Supposedly, they normally bred by energy or electricity. Eventually the Aryans succumbed into interbreeding with the lesser subhuman apelike races. The godlike Aryans were thus corrupted. This bull was at the heart of the occult Aryan-Nazi motivation of eugenics—the lesser bloodlines had to be filtered out to restore the Aryan blood to as much purity as possible."

"It's easy for us to get offended over this," Brian interjected, "but do you realize that the ancient alien claptrap you sometimes read about basically parrots this idea without the overt anti-Semitic language? Honestly, if there were no Gnosticism, Theosophy, and Ariosophy, the ancient astronaut idea wouldn't exist."

"The last major figure," Melissa moved on, "is probably a more familiar name: Alfred Rosenberg."

"The guy who was tried and hung at Nuremberg?" asked Malone.

"That's him. Rosenberg was an early member of the Nazi Party and held influential positions in the Third Reich. He was the major intellectual force behind political ideas like the Nazi creeds, the holocaust, and *Lebensraum*—that the Germanic super race needed more 'living space.' "

"I remember Andrew had me read his book," noted Malcolm, "*The Myth of the 20th Century*. It spelled out his racial theory."

"He was the Nazi evangelist for the Aryan rejection of Christianity. It's no surprise that he favored Nordic and Hindu religion. While Lanz captured the imaginations of Hitler and Himmler, it was Rosenberg who reached the masses with the ideas that Jews were a sub-race and that the Nordic Aryans descended from the gods from an icy northern homeland. That homeland is at times referred to as Thule, which is a Greek geographical term for the distant north. It's a synonym of sorts for Hyperborea, the term the Colonel used when talking to Brian."

"Isn't Rosenberg the one who said Jesus was a white Aryan—a German?" Fern asked.

Melissa nodded. "Rosenberg argued for what he called 'positive Christianity'—a term he used to describe a Christianity without Jewish elements. He taught that Jesus was a Nordic Indo-European opponent of the Jews. His book was published in 1930, and over a million copies had been sold by 1942."

"Believe it or not," Brian interjected, "it's the northern ice-homeland that brings us back full circle to the Indo-European problem raised by ancient India and Sanskrit. Rosenberg utilized the work of Bal Gangadhar Tilak, a famous voice for Indian independence from British rule and a Vedic scholar."

"It's sort of an odd twist of fate," Melissa said, "but Tilak, even though he was a native Indian, didn't argue that the Aryans came from an Indian homeland. He actually argued for an original homeland in the north."

"Was he a Nazi?"

"No. The movement was before his time, and he was only focused on the Vedas. He was convinced that they were extremely ancient and used astronomy to make his case. Tilak had an encyclopedic knowledge of the Vedas and was expert in Sanskrit." Brian heard an excited grunt from the other end of the table. He smiled. "Astronomy got your attention, Kamran?"

The young man nodded and tapped Madison's arm. He quickly signed something to her. "He wants to know how . . ." Madison translated as she watched, "how this Tilak argued his case."

"Well, the Vedas contain lots of references to positions in the heavens of celestial objects, including descriptions that can be correlated with the precession of the equinoxes—the sun being in certain constellations, for instance. There are other odd descriptions of days lasting long than twenty-four hours—"

"Didn't Ward mention that Weston was raving about that?" asked Clarise.

"He did," replied Melissa. "Those sorts of descriptions only make sense if someone is living at the North Pole, or at least very close to the polar region. Based on these sorts of references, Tilak argued that the Vedas must have been written around 4500 BC—1,500 years earlier than the earliest known writing from Sumeria or Egypt. Since the Vedas don't describe people living on ice, the idea is that in 4500 BC or earlier, the polar region wasn't covered in ice but was quite habitable.

"He published his results in 1893, and they were used by Nordic Aryan theorists in the Nazi era. More recent scholars have found flaws in his astronomy and some of his translations—mainly, some of the Sanskrit vocabulary is flexible and imprecise."

"It might sound shocking," Brian added, watching their expressions, "but Tilak actually credited a Wesleyan minister for some of his ideas—William Warren, who was a president of Boston University and Boston School of Theology."

"A Christian theologian?" Ward was incredulous.

"It's true. In 1885 Warren wrote a book called *Paradise Found: The Cradle of the Human Race at the North Pole*. Warren believed the North Pole was home to Eden and the original homeland of humanity. He also believed Atlantis was at the North Pole, as well as Hyperborea—so he had Eden and two of Blavatsky's continents in the far north."

"So let's think about where this brings us," Melissa said. "The photocopies Kamran and Madison passed out when we began contain a short summary of what I was hoping to cover. We've gone from the mid-nineteenth century to Nazism, tracing a set of ideas—ideas that the Colonel will be able to draw from for demonizing his extraterrestrial contrivance." Melissa pointed to the summary of points.

- *Extraterrestrial life forms existed before humanity.*
- *Theosophy has humans evolving from some of these original extraterrestrials.*
- *Ariosophy taught that only one race could trace their lineage to these extraterrestrials, who were viewed as the Nordic gods.*
- *The Nordic-Aryan master race therefore descended from gods—extraterrestrial gods.*
- *These sons of God in Blavatsky's thought were giant Atlanteans; their homeland, Atlantis, was wiped out in a flood. The last of these Atlanteans were the mighty men of renown in the biblical story—the Nephilim. In occult thinking, the sons of God and the giants are the same—and they're the good guys.*
- *These divine men or "sons of God" in Ariosophy were the Aryans; the interbreeding with lesser life forms—apelike creatures—resulted in their corruption and the dilution of their divinity.*
- *Since the Jew of the Old Testament does not descend from the giant clans*

> *and the giant clans are their enemies, this means that the Jew is the enemy of the Atlantean, or the Aryan—and so, the extraterrestrial gods.*

"It's a string of non sequiturs that lacks any basis in reality," Malcolm scoffed, "but when you summarize it all like that, it sounds coherent . . . in a sick sort of way."

"Now we can begin to process Melissa's Minoan genetics article." Brian looked at her with anticipation. "You'll all be able to follow what the Colonel could do with it."

Melissa gazed at her small audience. "Can anyone tell me where most historians who give Plato's Atlantis account any credence place that legendary civilization?" She could already tell from their expressions that they'd done the math.

"Crete," Malone sighed. "The cause of the destruction is thought to be the eruption of Santorini, or Thera, a volcano about seventy miles away."

"Correct," Melissa confirmed. "I'm impressed," she added.

"Hey, I've read a lot of Atlantis stuff. That one was easy."

She went on. "There's academic consensus that the explosion of Thera occurred at the height of Minoan civilization and wiped it out, causing its collapse, forcing a migration to Greece and farther north. Blavatsky and other alternative historians would debate the chronology, naturally, since they believe these civilizations were much older, but all the pieces are there . . . with a bit of a twist."

Brian took the cue. "Where would the Bible's 'Atlantis' be?"

"I don't follow," said Neff.

"The place where humans originated. It wouldn't be at the North Pole, since the biblical writers didn't know of any such place. So where did the races originate? It's a bit of a trick question."

"Ararat," Nili answered quickly, "where the ark landed . . . which is in Turkey."

"Right. And the ancient name of Turkey is . . . ?"

"Anatolia," sighed Malcolm. "If you thought like an occultist, you'd say that the ancient Near Eastern version of the story channeled to Blavatsky was that the giants, who would be the Atlanteans, originated in Anatolia and moved to Crete, establishing what Plato knew as Atlantis. They eventually lost their homeland in the flood catastrophe. Some escaped and moved north into what's now Europe—or maybe several places—and became the stuff of legend."

"That's a nice summary," Melissa replied. "Remember, all of these presumed events took place in remote antiquity. The distance in time would also allow you to say that the subsequent northern homeland that the Atlantean survivors migrated to was what the Vedas was talking about. And so we get a superior race from the north descended from the gods. At some point, their descendants migrated to other places, including into India—which is the Aryan-invasion theory."

Nili spoke up, some apprehension in her voice. "But the Bible would oppose all this. Surely there's no way to have the Bible connect Crete, this mythical Atlantean land of giants, with the biblical story of the Nephilim or giant clans . . . is there?"

Brian sighed. He had the appearance of someone burdened with bad news. "What's the Hebrew name for Crete?" he asked her.

"*Keretim?*"

"No, the *biblical* Hebrew name, not the modern one."

She thought for a moment. "I don't know."

"Caphtor . . . one of the points of origin of the Philistines—as in Goliath."

64

I'd like to see that land beyond the pole.
The area beyond the pole is the center of the great unknown.

—*Rear Admiral Richard E. Byrd*

"You weren't kidding," Malone said, smiling nervously. "Bizarre doesn't even begin to describe what I'm hearing." He glanced at Neff. "But it untangles a lot of ideas we've been trying to understand for a long time."

"I know," Neff responded thoughtfully, then looked at Brian. "We told you back at the college that we engage a lot of conspiracy material. Some of it ends up drifting into fringe topics like the ones you and Melissa have been discussing. We do that because we see an encroaching fascism and greater militancy in anti-Semitism and hostility toward Christians."

"No surprise there," Brian said. "For my money, I'd say we're already living in a post-Christian culture. But the Colonel presented himself and his cronies as above all that, as though they had bigger fish to fry. It seems the world could burn to a cinder so long as he got to fulfill his own fantasies."

"Where do you think this madman will go with these ideas?" Nili asked. Her face was lined with determination, but Brian could see some anxiety in her eyes. "His position gives him access to real power and others who hold power."

"I don't know. Honestly, the Minoan article is new to me, and I have no idea what Ward saw in Weston's briefcase. I'm going to need some time to track that stuff down and think through it. What seems clear at this point is that the Colonel wanted us to learn just enough so that we could see his pieces on the chess board and where they're positioned. Then he could let us fret about what he's going to do. It suits his ego."

"We'll have to figure out the rest of Becky's code to have a better idea," Melissa said, hopefully. "I have no idea what the rest of the numbers mean. We ought to finish off a few other items so we can go back to the drawing board."

"There's more?" Neff asked.

"Just the matter of the Antarctica fragments, which—to be honest—I don't think will end up helping us, but the Colonel could certainly use them for propaganda."

"Like he needs another ingredient."

"The fragments Becky's boyfriend produced are certainly genuine. There's little doubt that they detail a planned base on Antarctica. That said, I've found nothing to suggest that any such base was actually built. If the Nazis did carry on the dream of reviving the Reich—or at least keeping it dormant until the right time—they may have not needed to go any farther south than Argentina. They also may have gone north."

"Like you suggested about Kammler," Malone recalled. "Wow, a dormant Reich. Think of what the neo-fascists would do with that."

"What about the Admiral Byrd legend?" asked Ward. "The one about how he went to Antarctica to fight Nazis after the war. I've read some things online where people suggest it had something to do with UFOs."

"You're referring to Operation Highjump," Melissa replied. "Brian and I don't think there's anything to the story. It has significant problems in terms of sourcing."

"How so?"

"There's no doubt that Byrd went to Antarctica right after World War II ended, and it was serious. It's still the largest expedition ever to go to that region. Byrd literally had a small army with him—4,700 men, thirty-three aircraft, thirteen ships, including an aircraft carrier, an ice-breaker, and a submarine."

"Certainly sounds like a military operation."

"We agree. Byrd was outfitted for a stay of eight months, but he stayed less than two. Rumor has it that his expedition ran into an outpost of Nazis with some exotic weapons, including UFOs."

"So what's the official explanation?"

"It was a mission to train the Navy in polar operations based on the assumption that they'd have to engage the Soviets there at some point. Published articles from the time suggest that the military suspected they'd have to operate polar bases as part of a strategy for that."

"Makes sense," Ward offered, "at least for northern polar geography. But Highjump was aimed at the South Pole."

"True, but Highjump wasn't a secret operation. There were eleven journalists along on the expedition, which would be unthinkable if the expedition was looking for a surviving Hitler and his fleet of UFOs. The official Navy report was also published. There were three volumes and twenty-four annexes, none of which was ever classified 'Secret' or 'Top Secret.' While the material was initially confidential, it was all later made public."

"Admiral Byrd wrote a paper about the operation a couple years later," Brian added. "If you compare that to the now public reports, you won't find any contradictions. The Navy report also has specific maps of where the planes flew. They touched almost none of the territory claimed by the Germans when they mapped the region in the late thirties. There's no correlation when you compare the actual published material and what you'll read on the Internet and in conspiracy books."

"But didn't Byrd say something in an interview about flying saucers?" Malone asked. "I seem to have read that somewhere."

Melissa chuckled at the reference. "Byrd gave an interview to a Chilean newspaper called *El Mercurio* in 1947 where he supposedly said he was afraid the United States could be attacked by 'flying objects which could fly from pole to pole at incredible speeds.' That's a blatant mistranslation of the actual article. It's another of the items I asked Kamran to photocopy," she added and began circulating a piece of paper.

"What you have is the first paragraph of that article, in Spanish and English. The line about craft flying at fantastic speeds is a demonstrable distortion. The first highlighted portion clearly talks about planes flying over the poles—which is not at all unusual in terms of cutting flight distance. I'm sure Ward can confirm that, as well as the translation, since he knows Spanish. The context would be that the United States needed a presence in these regions to prevent or intercept such possible hostile acts.

"The second underlined portion is the one that contains the phrase about 'fantastic speed.' It clearly does *not* refer to the planes or any other flying craft. It refers to the speed of the world shrinking—a thought anyone who experienced World War II would understand. In effect, air travel and communications make it a small world after all. That's even truer today. The famous Byrd UFO quotation conflates the two separate lines; it's a fabrication."

> *El Almirante Richard E. Byrd advirtió hoy que es imperativo para los Estados Unidos de America el iniciar medidas de defensa contra la posibilidad de una invasión del país de parte de aviones hostiles provenientes de las regiones polares. El Almirante explicó que no quiere asustar a nadie, pero es una verdad amarga que,*

> ***en el caso de una nueva guerra, los Estados Unidos podrían ser atacados por aviones que pueden volar sobre uno o los dos polos.*** *Esta declaración se hizo como parte de una recapitulación de su propia experiencia polar, en una entrevista exclusiva con International News Service. Refiriéndose a la expedición de reciente finalización, Byrd dijo que el resultado más importante de sus observaciones y descubrimientos es el efecto potencial que tienen con respecto a la seguridad de los Estados Unidos.* ***La velocidad fantástica a la que el mundo se está reduciendo—recordó el Almirante—es una de las lecciones más importantes aprendidas en su reciente exploración antártica.*** *Debo advertir a mis compatriotas que terminó aquel tiempo en el que podíamos refugiarnos en nuestro aislamiento y confiar en la certeza de que las distancias, los océanos, y los polos eran una garantía de seguridad.*
>
> Admiral Richard E. Byrd warned today that the United States should adopt measures of protection against the possibility of an invasion of the country by hostile planes coming from the polar regions. The Admiral explained that he was not trying to scare anyone, but the cruel reality is that **in case of a new war, the United States could be attacked by planes flying over one or both poles**. This statement was made as part of a recapitulation of his own polar experience, in an exclusive interview with International News Service. Talking about the recently completed expedition, Byrd said that the most important result of his observations and discoveries is the potential effect that they have in relation to the security of the United States. **The fantastic speed with which the world is shrinking—recalled the Admiral—is one of the most important lessons learned during his recent Antarctic exploration.** I have to warn my compatriots that the time has ended when we were able to take refuge in our isolation and rely on the certainty that the distances, the oceans, and the poles were a guarantee of safety.

"Well, that answers that question," Ward said, looking up from the paper. "The Byrd quote I'm thinking of is terribly misleading."

"For sure, strange things have happened down that way," Brian said, "but there's no proof they concerned Nazi bases or UFOs."

"What strange things?" Fern asked.

"Well, in 1958 the US detonated three nuclear bombs in the Southern Hemisphere."

"What?" she gasped.

"It's true. And, like Highjump, that operation wasn't secret, either. Notice, however, that I said 'Southern Hemisphere,' not Antarctica. The Byrd UFO conspiracy crowd says the bombs were detonated over Antarctica to wipe out the Nazi base's communications or something like that. It isn't true. You can read about the detonations—though I wouldn't recommend it unless you understand the science. I did it just to say I'd done it, and barely got through the thing."

"What was the point of *that* exercise?" Madison asked in dubious tone.

"The project was called Operation Argus. The bombs were detonated 1,100 miles southwest of Cape Town, South Africa. They were testing the effects of nuclear explosions outside the atmosphere—whether charged particles and radioactive isotopes would affect the earth's magnetic field. That was important for answering whether such things would interfere with radar, ballistic missiles, and satellite tracking."

"In 2006," Melissa continued, "the British tested Antarctica for evidence of an atomic bomb explosion to see if there was any fallout in the atmosphere. There wasn't. That would basically be impossible had the bombs been detonated directly over the alleged Nazi base."

"The Colonel could use the fragments Becky turned over to prop up whatever story he writes to legitimize Nazi occult ideas, since their mythology includes extraterrestrial threads courtesy of theosophy and occultists like Serrano. Like he said," Brian added with a tone of resignation, "it's not about what's real, only what's believed. Honestly, there's more evidence for Nazi activity closer to the North Pole than the South Pole, though that trail ends quickly. But the north would make more sense given the SS mythology about the northern Aryan homeland."

"What evidence is there for that?" Neff asked.

"It's all circumstantial. The Nazis had outposts in Norway, Greenland, and Arctic Canada, mostly for the purposes of communications and monitoring weather. People in Greenland said they knew of other secret bases, though none were ever found. After the war, a handful of Germans said the same thing."

"Doesn't sound like much for evidence."

"It isn't. The only thing that I've found suggesting these postwar reports might have been correct is an article that appeared in a Vienna newspaper, the *Wiener Montag*, on December 29, 1947. Some Eskimos reported to American authorities that they encountered an SS battle group of about 150 men. That's it."

"I think we need to stay focused on the threads we know for sure, things the Colonel could exploit," Melissa said.

"Sure, but does the average person even know about any of this stuff?" asked Clarise.

"Not in an academic sense, but the public has unconsciously absorbed a lot of it through UFO books, TV, and film," Melissa replied.

"Kamran wants to add something," Madison interrupted, watching him signing. "He says comic books are filled with these ideas, especially aliens—and, of course, many of them have been getting made into movies, like *The Avengers* and *Superman*."

"He's right," Melissa agreed. "Comic books from the mid-twentieth century—the time of the UFO-contactee wave—follow the occult trajectories pretty closely. For example, Blavatsky taught that there were spiritual masters living on other planets who periodically came to earth to seek a human pupil. In her *Book of Dzyan*, they were called the Lords of the Flame. The spiritual guides of Blavatsky's *Secret Doctrine* specifically came from Venus. Later theosophical writers took that thread and turned it into a more detailed ancient-astronaut theory."

"Hmm," Malone mused, "that does sound familiar. That's George Adamski, the famous UFO contactee. We were all into his books in the sixties."

"Adamaski completely ripped off theosophy's Venusians," Brian noted. "But, aside from people from Venus, do you remember who else Adamski said contacted him?"

"Yeah ... oh ... a Nordic ..." Malone shook his head. "Good grief. I just didn't have the framework to make simple connections like that."

Clarise's phone went off, startling her. She looked at it curiously. "Who would be calling?" She picked it up, then looked at Madison with a wry smile. "It's Cal. You answer it—and don't say I never did anything for you."

Madison eagerly took the phone. "Hi, Cal!" she said enthusiastically. "How—"

The abrupt cut-off caught everyone by surprise. In seconds, the girl's warm, cheerful face drained of color, her features transformed into confused horror. She listened for a few more seconds. "Okay ..." Her trembling voice cracked.

She held out her phone toward Brian, her hand shaking. She swallowed hard and caught her breath. "Cal's in trouble. ... He says he needs you to pick up. The Colonel will only talk to you."

65

Courage is fear that has said its prayers.

—*Dorothy Bernard*

Brian took the phone. "Hello?" he answered tentatively. "Cal?"

"Dr. Scott?"

"Yes, are you all right?"

"Yeah. Look, I don't know who this guy is or what he wants, but he showed up here with an FBI agent and threatened to shut me down and turn me in to Homeland Security."

"Did he say why? If not, I hope you didn't say anything."

"No, and I didn't. All he said was that if I wanted the matter cleared up, I'd call the people who brought the priest's body to me—and I'd ask for you. There was no bargaining, trust me."

"Be very careful," Brian warned. "This is the guy who's responsible for killing Father Fitzgerald. Don't be fooled by the uniform."

"Understood."

"What phone are you using?"

"My cell."

"Is it secure?"

"Same as the ones you all use."

"Good. Put him on," Brian said, anger welling inside him. He quickly motioned to Melissa for her laptop. The others stared at each other in stunned disbelief, dumbstruck at the Colonel's success in finding their colleague. Brian put his phone on speaker and tapped madly on the laptop, his ear trained in dreadful expectation.

"It has to be the body," Clarise said in a low voice.

"It couldn't be," whispered Nili in a frantic voice. "We swept it. There was nothing."

"It's the only thing that makes sense," she came back. Neff motioned for silence, reading Brian's expression. The Colonel was on the line.

"Hello, professor." His voice dripped with arrogant self-assurance. "I'm so pleased to have found a way to stay in touch."

"Let him go, Colonel, and anyone else working there. Then we can talk."

"Are you worried about your friend?"

"I don't even know the guy, but yeah, I know what you're capable of."

"And so you know that you're going to do what I tell you to, don't you?"

"And what's that?"

"You're going to introduce me to your friends."

"I don't think so."

"Then I won't have any use for poor Dr. Olesen. What a pity. Frankly, you should find more intelligent friends, professor. It was easy to locate the body—as planned, of course. A simple injection of nano-particles that form an antenna for tracking did the trick. But I got tired of waiting for something to happen. Pardon my impatience."

"Congratulations. Now let him go."

"Apparently you weren't listening, doctor."

"It's *your* turn to listen, Colonel. Pay close attention."

Brian clicked a file on the laptop and held the phone's receiver close to the microphone. Shortly after their return to Miqlat, Madison had produced a transcript of the audio Brian had recorded in the restaurant, complete with segment breaks. Brian knew exactly what he wanted his enemy to hear. The table listened in rapt concentration as Brian played back the recording of his meeting with the Colonel, pausing it after the Colonel's confession of killing Andrew had played.

"Now let me tell you what *you're* going to do," Brian said through gritted teeth. "You're going to hand the phone back to Dr. Olesen, and it's going to leave the office with him. If I so much as hear he's caught a cold after this conversation, I'm going to send that file to every law enforcement agency in Nevada, every congressman and senator in Washington, every national news network, and every administrator at the Pentagon and the Air Force. I can't stop your plans, but I can cut you off from your position and your toys. *Understand?*"

Brian's heart pounded in his chest. There was no reply. He was trembling, both with rage and fear for the man he knew the Colonel would kill without remorse if he chose to do so.

Still no answer. Brian looked breathlessly at the startled faces around the table, each of them as uncertain as he was. Madison was crying, her hand covering her mouth. Brian glanced at Sabi. His eyes were closed in concentration, his hand clutching his prayer rope.

"Very well, professor." Brian started at the sound of the Colonel's voice. "Your friend is free to go, but understand this: threatening me was a very, very poor decision."

Brian heard the sounds of the phone being handed off. He quickly motioned to Neff to come to his side.

"Dr. Scott?"

"Cal, the Colonel is going to let you go. I'll explain why some other time."

"Are you sure? He looks pissed."

"Yes. I'm giving the phone to Neff, who can give you directions." He handed the phone to Neff.

"Cal, this is Graham. Don't take anything with you from the office. Just get out and use the network—Lewis and Clark. We'll pick you up in five days at the last stop. We'll take care of you. Now *move.*"

***

The Colonel watched as the young pathologist ended the call and slipped his phone into his pocket. He glanced out the window at the idling car where the FBI agent had been waiting since emptying the office of onlookers. The Colonel had ordered Cal to lock the front doors and turn off all the lights, save for the office.

Cal quickly shut the briefcase resting atop his desk. He pulled his coat from the rack and put it on, grabbed the briefcase, and turned to leave. The Colonel blocked his path. A chill ran through him as he saw the officer's hand. He was holding a scalpel. Cal started to retrace the day's steps. How did the scalpel get into his office? Was the drawer unlocked? But that was pointless now.

The Colonel noticed his expression and smiled menacingly as the young man looked up into his piercing blue eyes, now narrowed in focus. "Before you leave, doctor, I have a message for your friends. You're going to deliver it."

66

Precious in the sight of the Lord
is the death of his faithful ones.

—*Psalm 116:15*

"Sabi, it's me," Clarise whispered as she touched the prone figure's warm, wet cheek. It was a familiar scene by now, but she couldn't get used to it. She watched anxiously as Sabi jerked his head from side to side, eyes still closed. The sweat ran off his face, drenching his pillow and the collar of his shirt. She spoke soothingly to him, to ease his consciousness into awakening. After another minute or two, the thrashing subsided. He began to breathe evenly.

He opened his eyes, unsurprised at her presence. "Again," he gasped.

"You're safe," she said, patting his brow with a clean towel. "We're all here."

"Yes . . . for now."

She stopped and locked onto his eyes.

"What do you mean? You've never said anything like that after your dream."

"It was the same, but different."

"Tell me."

"The door . . . the same place . . . machinery, tools, papers . . ."

". . . and shelves and tables again?"

"Yes. And the fear—always the fear. The scream of a woman . . . darkness . . . the smell of blood . . ."

"But something else . . ."

"Voices, other voices, mingling together . . . I hear but cannot understand."

"What else?"

He paused and looked up at her. She could tell he didn't want to say more. She waited. He closed his eyes.

"Death," he whispered. "Death is in the room, but it is not alone. . . . I am not alone . . ."

"Are you afraid?"

"I am not afraid to die," he said, looking up at the ceiling. "Death is there, but the Spirit is present, as always." He turned his head to her and smiled, his eyes moistening with tears. "He is there . . . and that is enough."

67

It is a capital mistake to theorize before one has data.

—*Sherlock Holmes in* A Study in Scarlet *by Sir Arthur Conan Doyle*

"Oh . . ." Melissa moaned, eyes closed, stretched out on the couch. "That's amazing. You wouldn't believe how good that feels."

"You got that right," Brian replied, looking at Melissa's pleased expression as he massaged her bare feet. "I don't know how you can stand this."

Her lip turned mischievously. "Ticklish?"

"Extremely."

"Good to know."

"You've been warned," Brian replied, almost smiling.

"Whatever. Now pamper me a little," she sighed, knowing he was looking. "It helps relieve the tension."

Brian tried to relax as he gently proceeded. It was almost midnight, but the Pit was bustling. Normally everyone would be preparing for bed, but not tonight. Ward, Neff, and Nili were due back in less than an hour with Cal. Even though they'd retrieved him without incident, the Colonel's malevolent unpredictability had everyone on edge. The tension was heightened a bit by Neff's cryptic comment that Cal seemed disturbed and refused to share details of the experience until his arrival. By all accounts, Cal was a sturdy, capable soul who was accustomed to risk and danger, so this unexpected bit of news had proven disconcerting.

Brian looked out into the living space from the couch where they were seated. Kamran and Malcolm were playing video games to distract themselves. Fern and Malone worked on a puzzle. Sabi was playing a game of chess with Summit, Squish nestled comfortably on her lap. Brian watched her move one of Sabi's pieces for him. He laughed to himself, recalling Sabi's warning about playing her. No one could beat the girl since she'd started memorizing chess manuals. She had, of course, insisted it wasn't cheating.

Clarise and Madison were at opposite ends of another couch with books in their laps, though they were talking rather than reading. Madison had been terribly stressed, despite the clear checkpoint reports they'd received from Cal, precisely as expected. The route was a familiar one. He'd used it many times to get others to safety. Nili had designed it herself and had trained him on how to detect being followed—something for which the Mossad had earned a special reputation.

Brian saw Malcolm get up from his chair and head their way. Despite the latest panic, Malcolm had seemed to regain his equilibrium. Brian was struggling to retain his own.

"Dude," Malcolm said with a smile, "you should try that one."

Brian shrugged.

"He's hard at work, Malcolm," Melissa replied, eyes still closed.

"I can see that."

"He won't be excused for any reason." She sighed contentedly to reinforce the point.

"Doesn't look like a matter for God and country."

"It's close enough—and I know why you're here."

"Let's hear it." He flashed a toothy grin and sat down on the floor, legs crossed in front of him.

"You want to know what he's come up with."

"I do," he acknowledged, "but I'm more interested in continuing this morning's conversation."

"I don't think it's a good time," Brian responded.

"I listened to you, now it's your turn. You can't blame yourself about what you said to the Colonel."

"You mean what I *didn't* say."

"You know what I mean."

"If my head had been clearer, I'd have said something about returning Dee when I threatened him. I didn't. It's an opportunity lost."

"*Brian,*" Melissa said, opening her eyes. She propped herself up on an elbow and reached for his hand. He hesitated but took it. "There's no way you could have been ready," she said softly and released his hand. "It was totally out of the blue."

"And you don't know that it would have mattered," Malcolm added. "He could have said yes and laid a trap for you, or Melissa . . . or all of us."

"It was our best chance. We have no leverage now."

"We still have the recording," Malcolm reminded him.

"And no idea if we can contact him. Who knows if the method we used earlier is any good now. He didn't even try to trace us then; he'd surely do it now. For once we had the upper hand, and I blew it."

"That opportunity came out of nowhere, so another one can, too."

"I guess," Brian surrendered. "Let's change the subject."

"Fine with me," Malcolm agreed.

"I'd rather he get back to work on me," Melissa said, reclining again.

"Are you telling me your man can't talk and do that at the same time?"

Melissa started to say something and then stopped.

"Trapped?"

Brian smiled and shook his head.

Melissa opened one eye in his direction. "Make me proud."

"Fire away, Malcolm."

"Sweet," he replied, then looked at Brian thoughtfully. "I listened to the Colonel's lecture again today. I'm just curious about what you believe on a few things. He hit you a couple times with the fact that you don't buy popular end-times thinking. I'm sure you know that Catholic theology's pretty tame there. We'd say the kingdom began when Jesus came the first time, and when He comes again that's the end of earthly history. I'm wondering where you're at."

"I agree with you on the beginning of the kingdom—that's pretty obvious from what Jesus says in the Gospels about the kingdom being present or at hand, and the way Paul talks about the kingdom. My divine-council theology leads me to expect that human history doesn't end with the second coming, though. I think the final kingdom and eternal state are really one, and it will take place on the new earth, the new Eden. As far as the idea of a rapture, I won't say it's impossible, but it's really unlikely."

"I was taught all that stuff as a girl," Melissa interjected, eyes still closed. "I think it's nonsense, but why don't *you* buy it?"

Brian glanced at Malcolm mischievously. "A third party might throw off my rhythm. Maybe you should just listen."

"Oh, be quiet." Her eyes flickered open. She grabbed a pillow on the floor next to the couch and threw it at him. He deflected it with a laugh. "Answer the question."

"I'm bothered by the assumptions that underlie the whole idea," he said, turning to Malcolm. "The belief in a rapture is an interpretive choice that depends on other interpretive choices. There's nothing transparently evident about it in the text at all."

"What do you mean?"

"What would you say to someone who told you the Gospels were full of errors because they reported events and conversations differently?"

"I'd tell them they were different ways of talking about the same event, like in newspapers. The stories in two papers are never the same, but that doesn't mean any of the writers were wrong. They're just selective, and every writer has an angle or agenda. We need to put all the material together for a fuller picture."

"I'd say the same thing. The most logical approach is to harmonize accounts or blend them together. The problem is that the belief in a rapture depends upon the reader's decision to resist doing that."

"You lost me," said Melissa.

"A rapture only comes into view in the New Testament when people put passages about the return of Jesus into two piles. The rapture depends on separating passages that, for example, have Jesus touching the ground when He returns, from others that don't—maybe that have Him appearing in the air. The result is two separate, distinct events—one being the rapture, the other being the second coming. But if you harmonize all that's said about the return of Jesus, the rapture disappears—you only have one event, the second coming."

"So the problem is whether to be a splitter or a joiner?" Malcolm asked.

"Yep. Christians who believe in a rapture seem to harmonize passages on every other issue to protect the Bible from contradiction. But when it comes to end-times prophecy, they're splitters so they can get a rapture. It's an intentional method, not something that derives just from looking at the Bible."

"I see your point," Malcolm acknowledged. "But I don't think that invalidates Andrew's ideas about new Nephilim being part of the end times. He was convinced Matthew 24 pointed that direction."

"I think Andrew's idea is wrong for other reasons."

"Such as?"

"The whole notion rests on one phrase in Mathew 24:37—that the Lord's return will happen in circumstances 'as in the days of Noah.' "

"Genesis 6."

"Does that put everything in Genesis 6 into Matthew 24?"

"Maybe."

"That assumption has real problems. There are no Nephilim in Matthew 24. No UFOs either. Has anyone in the history of Christianity ever seen Nephilim or spaceships in Matthew 24?"

"Since when have you ever cared about being in the mainstream of Christian tradition?" Malcolm jabbed good-naturedly.

"You're right, I don't care much. I care more about interpretations that violate the biblical writers' original context. The point of the reference to Noah in Matthew 24 is that, just like people were caught by surprise by the flood, so people will be caught off guard by the return of the Lord. The passage refers to normal human beings, not the sons of God or Nephilim."

"What about the 'marrying and giving in marriage' wording? If you take a sexual view of Genesis 6, that seems to fit."

"Actually, it doesn't. Grammatically, the subjects of those verbs and others in the passage are people—men and women—not divine beings. The illustrations offered in verses 40–41 to explain the previous verses are explicitly said to be men and women—*people*. There's no exegetical warrant for saying that those 'marrying and giving in marriage' in verse 38 involve divine beings like in Genesis 6, but then arguing that the subjects change to normal people in the second half of verse 38 on through verse 41. People just make it read that way. They bring the idea *to* the text, as opposed to getting it *from* the text."

"You heard what the Colonel told him," Melissa said with a yawn, shifting her position a bit. "With Brian, it's always about the text."

"I don't know if this fits Andrew," Brian went on, "but some of the people who argue his viewpoint love to use *1 Enoch* to defend a literal view of Genesis 6 and then conveniently forget some of the details that don't support how they view Matthew 24. In *1 Enoch*—at least the Greek version—the Watchers descend in the days of Yarad, which was generations before the days of Noah's flood. It also has each Watcher taking only one woman, so the 'marrying and giving in marriage' would have been over and done with long before the flood—but people, of course, would have been doing that the whole time."

"What about Daniel 2:43?"

"The problems are just as obvious there."

"What does Daniel 2:43 say?" Melissa wondered out loud. "And answer without gesturing," she laughed quietly. "You're losing focus."

"Demanding, aren't we?" Malcolm grinned.

"I'm pregnant."

"When did that become a power play?"

"About two days ago," Brian answered, gently squeezing her feet. "Works pretty well, actually. Being beautiful helps, too."

Malcolm shook his head.

"Anyway, Daniel 2:43 is the other passage used to defend Nephilim being part of end times," Brian explained. "The chapter is Daniel's explanation of Nebuchadnezzar's vision of the tall statue, where parts of the statue's body are made of different metals. Verse 43 talks about the toes of the statue—the fourth kingdom—being made of both iron and clay. The whole point is that the *rulership* of the fourth kingdom is mixed. Verse 41 makes that clear—it describes the fourth kingdom as *divided*. And the language of verse 43 tells us why it's divided: mixed marriages, which historically lead to dynastic struggle and competition for power."

"But," Malcolm objected, "literally it says that 'they will mingle themselves with the seed of humankind.' That sounds like part of the mingling isn't human."

"If you bring that idea with you, it does. But what indication is there that Daniel was thinking about Genesis 6? And if you throw in the modern Nephilim ideas you read on the Internet about aliens—or demons posing as aliens—suddenly becoming experts at genetic engineering, the question is more telling: Why would Daniel be thinking about modern science? Daniel didn't even know what germs or molecules are. Those ideas are right out of the ancient-astronaut myths."

Malcolm shrugged. "I'm just saying."

"The real problem is what the second half of the verse says—again, very explicitly."

"What's that?"

"It says the mingling *doesn't work*—that it won't hold together. Verse 42 talks about a kingdom that is partly strong and partly brittle—the mingling has a deteriorative effect. So anyone who takes the verse to describe a divine-human sexual mingling also has to admit it doesn't work, which sort of defeats the whole premise. How do you get an end-times rise of Nephilim if the mingling doesn't work?"

"When you put it that way, it does sound awfully suspect," conceded Malcolm.

"The fourth kingdom is most likely Rome, since it's pretty easy to argue that the kingdom began during the time of Jesus. Some argue it refers to the Jewish rebellion under the Maccabees that arose in the times of the Ptolemies and Seleucids, which was definitely a mixed kingdom, both racially and in terms of competing dynasties. But Rome had plenty of that sort of thing, too. To me, what it comes down to is this: You either base your theology on what's present in the text or what's not in the text. The latter might be good for imagination, but it's not anything you could call biblical theology. By definition, a biblical theology must be tied to the text. A biblical theology can't be based on what's *not* in the Bible; it can only be based on what is."

"I understand what you're saying," Malcolm said, becoming serious. "Without anchors in the text, people can go astray. But they also go astray when they filter the Bible through whatever grid guides their thinking—like what you've been working on the last few days, all that Aryan Jesus Minoan migration wackiness."

"Don't I know it," Brian said glumly. "For the past few days I've been trying to look at Scripture in a new way—bringing an agenda to it."

"You know how the Colonel's gonna bring the threads together, don't you?"

Brian looked at him uneasily. "I sure hope not."

68

The Amorites founded Jerusalem. They formed the Nordic stratum in later Galilee; that is, in the 'pagan region' whence someday Jesus was to come.

—*Alfred Rosenberg*

"You might as well get into it," Melissa replied, rising slowly from the couch, her hand on Brian's shoulder to steady herself. "I'm going to get some coffee. You want anything?" she asked Brian.

"The usual," he replied. "Thanks."

"It's the least I can do." She bent over and kissed him lightly. "Coffee, Malcolm?"

"I'm good."

Brian watched Melissa navigate her way toward the kitchen. "Man," he heard Malcolm sigh.

"What?"

"You two. I don't want to hear another pessimistic word from you. God can make amazing things happen."

"I know. That's a thought we'll all need to hold."

Malcolm could see his mood had darkened again. He waited for more.

Brian got on track. "It's a disturbing exercise to play evil genius with the Bible, especially when you realize you can make terribly misleading ideas seem so coherent—all to manipulate people."

"You're onto him, and it's creepin' you out, isn't it?"

"Yeah. To be honest, it's scary. It's painfully easy to lead people astray and sound informed while you're doing it. All it requires is a command of the data you want to distort and no conscience."

"And an uninformed target audience," Malcolm added.

"True. Unfortunately, those aren't hard to find."

"So you think you know the angle the Colonel's going to play . . . how he's gonna marry Genesis 6 to all the occult bunk to set up his target."

"I don't know if it's exactly what he's planning, but it certainly could be. Let's put it this way: I don't know what he's going to build, but I know the tools that he'd have at his disposal. If I can tie the threads together, so can he."

"Lay it on me. Give me the short version."

Brian took a deep breath. "You've already heard me say something about how the Philistines, the people of Goliath and his brothers, are associated with Caphtor in the Bible."

"Which is Crete. Yeah."

"Jeremiah 47:4 and Amos 9:7 make the connection certain. From that point, it's probably easiest to look at the Anakim in the Bible."

"They're the giants that are linked back to the Nephilim in Numbers 13:33."

"Right. You run into them in the books of Deuteronomy and Joshua, too. They're specifically referred to as 'great' and 'tall,' so there's no ambiguity about their appearance. Joshua 11 has them living in a couple of places that are important for us—Gath, Gaza, and Ashdod. Ring any bells?"

Malcolm thought for a moment. "Those were three Philistine cities," he replied. "There were some others, too . . ."

Brian nodded. "Ashkelon and Ekron were the others. But those three are most important. The books of Joshua and 1 Samuel list those as Philistine cities, but Joshua 11:22 tells us something else: that toward the end of Joshua's wars, the remnant of the Anakim lived in those three cities. It's a clear link between the Anakim and the people Goliath lived among."

"And, therefore, between the Anakim and Caphtor."

"Yep. The Philistines settled in Canaan—in serious numbers, anyway—in the early twelfth century BC. The Hebrew name for them was *peleshtim*—the modern term 'Palestine' comes from that word."

"Keep going; I'm with you."

"Philistine pottery has been found in those cities that bears a striking resemblance to styles on Crete and other parts of the Aegean. Most everyone who studies the archaeology of ancient Israel knows that. Less obvious are things like the term *Anak*. It has no known Semitic etymology, but it has a precise Greek equivalent, *Anax*. That might seem odd, but Greeks—people from the Aegean islands and the Greek mainland—were in Canaan long before the Bible was put into writing."

"What does the Greek word mean?"

Brian smirked. "'Lords,' 'gods,' 'masters,' that sort of thing. In some texts it's found in the phrase 'lords of the oar,' which refers to sea migration. Basically, it's a term used of dynastic rulers and some of the Greek gods, a few of whom were Titans."

"Great. Them again. That connection would be easy to exploit."

"That it would."

"Wow, all these links. It's a lot more than just Goliath."

Brian looked up. Melissa was approaching the couch. "Here you go," she said and took a seat. Brian carefully took the hot cup of tea and placed it on an end table. "Where are you guys at?" Melissa asked.

"Goliath," Brian answered.

"Oh, haven't even gotten to the weird material yet."

"Not yet." He took a sip and looked at Malcolm. "We've gone through it all a few times together. I wanted Melissa to hear all the potential hooks into the esoteric philosophies."

"No shortage there," she said.

"Goliath is a good pivot point. The name isn't Semitic. It's probably either Lydian in origin—which would take us back to the Aegean sea and Crete—or Luwian, which is one of the Hittite languages."

"Which takes us back to Anatolia," Melissa added, "the point of origin for the people who settled in Crete and were part of what we know as the Minoan civilization."

"There are so many threads the Colonel could use," Brian said. "They're right under the noses of Bible readers, hidden in plain sight. Take the Hittites. How many people who say they study their Bible would know that the Hittites were here and in control of good chunks of Canaan even before the Philistines?"

"Not many. I didn't even realize that," admitted Malcolm.

"In Genesis 23, when Sarah died, who did Abraham buy land from—in the promised land of Canaan, no less—to bury her?"

"The Hittites?"

"Yep. By the time the Torah was written, the specific name of that place was Kiriath-arba, 'City of Arba.' It was later called Hebron. Is the name 'Arba' familiar?"

"No."

"According to Joshua 14:15, he was the greatest of the Anakim."

"No way."

"Look it up. Later in Genesis 27, the Isaac and Rebekah story, the Hittite women are called 'women of the land.' That shows they'd long been settled in the area. That's part of why Ezekiel 16 says what it says."

"And what's that?"

"I'll read it to you." Brian reached for his laptop and quickly produced the passage. "Listen to these first three verses carefully. Think about them against the backdrop of what we've been talking about this past week."

> *Again the word of the Lord came to me: "Son of man, make known to Jerusalem her abominations, and say, Thus says the Lord God to Jerusalem: Your origin and your birth are of the land of the Canaanites; your father was an Amorite and your mother a Hittite."*

Malcolm looked at him uncertainly. "It's no surprise that Jerusalem was 'born' in the land of the Canaanites. But the line about Jerusalem's father being an Amorite and her mother a Hittite—what's up with that?"

"A lot of Bible readers don't realize Jerusalem wasn't always an Israelite city. David conquered it from the Jebusites, but it had an even earlier history. Joshua 10 says that the king of Jerusalem in Joshua's day was a fellow named Adonizedek. After he heard how Joshua had conquered Jericho and Ai, he formed a coalition force with—get this—the *other* four Amorite kings. That means Jerusalem was Amorite territory. The kicker is that Amos 2:9–10 describes the Amorites as being as tall as cedars."

"Man, it's like you said—the threads are hidden in plain sight."

"Trust me, he's just getting started," Melissa said grimly.

"Think about what the Colonel could do with what you've heard so far. The Amorites are the people God mentioned in His covenant with Abraham in Genesis 15—the ones whose 'iniquity was not yet full.' The Old Testament tells the story of the Israelites, the people of Yahweh, moving into Canaan, the promised land, specifically to take it away from the giant clans by conquest. Those giant clans have a traceable heritage back to Anatolia and Minoan Crete, or Caphtor."

"Right to the place where the occultists have the Atlantean giants," Melissa reminded him. "It would be painfully easy to cast the Israelites as not only the enemies of the giant clans, but the enemies of the Aryans. The roadmap of ideas is all right there."

"Believe it or not," Brian continued, "this also creates a clear path to an Aryan Jesus."

"Come on," Malcolm said skeptically.

"If you can remember your seminary Hebrew, think through the name Adonizedek with me."

"Well, *Adoni*, that's 'my lord.' . . . *Zedek* would be 'righteous.' "

"Correct. The most obvious meaning of the name is 'my lord is righteous.' "

"I take it there's a less obvious meaning?"

"*Zedek* could also be a proper noun—specifically, a deity name. That would produce the meaning 'my lord is *Zedek*.' The name would be paying homage to the god *Zedek*, who appears in Semitic texts outside the Bible. Most of the evidence for that deity comes from the old Babylonian kingdom of Mari."

"Mari?" Malcolm paused, trying to remember. "Didn't that name come up when Melissa was going through her research?"

"It did," Brian confirmed. "Some of articles the police found in Weston's briefcase mentioned Mari. One of them talked about some tablets connected to Minoans and a place called Kabri. After the phone confrontation with the Colonel, we asked Ward to contact the police in Nevada handling Weston's case to get scans of the articles. I was able to find all of the articles he cites in the journal databases. We know exactly what Weston was reading—and why. We'll get to that in a minute."

"Okay, back to Adonizedek. Why is he important?"

"Well, what other biblical name ends with *Zedek*?" Melissa asked.

Malcolm had to think for only a second. He frowned. They could see by the look on his face he had the answer. "Melchizedek."

"Precisely. In the scenario I'm developing here, that name means 'my king is Zedek.' Now who was Melchizedek?"

"He was king of Salem, which is the shorter name of Jerusalem in Abraham's day."

"So let's connect some dots. Abraham, the Israelite—or, to the Aryan occultist, the Jew—paid tithes to Melchizedek as a superior."

"But that has to fit into Israelite theology," Malcolm said. "The priestly lineage of Jesus is the line of Melchizedek. Psalm 110 is absolutely clear on that."

"Of course it is," Brian acknowledged, taking another sip of tea. "But you're not thinking like the Colonel."

"Or nineteenth-century anti-Semitic occultists like Rosenberg or von Liebenfels—people who want to divorce Jesus from the Jews," Melissa added. "Try this plotline on for size: The Bible is clear that Melchizedek was not an Israelite—he was no descendant of Abraham. He occupied territory that the Jews would later take by force from the peaceful Hittites—people who had befriended Abraham. But Abraham's descendants were treacherous. They attacked and killed the descendants of the Atlantean kings, among whom lived the vestiges of the earlier giant lineages."

"Sounds like something I'd see on YouTube."

"Then you get the picture," Brian replied. "It's the evil Jew against the Aryan ancestors descended from the master Atlantean race. A clever propagandist would say that's where all the strife over the land of Palestine begins. Jerusalem originally belonged to the Aryans by means of the Amorites, descendants of the master race. Like Ezekiel 16 said, Jerusalem's father was an Amorite.

"Our propagandist would also say that Jesus' own priestly lineage is Aryan; His god was Zedek, the Righteous One. His association with Melchizedek distances him from a Jewish priesthood lineage. It's a Nazi occultist's playground.."

Malcolm sat speechless before them, his jaw slightly open.

"We're not done," Melissa said, nodding to Brian.

"Zedek shows up in the writings of Philo of Byblos, who is most known for his 'Phoenician History,' a work he wrote in Greek using fragments of a Phoenician source by someone named Sanchuniathon. Philo's work contains a theogony, an account of the generations of the gods. One of those gods is Zedek, spelled *Sydyk* in Greek. Sydyk was a descendant of the Titans, who are identified with the Watchers—the sons of God—in Jewish literature.

"And we already know that, for the occultists, the sons of God were the Atlanteans. So we have yet another ancient connection between the enemies of the Jews and the master race through Zedek. Again, what could the Colonel say? Melchizedek was loyal to the Watchers' descendants, the Amorites. Jesus inherited the priesthood of Zedek. He wasn't a Jew. He was their enemy, and they killed him."

Malcolm's expression became sullen. "I almost hate to ask, but what else is there in all this about Jesus?"

"Let's talk about Haupt," Melissa coaxed. Brian nodded.

"Paul Haupt was the leading Assyriologist of his day. He taught for many years at Johns Hopkins University—my undergraduate alma mater, ironically. He died in 1926, so what he wrote can't properly be called Nazi, but he fueled the fire and the scholarship of people like Alfred Rosenberg."

Melissa picked up the discussion. "Haupt poured his scholarly abilities into the idea that Jesus was not a Jew, but an Aryan. His most famous essay, 'The Aryan Ancestry of Jesus,' was published in 1909."

"How did he argue something that seems so clearly wrong?"

"Basically," Melissa replied, "Haupt focused on Galilee. Jesus was from Galilee, since Nazareth is in Galilee."

"But he was born in Bethlehem."

"Well, Haupt believed that the tradition about Jesus being born in Bethlehem was added later," Brian explained.

"Seems contrived."

"I'd say so, but he based it on John 7:40–41 and Mark 12:35–37. John 7:40-41 is one of the scenes where people are arguing about whether Jesus is the Christ. Part of the verse has some people in the crowd saying, 'Is the Christ to come from Galilee?' That, of course, sounds like the expected answer is 'no.' "

"Of course," Malcolm replied, "since Micah 5:2 has the son of David being born in Bethlehem, the city of David."

"The Greek text of John 7:41 has a negator in it—a word for 'no' or 'not' that doesn't get reflected in most translations. But if you translate the negator, the statement changes: 'Is *not* the Christ to come from Galilee?' Then the expected answer is 'yes.' "

"Which one is right?" Malcolm asked, some uncertainty in his voice.

"The first one. The negator isn't supposed to be translated. That particular negator in Greek communicates that the statement expects a negative answer. Everybody who works in Greek knows that. All the grammars discuss it."

"So how does anyone get away with translating it the other way?"

"Simple: They just do it. And if you're someone like Haupt, it becomes an argument from authority."

"Malcolm," Melissa said, "think about what you just asked. You're a priest. If this sort of thing inserts a seed of doubt into your mind, think about the average Christian."

"I am."

Brian continued. "In Mark 12:35 Jesus asks, 'How can the scribes say that the Christ is the son of David?' Haupt argued that Jesus asked the question to cast doubt on the idea. Sure, that ignores lots of other things, but it's a good example of interpretation by suspicion."

Melissa put down her cup. "Haupt also taught that Galilee was not Jewish territory—or, maybe more precisely, that Jews didn't live there."

"He argued that it was a Gentile region?"

Brian nodded. "Galilee is in the northern part of Israel. Haupt played off the Assyrians' destruction of the northern kingdom of Israel way back in 722 BC, long before the time of Jesus. Assyrians held the policy of deporting the people they conquered and then moving foreign people into a region to replace the population. That's what happened when Assyria conquered the ten northern tribes. Haupt argued that Galilee was therefore not populated by Jews. For sure, the northern parts of the country had mixed populations—as evident in the racism toward the Samaritans. But it's a hopeless case to argue that it was basically free of Jews and that no one from Galilee was Jewish."

"Again, how could other scholars let that ride?"

"They didn't. They published rebuttals. The point is, though, that there is a scholarly breadcrumb trail that the Colonel can use. He can use the work of a leading Semitics scholar from the turn of the twentieth century to revive and prop up Aryan mythology—in this case, a mythology that includes the giant clans, which includes Genesis 6, which is part of the occult philosophy that bleeds into Nazi ideology courtesy of people like Miguel Serrano."

"The Colonel is building a matrix of ideas, Malcolm," said Melissa. "And Weston was part of that at precisely the point we're talking about. We know that because Ward noticed that article in his briefcase about Kabri."

"What's Kabri?"

"It's an archaeological site that's known for its frescoes—paintings on plaster, usually on walls or ceilings," Brian answered.

"What's so special about the ones at Kabri?"

Brian looked at Melissa. "They're Minoan," she answered. "Now guess what region of Israel Kabri is located in."

"Judging by the way these conversations go, I'd say Galilee."

"Bingo."

"This is nuts."

"Welcome to Crazytown," Brian agreed. "But don't miss the point—the web of ideas. It doesn't have to pass peer review or be real. It doesn't have to go uncontested. It's just a set of data points from real scholars, not eccentric Internet trolls. The Colonel could use all of it to build his case, and we suspect he will do just that."

"Have you thought about his logic?" Malcolm asked. "Why does Ferguson care to make people believe in ET life only to turn around and make Christians resist it by staining it with all this garbage? Maybe he really is insane."

"I wouldn't rule it out," Melissa responded, "but he clearly stated that he wants Christians to forsake their faith. He thinks this will make that happen. Talk about a God complex."

Brian added, "He doesn't care if anyone else buys it. He wants that specific group to rise up against his alien myth just so he can manipulate them to embrace the last part of his hi-tech fairytale."

"Any idea what that is?"

"None," Melissa replied.

"But we know it has something to do with Jesus," Brian said. "I'm still troubled about his mention of a Jesus who was but wasn't Jesus. What's that supposed to mean? How are the other parts—his alien disclosure and then turning that into something evil—supposed to lead to his endgame?"

Their attention was suddenly arrested by a chime that signaled the freight elevator hidden in the house above them had been activated.

"They're here!" Madison shrieked excitedly and bolted from the couch. Everyone stopped what they were doing and made their way toward the door. Brian mentally replayed the moment of their own arrival barely a month earlier. While he and others had been topside and back any number of times since, this occasion had special import. He took Melissa by the hand and helped her from the couch.

"Oh, come on!" Madison groaned. The ride took only a couple of minutes, but every second was excruciating. She began to bob expectantly at the click of the lock.

Neff entered first, followed by the others. Madison clapped and ran straight for Cal, the only figure Brian didn't recognize, and hugged him tightly. Cal enthusiastically returned the gesture. Brian saw him lean over to whisper something to Madison with a smile. He looked a little younger than Brian, probably around thirty, and was six feet tall and had sandy-brown hair. Brian couldn't help being reminded of Matt Damon. He smiled as Cal was introduced to the familiar hugging ritual. It was nice that the frightful circumstances could bring another good memory to the surface.

As Cal moved through the round of familiar faces, he caught a glimpse of Brian, Melissa, and Malcolm. His mood perceptibly changed as he approached. He stood before Brian, seemingly unsure of himself.

"Dr. Scott?"

"Yes."

"Well . . ." He hesitated.

Neff interrupted, speaking loudly enough for all to hear, "Cal's been saying he has a message for you . . . and for all of us. The Colonel gave something to him, but he hasn't told us what it is."

Brian watched Neff's expression as he spoke, noting that Neff's eyes never departed from Cal's face. Brian could tell Neff was trying to get a read on the man's mental state. His mind drifted back to Becky, and a wave of alarm swept over him.

"Sorry," Cal said sincerely to Brian, then looked out over the small group, indicating to everyone that they were included in the apology. He turned his focus back to Brian. "First, thank you for doing what you did. From what Graham and the others have told me, the guy probably would have killed me."

"You're welcome," Brian replied, feeling a bit relieved but still absorbed with curiosity. "What did the Colonel want us to know? I'm sure it's a threat of some kind."

"Actually," Cal said slowly, "I'm not sure what to think." He looked around at the faces. "I've never seen anything like it my life. I hope you can tell me who . . . or maybe *what* . . . this Colonel really is."

69

The oldest and strongest emotion of mankind is fear,
and the oldest and strongest kind of fear is fear of the unknown.

—*H. P. Lovecraft*

"The Colonel wanted you all to see something." Cal reached into his pocket, then paused. Brian could tell that he was fingering something inside his coat, making sure it was there. "He also wanted me to tell you how I got it."

Cal pulled out a clear plastic baggie. Everyone instinctively crowded in to see.

"What the—" Ward squinted. Madison covered her mouth and turned away. Nili gasped and instinctively moved in front of Summit to block her view. Cal tried to hand it to Brian, but Brian could only gawk in appalled disbelief.

"It's a thumb," Cal said, gesturing with the baggie toward Brian. "*His* thumb. He wanted you to have it. He said you'd figure it out."

Brian gingerly took the baggie. "This is the *Colonel's* thumb?"

"Yeah," Cal said tensely. "I saw him cut it off . . . right in front of me. After I hung up the phone, I saw he'd picked up a scalpel. I thought he was going to stab me. Instead he looked right at me and told me to watch. He just sliced off his thumb like you'd cut a carrot. He took it off in one, fluid motion. He never said a word . . . never flinched. And *he didn't bleed.*"

"What do you mean?" gasped Clarise.

"There's no other way to say it—he didn't bleed. You can look at it yourself, put it under a scope. There's no blood. Not a drop. He just snickered and said it would grow back."

"Grow . . . back?" Nili had trouble even saying it.

"Let me see that," Clarise said urgently. Brian handed her the baggie. She examined it closely, turning it in her hand a few times. Skin tone, body hair, cuticles—it looked completely normal . . . too normal.

"You noticed the obvious, too, huh?" Cal asked.

"Why hasn't there been any degradation?" Clarise asked, looking somewhat alarmed. "Did you freeze it? Formaldehyde?"

"I haven't done a thing to it except carry it around. I put it in a baggie at the first safe house. It looks exactly like it did the moment he chopped it off. I didn't have any equipment to investigate it further."

"Well I do," she said. "Want to join me in the lab?"

"Absolutely." He hesitated. "Give me a bit, though."

"What else?" Neff demanded. Brian could see his own disdain for the Colonel was becoming contagious.

"I'm okay," Cal answered in an unconvincing tone. "I'd like to grab something to eat and then take a nap."

"We understand. It's been a rough week for you."

"Yeah."

Neff watched as Fern took Cal by his other arm and led him and Madison toward the kitchen. He looked at Brian but said nothing.

"The Colonel would scare anybody," Brian offered, "especially that stunt—if that's the right word."

Neff looked at him apprehensively. "Cal doesn't get scared. He's holding something back."

70

I think and think for months and years. Ninety-nine times, the conclusion is false. The hundredth time I am right.

—*Albert Einstein*

Madison nudged the slightly ajar pod door. It quietly swung inward at her touch. Brian and Melissa saw one of her familiar, impish grins forming. She looked back at them and put a finger to her lips. The three of them slipped quietly into Kamran's room, undetected. Kamran was seated in front of his computer, headphones on, jerkily bobbing his head to a tune only he could hear. Melissa had to suppress a laugh at the air drummer performance.

They looked around, unable to discern any of the features common to their own room—to all the pods. Clothes were everywhere, seemingly hung at all heights by magic on fixtures invisible to the eye. They couldn't tell whether the clothes were dirty or clean. Dirty dishes seemed to occupy every flat surface. Kamran had even taken books off the shelves to make room for more dishes.

"Needs a woman's touch," Brian said to Melissa.

"More like a Hazmat team."

"Or a flamethrower." Madison shook her head. "Watch where you step."

She carefully picked her way through the mess to tap Kamran on the shoulder. He turned around with a start, at first looking annoyed, but then catching himself. Melissa watched him closely as he began to sign to Madison. It was clear, at least to the women at Miqlat, that the young man was attracted to Madison. She was the most proficient person in sign language at Miqlat. The two of them seemed to be together constantly. That had changed now that Cal was present at Miqlat, and everyone knew it would be a hard adjustment for Kamran. The past several days had already produced a few awkward moments.

"I'll make it up to you," they heard her say. "We'll play some HALO tonight, just you and me." He nodded and then turned toward company, waving Brian and Melissa closer. Madison looked at them sheepishly.

Kamran quickly navigated through some windows on his computer screen, which was inordinately large, but perfect for his kind of work. He signed again to Madison, who watched in concentration.

"Kamran wants to know if you read through the material he gave you on the flash a while back, and if it answered your questions."

"I did," Brian answered, looking at him, "and I don't have any more questions. The article on Herodian chronology and numismatics resolved my concerns about the 3 BC birth date."

Kamran nodded his approval. He turned to Madison.

"He says he can proceed then."

"With what?" Brian asked. "Do you have something else to show us? Is that why you asked us to come?"

Kamran nodded and turned to his screen. He hit a few keystrokes and then looked back over his shoulder, beckoning them to watch. He did the same to Madison, with a look that sought approval.

The three of them peered at the screen. At first glance it looked only like a smattering of small white dots against a black background. A few astronomical terms in two of the corners made it clear, though, that they were looking at the night sky. Kamran pointed to one of the corners, which read "September 11, 3 BC." He signed to Madison again.

"He says watch the screen. He's made a video. He says pay attention to the constellations and the sun and the moon."

"We'll try," said Brian.

Kamran clicked his mouse, and the screen began to move. The outlines of constellations they recognized from his earlier presentation faded into view, as did the sun and moon, the planet Jupiter, and the star Regulus, all conveniently labeled. Kamran pointed to another corner as the constellations began to move along the visible ecliptic line that marked their course. At the tip of his finger was a counter marking the year, month, and day. It began to progress forward in time, gaining speed. The scene began to resemble an animation of an atom, where the circular paths of electrons are simulated. Kamran tapped Madison on the arm and signed once more.

"He wants to explain." She kept watching his hands. "He's made this video to show us the next time that all of the celestial objects and their positions present at the birth of Jesus will be in those same positions again."

She waited for him to continue, then resumed. "He says that some people on the Internet have done this, but they've accounted only for what Revelation 12 mentions—and that set of signs has been duplicated several times since 3 BC. He says that it's important to include everything, including what isn't listed in Revelation—things like Jupiter and Regulus, and a few other things he didn't mention in his presentation, since they were also signs to the Gentiles about the birth. The *complete* set of elements is very rare. He says—"

Kamran touched her arm to interrupt. He pointed to the screen to draw their attention. The celestial whirlwind of movement slowed to a halt. Kamran adjusted the window size and then tabbed to a still image of the September 11, 3 BC sky. He positioned the window with the still image next to the scene at the end of the video. The point was obvious: The sky was the same, each labeled item accounted for. Kamran followed Brian's eyes. He was looking at the date. He tapped Madison's arm again.

"Kamran thinks that if the Colonel is going to try to fake something about Jesus, he'll do it on this date or leading up to it—maybe a faked messianic birth or a return—"

Kamran interrupted Madison once more. She watched carefully and nodded. "He says all that assumes that the Colonel is working with astronomy and—this is crucial—it assumes he follows *all* the elements. If the Colonel's astronomy is imprecise and only following Revelation 12, the dates for us to watch will be different by years."

"I understand, but I'm not sure why that's significant," Brian confessed.

Madison took note of his answer. "It means that if the Colonel screws up the astronomy, it may create a weakness in the myth he'll create for public consumption. We'll just have to wait to see if the Colonel is following some sort of astronomical timeline."

Kamran clapped enthusiastically.

Brian smiled. "It's like Kamran's bugged the Colonel."

Kamran nodded with a grin.

"I like it. But," Brian added, becoming more serious, "we don't know that the signs of the birth have anything to do with the second coming. There's no scriptural comment specific to that. We don't know if the sign of the Son of Man's appearing in Matthew 24:30 is the repetition of the birth signs or something else."

Kamran's hands flew into a response. "He says that's true, but it misses the biggest point. If the Colonel wants to use signs in the sky to create his myth, it doesn't matter if the New Testament is clear. He will just convince people that the sign of the Son of Man is the event *he* has planned."

Brian stood up straight and sighed. "Yeah, I follow. That sounds like something he'd do."

"Well, we've got a good bit of time to find out," Melissa replied. "But I'm sure the Colonel will be busy until then."

"And what can we do about it," Brian asked, "other than watch it happen? Just like he told me I'd be doing."

Madison's phone beeped. She pulled it from the holder on her belt. Melissa wanted to tease her about being away from Cal too long, but she held her tongue.

"Hmm," Madison said as she read the text message. "Mom says she has an update. She wants everyone in the Pit, pronto."

71

The efficiency of God may be understood as either creation or providence.

—*William Ames*

Everyone was waiting for Brian and Melissa when they emerged from the hallway leading to the familiar center of Miqlat. Kamran and Madison had run ahead, sensing the urgency of Clarise's message. They were all gathered around the large wooden table.

"Sorry everyone," Melissa apologized, a little out of breath. "This is about as speedy as it gets."

"Hear you go." Fern had a seat waiting for her.

"Is this about the thu—" Brian caught himself mid-question upon receiving a quick pinch from Melissa. He looked at her and saw her eyes quickly dart in the direction of Summit, who was seated between Clarise and Nili. Squish's angular, feline face was peeking just above the table surface.

Brian took the hint and rephrased his question. "Is this about . . . what Cal brought with him?"

Clarise looked up from a small stack of papers she'd been flipping through. She nodded, the put down the paper she was holding. "I'll cut to the chase. We learned earlier that the printout Brian and Melissa brought with them out of Area 51 was the genetic profile for Dee's baby."

Cal suddenly leaned forward. "Did you just say—"

"Later," Madison cut him off. "I'll catch you up."

"Go on," Neff urged.

"Well, I've tested the . . . specimen . . . Cal brought with him," Clarise continued. "The Colonel's DNA is distinct from both Dee's and her baby's."

"Did you suspect it might match?" Malcolm asked, surprised.

"At this point, I suspect everything," she replied.

"Is there any genetic relationship between any of them?"

"No, there's no familial relationship. However, the Colonel's DNA has an anomaly and some biological . . . enhancement."

"There'd have to be, given there was no blood," Cal said. He glanced at Summit, choosing his words carefully. "So how could he just . . . do what he did?"

"I don't know why he didn't experience any pain," Clarise offered, "but the specimen had no blood because, apparently, the Colonel has no blood."

"How can he be alive, then?" Neff exclaimed.

"That's the obvious question," she replied. "Blood serves dozens of purposes in the human body. Sure, it carries oxygen, but it also carries all sorts of cells through the body to deliver nutrients or, say, to carry a chemical injected into the bloodstream as a curative. It carries hormones to the kidneys for cleansing and excretion. It's absolutely essential for human life—at least life as we know it."

"So he's human, but not human?" Malone wrinkled his brow, his mustache unsuccessfully camouflaging a skeptical smirk.

"I wouldn't say that," Clarise answered. "His DNA is human. But his DNA results show that he's missing something called the MLL gene. That gene is necessary for the development of stem cells that generate blood cells."

"So his body *can't* produce blood?" Neff asked in amazement.

"If the MLL gene is absent, even basic blood stem cells can't be generated. In known instances of this sort of thing—as in mutation—the absence causes a rare and fatal form of leukemia."

"So how is he alive?" Ward wondered.

"That's where the enhancement comes in—at least as far as I can guess. If you don't have blood, other mechanisms have to carry out the functions of blood."

"It just sounds impossible," Neff said. "Are there really alternatives?"

"Just some theoretical proposals."

"We learned last summer at Area 51 that the line between theory and fact is more blurry that most people realize," Brian added.

"Like what?" Cal asked Clarise, while casting another stunned look in Brian's direction.

"Well, you told me that there was no fluid evident in the specimen, right?"

He nodded.

"Given our history with the Colonel's technology, I decided to look at the literature on nanotechnology substitutes for blood function. There are nanotechnology options on the board, but all of the options I've read about would still produce a fluid."

"So what's left?" Malcolm asked.

"I think we're still dealing with nanotechnology, but combined with the synthetic biology the Colonel was bragging about. In theory—and we seem to keep running into things that make that phrase ironic—if all your body's organs could manufacture all the chemistry they needed precisely when and where they needed it, you wouldn't need blood. If your body needed some item normally carried by blood flow, and you had nanobots inside you that monitored that need and then produced the necessary item, then you wouldn't need a bloodstream."

"That's science fiction," Madison objected. She gestured at Kamran. "That was him talking."

Clarise surveyed the rest of their faces. "I came across some very advanced concepts in nanotechnology that I think could apply to what we have here," she continued. "I'm not saying they apply completely to the Colonel, but conceptually the ideas fit. Anyone ever heard of Ray Kurzweil?"

"Sure," Madison piped up. "He's a god to anyone working in artificial intelligence."

"It's not nice to call other people God," Summit piped up with a detached air, reaching for one of Clarise's papers that had caught her attention.

"Just take one," Clarise directed.

Madison looked ready to correct her but saw a mildly scolding expression on Nili's face.

"Sorry, Summit," she apologized. "You're right." The pink-haired girl said nothing, already absorbed by moving Squish's paws over the paper, as though the cat was analyzing it.

"Anyway," Madison sighed, "I've read lots of Kurzweil's stuff. Is the Colonel some sort of cyborg?"

"That's the part I don't know," Clarise replied. "The Colonel's body is a human body, but it's well beyond that."

"What's the Kurzweil angle?" Malcolm asked.

"I found an article on his website by a guy named Robert Freitas, a specialist in nanomedicine. Freitas has a theory—along with a full set of specifications—for something he calls a 'vasculoid,' by which he means a machine that fulfills all the body's vascular functions. In a nutshell, it would replace human blood with 500 trillion nanobots that coat the entire vascular system—anything that carries or absorbs blood and other fluids and chemicals. The nanobots would not only do simple things like carry oxygen, they would 'live' where they're needed. They'd effectively make the body immune from disease and aging, and even fix bodily trauma. We've seen that part work with our own eyes."

Everyone except Cal looked at Brian. The new resident took notice. "Why is everybody—?"

Madison elbowed him lightly.

"Okay, I'll wait."

"How would this vasculoid prevent disease and aging?" Fern asked.

"It would remove parasites, bacteria, viruses, that sort of thing," answered Malcolm.

Clarise nodded. "And, say, prevent cancer cells from metastasizing, even disassemble them when detected. It could also dramatically improve physical endurance and stamina with increased oxygen and adrenaline flow. It's a transhumanist's dream come true."

"There we are," Brian shook his head. "We shall be as gods. That had to be the Colonel's point. Another ego trip."

"Something like this vasculoid would also explain the lack of degradation, at least given the time frame so far," Malcolm suggested. "The nanobots, if that's what's going on, would keep doing their job. I presume you've put it under the electron microscope."

"Yeah," she answered, and reached for one of the pages in front of her. "Here's an image of what's inside the Colonel." She slid it over to Cal, and then passed a couple copies toward the other end of the table.

"That's incredible," Malcolm gasped, tilting the image toward Madison. Her eyes widened in disbelief. The image was a black-and-white close-up of dozens of rounded mounds. It had the look of a bad case of goose bumps, but the mounds were more tightly clustered and had definable borders.

"Let everyone get a look," Clarise said. "Each one of those bumps is three thousand times thinner than a human hair. I have no idea what they actually do. The science we're looking at here is way off the charts when you're talking adaptation to a biological organism. It's unthinkable."

"And yet it's sitting in your lab," Ward said, glancing at the page as it came his direction.

"But why would the Colonel need to be . . . what he is?" Cal asked.

"I don't know."

An unexpected playful giggle drew their attention.

"Squish likes the little balls," she said, looking down at the page in front of her, using the cat's paws to bat at the round images. She laughed again. "They remind me of dancing," she looked up at the ceiling in a happy thought, "and my birthday."

Nili gazed at her, perplexed. "Dancing? Your birthday?"

She nodded. "At home . . . my class . . . it was fun."

Nili glanced quickly at Clarise, then back to Summit. "Why does the picture remind you of your dance class?"

"Ahuva would take me," she replied, ignoring the question. "Then we would go to Dafna's house. I like her. I know where she lives."

"Ahuva was Summit's aunt," Nili explained to the others. "She thought dancing would be a good social experience for her. Dafna was her teacher. She lived in East Talpiot, a neighborhood in Jerusalem."

"Did she go on her birthday?" Fern asked from across the table.

"No," Nili answered. "Summit, you didn't go dancing on your birthday."

"I know *that,*" Summit replied with bored disdain, still looking at the picture. "Talpiot is my birthday."

Nili's brow wrinkled with confusion. "I'm sorry, Summit. I don't understand. Talpiot is a place, not a number."

"The Talpiot number," Summit answered unwaveringly and looked at Clarise. "The old boxes. Clarise showed me."

Everyone looked at Clarise. Brian watched in bewildered fascination as her confused expression suddenly morphed to an anguished grimace, like she'd been overtaken by a stabbing pain. Clarise cupped her face in her hands for a moment, concentrating, and then looked at Summit. She shook her head in denial.

"It's *sixteen* . . ." she whispered. She lifted her head, her eyes moving from one confused face to another. "It adds up to sixteen!" She jumped up out of her chair.

"What's wrong?" Ward turned his chair in alarm.

"Please be wrong, Summit . . . *please,*" she said anxiously under her breath, "just this once." Clarise bolted out of the Pit toward one of the hallways.

"What's going on?" Neff asked helplessly, agitation in his voice.

"I don't know," Ward replied, now standing. He, Neff, and Malcolm took off after Clarise, leaving the rest of the table in stunned silence.

"What do you make—?" Melissa turned to ask Brian, but stopped in mid-sentence. He was staring out across the table, his palms flat on the surface, his jaw drooping slightly, fear in his eyes. "Not you, too," she said, exasperated. "What is it? What does the number mean?"

"It means I hope she's wrong, too," he said ominously, turning toward the girl, who was now sitting quietly, stroking Squish's back.

"I'm not wrong," she said innocently. "My brain doesn't lie."

72

The average evangelical church lies under a shadow of quiet doubting. . . .
It is the chronic unbelief that does not know what faith means.

—*A. W. Tozer*

"Brian," said Neff's voice.

"What's up? Did Clarise find what she was looking for?"

"No, net yet . . . we're in the library now. We stopped by her lab first. Clarise needed something there. She wants to talk to Summit."

"Okay," Brian replied. "Everybody's still here at the table."

Brian hit the speaker button on his phone and put it in the middle of the table. "Summit," he said, "Clarise is in the library. She needs you to tell her where to find something."

"Sure," Summit said quietly, releasing Squish, who leaped with effortless grace onto the floor.

"Summit—can you hear me?" It was Clarise.

"I hear you. Your files are in the library."

"I'm sure they are," Clarise answered. "But the files aren't numbered. You know we're looking for the number."

"Why are you looking for a number?" Summit asked.

There was silence on the other end. Clarise spoke again after a few moments. "You know what I mean," she said, some tension surfacing in her voice. "The last number in Becky's series."

"Who's Becky?"

"Never mind." Everyone at the table could hear the frustration in Clarise's voice. "If you knew about the number, why didn't you say anything before today? We've been trying to figure that out for weeks!"

"I just saw the number in my brain . . . 80503. No one asked me about it before."

There was silence again.

"Summit is telling the truth," Nili spoke into the phone. "After the first number frightened her, we've kept her away from our work. She's never seen the full list."

Brian heard an exasperated groan through the speaker.

"Clarise," Sabi said calmly, "do not to be angry. God has used Summit despite our mistakes."

"You're right," Clarise said in a calmer voice. "I'm sorry, Summit. Do we have a folder labeled 'Talpiot'?"

"No," she answered immediately.

"I can't believe I'm asking this but . . . are you sure?"

"Of course."

"But you're talking about my Talpiot articles from . . . I haven't used them for several years."

"Yes. I filed them."

"Where can I find them?"

Summit blinked a few times. "Archaeology . . . then the New Testament tab . . . then Jerusalem . . . then osswa—osso . . . that's a hard word."

"Ossuaries." It was Malcolm's voice. "Got it. Brian, are you tracking on this?"

"Yeah, 80503 is an ossuary number . . . and I'm pretty sure I know which one," Brian said, slumping back in his chair.

"Oh, man, I remember hearing about this. I can't believe it."

"Believe it."

"You know what this means! It's . . . I don't even want to think about it."

"Bring everything out here," Brian said in a subdued tone.

"We'll be with you guys in a minute."

Brian ended the call and sat silently for a moment. A dull ache crept through his chest.

"Professor," Nili said. Brian turned toward her. He could see fear and anger in her eyes. "I think I understand what this means . . . what this Colonel means to do. He is an evil man."

"Let's wait till everyone gets back."

"No one takes this theory seriously . . . at least in Israel," Nili fumed.

Brian held up his hand and sent her a gentle look. She nodded. The he looked at Melissa, whose face was drawn with anxious confusion.

"What's an ossuary?" Malone asked.

"A bone box."

"Why is this one so important?"

"You'll see in a few minutes."

Brian looked at Summit. He watched the girl, off again in her own little world, tickling Squish's nose with a few strands of her long, pink hair. Laughing whenever the cat tried to bat them away. *If only things could be that simple.*

"I hear them coming." Fern craned her neck to see the hallway.

"You did a great job, Summit," Madison congratulated her.

"Yes, you did," Brian echoed.

Summit looked up. "Don't be sad."

"I'll . . . I'll try," he replied, a little taken aback.

Melissa leaned toward him with a whisper. "You know that Summit may not look at us, but she studies everyone."

Brian forced a smile.

"But you're an easy read. What's troubling you?" she asked.

"Dr. Scott," Sabi said in a calm voice. "When doubt seeks to crush the soul, we must remember. . . . You must examine the record of your life as closely as you would engage your research. You have seen much tragedy—and many, many providences. *Consider them and believe.*"

Brian sighed. "I do, and I will."

"None of us could have ever imagined our lives would converge in this way," Sabi continued, "at this place, for this purpose. We are all living proof *to each other* that God has His own agenda. He enjoys the unpredictable. Whatever this fiend is planning, it will *not* go unnoticed by the Most High. He will show us the way."

Their four colleagues emerged from the hallway, Clarise and Malcolm both carrying thick folders stuffed with papers. They quickly took seats and started rifling through the content without saying a word.

Clarise pulled a page from her folder and turned to Malcolm. "Did you find it yet?"

He handed her a few stapled pages.

"Summit was right," Clarise said, flipping through the pages of the article Malcolm had handed her. "She's not only identified the number, but now I remember where I saw that DNA profile before—the one for Dee's baby. It's all here."

Clarise folded the article in half, exposing a page that contained what everyone recognized by now as a vertical-bar visualization of a DNA sequence. She grabbed the page from her stack and positioned it next to the photocopied article. "You see that? The profile sections are the same."

"Sure looks that way," Neff said, leaning in. "But if that's the case . . . the other had something to do with the New Testament. Whose profile is the other one?"

Clarise looked anxiously at Brian. "It's the result of a DNA test on bone fragments found in a tomb in Talpiot—that's the association that Summit recalled. The fragments came from on ossuary in that tomb, one that was given the catalogue number 80.503."

"Is there any significance to the ossuary?" Ward asked.

"Yeah," Brian answered. "It had an inscription on it . . . a name: 'Jesus, son of Joseph.' "

73

The individual is handicapped by coming face to face with
a conspiracy so monstrous he cannot believe it exists.

—J. Edgar Hoover

"*What?*" Neff blurted out.

"The ossuary was marked 'Jesus, son of Joseph,' " Brian repeated.

"Well, it couldn't have held the bones of the real Jesus," Neff protested. "The *real* Jesus rose from the dead."

"I agree," Brian said, "and most archaeologists and biblical scholars don't think this ossuary held the New Testament Jesus, regardless of whether they believe in the resurrection. But the Talpiot tomb isn't explained away by quoting the New Testament. I'm surprised you haven't heard of it. It was all over the mainstream news outlet back in 2007, as I recall."

"I don't watch television. I'm basically off the grid when it comes to that sort of thing. Do any of the rest of you remember it?"

"Vaguely," Malone admitted. "I assumed it was bunk. I never gave it any time."

"Same here," added Melissa. "I wasn't exactly interested in Christianity back then, but I assumed it was sensationalism."

Ward nodded. "Same here. I thought it was a hoax or something. Was it?"

"No, it's no hoax," Clarise said. "I followed the discussions after it aired on TV and read the article on the DNA work. It just sort of died out after scholars began to expose the problems with the interpretation of the data—the whole thesis, really. I lost interest."

"Most people did," Brian said. "And you're right about the academic response. The tomb itself was actually discovered in 1980, but it only became news in 2007."

Ward laughed. "Why did it take twenty-seven years for the world to hear about it?"

"Because the archaeologists didn't claim it was Yeshua of Nazareth," Nili answered angrily. "All the Israeli archaeologists knew about it. But Yeshua was a common name in the first century, and there are other ossuaries with the same inscription: 'Yeshua, bar Yoseph.' In Israel, this is not taken seriously."

"There's more than one 'Jesus, son of Joseph' bone box?" Madison laughed. "That ought to end the theory right there."

"It didn't because there were other ossuaries in the tomb, all of them with names of people associated with Jesus in the New Testament. There was one for 'Jude, son of Jesus'; 'Matthew'; 'Mary'; another whose inscription may read 'Mariamne' or 'Mary and Martha' or 'Mary and Mara'; and there was one for 'Joseph.' "

The table fell silent. Brian looked at everyone's expressions, which were exactly as he'd imagined they would be when he'd contemplated having the discussion. He felt suddenly emboldened, almost angry. "*What's the problem*?" he demanded.

A faint smile came to Sabi's lips.

"I know you're not all familiar with the data here, but what are the *obvious* questions here?" Brian prodded. "*Think*."

"Well," Fern began, "even with the other names, why haven't most scholars been persuaded that it's really Jesus and His family and friends?"

"Good. What else?"

Malone jumped in. "Jesus is a common name. Are all the names common?"

"Another fitting question. Let's hear more—think like a detective." Brian looked at Ward, who was quick to pick up on the nudge.

"Do we know if any of the people in the tomb were actually related?" Ward asked. "And if they were, are they related the way the New Testament has them related? If not, the whole thing's a wash."

"Excellent," Brian said, sitting up straighter and leaning toward them. "The facts are, the names *are* common, despite insistences to the contrary. Scholars went after that right away. Of the six ossuaries with names on them, only two have patronyms—statements of family relationship, like 'son of.' That means we have no idea which people are related and exactly how they're related, except for those two instances.

"In the case of the ossuary that seems to have two names, 'Mariamne' and either 'Mara' or Martha,' scholars don't even know what gender the second name points to, since the spelling was used for both men and women. They might have been sisters, or mother and daughter, husband and wife, father and daughter—who knows?"

"He's right," Clarise interjected. "Only two of the ossuaries had any bone fragments in them, and they were very small—literally just tiny chips. The bones had been removed. It's not even clear if the fragments left came from the ossuaries in which modern archaeologists found them. The tomb had been disturbed."

"I'm not following," Neff admitted. "Who took the bones?"

"The orthodox Jewish authorities claimed the bones of all the ossuaries just days after the discovery," Nili informed them. "They buried them in an unmarked location. That is the common practice in Israel. Archaeologists sometimes try to hide discoveries if they contain human remains so they can remove the bones unnoticed. If word gets out, the religious authorities will stop at nothing to inter them properly—even risking their own lives."

"The Talpiot tomb had also been violated in antiquity," Brian told them. "The initial discoverers note that in their reports. There were many ossuaries in the tomb, and they found bones and skulls scattered around it. Tomb robbers tend to discard the bones as they look for objects of value buried with them."

"So that's why they can't really even tell which boxes the bones originally belonged to," Ward reasoned. "Some could have been tossed out and then put back into a different ossuary."

"Right. It's not the neat and tidy picture that you're led to believe it is when you first hear about it. Most people—and I think some of you just experienced it—just get shocked by the names. All things considered, there are very few specialists in the field who believe this tomb really was the tomb of Jesus' family."

"But keep thinking," Brian continued. "If all the ducks were in a row, what would be the obvious question to ask then? It still hasn't been answered by the few advocates of the tomb."

"How about this," Melissa said, eyes narrowed in concentration. "This was a family tomb, right?"

He nodded.

"And it was marked on the outside?"

"Right again."

"So, it stands to reason it would have been visible in antiquity—why else put a symbolic marker on it? You wouldn't do that if you intended to hide it from view."

"No, you wouldn't," Brian agreed.

"If this were the tomb of the real Jesus— who died quite publicly, to say the least—and friends and family were added to it now and then, how would the apostles' story have survived? As soon as the early Christians started preaching about the resurrection, why wouldn't people in Jerusalem have just waved their hands and said, 'Hey, the guy's buried right over there'?"

"How indeed," Malcolm smirked. "It would have been painfully easy to undermine the whole gospel story. The tomb was out in the open and visible. Everyone in the city would have known about it, including the Romans. They could easily have used it to put a stop to the new religion that would cause uproars in the city and other parts of their empire. But none of that ever happened."

"Speaking of obvious questions," Neff remarked, "if there were only tiny chips of bone in the Jesus ossuary, and Israeli authorities took them and later tested them, how could the Colonel get the DNA sequence? Was it published somewhere?"

"No," Clarise said. "What you see in articles like this and my own printouts is a genetic summary; it's not the whole sequence. I don't know where he'd have gotten it. You certainly couldn't guess and get it right."

"There's one possibility," Brian said, turning to Malcolm. "Can you find the site reports in that folder, or maybe a newspaper article about the original find?"

"I think I know why you ask this," Nili said thoughtfully. "Sometimes collectors or antiquities dealers will hire small boys to slip into unexcavated tombs to steal things. There is money in such things."

"That's exactly what I'm thinking," Brian confirmed.

"Hey, look at this." Malcolm was holding a piece of paper and scanning the contents. "It's a summary by a professor in North Carolina. Listen to this."

> *The tomb was exposed by a dynamite blast on Thursday morning, March 27, 1980. This was just before Easter weekend with Passover falling on the following Monday evening. The district archaeologist applied for the license to excavate on Friday, March 28. The license was issued on Monday, March 31, the day before Passover, but some work was had been done on the site on the Friday morning of the license application.*
>
> *At noon that Friday, the day after the tomb was exposed, an eleven-year-old boy from an Orthodox Jewish family saw the exposed tomb on the way home. His mother called*

> *the Department of Antiquities to report the exposed and unguarded tomb, worried that it might be plundered. She was unable to reach authorities as the office had closed for the Sabbath. She and her son looked inside the tomb and saw that items had been disturbed, including skulls and bones. The next day, the Sabbath, the boy's mother reported that she had seen boys playing soccer with one of the skulls. She and her husband ran them off and gathered the bones, even going door-to-door of those children known to her to ask parents to make sure all the bones were returned. She delivered the bones she had collected to archaeologists on Sunday morning.*

"Interesting," mused Ward. "That means it's possible that there were bones or bone fragments from that tomb floating around in private stashes, as mementoes, or maybe to save for later sale. We can't assume everything was given back. The Colonel could have heard about fragments and taken them."

"Regardless of how he might have gotten anything, do you all see what the Colonel can do with this?" Brian asked. "Dee was carrying his Jesus. The Colonel has handed us the blueprint, just to mock us."

"Think about what he told Brian," Malcolm pressed. "The part about the resurrected Jesus who was real but not real, how he and his associates would steer people toward a conclusion that would have them believe in a lie without ever knowing it."

Brian kept going. "First he gives the world a new hope, a belief in the sort of gods everyone hungers for—the benevolent alien here to solve our problems. Then, when the path to human evolution and Utopia suddenly gets sullied by other staged revelations, leading to an attack on Jerusalem, Jesus shows up to save the day—just like the Bible says. Who wouldn't believe in Him at that point? Every phase of it is a lie, but it's all real."

"And how much do you want to bet that his Jesus will also have no blood?" Clarise said solemnly. "Just what the New Testament tells us to expect."

"But what about the tomb?" Nili protested.

"That's not hard to figure out," Brian said thoughtfully. "It requires redefining the resurrection. It won't be hard since a lot of scholars already argue that ancient Judaism viewed resurrection not as a rising of the original intact body, but the reconstitution of that body in the last days. After all, there will be millions of dead raised for whom there is no body to raise—people who were lost at sea, incinerated, or whose remains are completely turned to dust. The Colonel will say that his Jesus is the true Jesus, wholly reconstituted in the flesh."

"But that isn't what the Gospels describe—or Paul, for that matter," said Malcolm.

"I agree, but if this Jesus appears, those passages will be reinterpreted in light of the reconstitution view of the resurrection. And that's the trap: millions of believers will put their faith in a real but false Jesus."

"There's one missing detail—a missing expectation about Jesus," Cal spoke up quietly, his voice full of apprehension. "One that I can tell you the Colonel hasn't overlooked."

"What do you mean?" Madison asked, her ears catching the fear in his voice.

Cal looked around the table. "I didn't tell you everything that happened back at my office."

"Really?" Neff asked inquisitively, eyebrows raised.

"Please know I'm not crazy," Cal said, looking at the faces gathered at the table. "It's me—I'm still the guy you all know. Fern can give me any sort of psych evaluation she wants. I'm not out of my mind."

"We trust you," Madison said, touching his arm, unsure of what was coming. "Just say it."

"Well ... after he cut off his thumb and said what he had to say, the Colonel just turned around and ... he turned ... and walked through the wall. It was like he just dissolved right into it and was gone, like he just told every molecule that was him to stop being physical. I swear, I saw it. He *wanted* me to see it."

No one said a word. They were all astonished by the revelation.

"I believe you," Sabi said quietly. "It seems that Dr. Scott had a similar experience in the restaurant, without actually seeing what you did."

"Even though my mind can't accept it," Clarise said, "I believe you, too. We can sit here and theorize how the Colonel's techno-body could just disassemble—how we're all just matter, held together as a solid by the vibration of the atoms that compose us—but even if we understood it all in theory, it doesn't change the impact. We're looking at a bloodless body, impervious to disease, that can walk through walls."

They all understood the implications: When Dee's boy grew up, he'd be all that, and likely more. There would be no doubt.

"It was right in front of my eyes!" Brian suddenly exploded in exasperation. "How *stupid!*"

"What?" Melissa exclaimed, caught off guard by the outburst.

"The tip, $153!" Brian blurted out, remembering the exorbitant tip the Colonel had paid at the restaurant. "We had fish ... at a restaurant called the *Galilee*. How could I have been so blind?" he berated himself. "The whole thing was orchestrated to ridicule me—us. What was it he said? That he had one more revelation for me about himself and his associates. He sat there right in front of me counting it out, $153, and I never saw it."

"That number, 153," Melissa echoed, "it comes from Jesus' conversation with Peter after the resurrection by the Sea of Galilee. Jesus was roasting fish. It's gematria, isn't it?" Melissa asked.

"Yeah. There are several possibilities for converting the numbers to text, but I already know which one he intended."

"Yes," said Sabi unexpectedly. "I do as well."

Brian looked at him in surprise.

"The early fathers write of this," Sabi explained. "It now becomes clear. Jesus was speaking of His children—the metaphor for His body. The Colonel wishes us to think of that divine body . . . and one thing more . . . to identify himself with the rulers of this world." He stared knowingly at Brian.

"By Hebrew gematria, the number 153 converts to *bene-ha-elohim* . . . 'the sons of God,' "

74

The trust of the innocent is the liar's most useful tool.

—Stephen King

Brian took a deep breath, filling his lungs with the cold, crisp, Montana air. It was good to be outside again. The last week had been filled with life-altering decisions. The rapid-fire revelations of the past few days had unnerved Melissa—so much so that two days ago she'd asked Clarise to perform an amniocentesis for a DNA analysis of the twins. The procedure had gone well, and today Melissa had insisted she felt vigorous enough to come topside, if for no other reason than to remember what the sun looked like.

Presuming the test yielded no surprises, Melissa had agreed to deliver the babies in Miqlat's infirmary and surrender them to Miqlat's network rather than an adoption agency. One of the pods would be modified to serve as a temporary nursery. Ward and Neff needed to prep the helicopter for a quick flight into Bozeman for materials and "baby gear," as Fern had called it. Brian, Malcolm, and Melissa had tagged along for the change of scenery.

"Aw, crud," Ward said, feeling his pockets as they stood next to the helicopter, his breath floating in wisps toward the others. "Forgot my flashlight. There's one in the house. I'll run and get it." He turned and started jogging back to the house.

They'd made other decisions as well. After some earnest coaxing, Brian and Melissa had decided to stay rather than adapt to another set of new identities. Malcolm would do the same, though he was still undecided about his future. He'd joked that he wanted his last act as a priest to be marrying Brian and Melissa.

The decisions had come with demands. As part of the Miqlat team, the three of them would have to learn the entirety of the network of finance, safe houses, and supply trains. Training in self-defense, first aid, tactical arms, and protocols and operations for use of all communications devices was mandatory. They all promised to learn sign language as well, and Neff and Ward had decided that all of them should get experience driving the range of vehicles used by the network, along with basic maintenance. Flight training was, for now, optional, but at minimum it was expected they would learn how autopilot functioned and how to land in an emergency.

Once Melissa was physically able, the three of them would accompany Miqlat team members on missions, first as observers, then as participants. They'd all agreed the work would be fulfilling, though they didn't know how their own research would be useful. Brian and Melissa both had a clear sense that they were supposed to keep doing it, if for no other reason than to tune their senses to whatever the Colonel would do in the future.

"What's in there?" Malcolm asked Neff while they waited, pointing to the wide two-story building nestled into the tree line about forty yards away.

"Lots of stuff," Neff replied. "Riding mowers, yard tools, some maintenance equipment, a woodshop, softball gear, medical supplies, old equipment . . . We use it to stage things we'll load onto the choppers to take on missions or move to safe houses or orphanages. We try not to just throw things away."

"Here," he said, pulling a key from his keychain. "Go have a look. You should know where everything's at around here. Grab me a pint of engine oil and a funnel from the shelf above the workshop desk. It's toward the front of the garage."

"Cool. Let's go," he said to the others.

Neff watched the three of them traverse the short distance to the garage over another shallow layer of white powder. He was glad things had worked out. Miqlat would be in good hands for a long time to come. He unlocked the chopper door and then headed around the front of the bird. He heard the crackle of his radio followed by his name and grimaced a bit.

"What is it Ward? If you can't find your light—"

"Graham, we have company. . . . We've got the front gate motion detector light going off inside. . . . Look at the driveway—a little into the tree line. . . . I've got glasses on him now."

Neff turned and immediately stiffened. A lone figure was walking into view, erect, deliberate. He wore a brown leather bomber with a white woolen collar. Neff's stomach fluttered.

"I don't know him. Do you, Graham?"

"Yeah . . ."

"Who is it?"

"A nightmare—*our* nightmare."

"Where's everybody else?"

Neff slowly raised the radio to his lips again. "They're in the garage. I don't know if he saw them. They won't know where the tunnel entrance is inside the building. I'm unarmed. Get Nili topside—fast. Tell her to bring whatever's handy. But lock everything else down. *Code red.*"

Neff suddenly caught some motion out of the corner of his eye. The front door of the garage had opened. Brian stepped through. The noise didn't go unnoticed by the trespasser. Neff waved to catch Brian's attention, then pointed.

"Neff, we can go through the tunnel and—" Ward began.

"No, he knows they're in the garage. He's headed that way."

"The freight elevator's too slow!"

"Negative! You'll come up inside after he gets there, and he'll know we're underground. We can't risk that. Get Nili topside and come across over-ground. I'm going to engage. *Do the best you can to hurry.*"

***

"You can't be serious!" Melissa shuddered, terror in her eyes.

"It's him," Brian said breathlessly, locking the door.

"Holy Mother of God," Malcolm whispered as he peered through the glass of the front window. "Where did he come from? How—aaagghhh!" He looked at Brian, wide-eyed with terrified rage. "It's the thumb! He gave it to us knowing he could track it."

"Does Neff see him?" Brian asked, panic rising inside him.

"Yeah, he's calling to the Colonel . . . moving toward him . . . no response. He's still headed this way."

"Melissa," Brian said, trying to stay clear-headed. "Hide—anywhere you can find. I'm the only one he's seen. Cover yourself with something. Whatever happens, don't make a sound. Stay hidden—no matter what. *Do you promise me?*"

She nodded, unable to speak, and moved toward the rear of the building.

"Brian!" Malcolm motioned for Brian to join him at the window.

Neff had broken into a run toward the Colonel, who had not changed his pace. The Colonel only halted his advance when Neff positioned himself between him and the garage about fifty feet from they were watching. Neff said something. Brian felt the familiar chill run through him as saw a sadistic smile crease his enemy's face. Neff pointed at him and shouted.

Without warning, Neff's body careened through the air in their direction. He hit the exterior wall with a startling, violent crash. Then there was silence. The smirking Colonel turned his attention to the window next to the door and locked eyes with Malcolm. He started moving in their direction again.

Malcolm bent down and withdrew a handgun from his ankle holster. "It may not do any good," he said, standing up, "but I'm gonna use it until I know there's no point. *Find a weapon*—gas, a torch, some chemical, a shovel, anything!"

***

"Hurry!" Madison screamed as Ward and Nili sprinted into the Pit, shoulder holsters draped over their arms. Ward's alert had spread through Miqlat like wildfire. Madison had been watching a video camera that panned the outside front of the property and had seen Neff go down. Nili quickly punched a code into a gun safe adjacent to the front door and grabbed a TAR, handed it to Malone, then took another. Summit took off running to her room in tears. Clarise and Sabi were watching the screen with Madison.

"What's happening?" Nili shouted as they headed for the door out of Miqlat. She threw a handgun to Cal. "Stay here with Madison, but be ready!"

"He's heading for the garage. Neff's just lying at the bottom of the wall. He isn't moving!"

"Lock down!" Ward yelled at Clarise as he opened the door. "Invasion protocol!"

Seconds later, they were gone, rushing to the elevator platform.

Clarise grabbed the handles of Sabi's wheelchair and headed up the nearest ramp. She steered him toward his room.

"Sabi, get inside your room and lock down."

"Clarise," he said with a calm that stopped her cold. "Please take me to the tunnel."

"What?"

"The tunnel . . . that goes to the garage."

"Are you crazy? There's no way—"

"It is time," he said softly, looking up at her, completely composed. "The garage is the *only* place I have never been at Miqlat. That is the unseen place . . . where the tunnel in my dream leads."

Clarise stood over him, dumbstruck. In all their missions, she'd always known exactly what to do, but now she felt completely unprepared. "I can't do that," she finally managed to say.

"You must. God wills it."

"But—"

"Take me to the tunnel. There is little time. My chair will make the journey."

"But what are you going to do?" She started to tear up. *"He'll destroy you."*

"I am not afraid to die. You know this."

"I can't just turn you over to this monster!"

"Clarise, if you fail to act now, we will be lost. God bids me to defy him in that place. He has a reason. Take me *now*."

Clarise choked back tears. She grabbed the handles of the chair and began to push it at a run.

75

Life and death are balanced on the edge of a razor.

—*Homer,* The Iliad

Brian watched the door, illogically expecting it to burst open, spraying splinters into the front section of the garage. Instead he saw the Colonel's form seep through the doorway.

The Colonel stared at him, enjoying his fear.

"I warned you to find more intelligent friends, doctor. I've had more difficulty finding my keys."

"What do you want?" Brian asked, being careful to not sound demanding. "You've already told me what you're planning, and how you can't wait to see my reaction."

"All true. I told you on the phone I wanted to meet your friends. Perhaps I would have let you pick a neutral location had you not acted so rashly."

"I'm having a hard time believing that."

"You're probably right," he said with a twisted smile. "But that was then; this is now. I'm content to kill your friends at this point. I might leave a few of them alive if I leave here with every electronic device in that house. I want that audio file destroyed. Your friend outside was using a radio, so I'm thinking the house isn't quite empty."

"I'll gather everything myself if you just leave," Brian said, stalling.

"I don't want to do that. At the very least, I'd like to say hello to Dr. Kelley. The two of you make such a cute couple. Oh, and Dr. Bradley," he called, raising his voice, "Dr. Harper sends her greetings." He chuckled and looked at Brian. "When she can speak, that is."

Brian could feel his fear giving way to rage. "Neff was radioing someone off-site," he lied. "We're the only ones here. Now let me go and I'll get what you want."

"You're a very poor liar. Your words strike the right chord, but your eyes tell me otherwise."

"It's the truth."

"No, it *isn't.*" The Colonel looked around the garage, surveying the equipment and scattered tools. He picked up a staple gun and slid its row of staples into his hand. He held them up in front of his eyes. "A clever, but primitive, tool."

The words were scarcely out of the Colonel's mouth when the staples disappeared—at least that's what Brian thought. A second later he felt excruciating pain in his thigh.

"Aaahhh!" he cried out and fell to the floor. He looked at the source of his agony. The row of staples was firmly buried in his flesh. He gasped, raising himself up on one elbow. The Colonel took a few slow steps toward him, strolling around him in a circle. He knelt down, positioning his face inches from Brian's.

"You know, I'm not here to kill you, Dr. Scott. That would be like turning off a favorite show just when things were getting interesting. However . . ."

Brian cried out again and twitched on the ground. He could feel the staples burrowing deeper into his thigh.

"You'll heal, of course," the Colonel soothed mockingly, "but I can cause you pain in a thousand ways. I'll give you a minute to clear your head while I kill Dr. Bradley. Then we can go to the house to get acquainted."

***

The soft, steady whir of the wheelchair reverberated through the paved tunnel. Their path was unobstructed, save for the occasional spider web that Sabi could neither avoid nor clear with his powerless arms. He had asked Clarise to gather with the others to pray after he left. He'd also said goodbye, telling Clarise thank all those who had cared for him at Miqlat in case he did not return. He prayed continuously while his chair moved slowly, relentlessly, forward.

He could see the door now. He began to hear the voices, unintelligible syllables that beckoned him to deliver the message God had embedded into his consciousness, night after night. He rolled the chair to a stop and prayed a last, brief, silent prayer. Then, as he'd done dozens of times in his twilight mind, he rammed the chair into the door. It didn't move.

Surprised, he urged his wrist forward, propelling the chair once more into the door. No effect. He looked at the adjacent walls for a speaker, some biometric device like those scattered all over Miqlat. A devastating realization swept over him: This door was different because this place was different. It was the only location he'd never seen for the simple reason that it lay outside Miqlat. Anyone wheelchair-bound would have no reason to leave Miqlat or go across the property on his own.

He looked upward and squinted, his mind rebelling at a dull, silver protrusion that was faintly visible through a thin layer of dust. A deadbolt. The door was locked.

76

The day which we fear as our last is but the birthday of eternity.

—*Seneca*

"I'm curious, Dr. Bradley," the Colonel said evenly as he knelt beside Brian, watching him writhe on the hard concrete floor of the garage, blood streaming from the wound in his leg, "how long are you going to let your friend suffer on your behalf?"

He stood up and looked around. "I know you're here, Malcolm," he taunted. He peered into the dark interior of the garage, listening intently. He stood up and stepped around the disabled Brian toward the open, concrete expanse before him. He took note of a light switch affixed to a support beam. He flicked it on. Lights cascaded in unison through the interior. He smiled and watched, looking for an unnatural movement in the stillness.

"Up here."

The Colonel jerked his head upward. His eyes were drawn immediately to the barrel of the handgun in Malcolm's outstretched arm only a few feet away. Malcolm pulled the trigger, firing rapidly into the object of his hatred, again and again.

Malcolm suddenly felt his own body go rigid. He struggled to react, but was completely immobilized by some unseen force.

"How imprudent, Dr. Bradley," the Colonel snarled, looking up at where Malcolm had perched himself on a ledge, partially obscured by some large boxes piled atop each other. He'd been kneeling on a partially completed plywood floor. "Had you not said anything, you may have injured me, albeit slightly. But in any regard, this body repairs even more quickly than your friend's."

"Bbbllld," Malcolm croaked through his unmoving jaw.

The Colonel looked into Malcolm's eyes, but they weren't trained on his face. They were directed at the floor. The Colonel looked down. He was standing in a small pool of blood. He took a step back and stumbled over Brian's prone body. The blood was Brian's.

The Colonel glared back up at Malcolm, who was still fastened to his ledge by the Colonel's power. *"You fool!"* the Colonel raged. *"I decide who lives and dies here!"*

In a rush of fury, Malcolm's body hurtled from the rafter down to the concrete and then was once more jolted through the air toward one side of the garage. He smashed into a pegboard wall, sending the tools fastened against it flying in all directions. He groaned but was immediately lifted into space again, this time hurled into the door of the garage. A loud crack shuddered through the space, accompanied by a brief yelp.

The Colonel walked over to the motionless form, but his eye caught an unexpected sight—a face at the bottom corner of the window. It was Neff.

"Please *join* us," the Colonel growled viciously. The window exploded, spraying glass in every direction as Neff's form went sailing through it into a shelf full of tools next to the pegboard wall.

The Colonel looked at the prone figure, and then back at Malcolm. They weren't moving—and neither was Brian.

77

At the edge of chaos, unexpected outcomes occur.
The risk to survival is severe.

—*Michael Crichton*

Melissa closed her eyes tightly, squeezing a flood of tears onto her soft cheeks. She'd seen everything, heard everything. She'd managed to find a space between the legs of a large, rusty table saw and a drill press. Both had been covered with heavy canvas tarps, which overlapped, allowing her to crawl through for coverage and, at the right angle, provided a tiny viewing slit.

She'd managed to crawl underneath leaving everything undisturbed—everything, that is, except the dust that her coat had swept through while she crawled on her hands and knees. She realized after she was in position that she'd left a detectable trail. But it was too late. There was no time to move elsewhere.

She wanted to burst out of hiding, to go to Brian. She'd seen him hit the floor and knew instantly that at least one of Malcolm's bullets had found the wrong mark. She'd watched the trickle of blood become a pool. He was bleeding out. He was dying, and there was nothing she could do.

Melissa watched helplessly as the Colonel knelt next to Brian. To her surprise, he felt for a pulse, then shook his head.

"Such an inept species," he muttered, then stood up. "You do not have my permission to die, professor," he said with a casual sniff. He removed his jacket and laid it on one of the work benches. "When you're done entertaining me, then *I'll* kill you, not before."

Brian's body began to rise from the floor. Melissa suppressed a gasp. Her astonishment was tempered when she caught sight of the blood dripping from a gunshot wound somewhere in Brian's torso.

Silently, the Colonel placed his hand on the right side of Brian's chest. After a few seconds, he did the same with his other hand on the underside. The trickling stopped. With Brian's body still suspended, the Colonel turned in Melissa's direction. She carefully moved her head an inch to the side and held her breath. There were no footsteps, only some shuffling.

Subduing her terror, she tilted her head back to the vantage point that allowed her to see. She saw the Colonel grab a soiled towel that had been draped over the edge of a barrel. He wiped Brian's blood from his hands. In the same instant, she felt a piercing pain in her abdomen. A contraction. *Not now!* She sat back and gritted her teeth, then bit into the thick sleeve of her coat as the pain coursed through her.

Hearing the subtle crack of glass under pressure, she moved to look through the slit again. Neff had come to and discovered that he'd landed atop Malcolm's gun. He'd risen to one knee and taken aim, but was unable to hold the weapon steadily. He was shaking. He grunted in pain and fired.

The shot was well wide of its mark and smacked something metal beyond Melissa's location on the distant back wall. The bang of the gun had startled the Colonel, causing Brian's body to drop to the ground with a sickening thud. The Colonel turned and saw Neff collapse.

"Those things are dangerous," the Colonel scolded sardonically. He held out his hand, and the gun rocketed into it. He popped the magazine and looked at it. "Excellent. I'll only need two bullets."

***

Nili leaped off the platform as it came to a rest in the upstairs pantry, followed closely by Ward and Malone, all of them fully armed. "Finally!" she exclaimed in desperation. The three dodged the furniture in the house and bolted out the front door, into the snow. Malone quickly lost pace as Ward and Nili sprinted ahead toward the garage, weapons at the ready.

***

Sabi sat trembling in his wheelchair. He'd heard the gunshots, the angry voice, the thunderous crashes. He'd tried repeatedly to move the door, knowing it was futile. He'd finally ceased and silently vented his frustration to God.

His prayers had been abruptly answered by a loud ping and a whistling sound next to his ear. He knew within moments that he'd nearly been killed, a stray bullet fragment ricocheting within inches of his skull. He closed his eyes and gradually gained control of his breathing—in, then out . . . in, then—

The quiet was suddenly broken by another gunshot. Then silence resumed.

His pulse quickened. In desperation, he powered his chair into the door, and it gave way. He looked up at the lock, which was now nothing more than a mass of protruding metal and splinters. He pressed forward, but the heavy door resisted. He rammed it again and gained, slowly gaining more ground. He backed the chair up for another run . . . and heard Melissa scream.

78

Jesus said to her, "I am the resurrection and the life.
Whoever believes in me, though he die, yet shall he live,
and everyone who lives and believes in me shall never die.
Do you believe this?"

—*John 11:25–26* ESV

Melissa had turned away, unable to watch as the Colonel fired a kill shot into Neff's head. She began to weep again, trying desperately to keep her promise to remain hidden. The shot was followed by silence. She mustered the courage to look.

The Colonel carefully sidestepped the pool of blood that had formed from Brian's wound. He moved to step over Neff, but stopped. He crouched over Neff's body and seemed to take in its scent, like an animal inspecting a carcass. Melissa watched in transfixed horror as the Colonel put his hand to Neff's head wound and then put his fingers, soaked in blood, to his nose. His face conveyed curiosity. Suddenly he licked the blood from his fingers. Melissa's stomach heaved.

The Colonel stood up and walked over to Malcolm, who had begun to stir. "Goodbye, Dr. Bradley. Tell dear Andrew that it was more fun to kill him than you."

Melissa's instinct overtook her. "*No!*" she screamed, expending all the energy she had.

The Colonel's head jerked in her direction. His brutal, wicked smile quickly returned. "Well, finally a pleasant surprise."

He turned in her direction. He could see Melissa's tussled red hair and frightened face peering out from behind the corner of the tarp. "I'm sorry we couldn't meet again in better circumstances, Dr. Kelley. Please, won't you join me?"

Melissa struggled to move. Another contraction hit suddenly, and she slumped to the floor, gasping in pain.

"Oh, come now, professor."

Melissa groaned loudly. The Colonel watched as her hand clawed the side of the table saw. He took a step toward her and stopped.

"What is *this*?" the Colonel demanded.

Melissa looked up at him, startled by the shock in his voice. She lowered her head, gasping and gritting her teeth through another contraction.

"You're *pregnant*?" He got down on one knee and grabbed her by the hair, forcing her to look at him. "Who is the father? How are you pregnant?"

Melissa stared at him, her senses beginning to blur. The question made no sense. "Brian," she murmured weakly.

"You lie!" he snapped. "You can't have children. We examined you at the base. Now tell me how you're pregnant."

"I told—"

"The truth! Now!" He gave her head a vicious jerk.

"I don't know," she answered in a barely audible moan.

The Colonel stood up and took a step back. He looked around at the mayhem he'd caused, and his eyes fell on a utility knife. He held out his palm, and the knife flew from its resting place to him. He grabbed Melissa again by the hair and pulled her from her hiding place. Muffled whimpers arose from her throat. She was too weak to scream.

"I must know ," he sneered. "I'll just have to take it with me." The Colonel moved around to Melissa's side and exposed the blade. He pulled her sweater up.

A still, calm voice penetrated the air. "No."

The Colonel looked behind him over his left shoulder. He lowered the blade, dumbstruck at the source of the voice.

Sabi sat in his wheelchair a few feet from the stricken Melissa, whose legs were now spread, the mound of her abdomen exposed before the kneeling Colonel who was ready to tear into her womb.

"Is this a joke?" the Colonel jeered.

"You will not touch the woman again," Sabi said quietly. "The Most High commands you to leave."

The Colonel erupted in laughter. He got to his feet and turned toward Sabi. "How dare you?" he snarled. *"How dare you command me?"*

"I did not command you. The Most High commands you. You will not touch the woman. Leave this place—now."

"I'm not going to leave this place!" the Colonel bellowed, his rage building. "I'll take your head off and then get back to business."

"How stupid," Sabi said in quiet defiance, "to threaten one such as me with death. Look at me. I *welcome* death. You may kill me today, but you will not touch the girl. The Most High has decreed it."

The Colonel stared down at the frail figure. Sabi looked into the cold, blue eyes. Melissa grimaced through another contraction.

"Yes . . ." the Colonel said slowly. "Death would be a gift for you. I could cut you in a hundred places, and you'd never feel it. It would be more fitting to increase your misery . . . perhaps remove your eyes . . . or your tongue. *Yes.*"

"You may do as you wish to me," Sabi replied, "but whether here or in the life to come, I will know that you did not touch this woman . . . that you hearkened to the voice of the Most High as your master, or suffered His punishment. Hear my words. You *know* He is real. . . . You *know* I will see it . . . *Watcher.*"

The Colonel took a step back. Melissa was still conscious. Afraid to move, she'd listened in terror to the exchange. The word itself was paralyzing. She turned her head. Incredibly, the Colonel appeared startled.

"I know who you are, Watcher," Sabi said serenely. "The question in your mind should now be . . . *how*? How would this weak, pitiful man know what others do not? There can only be one answer." Sabi started to smile. "It is because God has shown me . . . and if that is the case, He has truly given me the message you have heard. This is your opportunity to escape punishment. Now *go*."

Melissa watched as a silent face-off ensued. The seconds seemed like hours. Terror began to well up in her in anticipation of an explosion of violence. But Sabi was still smiling, wide-eyed and expectant, as though on the verge of some long-anticipated thrill.

"Are you insane?" the Colonel broke the silence. "Yahweh sends a crippled village idiot as His Marine. *What are you smiling for?*"

"I wait," Sabi answered. "I wait to see if you will obey . . . or perish. It is time to decide."

The Colonel gritted his teeth. His face began to turn red. In a flash, he spat violently at Sabi, then repeated the action. The crippled man remained erect, unmoving, as gobs of spittle dripped off his nose and clung to his beard.

The Colonel stooped and pressed his face toward him. "Watch what I do now," he growled, quaking with anger.

Sabi watched in dismay as the Colonel whirled and strode toward the fallen men. Melissa was abruptly seized again by pain. She tried to breathe evenly, turning her head to see what was happening. Objects on the floor and the walls began to hurtle toward the prone figures of Malcolm and Brian, pelting them repeatedly in a spastic fit of the Colonel's rage. But just as quickly as the tantrum had commenced, it stopped. The Colonel had come to some silent realization. A low, menacing laugh gurgled from deep within his chest.

The Colonel turned abruptly and knelt next to Neff's corpse. With one merciless motion, he slit his throat. Melissa closed her eyes. She heard the Colonel throw the knife aside and looked again, only to see the sickening sight of him plunging his fingers into the open wound.

The Colonel stood up, Neff's blood dripping from his hand, and moved to Brian, kneeling once more. He turned and looked at Melissa. Without breaking eye contact, he dug his blood-soaked fingers into Brian's leg wound, raking the staples aside, grinding his hand into the deep gash. Brian started to move, the pain nudging him into consciousness.

"Now," the Colonel growled and stood up, "to finish this affair."

The Colonel strode the short distance to where Melissa lay, but his attention focused on Sabi. Without warning, his form began to swell and glow. The earthly façade of a man faded into distorted pixilation, replaced by a towering figure with brazen, shimmering skin, his body at once undefinable yet displaying a coherent form. The entity's face had an angular shape, with deep, black, unblinking eyes, simultaneously reptilian but still somehow anthropoid. Melissa tried to scream but couldn't.

The tall figure bent slowly, pressing its face toward Sabi.

"Behold my glory," it hissed.

"I have seen your kind before," Sabi said, unmoved. "You will not touch the woman in any form. *Now obey the Most High.*"

"This is my domain, mortal. *I do what I please.*"

With an unearthly wail, the creature lunged at Melissa. She closed her eyes, expecting to feel her body torn open, but she felt nothing. In her mind, she saw her frame being broken and shredded. She shook violently, rocking back and forth, trying to deflect the pummeling of repeated, powerful blows that rained down on her . . . but only in her mind.

"Dr. Kelley . . . Melissa." Sabi's voice penetrated her panicked consciousness.

A contraction jolted her to reality. She arched her back and then was still.

"Melissa!"

She cautiously opened her eyes. Sabi was leaning over the arm of his wheelchair. His kind face gazed down at her. She heard the door burst open . . . shouting . . . a woman's voice . . . Nili.

"Be brave," Sabi said softly. "He is gone."

"Wha—what happened to it?"

"I don't know, but you need not fear."

Two weeks later

79

We felt that we had received the sentence of death.
But that was to make us rely not on ourselves,
but on God, who raises the dead.

—*Second Corinthians* 1:9

"Did you tell him?" Melissa asked, tying her robe.

"He knows," Clarise said somberly as she folded some linens.

"Everything?"

"All of it."

"I'd like to go see him."

"Sure. He's up to it today."

Clarise looked away. Melissa moved to leave, but stopped. She took a step toward Clarise and touched her gently on the arm. Clarise looked into her eyes.

"You've been here for us," Melissa said, trying to find the right words. "And we want to be here for you."

Clarise started to cry. She offered no resistance. She'd been overwhelmed with grief every day since the events at the shed. Melissa put her arms around her, absorbing her anguish.

Everyone at Miqlat was an emotional wreck, but they had reacted with swift precision. They'd determined almost immediately that they needed to abandon their home base. The evacuation itself was accomplished in less than twenty-four hours, but the logistics of handling the fallout had been a nightmarish challenge.

Clarise and Fern had first attended to Melissa with medication. Her contractions had subsided soon thereafter. Ward had taken Malcolm to a local hospital, claiming he was a victim of a hit and run—a plausible screen for the two broken collar bones and linear skull fracture he'd suffered.

Brian had been much trickier. Internally, Brian's body would show evidence of a gunshot wound and blood loss, but the external wounds had been closed by the Colonel's bizarre intervention. There was simply no explaining the contradiction, much less what doctors might find in his blood if they looked closely. Cal had therefore been pressed into duty to keep him sedated until Clarise could perform surgery to remove bone fragments adjacent to his right lung and dress the wound in his leg.

Thankfully, only one rib had sustained serious damage. They hoped that his unique bloodstream would again work its wonders. After a week, that appeared to be the case. Despite his having lost a lot of blood, Brian's wounds were healing more quickly than expected. Clarise had theorized that the nanobots were self-replicating and had been triggered to reproduce by the trauma.

In the urgency to abandon Miqlat, Brian was moved less than ten hours after surgery to the safe house they were temporarily calling home. Malcolm had arrived yesterday, following his release from the hospital. Ward was working with police on what he'd make sure was an unsolved hit and run.

The contingency plans for Miqlat's evacuation meant that the topside house would be burned nearly in its entirety. They'd deliberately deferred having insurance, a planned safeguard against layers of investigation. The calculated burn would leave the pantry area with the freight elevator intact, and everything underground would be left untouched. The entire compound had been built with the plan in mind. The house would be rebuilt and perhaps someday reoccupied, but no one was considering that a serious option at the present. Everyone would migrate to Miqlat II in Belize. Neff, whose body was being temporarily stored by a mortician in the network, would be buried there after the move was completed.

They dissolved the thumb that had led the Colonel to their location in acid, then dumped the residue into a stream at the edge of the property. But that was only one effort to assuage their fear that someone would follow the Colonel to Miqlat. Madison managed to convince everyone that the only explanation for the Colonel's mysterious appearance was UFO transport. At first everyone had doubted the idea, but it seemed the only reasonable conclusion, since they hadn't found a vehicle or tire tracks, and the gate was intact.

In a stroke of genius, Madison had pulled audio of the Colonel's voice from the recording at the restaurant and then made contact with whomever had brought the Colonel, using the radio they'd found in his jacket. Someone had picked up, only to hear the Colonel's voice tell them to leave the area and await future contact. It had been extraordinarily risky but had apparently worked, since no one came looking for him.

Clarise released Melissa and wiped her eyes. "It's going to take a while for all of us—a *long* while. I just can't believe Neff's gone."

"I know," Melissa replied.

"You know everything there is to know now. But the Graham you knew—he was real," her voice trembled. "He was the most changed man I've ever known. We loved him, and he loved us. There's no pretending here. We all know what it's like to be truly forgiven and made new."

"Me, too."

"I'm here when the two of you want to talk."

"Thanks—I'm sure we'll need that."

Melissa waddled slowly down the hallway toward Brian's room. Reaching it, she gently knocked on the door and pushed it open. Brian was seated in a wheelchair, staring out the window.

"How did you get in that chair?" Melissa asked, trying to make the question sound like the rebuke it was. She walked over to the bed and sat down on the end.

"I managed," he said without turning. "I wanted to watch the snow." He sat quietly for a moment, then said, "Clarise was here about an hour ago. I presume you know what she had to say."

"We need to talk," Melissa said. "You know I love you."

He turned toward her, his face betraying a deep insecurity. "Melissa, you know this changes everything."

"It changes *nothing*," she said, her eyes flaring.

"You're not thinking clearly."

"*You're* the one not thinking clearly. In fact, you're thinking selfishly."

"I'm thinking of *you*," he shot back angrily, then caught himself. "I—I don't know what to say." A tear started its path down his unshaved cheek. He turned back to the window.

"Brian, having HIV isn't the end of the world. . . . It's not the end for us, either."

He shook his head and awkwardly turned the chair toward her. "All it would take is one mistake, and you'd be like me. I couldn't live knowing I'd given you a death sentence."

"You're overreacting. Neff lived with AIDS for years. He was in terrific shape; he took good care of himself. That's what you'll do."

"He wasn't having sex with anyone," he retorted. "It's how he got AIDS in the first place!" Brian raised his voice in exasperation.

"Brian, he was a *pornographer*. He was careless. Weren't you listening to Clarise? Didn't you hear about his lifestyle?"

"Her sister *died* from AIDS—were *you* listening?"

"Her immune system was already compromised from drugs and other illnesses. It's not the same! And Clarise was careful."

"Clarise only worked for Neff a month and got out because of her sister. She was lucky." He turned back to the window.

"Since when do you use the word '*luck*'?" Melissa asked him piercingly.

A sarcastic reply flickered in his mind, but the sound of soft sniffle stopped him cold. He turned back to her. She was crying. He'd seen the image before, back in his room at Area 51, the night she'd tried to ruin him. He remembered grabbing her by the arm and shouting at her . . . then he'd seen her eyes, filled with tears. The scene was seared into his brain.

"I'm sorry." His own eyes welled with tears as he got up, awkwardly, and joined her on the bed. They held each other tightly. He rocked her gently and stroked her hair. Time seemed suspended. "Just don't leave me," his voice cracked, "please."

"I'm not going to leave you," she whispered in a trembling voice, her head resting on his chest. "I'm yours." She sniffed. "We'll figure things out. We'll talk to Clarise."

Brian didn't reply. He held her close, listening to her breathe.

"Brian," Melissa said, breaking the silence. Brian heard fear in her voice.

"What is it?"

"The Colonel—he had no idea I was pregnant. He was absolutely shocked. How could that be?"

Brian stroked her back. "I don't know."

Six weeks later

80

הרנינו שמים עמו והשתחוו לו כל אלהים
כי דם בניו יקום ונקם ישיב לצריו
ולמשנאיו ישלם ויכפר אדמת עמו

—Deuteronomy 32:43 in the Dead Sea Scrolls (4QDeut^{q})

"They're beautiful," Fern whispered, lowering the second of Melissa's twin girls into the newborn bassinet. "Just perfect."

"Thanks, Fern," Clarise said with a smile. "I can handle the PKU. Why don't you go check on Melissa."

"Of course," she said enthusiastically, "but I'll be back. It's so exciting to have little ones around."

Clarise watched Fern disappear through the door and then stood over the tiny newborn girls, each of them wrapped snugly, their eyes closed in peaceful slumber.

Clarise looked at the sterile needle kits and the bandages on the tray next to the twins. She put on her surgical gloves, picked up one of the needles, then paused to take a breath. She knew now how Melissa's pregnancy had happened. The process that had produced her twin girls had a name: parthenogenesis. *Virgin birth.*

Melissa would have to know, too, as scary as it sounded. But the name offered no clarity. The situation defied explanation. Parthenogenesis could not biologically occur naturally. There were no known instances in any mammal. The only explanation was implanted cloning. That wouldn't have been a shock, since it confirmed their suspicions. But the Colonel had not known. They knew the how, but not the who. No one had expected that state of affairs.

Clarise drew one of the newborn girls out of her bliss. She carefully unwrapped the tiny bundle and then placed her back in the bassinet. She couldn't help smiling as she watched the little legs kick the air awkwardly. She removed the needle from its sterile sheath and set it on the table, along with the blotting paper needed for the blood drops.

Bending over, she lifted one leg, took the needle, and pricked the tiny heel. She turned to retrieve the blotter, feeling the baby squirm ever so slightly with her other hand. She quickly brought the paper to the heel and then froze. She reached for the needle again, inspecting its tip. Her heart began to race. She lowered the needle and pricked the heel again, this time more slowly, with pressure. She watched the tip disappear into the soft, pristine flesh and then removed it.

Nothing.

Postscript

A handbook to *The Portent* is available at ReadThePortent.com. The handbook contains links to research used for the book, as well as expanded discussion of important concepts and points of dialogue.

The passage used for the final chapter's quotation, presented in Hebrew, offers a clue about the meaning of the circumstances of Melissa's pregnancy and the birth of her twin daughters. The handbook contains a second clue, another passage also in Hebrew. Both passages are essential to unraveling this puzzle. The first, found here at Chapter 80, is accessible to English readers only in the English Standard Version (ESV) and the New Revised Standard Version (NRSV). The second, which you'll find in the handbook, is found in any English translation.

While readers will find English translations for these passages, there is something resident in the Hebrew text of both that I'll draw on as part of the story in the next novel. You must consider the passages in tandem or you will be misled in that regard. The solution to the puzzle is no surface reading or familiar popular interpretation of any of the passages. I don't care about popular thinking. I care about the text.

The first reader who solves the riddle accurately (i.e., in satisfactory detail) will have a character bearing their name in the next installment of Brian and Melissa's journey. Readers may email their guesses to me via the address on my homepage. Multiple attempts are permitted.

Acknowledgments

The Portent, volume two in *The Façade* saga, has been a long time coming. I'm thankful to the many fans of the *The Façade* and their persistent encouragement (sometimes demands) to continue the story. Some names deserve special mention, not only because of the way they have faithfully promoted *The Façade* on websites, in podcasts, at conferences, and in other outlets, but because they've become friends in the wake of the response to *The Façade*. Readers will take note that some of the names that follow are the source for the names of characters in *The Portent*. Other character names are explained in the companion handbook described in the Postscript.

Guy Malone, Joe ("Free") Ward, and his wife Amy (middle name, Clarise) are dear friends. Their work in Roswell, New Mexico, to inject a Christian presence (not to mention creating worthwhile events) into the annual UFO festival has produced fruit in many lives. I enjoyed participating at the Ancient of Days conferences each time my schedule permitted me to be there. Guy read an early draft of *The Portent*, and his suggestions were helpful.

Doug Vardell has been a steadfast friend and supporter since my college days. (How many times did you read *The Façade* to your kids?) It was Doug who played publicist for *The Façade* and got me on Coast to Coast AM with Art Bell for the first time. Doug also read a draft of *The Portent* and provided some important insights for the final product.

Sometime after my first Roswell trip, I met Mike Bennett ("Dr. Future"). Mike is a constant encouragement, one of those people who manage to be a blessing with every conversation. He didn't realize it, but certain things he said directed my thinking for some of the subplots in *The Portent*. Other readers of the initial draft, Brian Godawa and Sharon Shipwash, also contributed to its improvement in specific ways.

The late Fern Hieser also deserves recognition. Fern and I became friends through *The Façade*. Fern's last name is pronounced the same as mine, though the spelling is different. She heard me on Coast to Coast AM shortly after her husband—Mike—passed away. The startling providence prompted her to contact me. We were able to meet once while I was traveling through Indianapolis with my family. I told her I would name a character after her in the next volume. Although she didn't get to see that, members of her family will.

I've also enjoyed the friendship of Derrel Sims (a.k.a., "Alien Hunter"). If there's a real Fox Mulder, it's Derrel, for lots of reasons. He's always interesting and fun. There's a little bit of Derrel sprinkled here and there, and one of the characters shares his last name.

Special mention is due to Becky Woithon. I met Becky via Facebook after discovering she'd read *The Façade* six times. That sort of dedication deserved a character namesake, and so she has one in *The Portent.*

Speaking of dedication, I'm blessed to have Elizabeth Vince as copy editor. Sorry for creeping you out (again). Dan Pritchett of Acid Test Press also deserves thanks, as well as the folks associated with Kirkdale Press—Kyle Fuller, Ryan Rotz, Jack Chambers—for producing the special edition of *The Façade* and provoking the writing of *The Portent* when they did. I needed the shove. Lastly, Brannon Ellis was a key force behind the most recent edition of *The Façade* and *The Portent.*

Publisher's Note

We hope you enjoyed *The Portent.* If this book left you on the edge of your seat, challenged you in what you believe, or impacted you in any way, we'd love to hear your feedback. Visit Kirkdale Press on Facebook, leave a review on Amazon or Goodreads, and stop by Michael S. Heiser's homepage, DrMSH.com.

For background on the author and the book, and to dig deeper into the research behind the work, be sure to check out ReadThePortent.com.